BLACK AURA
VB SCOTT

NO BARRIER PUBLISHING

Copyright © 2022 by VB Scott

All rights reserved.

No part of this publication may be reproduced, distributed, scraped, or transmitted in any form or by any means, including photocopying, recording, or other electronic or mechanical methods (including feeding artificial intelligence), without the prior written permission of the publisher, except as permitted by U.S. copyright law. For permission requests, contact VB Scott via vbscott.writes@gmail.com

The story, names, characters, and incidents portrayed in this production are fictitious. No identification with actual persons (living or deceased), places, buildings, and products is intended or should be inferred. Names of bands and music artists contained herein are referenced in the Soundtrack at the end of the book.

eBook cover designed by VB Scott. Paperback cover, band logo, chapter and scene break images and editing by Ollie Ander under Acidic Ink Publishing

Absolutely no form of artificial intelligence was used in the making of this book.

ISBN: 9798230199922

First Edition Published in 2025

10 9 8 7 6 5 4 3 2

Contents

Dedication	VII
Content Advisory	VIII
Preface	IX
Opening Verse	X
1. Tranquillum Tranquility In Chaos	1
2. Succubus Hell's Groupies	17
3. Serpenus Snakes, Trouser and Otherwise	29
4. Auraneae Auranna's Spider	38
5. Viscera Our Lovely Bassist's	51
6. Sanguine Mixed Blood	60

7.	Daemonium Who's the Demon Here?	70
8.	Foetidus Oh God, the Smell	78
9.	Vespertilio Bat, Head Intact	87
10.	Polypus Sexy Octopi	94
11.	Lepores Pati Suffer the Bunnies	104
12.	Deliramentum Is She For Real?	115
13.	Mors Voluntaria Suicidal Hopefulness	124
14.	Nudus Isn't This What You Came For?	135
15.	Aestus Hell is Hot… And Crowded	148
16.	Orandi Deliver Me, O Metal Gods	160
17.	Ecclesia The Metalhead's Hell	172
18.	Poena Punishment Rendered	183

19.	Oculos Eyes of Angels	193
20.	Hymnus A Heavenly Voice	204
21.	Advocatus Lawyers in Hell. Punchline Complete	214
22.	Rota Wheel of Torment	225
23.	Retrosus Backward Logic	236
24.	Negotium Soulful Negotiations	247
25.	Angelus Angels and Their Chariots	265
26.	Caelum Sex and Metal in Heaven	274
27.	Salvatio Imperfect Crescendo	284
28.	Solutio Figure It Out For Yourself	294
29.	Liberandum Final Desperation	305

Epicinium 319
Epic Finnish

Audite Periculo Tuo	335
Soundtrack {Listen at Your Own Risk}	
Special Thanks	342
Sneak Peek	343
Devil's Sorrow	
About VB Scott	346
Also by	347
VB Scott	

Dedication

Dedicated to Michael Kamen and the music department that put together the soundtrack to *Last Action Hero*, responsible for shaping my hard rock and metal tastes from an early age.

My music life would have a giant hole in it without the visceral experience of cranking "Angry Again" by Megadeth as loud as possible. I get chills every time Jack Slater IV's opening credits explode from the screen.

Also dedicated to Richard, Roger, Hiroshi, Yoshie, Lilly, and Howard.

Gone way too soon.

Content Advisory

The following book contains:
  Graphic, bloody violence and gore
  Strong sexual content (briefly graphic)
  Fetishized choking
  Allusions to rape in dreams
  Theoretical depictions of Hell
  Theoretical depiction of Heaven
  Satanic iconography
  Heavy Metal iconography
  Suicide and suicidal ideation
  Brief self-harm (cutting)
  Cannibalism
  Purposeful misuse of pronoun capitalization between the main character, Satan, God, and the Bible (the true horror!)

Preface

Black Aura is a love letter to the Metal and Hard Rock genres. The book references and paraphrases over sixty years of real bands and their music. Every effort has been made to not quote lyrics directly. Any passage or set of words that have been included in that same order from an actual song is purely coincidental and unintended.

What *is* intended is for metalheads of all eras, ages, and genres to find the dozens of Metal Easter eggs hidden throughout these pages. There are eggs filled with overt and oblique references, and some are simple vibes and atmosphere inspired by certain songs or albums. There are often clues in plain sight, but you might need to consult your local metalhead to find the rest. (Apologies if you *are* the metalhead in your community. You fuckin' rule!)

A soundtrack is provided at the end of the book for those who would like to experience Black Aura's journey and celebrate Metal's history in all its myriad permutations.

Opening Verse

Exodus 23:20

"See, I am sending an angel ahead of you to protect you along the way and to bring you to the place I have prepared."

CHAPTER ONE
TRANQUILLUM

TRANQUILITY IN CHAOS

A THOUSAND BEINGS ASSAULTED RACHEL Kimura with heat and sweat. They reeked. They pushed. They jabbed. They groped. They screamed. They cursed. They sang. Rachel's head thrashed and swelled with violence vibrating behind her eyes. Their Queen shrieked, growled, and screeched, exhorting the denizens of the pit beneath the starless sky. Feral men slouched at the edges, catching their ragged breath before getting pushed or pulled back into the whirling center.

Chipped horns, stomped tails, broken wings—costumed worshippers weren't spared the rambunctious fury of the metalheads. They cared not for the hours of prep that went into the designs and implementation, nor for the fracturing of their fellow fanatics that strayed too close.

A woman fell hard to the ground at Rachel's feet on the edge of the pit. She stooped to pick the woman up, then pushed her back into the fray at her insistence. Rachel wished she had the fortitude to join, but she feared her piercings being ripped out above any other injury she witnessed from the edges.

Someone jostled her too hard from behind and she fell to the bottom of the pit. The woman she assisted already disappeared from view—consumed by the throng, and Rachel was next. A boot crushed her hand. A knee connected with her ribs. A cord of muscle and testosterone tumbled over her back. She grimaced, picked herself up, and received an elbow to the jaw.

Before further reckless abandon befell her, her boyfriend found her and cleared a path back to the edge of the pit, then dove back into the scrum.

Oh yeah, it's fine, Justin, thanks for asking. She flexed the hand sporting a new muddy boot-print.

Worried she might have broken it, Rachel stepped away from the pit. She turned around, bumping into another metalhead, brushing her possibly broken hand against the woman's sweaty black bra.

"Sorry!"

"What?" the woman yelled.

"About your... Never mind!"

"What?"

Rachel shrank away from the glare of the woman, whose piercings and tattoos were gorgeous. Too bad she had such a foul attitude because Rachel would have invited the woman to Justin's van after the show.

She pushed her way through the groping zombies at the edge of the mosh pit, who weren't interested in the activity so much as the women that fell out of it. With no clear path out, she focused on at least making it to the mixer tent to catch her breath.

She leaned against the front pole of the tent and re-focused on their Queen's haunting, mesmerizing, beautiful voice. Their Queen graced Rachel's bedroom walls on posters, photo-shoots, and album covers. Her voice filled headphones at the gym and work, and speakers in the car and house. No one followed Her Highness longer than Rachel.

Justin's unhidden love for their Queen didn't hurt Rachel's feelings. Approaching royal perfection was a fantasy—something to be dreamt of but never hoped for. She'd be a hypocrite if she had a problem with his worship of Her. Hell, if she were to ever meet their Queen, she might endeavor to steal a kiss on Her cheek, if only to feel that godlike skin and brag to her friends. The likelihood of receiving a beating from the Queen's protectors for her transgression would be worth it to gain the renown and jealousy of her fellow worshippers.

Rachel forgot the pain in her hand as their Queen hypnotized the crowd with Her fingers and voice during "Obsequious Obeisance." For the briefest moment, their Queen stared straight into Rachel's eyes. She jolted as if struck. That had to have been her imagination, right? How could their Queen ever pick her out in a crowd? Rachel used to think her piercings made her stand out from regular people, especially among other Asian Americans, but whenever she came to shows—with thousands of others dressed and pierced like her—she was forgettable again.

Their Queen averted Her gaze back to Her instrument. Rachel came out of her hypnosis and looked around, wondering if anyone else noticed their "moment."

Everything changed in a flash of black.

Though Rachel stood in the same spot, all the people around

her morphed into visions of night terrors of various sizes. Had she been dreaming the whole concert? Her hand didn't hurt anymore, so... Maybe? But the night terrors that used to plague her hadn't petrified her in the last five years. At least these ones ignored her instead of reaching out with their smoky appendages while she cowered beneath blankets. At that thought, though, each one pivoted in her direction. Her heart double-timed and she took several trembling steps backwards.

A dull rhythm echoed from the stage, pulsing with her heart and syncing to the flow of her blood vessels. The five musicians that made up Black Aura stared at her. Even the keyboardist, whose body remained square to the keyboard, twisted her neck at an unholy angle to meet eyes. They were all shinier versions of the night terrors populating the grounds below them, bedazzled with white light from their eyes and metallic accessories.

Rachel needed to wake up. She slapped her face hard to no effect but to sting her cheek. The night terrors and musicians continued staring at her. She backed up further and bumped into something solid and about her height. She turned to find a hooded, ragged, black-robed figure. The shock knocked Rachel on her butt. The void beneath the hood stared into her soul. It raised a tremulous, bony finger to her, then to the top of a cliff face in the distance.

Rachel blinked and she overlooked a dark red landscape surrounded by a jutting precipice of rock. Down on the black plain, the stage flashed multi-colored beams of light with the throng of night terrors swaying around it. The dull rhythm continued.

What the hell is going on?

Rachel shivered even though the air around her sweltered. Only, that wasn't quite right. The air was alive, like it was sweating, well beyond natural humidity. Why was she so cold, then? Behind her, a dark forest loomed, maliciously moaning from the creaking trunks and swaying branches. She surveyed for a path that might skirt the forest's edge, or a slope to slide down to get back to the concert, but nowhere seemed safe.

Had she blacked out after their Queen looked at her? Or did Justin or some asshole at the water booth slip her something? If she found that to be the case, she'd personally pierce them with no anesthetic, and the large implement she'd use wouldn't be sanitized.

"Justin? Justin! Are you here, too?"

Groaning trees answered, though no discernible wind created their ominous wails. Screams came from beyond the trunks, animalistic but still human. The horizon in every direction and over the tops of the trees glowed red as embers. She hugged her arms over her tight Black Sabbath T-shirt that she'd sewn herself and bent her posture inward to generate warmth. Her efforts provided no relief from the odd chill wrapping around her bones.

"Where am I? What is this place?" she asked, receiving no answer.

If she stood in one place long enough, someone had to find her. Wasn't that the right thing to do when you were lost? She remembered her cell phone then, but it only displayed black. How did it die so quickly? Oh right. The flashlight drained the hell out of it at the concert. Still, there should have been a little left... Next time she'd bring a lighter.

A whisper came from the foreboding forest. It could have been the wind; it sounded like the dead.

"Follow the darkness," the wind squirmed through her ears.

Rachel hesitated, looked back one more time to the strange valley below the cliff she stood on, then proceeded into the trees. An overwhelming sense of being watched enveloped her from all directions. She turned back to where she'd entered the forest, but there were only more trees. The opening and the sprawling red and black vista disappeared. A void with no stars or moonlight replaced the glowing red of the sky.

Dim orange lights floated a hundred yards from her in a circle, illuminating only the trees surrounding them. No path presented itself, and no light guided her in any particular direction.

Against her better judgment but not knowing what else to do, she took a few more steps forward. Skittering little feet against the fallen detritus of the forest floor startled her. Puffs of air bumped into her sides. The sensation was like being on the edge of the mosh pit she'd been at only moments before. Unlike Rachel, Justin regularly threw himself into the fray while she contented herself with being bumped along the outside of the circle. Not even getting horribly injured at the Lamb of God concert during "Black Label" kept Justin from aggressive moshing.

And the one time she fell in, all this happens? This had to be a dream, warning her against attending the concert the next night.

...Right?

"Justin? Are you there?"

The words died in her mouth, like talking with tightly secured earbuds. She put her fingers to her ears, but they were only cold and still ringing from the concert; the screeching guitars and crashing cymbals that had buffeted her the last two hours had been replaced with dead silence that made the ringing worse. The little feet and trees had become silent.

As she ventured deeper, glowing red eyes appeared and tracked her movement from the branches, from the floor, and in the distance. They danced like flames to the new rhythm reverberating through her bones as a new song began from behind her. The orange lights remained the same distance as when she first noticed them, even though she'd moved a considerable distance since then.

A new chittering spawned from around her feet. It was so dark in the immediate area around her that she couldn't see her own chest when she looked down. A creepy, tickling, disgusting feeling of tiny pressures made their way up her legs, higher and higher underneath her plaid skirt. She shook them away and ran towards one of the many orange lights. It didn't get closer, but she was relieved from the crawling things for a moment, whatever they were.

She ran; her legs moved up and down and forward, but no distance appeared to be gained in the slightest. It really had to be a dream, after all. She pinched herself, hoping a cartoonish solution would be the ticket out. She winced and held her arm up closer to her face, but she couldn't see anything in the blackness. She rubbed her hand along where she felt the pain and there was a sticky wetness. Pungent iron tickled her nose.

The rhythm picked up its tempo. The orange lights throbbed, making her eyes vibrate the longer she looked at them. She ran at them again. This time they allowed her to come closer.

She stopped in front of one and held her arm up to the light. Her arm oozed blood from the spot she pinched, while spiders, scorpions, and centipedes crawled all over her. She brushed them off in a panic. They disappeared into the blackness outside the glow of the floating light.

The low pulse of the rhythm, distant and dull, grew deeper and slower. The orange lights floated away, disappearing into the inky void. Large red eyes, each as big as her body, opened from the darkness behind the light. They didn't blink. Something inside told her they never blinked.

The eyes floated up and loomed over her, stories high. Its presence weighed down the air in front of her. It smelled like a wet dog with its fur on fire. Her blood froze, as did her feet to the ground.

Rachel screamed, but no sound formed. She thought in

desperation:

– What the fuck is happening? –

You have been chosen, Rachel Kimura.

Rachel held her hand to her ears as the terrible voice engulfed her mind. Whatever was talking held her brain on its tongue inside its mouth.

– How do you know my name? –

I know everything about you.

– Yeah, well I don't know you! What am I doing here? What have I been chosen for? –

You are her currency.

– What are you talking about? A currency for what? For who? Why are you doing this to me? –

The unidentified being ceased responding. The air around her squeezed and picked her up to be closer to the red eyes which regarded her, scrutinized her. She vomited into the abyss as the air constricted around her, violating every part of her. Its gaze caressed every inch of her skin, tweaking and tearing as it went. Her piercings tore out from along both ears, eyebrows, nose, lips, tongue, nipples, belly button, and elsewhere. She opened her mouth to scream but the presence rushed into her throat, into her core, spreading through her veins.

This particular pain is only temporary. Soon you will be a part of my army and you will gain knowledge of new sensations. But first—improvement.

She struggled against the air, but it only squeezed tighter. It tore the clothes from her with its invisible claws, raking through her skin. Rachel was accustomed to the pain of new piercings, but a thousand septum rings couldn't have prepared her for the new torture. Hoops, barbs, rods, studs, screws, labrets, pins, and chains drove into her flesh anew. Rachel regretted wishing for un-anesthetized piercings on her enemies.

An unfamiliar discomfort pushed from inside her skull,

out of her forehead, and through the skin above both eyebrows.

The salt of her tears and blood mixed with mascara running into her open, soundless, screaming mouth, tasting of metallic tang. Her eyes rolled out of her head like there'd been nothing holding them to begin with. They slid down her cheeks, neck, breasts, stomach, legs, then bounced off her feet into the blackness. She blinked her lids over the emptiness in her skull. When she opened them, a new sight came to her.

She saw the dingy, matted fur of the large black shape with flaming eyes holding her; the two hard protrusions above her eyes curled out and up from her forehead; the trees below were visible, as was the hellscape she'd seen from her perch on the black rock; the multi-colored lights that strobed and waved in all directions as the black figures in front of the stage, rising with the crescendo of the rhythm, continued to reverberate through her bones and new piercings.

The sky's dull glow along the horizon grew in red and orange intensity. The creature placed Rachel back down on the jutting precipice. The feeling of pervasive remolding dissipated. She looked up and there was no trace of the giant being that had given birth to her new form. She noticed something new pulling at the end of her coccyx. Running her clawed fingertips down her spine, a protrusion extended into a long, fleshy tail. Where her feet used to be were two goat hooves. She stamped them a bit, getting used to the new movement and backward knees.

It was all...kind of cool? Once the pain wore off...

The chill left her bones. The air matched her warm, naked skin, glistening and dripping with sweat and blood. Rachel peered out to the mound. The lights shot straight down onto the center of the stage, covering it in white. She bowed down to her Queen, then trotted towards the black forest. The hooded figure from the plain below waited outside the entrance. It held out its bony fingers for Rachel's hand.

Auranna Korpela thrust her guitar pick into the night sky as white light bathed the stage. Twenty-five-thousand screams blasted her. She soaked it in, letting their chants wash over her. Stephanie Creighton stood to her right, with her bass guitar slung over her shoulder and hanging off her back, holding her arms out as if to hug the adulation but it was too large to get her arms around. To her left, Alex Kerrington had one hand on the neck of his guitar while holding the Devil's Horns up with the other. Two drumsticks flew over Auranna's head into the throng, tossed by Desmond Fuller. Carrie Stafford walked out from behind her keyboards to toss unopened bottles of water from the stage out into the abyss.

Auranna flicked all the extra picks from her guitar's neck and microphone stand into the crowd along with a couple of sweaty bracelets, then bowed one last time. Stephanie and Alex followed. The band would have loved nothing more than to play a third encore, but there was only so long they could keep up their stamina, even when the crowds fueled them as deeply as they had that night.

They handed their instruments to the techs and made their way through the line of backstage fans—shaking hands, signing autographs, and posing for photos with death stares in their melting corpse paint. A documentary crew, consisting of Lisa Nocnitsa, the director, and Joel Prescott, the cameraman, trailed them as always. Auranna had gotten used to them early in the tour and mostly ignored them. It was hard to resent their presence after the promises Lisa made of what the film would do for the band's "already-epic" stardom.

"Wait until we're playing in front of a stadium or former air base before you start throwing that word around like it's nothing," Auranna had said.

In the dressing room, Auranna exhaled all the energy she'd gathered from the evening. One of the roadies had already prepared her teas and honey to soothe her throat. She hummed to herself while removing the heavy black and white corpse paint and fake blood from her face, then tied a high ponytail out of her messed and matted long, wavy, ash blonde hair. Finally, she changed into black sweats and a form-fitting Immortal T-shirt.

Auranna tossed her spiked leather armlets, spiked black platform boots, and spiked single-shoulder pad into a trunk and laid down on the cheap, scratchy couch supplied by the event promoters, covering her eyes with her arm as she brought her voice down from two and a half hours of screams, screeches, shrieks, and death growls.

Her heavily calloused fingers throbbed and pulsed along with her slowing heartbeat. She almost dozed off when a soft knock snapped her out of it.

"Come in, Steph."

Stephanie opened the door a little bit to verify Auranna was alone, then slipped in and locked the door behind her. She leaned back into the door, exhausted, and smiled. Auranna returned it. Stephanie's bright red dyed hair hung down for the night, dancing along her shoulders like flames. She had changed into a knee-high plaid skirt and a Venom T-shirt. Unadorned from her stage outfit, she looked like any other fangirl in the crowd.

"Forty-five minutes, then Gerald says the bus is leaving with or without us," Stephanie said.

"Right. So... How was that for you?"

Stephanie shrugged her shoulders and looked up for a moment. "It was better than sex."

"Even with me?"

Stephanie contemplated the question with a cute, bashful little smile and a red glow emanating from her cheeks. "Mm-hm. Sorry, Aura."

Auranna beckoned her to the couch. Stephanie straddled Auranna's stomach and kissed her, enjoying the taste of honeyed teas on her tongue. She pressed into Auranna, while Auranna's hands reached up Stephanie's thighs underneath the skirt and traced the outline of her underwear.

Auranna paused to catch her breath and whispered, "I don't think we have time for this tonight. Maybe if we hadn't performed the second encore…"

"The second was better than the first. You can't beat that feeling, anyway, so why try?"

Stephanie relaxed between the couch's crevice and Auranna's torso and kissed her neck, then rested her head against the front of her shoulder. She traced her fingers along the sharp patterns of Scandinavian metal imagery tattooed along Auranna's arms, ending on the branded inverted cross on the underside of her left forearm.

"You better stop talking," Stephanie yawned. "Let your voice heal up for tomorrow night. I'll talk to the documentary crew tonight on the bus. You should get your rest."

Auranna hummed in response. Stephanie could listen to Auranna calming her voice down for hours. Auranna often did so in her sleep. It was more soothing than anything else Stephanie had tried putting herself to sleep with, when the adrenaline wouldn't fully die down after a performance. They both dozed until a knock startled them awake. The doorknob shook. Carrie yelled through the door that the bus was leaving in ten minutes.

Stephanie helped Auranna off the couch. They kissed again, then left the room, entwining their fingers together.

They followed a roadie through the labyrinthian tents as they were struck for the journey to the next venue. The rest of the band and documentary crew were already inside Black Aura's tour bus.

"How many guesses do I get for why you two are the last ones on the bus again?" Desmond asked.

"You'll never guess that we were only sleeping, Dezzie," Stephanie said, though her face turned crimson at his accusation.

"I'm not trying to shame you, Steph. But we spent all this money on a tour bus with multiple beds. Why don't you get out of your outfits and come straight to the bus?"

"It's a little crowded in here, dude," Alex said from the dining table, eating whatever he could take from the venue's catering service. "Sometimes it's nice to stretch out in some of the larger dressing rooms. Besides, what would you prefer, they do their thing alone? Or in here, within earshot of the rest of us?"

"What'd you bring us, Alex?" Stephanie asked, eager to change the subject and not be the focus of her bandmates' attention.

Alex slid bags of plain chips and desiccated-looking sandwiches across the table. They took one of each.

"What'd you do, take all the good stuff for yourself?" Desmond asked while he popped open a chip bag with a bang.

"It was all the same. You think I'm that sneaky?"

"We'd never know. I don't know how you eat as much as you do and never seem to gain weight," Carrie said as she looked down at her stomach beneath her X Japan T-shirt and sighed.

"You're the only one here that looks healthy, Carrie. Settle down with that," Alex said. "By the way, I liked the way your new dye looked tonight. You should settle on red for the rest of the tour."

"I'm done with it. Stop asking me to dye it red. I've had enough. I don't want to look like I'm copying Stephanie. What do you think about the new length, though?"

Alex went back to his sandwich.

"I don't like it falling in my eyes all night!" Carrie blurted.

Alex thrummed his fingers on the small table and looked away. None of her other bandmates looked at her, either.

"What's with metalheads and hair length?" Carrie muttered and went back to eating.

Auranna ignored the food and grabbed a water bottle from the fridge, then prepared more tea. Stephanie sat down on one of the couches in the living area. She ran her fingers through her hair and waited patiently while Lisa fiddled with the black box and microphone clipped on Stephanie's skirt and shirt. Lisa signaled for Joel to start rolling after adjusting her thin black glasses and moving a stray strand of her black hair behind her ear. The bright light at the top of the camera briefly blinded Stephanie.

"So, are we talking about the music tonight, Lisa? Or that other thing?"

"Since you brought 'the other thing' up, disappearances haven't stopped. Every venue on the tour this year—the same as every venue over the ten years Black Aura has been touring."

"Hold on. Have you found proof that these people are disappearing during the concerts now? You continually imply that it's related to us. I get that you have to have a theme for your documentary, but the accusations are getting tired at this point. Do you have anything new to add?"

"Just to update you on the numbers, that's—"

"We're not blind or deaf to all this," Stephanie interrupted, tired of repeating herself in front of the camera. "But constantly bringing it up to us after every show isn't going to unlock any new clues or bombshells. Why don't you talk to the police in these towns that can't seem to ever find anything?"

"We do interview them. The ones that allow us to, anyway. It's always the same—the victims vanished out of thin air, leaving no evidence whatsoever."

"Do you ever see any of us leave the stage in the middle of a set? We have cameras and tens of thousands of eyes on us at all times. We're not involved in any of these disappearances."

"There's been an outcry from parents in many towns, before and after your shows, that your Satanic imagery and lyrics are fueling something. Like people are forming cults and carrying out ritualistic behavior with the victims."

"Would you can it with that shit?" Desmond said, sitting in front of the muted TV. "We can't control what some idiots choose to do with their time. We aren't inciting anything but mosh pits. Why don't you do an exposé on the security companies not doing their jobs at the venues and stop blaming us?"

"Don't you feel bad that one of your fans from each show vanishes without a trace?"

"Of course! We want these sick assholes to be caught and punished as much as anyone!" Alex said as he sat down next to Stephanie and pulled the microphone from her shirt. She swatted his hand for getting so close to her chest. He apologized for his carelessness.

"Have you considered shutting down the tour until a breakthrough can be made in any of the cases?" Lisa continued.

"Do you shut down public transportation systems when someone goes missing from a bus or train?" Alex said. "Do you unplug the Internet whenever someone gets lured into a trap and abducted? Do you stop making movies because some nutjob commits some heinous act directly after watching? Should we go hang ourselves because some puritanical politicians and parents can't figure out how to take care of their own kids and need an easy scapegoat?"

"There seems to be a very heavy cause and effect at play

with your concerts, though. Don't you agree?"

"If it's so heavy, Lisa, why has no one ever caught a single one of these people? No, if something is unexplainable, let's blame the young people and their black makeup, metal clothing, tattoos, facial piercings, and loud music, right? Rotting Christ!"

Alex stood up in disgust, handed the microphone back to Stephanie, flopped on his bed, and threw on his headphones. He pulled out his lyrical notebook and they could all hear him nearly tearing through the pages with his pen.

Stephanie half-smiled at Lisa.

"We're not going to stop touring because of this, unless there's some actual concrete evidence and there are no other possible explanations. Anything else you want to talk about tonight?"

"That's all, Stephanie. Thanks, Black Aura."

Lisa motioned for Joel to cut.

"I love the anger and frustration from you guys," she said. "You all 'doth protest too much.' This movie is going to be amazing. It'll be my winning ticket to bigger budgets and stars."

"You realize that makes you no different than us, right?" Auranna said from the little kitchen table.

"I happen to agree with you all. That's not what's going into the film, though."

"Okay. Just so we're all clear."

CHAPTER TWO

SUCCUBUS

HELL'S GROUPIES

AURANNA STARTLED AWAKE. IT WAS her turn on the big bed in the back and she was alone. She got up and discovered that the other beds and couches were empty. She hugged her arms and shivered in her Dissection tank top and thin pajama bottoms.

"Guys? Steph? Lisa? Please tell me this is a prank."

It wasn't going to be. It never was. But she always held out a little hope, which made the coming pain a tiny bit more bearable.

Her duffel bag wasn't underneath the bed. She opened one of the closets that housed their jackets, but it hung bare. She crossed her arms and held her hands in her armpits to keep them warm as she walked to the front of the bus. The still blackness outside didn't bother her. In fact, she adored darkness, especially when it contrasted with the snows of Finland. She loathed what lurked in the dream darkness, though—always watching, always waiting to inflict unimaginable pain.

She sighed at the coming agony, an inevitability she'd

come to expect. She couldn't escape it, so she didn't try anymore. Getting it over with quicker than the last time was all she could wish.

"Can you please not rip me asunder this time?" she asked, knowing no one would answer, no matter how politely she queried.

She pushed the button on the front console to open the door, then stepped out into the blackness, onto a jutting rock over a void. Behind her, the bus disappeared, revealing an endless line of black trees, barely discernible in the low light except by the dull red glow above their ragged peaks. She sighed and shook her head as memories of all the pain and suffering she'd endured in that forest rushed back to her.

Knowing there was no other way out of the dream on her own terms, Auranna trudged into the dark embrace of the looming black trunks. The little red eyes of the imps that inflicted most of the pain when His attention pointed elsewhere stared at her. Their hissing whispers filled her head the moment she entered the forest. Their voices overlapped, irritating as a mosquito buzzing inside her ears.

The Queen! The Queen is here!
Not our queen. Unworthy. Pain deserved. Hope unearned.
She is the only one to withstand Him. She will save them all.
Foolish pride. Only a musician's life interests her. She will forget them all. She will fail them all.

Their taunts had stopped having an effect on her about ten years before, after she formed Black Aura, and they had started eight years before that. It wasn't worth arguing with them when she didn't know what the hell they were talking about, and half of them seemed to argue "on her behalf" anyway, so she did her best to fill her thoughts with music to drown out their incessant whispering.

She learned long ago the distant orange lights wouldn't come closer no matter how fast or far she ran unless she chose the "correct" one—the light that wanted to converse.

She took a step towards each one in turn until one grew closer, then she jogged to it. Once close enough to see with the light it provided, she checked her skin. There were no creepy-crawlies. Sometimes there were, sometimes there weren't; it all depended on what the dreamworld wanted to show her or make her feel. It seemed to have moods, like the weather. It wanted her to feel every sensation a human being could but delighted in nothing more than pain.

The air swept around her warmly, pleasantly. *Seductively*. Usually, the air was more interested in raping her than making her feel good, so it was a welcome deviation. Her hands followed her body's contours in sync with the invisible pressure, exploring every part of her without force. She wished she could pull Stephanie down into the blackness with her, to experience the pleasure together. On Earth Auranna couldn't hope to come close to giving Stephanie anything resembling the sensations the forest could bestow, when it wasn't in a bad mood...

A clip-clopping approached from a distance. The air pressed into her tighter as the being grew closer. In the orange glow, the silhouette took shape. It had goat's legs up to its knees, supporting a young woman's voluptuous naked body. A fleshy tail whipped the air behind it like an agitated cat's. Its forehead bore two ram horns above inky black eye sockets. Medium and large-hooped golden rings glinted in the low orange light, hanging from its ears, nose, eyebrows, lips, chin, nipples, neck, sternum, stomach, and between its legs. The piercings dangled, perfectly spaced all in a row, every few inches. Its face was both hideous and gorgeous to behold. Its voice was terrible and lurid in Auranna's mind, as if speaking to her underwater.

My Queen. How I have longed to meet You. It has been an eternity.

– Your...queen? I'm not a queen. –

My Goddess. My Love. My Life.

– What? I don't know who you are. My girlfriend is back on Earth. I think you have me confused with someone else. –

She cannot please You like I can. Like I will.

– Usually, the wind either blows up my skirt or tortures me and lets me go at this point. –

There will be no wind this time. You will beg me to never let You go.

– I know I'm dreaming, ok? Could I request this sort of dream more often, though? Without the pain afterwards? –

You will wish You were not dreaming.

– Are you going to talk all night or get it over with? You're already giving me some great lyrics. I want to write them down before I forget them. –

We will make the most beautiful music together.

The creature disappeared in a puff of smoke that moved to Auranna, enveloped her, then laid her down onto the forest floor. The smoke reformed into the hooved creature laying over her. Its tail whipped down, around, and up her pant leg, snaking through the pants and underneath her tank through her cleavage. It cleanly tore the clothes from her body in one twitch. The tail wrapped itself around her leg and pulled it aside. The creature's mouth opened to reveal three pierced tongues that lapped at her neck, then proceeded to explore every part of her. The tongues never seemed to dry or tire with the strain.

The voices of the imps threatened to overwhelm Auranna's mind. Though she battled to keep them from ruining the moment, their taunts didn't go away.

The Slut Queen will not save them. She cares only for sex and music.

Does the newcomer know there must be more pain than pleasure? He commands it.

Our Queen deserves hope. She deserves more than pain.

Slut Queen, your succubus is in eternal pain. Making love to you hurts her. She resents you. She lies to you. She is coerced.

Our Queen will save her. She will save them all.
Deluded. Salvation is beyond her detached grasp.

Sweat and saliva glistened on Auranna's skin like a golden statue under the orange glow. Every part of her tensed with pleasure. The creature knew exactly where to touch, where to press, where to squeeze, where to caress, where to hover, where to tease, where to pinch, where to kiss, where to lick, where to bite, where to pull, where to be gentle, and where to be rough. A symphony of pleasure worked feverishly towards its crescendo while Auranna's fingers formed furious chords along the creature's flesh. She transferred each sensation into a new composition. A ripping, tearing squelch came from the creature's back as they both climaxed at the apex of the new song. The creature rose to stand over Auranna, unfolding and flexing its new leathery wings. Its sultry voice filled her head again as Auranna caught her breath.

Thank You, my Queen. I did not expect Your reciprocity, nor that Your music would unleash these. I did not believe the old woman.

The wings flapped, then picked the creature up. It held itself a couple of feet over Auranna's body, its black eyes piercing hers, her eyebrows communicating gratitude and sorrow.

I am sorry to leave You to them. I hope we meet again.

– Who are you? What old woman? –

Auranna received no reply as the demoness flew out of sight. Many small red eyes opened around her then. They glowed, burning as Hell's fire. She propped herself up on her elbows.

– Alright, guess fun time's over. Get it over with. –

The eyes rushed in, their taunts drowning out all other thoughts as they ceased whispering. They flicked out their razor claws and revealed pointed teeth.

Auranna woke gasping for air. Her flesh burned and tore. Her hands explored her body frantically. It was too dark to see in the back of the bus. She grabbed a flashlight from her duffel and examined her arms, legs, chest, and stomach. There were no burns or scratches. She had felt every one of their claws and teeth tear into her, as if eating her alive. They were enough to make her forget all about the beautiful, hooved creature's gift to her, but only briefly. The evidence of the sexual encounter soaked her sheets and pajamas and brought the sweeter memory of the dark forest back to her.

Why did the dreamworld feel different in the presence of that demon? Some of them attempted the pleasure-before-pain bit maybe once or twice a year over the previous eighteen years, but nothing was ever like that. Had He approved that?

The others slept on without a care in the world, so she changed into a fresh Ulver T-shirt and sweats. She grabbed her notebook and plopped into the passenger seat at the front of the bus.

"Evenin,' Gerald."

"Mornin,' Aura. Couldn't sleep?" Gerald asked while keeping his eyes on the road.

"Too many ideas came into me tonight. I need to write them all down before I forget."

"Don't you mean 'came *to* you?'"

"Hmm?"

Gerald cocked his eyebrow when she wouldn't justify or change her odd phrasing. Her English was nearly flawless, but sometimes Auranna would say a word or phrase that betrayed it wasn't her first language. She meant what she said, though. A little curl of a smile out of Gerald's sight broke her pursed lips—she didn't often feel like being lewd out loud, but the dream put her in a mood.

"I could hear you moaning from here. It's a good thing the others are such heavy sleepers."

"Oh, sorry about that. It was a really painful dream."

"Didn't sound like pain to me, but whatever. It's not like we have control of our dreams, eh?"

"Wouldn't that be lovely?" she murmured while drawing imagery accompanied by lyrics, emotions, and the chords she attributed to those feelings.

Gerald knew to keep quiet when she wrote in her notebook. Auranna loved writing next to someone who understood her need for silence during pivotal moments of inspiration. She valued the dark and quiet when she worked. After an hour of writing and drawing, she fell asleep in the seat. Someone put a hand on her shoulder and shook her awake.

"Hey, Aura. Wouldn't you be more comfortable in your bed?" Stephanie asked.

"No, I would not, my love. It's a mess back there," she yawned and closed her eyes again.

"Ok, well, at least come sleep in my bed. I know how groggy you get at rehearsals when you fall asleep up here. Come on."

Stephanie pulled her up by the hand and steadied her in the aisle. Auranna put her hand on Gerald's shoulder and thanked him.

"Of course, kid."

Stephanie grabbed Auranna's shoulders and guided her back to her own bed. They'd spent enough nights together to be comfortable cuddling in such a cramped space. Stephanie'd had her own trouble sleeping and hoped Auranna would hum. After five minutes, she hummed a tune Stephanie never heard before. The sound captivated her. She tried committing it to memory so she could go over it with Auranna in the morning, but sleep caught up to her before the chorus did.

Auranna and Stephanie sat together on the edge of the stage, their bare feet flirting as they dangled together. They went over the imagery and lyrics that Auranna had recorded from the night before while the crew set up the stage equipment and prepped for sound check.

"You...were raped by a demon? Jeez, Aura. I don't know that we need more songs with abusive subtext."

"I didn't use that word. I said *seduced*. It was...exquisite...for both of us. Mmmm, I wanted you there with me so much."

"Wake me next time you feel that hot and bothered. You know I'm quiet. I don't mind how sweaty you get. I don't sleep very well, anyway."

Auranna put her hand over Stephanie's, always taken aback by her unconditional and sweet love. Stephanie was the only person Auranna had ever been with that didn't at some point make some passive-aggressive comment about how much she sweat during her nightmares.

"I'll show this new stuff to the band tonight. Maybe Alex can make something out of it all. I feel like there was a lot I forgot once I was— ...once the dream ended."

Auranna looked into Stephanie's concerned eyes. It was a good thing Stephanie still thought Auranna only dreamt of these things, and she never ridiculed her stories. It was hard to express to anyone else the pain Auranna suffered. It would only sound hyperbolic to anyone who wasn't there with her. Auranna wished Stephanie would never feel the same pain.

One of the techs handed over Auranna's Vantablack™ ESP EC Black Metal guitar. She tried recalling her fingers' movements along the flesh of the creature from her dream, but the harder she concentrated, the quicker the details fluttered away into ephemera.

"Am I supposed to get my own bass?" Stephanie said out of earshot of the departing tech. "Freakin' roadies kiss your butt so much, Aura. I'll probably have to tune it myself, too."

Auranna sympathized with Stephanie, and smiled at how she couldn't simply speak up for herself and tell the roadie to do his job. But Auranna couldn't spare her the distraction. Stephanie went back to the instrument cases. Auranna closed her eyes, hoping to conjure the creature back into her mind. She strummed a couple more chords back from the abyss.

A scream pulled Auranna out of her trance. Stephanie had dropped her bass onto the stage and held her arm. A melanistic adder slithered away from Stephanie's guitar case towards Auranna.

Auranna reached down—hoping it would slither up her arm—but it went through her. The serpent floated to the ground in front of the stage and slid away, escaping through the feet of dozens of oblivious people. Auranna stared in wonderment until it disappeared by the mixer tent. Stephanie's whimpering brought her attention back to the commotion on stage.

Desmond and Carrie huddled around Stephanie, scratching their heads as they examined her arm. Auranna put her guitar aside and went to stand next to Stephanie. Trickles of yellow seeped out of two holes in her forearm.

"What'd you say happened?" Carrie asked.

"I don't know! Something stabbed me when I opened my

case, but I didn't see anything! Nnngh, it hurts!"

"Carrie, you don't see her arm?" Auranna asked.

"I see she has an arm, and I see she's holding it, Aura. Jeesh."

"You don't see the bite marks?"

"Bite marks? What could have bitten me? I didn't see anything! It feels like I've been *stabbed*!" Stephanie cried.

"You don't see them either? Dez, do you see them?"

He shook his head, then put his hand on the back of Stephanie's head to help soothe her.

"Are you sure you didn't scrape it on the clasps? Your case is pretty old..."

"No, Dezzie, I didn't 'scrape it on the clasps.' I opened the case, picked up my bass, and something stabbed or bit me or something. I didn't see it."

"Guys, go grab a medic, please. I'll stay with her," Auranna said.

Desmond and Carrie exchanged looks and walked away.

"Why's she being so melodramatic today?" Desmond said.

You're not out of earshot yet, Dez, Auranna thought, then put her concentration on Stephanie. She grasped the arm and inspected the wound closer.

"Tell me if this hurts, Steph."

Auranna pressed her fingers around the area, then over the holes. The yellow liquid oozed out at even a slight amount of pressure. Stephanie winced and closed her eyes. Auranna hated seeing her in so much pain.

"So you're feeling this but you can't see what's causing it?"

Stephanie nodded as tears escaped her tightly closed lids.

"Alright, my love, I'm going to try something. It'll seem strange, I'm sorry. I want you to think about how you can infuse all this into your art, though, while it lasts."

Auranna bent her head down and licked the yellow liquid, which she assumed to be the ghostly snake's venom. It tasted bitter but for an unexpected, subtle sweetness behind it. She clamped her lips around the wound and sucked the liquid into her mouth.

She knew the sucking method wasn't actually how one should go about treating a snake bite, but that wasn't exactly a normal snake. After a tablespoon or so of liquid filled her mouth, she spit it out, then clamped down again.

"What are you spitting out? There's nothing coming out of your mouth."

Auranna held up her finger and continued. The liquid grew more metallic in taste as she sucked out the venom and hit fresh blood. She spit the rest out. The holes closed, as if they were never there; all that remained was a dark brown mark from where her mouth had sucked at Stephanie's skin.

Footsteps approached the pair. "What is this? You wanted me to look at a hickey? Quit fucking around, guys. Only get me when there's a real emergency!"

The medic stormed off. Desmond, Carrie, and Auranna all looked at Stephanie.

"I—I—I don't know what's going on. It doesn't hurt anymore. It's a little tender around that brown mark is all."

"Steph, there are simpler ways to have someone suck on you," Carrie said, shaking her head. "You don't need to come up with some elaborate song and dance. I'm sure Aura will be happy to take care of your needs in the dressing room after the show. There're plenty of groupies who'll do whatever you want, too."

"Come on, Carrie, we're up for sound check. Alex is waiting for us," Desmond said, then gave a little conspiratorial smile over his shoulder as they walked away. "It's so fuckin' cute that she gets all bashful when we talk about sex around her."

"Guys, I'm not crazy! Ask Aura! She saw whatever it was and made the pain go away."

They laughed and went back to their instruments. Auranna smiled sympathetically and shrugged.

"I don't know, Steph. It was preternatural, certainly. I saw the snake and bite clear as I'm seeing you now. I tasted venom and your blood. That's what I spit out."

Stephanie stared at her, then looked sad.

"You sound as crazy as I do."

Auranna kissed her, loving her blushing face as much as her bandmates, and grabbed the bass. She waved a tech over to tune it, then picked up her black-as-death guitar and joined the others for sound check.

CHAPTER THREE
SERPENUS

SNAKES, TROUSER AND OTHERWISE

WHILE THE TWO OPENING ACTS performed, Auranna liked to get extra sleep in the likelihood Black Aura played another multi-encore set. She only ever demanded of her bandmates that they do everything in their power to earn the encores, never allowing them to consider it a right, but a privilege.

The couch in the venue's dressing room was far more comfortable than the last and made it much easier to doze off. She set an alarm to go off twenty minutes before they were expected on stage. She loved the music of the opening bands, but the longer the tour went, the less she wanted to hear the same songs night after night. Eventually the repeated music helped her fall asleep.

The black forest appeared before her. Auranna rose from the couch and walked inside. Hissing and slithering filled her mind. She took steps towards the lights until one moved towards her. As she got closer, her bare feet grew heavier.

Only one thing could be holding her back. She stopped

and they wriggled around her feet, pulling at the black nylon up her calf and thigh, licking and tickling all the way up. She ignored them and pushed forward as if trudging through thigh-high snow back home in Finland.

The hundreds of snakes surrounding her became clearer the closer she got to the orange light. When she stopped, an undefinable number of them lunged at her. They pierced her skin dozens of times, over and over; relentless. Her legs buckled and she fell down on all fours. They struck at her arms, legs, stomach, breasts, butt, back, and neck while slithering around like a mass of live wires.

– Why...are you...doing this...? Who...are you? –

About twenty feet in front of her, a dark figure, blacker than the black surrounding it, slithered forward. It appeared to be a giant snake—man-size in girth and height.

My Queen. I heard Your entreaty in our realm and Yours. You wished for the one named Stephanie to join You in the pleasures of this place.

– No! That was selfish, idiotic thinking born of unbridled lust! I don't wish for her to see it! To...experience it! –

My black adder has connected her to our realm.

– Wait! Wait! You said I'm your queen! I command you to leave her alone! She doesn't deserve to feel the pain this place bestows! It's not for her to bear! –

I fear it is too late. Maybe I can find a way to... I...wish You had the power...to...

The snake-man shivered and convulsed. All the snakes that had been attacking her engulfed him instead, like a writhing snake orgy. The silhouette faded and disappeared, replaced by the giant red eyes she dreaded more than anything else the dreamworld ever conjured.

– No, not You. Please. I'm so sorry. –

The air around her constricted and lifted her, pulling her up several hundred feet—the eyes always in front of her. Auranna knew that the eyes would make her feel the exact opposite as the creature from the night before. Its malicious intent was palpable.

You hoped to see Rachel again instead of me. Perhaps you desire a reciprocated gift from her?

– What are You talking about? Who's Rachel? What gift? That creature? She's always been here, hasn't she? Haven't You all? So what do I have to do with it? Why do You keep bringing me here? –

You have always entered the forest willingly, seeking truth and knowledge.

– I've never chosen to come here! There's no alternative to entering! Stop bringing me here! As your Queen I command— –

The air around her emanated rage, suffocating her. She struggled through the futility. It squeezed her muscles so she couldn't move.

You are NOT my queen. None command me. None are my equal. Your devotees—your army—may call you what they wish—it matters not.

– Please, please don't do this. I didn't mean to anger You. I beg of You. Not this time. I'm so sorry, my Lord. –

The giant red eyes betrayed the hint of a smile when their corners synched ever so slightly in the dark. The air loosened around her, then let her drop into the void below. She fell for hours.

Ever falling and unable to orient herself to up or down, Auranna screamed soundlessly into the void. Though she couldn't see how close she was to the bottom, her body kept expecting to feel the end of the fall at any moment. Breathing became impossible as she tensed more and more in anticipation of the inevitable collision. Her lungs burned from withheld breaths, but she never died.

Faintly she noticed a sound behind her, but she was unable to turn to discover its source. She concentrated, placing the sound of leathery wings. It was the hooved creature from the previous night, flying with the wings Auranna had strummed from her shoulder blades.

A light touch re-oriented Auranna, vertical to the rush of wind below her.

Wake, my Queen.

Auranna stood on the couch back in the dressing room. Stephanie stared at her from the make-up mirror, mouth hanging open, her mascara pen clattering to the floor.

"I thought sound check was as strange as it was going to get today. You shook on the couch like you were getting electrocuted, then stood bolt-upright without bending your knees! How the heck did you do that?"

"I shook? Did I say anything?"

"Not much. I only heard the name Rachel. The shaking was only for a couple seconds or I would have gone for the medic... Though she may not have come after what happened with my arm."

"Rachel? Do we know a Rachel?"

"Mmm-mm. Not that I know of."

"How much time do we have?"

Her phone alarm went off before Stephanie answered. Auranna threw off her Morbid Angel T-shirt, opened her trunk, and pulled out her spiked gear. That night she felt like wearing a black leather bra, spiked shoulder pad, and high-waisted torn black jeans with a studded belt. She kept her hair down for thrashing, but put a tall, spiked tiara at the front of her hairline to keep it out of her eyes. Stephanie had already tossed her Judas Priest T-shirt aside and was tying her new top as tight as possible. Auranna helped her out once her own gear was in place, but it was hard to concentrate with the irresistible outfit Stephanie chose to wear. She always wore a T-shirt and jeans on stage. The change was jarring, though not unwelcome.

"Hellbent on this black and red leather corset? Nice," Auranna said. "I love this look with your hair."

"I know. Should I go exaggerated cat eye or crying girl?"

"You have to ask?"

"Cat eye, it is, then."

"How's your arm doing?" Auranna asked as she caressed the spot she'd extracted the venom from earlier.

"Like it never happened. What the heck was that? How could I feel it and you see it, but no one else could?"

"I don't know. We both didn't get much sleep last night. Maybe our hallucinatory states melded and birthed the snake and bite."

"That sounds...really stupid, Aura." Stephanie sputtered trying to stifle a laugh.

"What would sound better? Satan was punishing you for flubbing that note last night during 'Forsaken Fury?'"

"Screw you." Stephanie frowned in her corpse paint and swatted Auranna's arm. "Just because you've never missed a note in your life..."

"*I* wasn't judging, my love. *Satan* was."

"Right. If I do it again, will He flay me alive with a rusty fishing hook?"

"Don't give Him any ideas. You might end up like the girl in 'Bleed for the Devil' and I'm afraid I'd be unable to suck you out of that predicament."

Elijah and Tristan bobbed their heads to the unrelenting, unyielding rhythm of Black Aura's monolithic masterpiece "Selfish Sacrifice." They'd dreamt of the moment for years. The band always skipped their town on tours, but that year they played close enough that it justified the short trip. In the dark, pressed against thousands of other fans, the two held hands without fear of judgment. Endorphins flooded their systems. An uncontrollable urge took them over as the song rose to its first chorus. They embraced and kissed without shame thanks to their heavy corpse paint.

When they broke from their kiss, the music changed abruptly. The people around them had transformed into floating, blurry shades. The spikes on each of the band members' costumes grew out longer and longer. They continued playing but it was as unfocused as the shadows in the crowd. Elijah glanced at Tristan, jaw slack and eyes wide.

"What— Are you seeing this?" Tristan asked.

"Where are we?"

Their hands, slick with sweat, squeezed together in fear. They crept around the shades floating in place, only to realize that they could walk through them without feeling or moving them. Though the sound didn't carry from the stage or speakers, the familiar rhythm of "their song" pulsed through their blood. They made it to the front of the stage and looked up at the Goddess of Metal.

Shadow covered her magnificent visage, but her spiked tiara stood out clearly, threatening them as it thrashed back and forth towards their faces, growing longer with each thrust forward. When the melodic interlude started, flickering firelight sprouted from the darkness around them. They turned to see the shades holding up flames from stubby, smoky appendages.

"Are we... Did someone spike our drinks with something? Are we hallucinating?"

"I don't know, Eli. I feel like I'm dreaming. Maybe we *did* get spiked. I can't think of anything else. Maybe if we lay down, we'll wake up?"

Tristan lay on the field, then shot back up, brushing his clothes in a disgusted panic.

"What? What is it?" Elijah cried.

"The fucking ground is moving! Like, *living!*"

"Oh fuck, we are completely tripping. Let's see if we can find some water or something back at the concession tent."

"How are we going to find it? Everything is so goddamn black here!"

"I think I remember how to get back to the entrance. Use the mixer tent as a point of reference. We were just there. Let's go."

"Do you have any money left? I bought three band shirts and now I have nothing."

"I'll fucking *steal* some water, Trist! They can arrest me at this point."

It only took a couple feet before they realized the mixer tent wasn't getting any closer. They turned around to find the stage hadn't moved, either. The five band members stared at the two of them with their horrible, shadowed non-faces. Auranna Korpela played into her most renowned solo but didn't move her head from their direction. The music bore into them, and Elijah and Tristan were overcome with sudden lust and passion. They tore the clothes from each other and did things they never imagined they'd ever do—let alone in front of a mob of specters—all while Auranna's svelte fingers plucked at their veins.

The solo rose into the climactic chorus, then came down

on the perfect dramatic outro. Elijah and Tristan collapsed on each other's shoulders so they wouldn't have to touch the ground. Elijah turned his head and jumped at the sudden appearance of two gigantic red eyes.

"Oh! What the *fuck*?"

Tristan stepped backwards when he saw them, too. A low, resonating voice filled their heads.

You have been chosen, Elijah. Tristan.

Elijah tried to speak but no sound came out. Tristan seemed to be experiencing the same thing.

I can hear your thoughts, children. You have been chosen.

– What? That doesn't make any sense, even if you say it twice. What are you on about? –

Elijah nodded at Tristan's bewildered expression, confirming they were able to hear each other's thoughts along with the evil, disembodied voice.

Two, for the price of one. Your queen has paid it.

– Our queen? This is America, asshole. We don't have a––
–

The air restricted and lifted them, thrusting them towards the stage where Auranna's black, empty face peered into their souls.

– Her? It's not like we worship her or anything! We don't even know her! How could she choose us for anything? We're nobodies! –

You are her currency.

– Make sense, motherfucker! Let us go! We've done nothing to no one! –

Not yet. But you will. Together. There are no judgments for you here.

The air swirled around and twisted both of them, positioning them back-to-back. Their hair tangled together and pulled in opposite directions as if their heads were in a tug of war to claim the others' scalp. Their screams echoed in each other's heads as their skin and bone fused. From their coccyges to their spines to the back of their skulls, they became one. The air set them down, then bent their knees—as if they were sitting back to back—and extended their genitals, giving them independent, prehensile control. They were like a threatened tarantula, rearing up on its hind legs.

You will join my army. They are waiting for you up in the forest.

The air lifted them up, placing them onto a cliff lined with black trees. It nudged them toward the path inside. They attempted to walk "forward" but side-shuffling wasn't comfortable, all things considered, on their knees. Elijah turned them at a ninety-degree angle and walked forward while Tristan walked backwards. Then they swapped at a one-hundred-eighty-degree angle. It didn't take long to get used to the new movement. They looked down at the distant stage in turn, then scuttled away from the cliff.

A hooded figure waited for them at the entrance of the forest.

CHAPTER FOUR
Auraneae

Auranna's Spider

AS AURANNA REGAINED CONSCIOUSNESS, STEPHANIE'S legs came into focus, then she noticed the pain in her cheek as it pressed against the stage. Stephanie looked down at her with concern but kept her bass on point. Auranna lifted her head to the sound of the crowd swell. She pulled herself up, fueled by the power of the crowd behind her, chanting her name. Her guitar lay at her feet. She scanned around for the other band members. They all seemed concerned but continued playing—there was no denying the crowd's hungry energy. She bent to pick up the guitar.

Auranna recalled the "death" of Yoshiki on stage in an X Japan documentary. Had she collapsed through sheer exhaustion? Through ecstasy? The crowd's reaction to that performance in the movie was a feeling she could only dream of—to have been witness, or to perform that spectacularly herself someday. To die for her craft was the only way Auranna could meet her ancestors without shame.

She remembered playing the solo of "Selfish Sacrifice" and the terrifying sight of her guitar strings turning to fleshy veins of blue and red. Through that horrific and disgusting image a vision of two young men having decadent sex played through the chorus, ending with the two of them being tossed around by invisible forces and disappearing back into the crowd. She blacked out before seeing what became of them.

Auranna stood with her back to the crowd as the chants increased in volume and intensity. Her bandmates held their notes for her to intercept and take off. Blinking away her daze, Auranna seized the moment and lifted her pick to the sky. The crowd's voice rose, rapturous for her to launch into the next title. She juiced their anticipation for all it was worth, then exploded into their fastest, most difficult song.

After Auranna put on her Van Halen shirt, she allowed the rest of the band to congregate in the dressing room.

"Are you sure you're okay, Aura? That was pretty scary, as theatrical as you made it all seem," Alex asked.

"I'm telling you, guys, I was overwhelmed with emotion. You know I love that song. I guess I ran out of gas at the end."

"That's putting it mildly. You did a full faceplant! I thought you had a heart attack!" Carrie said.

"Yet you all kept playing. Don't get me wrong—I'm glad you did. I love the priorities in a moment like that. The crowd and music are the thing, and you all sensed it. Next time, though, wipe the worry off your faces when we're on stage. If there is a next time. I didn't plan it and I won't ever fake something like that."

"You 'ran out of gas,' yet launched into the beyond-*prestissimo* as if it was nothing?" Alex raised an eyebrow. "Were you trying to die?"

"Yes. I'm playing at a killer pace."

"I see you're well enough to make jokes," Alex said with a quick glance at her shirt. "That's a relief."

"Look, weird stuff has been happening over the last twenty-four hours. I'm going to put valerian root into my teas tonight. Maybe if I get some real sleep I'll get back on an even keel. The day off in a few days should help as well."

An obtrusive banging on the door made them all jump.

"Hey! Ten minutes! Get your asses on the bus!" Gerald yelled through the door.

They all rolled their eyes and shrugged their shoulders in turn, then filed toward the exit of the venue.

"What's the big goddamn hurry, Gerald?" Desmond said as they walked through the living area of the bus.

"Someone's got to keep you people on schedule. The sooner we're at the next city, the more time you'll have to relax, and I'll have less time to worry about traffic and whatever mechanical mishaps always arise before a gig."

Lisa greeted them as they boarded, then pulled Auranna aside.

"Can I talk with you about the show tonight? Can you tell me why you fainted?"

"Sorry, Lisa, I'm too tired. I'm going to have some tea and go straight to bed. Who's turn is it to use the big bed?"

"Mine," Carrie raised her hand.

"Ok. I'll double check the crew got around to cleaning it today."

"No one cares you're so sweaty when you sleep. It's not like you wet the bed, right?" Carrie's smile died when Auranna didn't immediately deny it. "Please tell me it was *adult* 'wetting the bed'... That's still gross, but...less so, somehow."

Auranna blew on the surface of her tea, raising her

eyebrows a couple times rapidly over the mug. Stephanie laughed while Carrie sighed and went to investigate the bedding situation herself.

The next morning Auranna felt much better. The dreams and visions didn't interrupt her sleep at all. The bus brought them to the next city without incident. The band ate breakfast at a diner, unrecognizable without their corpse paint, leaving them unbothered by any local finger-waggers or autograph hounds, although their metal band T-shirts got them a few squinty, distrustful looks. Auranna wore an innocuous Black Sabbath shirt. Innocuous to her, anyway.

While the rest of the band went sight-seeing, Auranna visited a magazine journalist at a guitar store for a pre-planned interview. Until the journalist arrived, she signed autographs for the patrons and corroborated the salespeople's advice to customers on guitar suggestions. When the journalist arrived, Auranna went with him to the soundproof room in the back of the store for privacy.

"Alright, I'd like to start recording, if that's okay with you? Okay. This is Stanley Crawford and I'm here with the lead guitarist and vocalist for Black Aura—Auranna Korpela. I appreciate you making yourself available for this interview. Your band has been touring endlessly over the last few years; it's been tough to pin you down."

"Yes, well, we've been endlessly inspired by our fans and the cities and towns across the world, the U.S. in particular. We feel like we'll have more than enough material for our next album that we'll start recording next year in Finland, then we'll get right back into touring. It's been busy for everyone."

"Anything you can tell us about the next album? Will it veer towards some of your earlier melodic work? Will you be maintaining your speed titles in the guitar community? Or will it be something new entirely?"

"We're always trying new things. Right now it's about imagery and lyrical exploration. As far as the speed records and all the other titles and awards we've held over the last ten years—that's all incidental. We're making the music we want to make, and we're privileged so many people support us in doing that by coming to our shows and streaming our albums."

"I'd be remiss if I didn't bring up the rather morbid statistic on the disappearances of some of those people: your fans. Over one thousand have gone missing from your concerts."

Auranna shrugged at him as if to say, "what do you want from me?"

"There have been calls from parents, churches, media, and many law enforcement groups demanding that your band stop touring. Is there anything you'd say to those groups if you had the opportunity?"

"We always wear black. We're judged and can't go back," Auranna smiled.

"Do you really want me to print that you only paraphrased Pantera as an answer to that question? I mean, I *personally* appreciate the reference, but the groups I mentioned might not see the amusement in it."

Auranna stopped smiling and cleared her throat.

"We won't be held responsible for the actions of criminals. Millions of people are able to listen to our music without becoming violent. As far as the parenting groups are concerned—are we forcing their children to listen to our music? Are we leaving their poorly supervised digital devices unlocked?

"My advice for them would be to spend less time trying to punish creators and more time policing their little *spawnlings*. Quit ruining the pastimes of responsible, discerning adults who don't need or want their overbearing, puritanical permission to live their lives."

A movement by Stanley's feet caught Auranna's attention. They were well past the Southwest part of the tour, so she puzzled to discover a large tarantula crawling around. She stared at the spider as it creeped out from under Stanley's chair and made a beeline towards her.

"I hope you don't edit out how much I hate those types of people," Auranna said.

She leaned down to allow the tarantula to crawl up her arm, delighted it didn't smoke through like Stephanie's black adder. It scurried up to the underside of her elbow and stopped. It didn't weigh anything, like a hologram. The spider's presence was a curiosity on its own, but the creature also appeared to have two heads. Stanley shook off a befuddled expression and continued with the interview.

"Um, no, that came through loud and clear. So, uh, do you believe there's more you could be doing to stop these disappearances? Such as telling your crowds to keep an eye out for suspicious activity?"

"The venue organizers are doing that already. Security teams are already on it. I don't know what more anyone could want from us. First, it's scapegoating the music, and now they want to put the onus on *our fans* to do everyone else's job? Not to mention how dangerous it would be to point someone out in a crowd of people. You've been at enough concerts to understand mob mentality, right?

"I once asked a crowd of metalheads which one of them threw some trash at my bandmate and in the blink of an eye the metalheads had the culprit in the air and crowd-surfed into the waiting arms of security. No, you'd be lucky if any semi-suspicious—or worse, *innocent*—individual didn't get torn into a million pieces if you ask the crowd to get involved."

Auranna held her arm up while the spider crawled higher, bridging across her shoulders, then to the other arm.

"There's never been a precedent for what's going on at your concerts. I think authorities are as frustrated by the lack of clues as you are at the scapegoating... Um, are you okay, Miss Korpela?"

"Can you turn the recorder off, please?"

Stanley complied. Auranna leaned in.

"Stanley, you've been interviewing every genre of metal bands for decades. There's no precedent for this? *At all?*"

"Honestly, I can't think of even a single urban legend or myth that comes close to what Black Aura is experiencing as far as scale. Someday your name will surpass Mayhem as the world's most-cursed metal band. Hell, that may already be happening."

"What would you do in our shoes? Cut the tour? A lot of people depend on us for jobs, and we've got to make a living."

"As a parent myself, I would recommend you take a break, cut a new album, re-form the band with new members, change the name of the band, almost anything but continue touring. But I understand that you'd lose a lot of fans and jobs if you did that. It's a shitty situation, for sure."

Auranna sat back and folded her arms in thought while the spider crawled up to the top of her head.

"Your suggestion to break up my band better not make it into your article. That's all anyone would need to speculate and create rumors that we're even thinking about it, and they'd run away with it.

"I'll die before I break up this band. If you want to keep asking me questions with the recorder, go ahead. Please steer it away from this topic, though, if you would."

She answered the same generic questions she'd been

asked in a hundred interviews before. It was second nature to a point where her mind could wander while she talked. She caught Stanley staring at her with a bewildered look, like he thought she might be insane. Or high. She received that look sometimes when talking about their music. She raised her eyebrow to him.

"Are you not seeing this?"

"Seeing what? You bent down a little bit ago and picked up nothing, then you've been waving your arms around the whole interview. What are *you* seeing?"

"You don't see this giant...mmm. Never mind."

"Umm, well, I guess I'm done here. Thank you for—"

"Wait, Stanley!" Auranna grabbed his wrist. "Look into my eyes. Do I look high to you? I haven't been sleeping well the last week or so. That's probably all it was."

"Alright, I believe you. I won't publicize that part of the interview. But I really do need to go. Again, thank you for answering all my questions. Good luck on the rest of the tour."

Auranna wasn't sure she believed him. A hallucinatory Satanist whipping up ritualistic kidnappings? Suggesting to her that the band should break up? Stanley seemed like a cool guy, but those were some tempting storylines for his article. She put her hand to her head and let the spider crawl onto her palm.

"Thanks for making me look even more crazy, little guy."

Truthfully Auranna felt fine, so she decided to walk around a bit more instead of going back to the venue. She spent many tour days hanging around the different venues, outside of town and city limits, or being cooped up inside the bus. After such a potentially disastrous interview, the fresh air would clear her head. She walked without purpose, looking for anything interesting or inspirational.

The tarantula followed her like a socialite's fashion accessory toy dog. It emitted a black glow against the grayness of the sidewalk. When she stopped, it stopped behind her. When she continued, it tailed her.

"What do you want, bud?"

A couple passed her, creating a wide, distrustful berth. She smiled and continued on her way. Two blocks ahead a heap of trash piled high up against a building. The tarantula took off with unnatural speed to the garbage mound and disappeared underneath. Auranna followed it. As she approached she noticed a shrouded figure in the middle of the trash, humming to itself. She bent down and put a twenty dollar bill in front of the figure.

When Auranna turned to continue down the sidewalk, the figure appeared in front of her, blocking the path. She jumped back. A quick double-take revealed nothing against the building anymore. No trash, no tarantula, no figure. Only her money getting blown away by a breeze.

The hood tilted up, though its face beneath remained shrouded. A grimy, decaying feminine hand reached out and delicately grabbed Auranna's wrist. Auranna leaned in closer to get a better look.

"Are you okay, ma'am? Is there anything I can do for you?"

The crone's fingers grew ice cold, as did Auranna's wrist, then arm. She tried to pull away, but the grip tightened.

"Hey, let go of me! That hurts!"

The crone pushed her into the side of the building, then sat her down hard on the sidewalk like she was a naughty child. Auranna looked up into the void of the shroud. The hood grew closer to her, then swallowed her into the void. Everything turned black, but she didn't experience the sensation of falling asleep and waking up in the darkness, as happened most of the time when she found herself in the dreamworld.

The black forest was nowhere in sight. The outline of the buildings and the sidewalk shimmered at their edges. The blue sky changed to black tinged with flickering red.

The crone no longer hovered over her, no longer gripped her wrist with frosted fingers or ate her with its hood. Auranna peered around and spotted the shrouded figure a couple of blocks ahead, shuffling away with a long walking staff. It beckoned her to follow with its slow, decrepit hand.

Auranna stood and hit her head against something fleshy and tube-like. She looked up to see the underside of a spider lowering itself towards her. She backed up and gawped in fascination and sickness at the creature. She recognized them—the two men she watched have sex at the concert the previous night. They'd been fused together, forming a ten-appendage monstrosity that even Auranna couldn't have dreamed up.

Our Queen. Thank You for following us.

Auranna touched their biceps, then their cheeks. Her mind raced to form lyrics and chords for what she was seeing and feeling.

– Who's that figure in black pointing at me? I don't feel like getting attacked today. –

She would like to show You something. We will take You to her if You are weary.

Before she could answer, they grabbed her with their four arms and placed her underneath their legs. One membrum virile wrapped around the other and rubbed back and forth over her body as they held her in place.

– Oh god, please, no, don't hurt me! –

Their expulsion emitted innumerable ropes of gossamer that spun around her just as a spider would entomb its meal in silk. The sudden bleachy smell from the ropes wrapped around her mouth, stopping only below her nose to allow her to breathe. She vomited into her closed mouth, forcing her to swallow it back. Her throat was on fire. They dropped her on the ground and scuttled after the crone, pulling Auranna's cocooned body behind them. They weren't mindful enough to take care of her head, which scraped and bounced off the black pavement for several blocks.

– I could have walked, guys! You took that completely the wrong way! –

We are sorry, our Queen.

– Great way to treat your Queen! –

We still learn our place here. He gives us free reign but does not teach us our purpose.

– If I'm your Queen, your purpose is to serve me! Don't wrap me in a cum cocoon and drag me on the damned ground! –

Apologies. We will have You cut loose.

– Cut? No! Not those things! –

Red eyes appeared all around, their taunts filling her head, then descended on her, cutting through the ropes, her clothes, her flesh. She screamed as their clumsy claws cut away the restraints. Once freed, they scattered and disappeared again, clearing their voices from her mind. Her clothes hung in tatters from her bleeding skin. Every incision and tear oozed black blood.

– Why is everything about pain here sooner or later? – Auranna thought as she dragged her lacerated body up and stood next to the spider boys.

Our pain is Yours. Yours is ours. Your beautiful, terrible music demands it.

– Demands? They're only words! Why does everyone take us so literally? –

Your confusion betrays Your gifts. You do not embrace them?

– What gifts? The gift of screeching? Of hoarseness? Of

eliciting hellish imagery? –

Your fingers. Your haunting, evocative extremities.

– What about them? –

The horrifying spider pulled back when the crone teleported in front of them, then a hundred yards ahead.

She has something to show You.

– Fine. I'll walk myself. No need to carry me this time. –

The crone waited in a large open area away from the buildings of the town, leaning on its staff. Every step Auranna took hurt. The incision-happy imps had torn up her shoes and cut into the soles of her feet. She wanted to wake up to alleviate the pain, but since she was already there, she might as well see what the old witch wanted.

Auranna caught up to where the crone had stopped and looked around at the open area. It was indistinguishable from any other open area; the skies of Hell never changed. The cliffs were either close or far-off but always there with their endless crown of black trees. At least there were no orange lights for her to waste time chasing.

The crone stood in place and offered no additional guidance. Auranna couldn't discern why she'd been led there.

– What are we doing here? Who are you? –

This one cannot speak or mindspeak.

Auranna jumped at the sudden presence of the spider. She thought they'd stayed behind when she walked into the field. They were surprisingly quiet for their size and number of appendages.

– How do you know what it wants if it can't speak? –

It found us outside the forest. Your aura drew us to You.

– My aura? Is that how you things keep finding me no matter where we're touring in the world? –

Not all of us here can find You. Only the ones You've chosen.

– What do you mean by chosen? –

The spider shrugged its four arms. Auranna sighed. In the absence of a distraction, she remembered the pain from all the cuts and tears all over her body.

– Please, let me wake up. –

The crone turned its hooded head towards her. Auranna approached it and pulled the shroud back. The old woman underneath had black eyes, rotting hair, and a mouth sewn shut with barbed wire. Even with the mutilation of her face, Auranna sensed a familiarity with the woman. She covered her mouth when the recognition hit.

– *Mummo*? –

When she brushed her fingertips against her grandmother's skin, she woke up.

CHAPTER FIVE
VISCERA

OUR LOVELY BASSIST'S

AURANNA RETURNED TO THE REAL world sitting on the sidewalk, hugging her knees. The pain from the imps dulled, then disappeared. Sweat soaked through her clothes. She shielded her eyes from the sun and found a police officer looming over her.

"No vagrancy in this town, miss. Move along."

"Oh, apologies, officer. I got lightheaded and sat down to recuperate. I'll head back to my tour bus."

"Tour bus? Are you in one of the bands playing tonight?"

"I am. I'm the lead—"

"Why don't you people pack up and get out? Take your ritualistic bullshit with you and leave our sons and daughters alone."

Auranna stood up without breaking eye contact.

"We have every right to be here."

"It's bad enough our kids won't stop listening to your music and you won't stop making it, but to add kidnapping and murder to each of your shows is unforgiveable. We've lost two in the last two years you've come through here. I'll be damned if you take another tonight."

"We aren't kidnapping or killing anyone. We don't want that any more than you do. What are you doing tonight to prevent it from happening? Hm? You and the security staff? Going to stand around while another person gets taken? We're on the stage, playing nonstop for three hours. All I see when I look out is an ocean of faces and very few police acting like they're doing their jobs."

The officer's face turned red and his lip curled. Auranna braced herself. This wasn't the first such argument she'd had with police and parents throughout the world in some of the more religious communities. Auranna hoped that the cop had the common sense not to bother arresting her. It led to postponements and thousands of angry fans turning their wrath on officials. In the past, they'd let her and the other band members go to avoid the headache.

"Look, before you start cracking my skull or tasering me, can I say something? I want the disappearances to stop like everyone else. What... What could I do at the concert to help you?"

"Get onto your bus and ride back to wherever you came from and put your devil worship behind you. Be a part of bringing this Satanic system down, not propping it up."

"We never run, summon, or hide from Him. It's all a part of the sho—"

The officer walked away from her. She waited until he was out of sight, then studied the buildings to get her bearings. She replayed the dream and followed the path her grandmother laid out for her. The buildings thinned out and the wide-open area was actually the location of the concert that night. The gigantic field had a large area cordoned off for parking and dozens of people milled about the concert stage in some form of preparation.

Auranna wished she'd been paying more attention to the number of steps to "the spot." She guessed where the area was that her grandmother had brought her, an unremarkable, random spot in the great open space. She noted its location in relation to the stage and the mixer tent being constructed next to her.

She called Carrie and asked if she was on or around the stage.

"Can you see me out here? I'm standing alone, waving. Can you take a picture of this field with me in it? You don't need to zoom in, I need a picture of the whole field. Thank you, Carebear."

She met up with Carrie on the stage while techs and roadies worked around them. Auranna held up the photo and placed where she would have been standing out in the field.

"What's going on? What's out there?" Carrie asked.

"I'm not entirely sure. I'm guessing we'll find out tonight. Keep that spot in your mind, though. I'm going to be watching it as much as possible. Where's Steph?"

"Oh, she said she didn't feel too good. She's been trying to get some sleep on the bus. I told her I'd get her bass ready to go at sound check and we'd grab her before the show."

"Thanks. I'll go check on her."

When Auranna arrived at the bus, the doors were locked. She pulled out her key and opened it. Several black snakes slick with gore slimed down the steps. They wriggled, squirmed, and slapped on the grass before dying and sinking into the ground. The horrid, combined smell of bile, urine, excrement, and blood walloped Auranna as she took the first step onto the bus. Disgusted and alarmed, she called out to Stephanie, but received no answer.

Her shoes squished in viscera and gore as she ventured further into the bus. She gagged at the worsening smell and vomited into a trash can. Why did she even bother with the trash can, considering what she walked through? It was nothing compared to what she'd experienced in the dreamworld, but to see it all outside of the inky blackness, in color, was a new assault on the senses.

"Steph? Are you in here?"

Auranna's heart stopped at the sight of Stephanie's body, splayed on the big bed in the back in an Alice Cooper T-shirt. Vomit and blood covered her face and chest. Her eyes were open, filmed over, staring at the ceiling. Her legs and short skirt were soaked in black blood, fleshy bits, internal organs, and all other bodily fluids and solids. They'd all exploded from between her legs, covering the bottom half of the bed and floor around it.

"Oh, my love," Auranna said as she lay on the bed next to her.

The wet squishiness of the bed didn't bother her. Even though everything was in color it didn't mean she couldn't get over the low-level unpleasantries for which Hell had prepared her over the years. She cupped Stephanie's cheek and pulled her face over to look into her lifeless eyes. Auranna's tears dripped into the muck of the bed.

"I'm so sorry," she whispered.

She leaned in closer to her face, ignoring the bile and blood. She kissed her lover's slippery, cold lips. When she pulled away, Stephanie's eyes blinked.

The blink had to be either a figment of her imagination or some sort of death reflex. Auranna put her hand over Stephanie's heart and felt nothing. She grabbed her wrist and checked for a pulse, but again, nothing. Stephanie's fingers twitched and curled. She appeared to be waking from a long sleep.

"Aura?"

"It's me, love."

They embraced on the bed.

"Okay," Auranna said, "I'm overjoyed you're alive, but you're as disgusting as this bed and bus right now. And...still cold..."

She lifted Stephanie's shirt and felt her stomach and chest. They were as icy as her lips and fingers, and she still couldn't detect a heartbeat.

"How... How do you feel, Steph?"

"I can feel your hands," she said while pressing Auranna's hand harder over her left breast. "How do *you* feel? You're surrounded by this...black...well, I don't know how to describe it—you have a black aura around you I've never seen before."

"Really? Well, that's less concerning than what you've gone through. Do you remember anything?"

"I gave birth to dozens of snakes from every hole in my body. I blacked out at some point, I guess."

Auranna pulled her hand out of Stephanie's shirt and held it against her own thigh to warm it back up.

"Can you stand? I mean, your lower half got the worst of everything."

"Hmm. Feel fine."

"Steph, some of the things that came out of you... I mean... I'm afraid to look."

Stephanie put her hand between her legs and felt around for damage.

"All this blood must have been a wicked lubricant. I don't feel any tears or anything."

"That's a relief and a disgusting image I can't wait to put in a future song. Well, how do you feel about the show? It's weird asking you that after it looks like you just died, but you've taken this all very nonchalantly."

"And you haven't? I guess with the lyrics you write this is all pretty mild, right?"

"Mild or not, if you bring this smell to them on stage, it'll be too awkward to explain. Let's get you in the shower."

"I can handle it, Aura. What are we going to do about this bus, though?"

"Burn it. Maybe we can bum a ride from one of the other tour buses. Or ride with the roadies. We'll think of something."

As Stephanie washed herself off, Auranna gargled with mouthwash to get the taste of blood and vomit out of her mouth, then washed her face. She searched for Stephanie's duffel under one of the beds when the bus door opened. Gerald boarded.

"Oh hey, kid. Don't mind me, just came back from lunch and picking up some wiper fluid."

Did he not see the viscera all over the floor, or the blood and vomit spattered over her clothes?

"Hu—hey Gerry. How was...lunch?"

"Amazing! I love these small-town diners almost as much as I love truck stops."

"I'm...glad to hear that. Try not to have any heart attacks while you're driving us around, ok?"

Gerald laughed and sat down in the driver seat to update the log on the day's expenses. Auranna approached him, still hearing and feeling the sickening squelch of her shoes on the soiled carpet.

"Gerald?"

"Yeah? What is it?"

"Do you...smell...anything?"

"Hmm...not really. Nothing out of the ordinary. Why?"

"What do you...see...in here?"

"What's with the strange questions? I see the bus, and you in a Death T-shirt that's a little too tight. Am I missing something? I hear the shower in the back, I guess. That's about it."

"Okay, thank you. I spilled some tea in the back and I just wondered if I cleaned it up well enough."

"Must have. Don't smell a thing," he shrugged and went back to his log.

Auranna moved some of the gore and viscera around on the floor, wet but weightless like the spider. How could he not smell, see, or hear it? She went back to the bathroom and opened the curtain to the shower on Stephanie.

"Hey, Aura. You want to fuck right now? Seems kind of soon but I'm up for it."

Auranna ignored the invitation, and the mild shock of Stephanie talking so uncharacteristically lewd, and knelt down to pick up some of the chunks of flesh that had slid from Stephanie's legs but were too big to go down the shower drain.

"Can you see this, Steph?"

"Mmm-hm. I was going to throw it all out when I finished in here."

Auranna grabbed a large piece and laid it over the drain. The water went right through as if nothing was there at all. She held her own hand over the drain and the water backed up. After a moment of speculation, she pinched the lump between her fingers and held it over the drain. The water backed up against it as long as her fingers were also touching it.

"Whatcha doin'?" Stephanie asked.

"Experimenting."

"My favorite word. Are you sure you don't want—"

Auranna rose and put her fingers to Stephanie's cold lips.

"I can't deny my heart racing at the sight of you all wet like this, your makeup running, your red tentacles of hair licking your shoulders. And it's not like metal isn't the playground for necrophilia, but this is becoming... I mean, I guess not weirder than birthing snakes, but still. I think this macabre scene in the bus is like the snake that bit you earlier. No one else can see it, but this time you can see it with me.

"I don't quite know what I am in this context, but you appear to be like me, now. I felt and tasted your snake bite. Your blood and other stuff are coming off of you in the shower, but the world doesn't interact with it the same way unless you or I are physically touching it. Can you see your blood, vomit and...other stuff on my clothes?"

"Yeah, looks like we'll have to burn your clothes, too. It's too bad. I know you liked that shirt," Stephanie said.

Auranna closed the curtain. She laid out clean clothes for Stephanie and looked for another Death shirt to use once she'd had her own shower, but it had been her last one. She grabbed an Exhumed shirt instead. Once they were fresh and clean, they sloshed through the soiled bus barefoot and stepped outside. They wiped their feet in the grass and put clean shoes and socks on. Auranna forgot what the world smelled like, that everything wasn't as rancid as the insides of her girlfriend.

"I'm trying to get a bearing on these new rules for you, Steph. I never bothered understanding this weirdness fully, because it's never affected anyone else. Did you also smell everything in there?"

"No."

"Okay. Just confirming. Are you sure you want to perform tonight? I can always ask one of the bassists from the opening bands to play your spot."

"Fuck that. No one replaces me. I'm playing."

Auranna held up her hands in surrender, not used to the edge in Stephanie's voice. They made their way to the stage and grabbed their instruments from the techs. Carrie came up to Stephanie and hugged her, then recoiled when their cheeks brushed.

"Rotting Christ, you're freezing! Are you okay?"

"Yeah, I feel fine, Carebear. I'll show both of you how fine

I am. Watch this shit! See if any other fucking bassist could do this," nodding to Auranna.

On the spot, Stephanie played her most famously praised solo without a single flub. Carrie shook her head after Stephanie finished her performance.

"I didn't say you didn't know how to play, I meant you were sick and now you're ice-cold. What happened? When did you start swearing so much?"

"'I'm fine,' I said. Don't fucking worry about me."

"Oh...kay. Well, let's get sound check over with so we can go have dinner before the show."

Chapter Six
Sanguine

Mixed Blood

AT THE DINER GERALD HAD recommended, Auranna sat between Stephanie and Alex, opposite of Carrie and Desmond. Stephanie was clingier than usual, holding Auranna close while they sat, attached to her hip the whole walk to get there. They never hid their relationship from the band, but they weren't outgoing with displays of affection to avoid seeming obnoxious to their bandmates.

Stephanie refused to order anything, claiming she wasn't hungry at all even though she never skipped meals before. She laid her head against Auranna's shoulder, hugged around her waist, and dozed off.

After their meal they ordered a round of coffee to kill some time. While their server bent over the table to fill mugs, a small child that had been running around the dining room woefully unsupervised tripped into her legs, knocking her onto the table and upending the steaming pitcher of coffee all over Stephanie. They all gasped. The server's mouth dropped open, stunned and overwhelmed thinking over which level of apology was appropriate for covering a customer in third degree burns.

Stephanie didn't stir awake in the commotion or react at all to the steam rising from her wet skin and soaked Dethklok T-shirt. Her skin didn't visibly burn. A small amount of the coffee spilled onto Auranna's arm, too, but she hissed at the pain and wiped it off to avoid damaging her tattoos. She poked Stephanie, who blinked and regained awareness, then looked down in confusion. She held up her dripping arms to examine the inexplicable wetness.

"The fuck happened? Why am I all wet?"

"Aren't you...burned?" Desmond asked with wide eyes.

"Hmm? Not at all. I feel gross and wet, though."

The server turned, looked back, and turned away again, unsure what she should do. She retrieved a towel and cleaned up the table, looking at Stephanie with an arched eyebrow, as if expecting her to retaliate at any moment.

"So, you feel the wetness, but you can't feel its heat?" Auranna asked.

"It was hot? Are you sure? Feels lukewarm and clammy to me."

A thought occurred to Auranna.

"Was your shower hot earlier?"

"Well, no. I thought it was a little odd. I turned the knob all the way up to the H but it felt very...neutral. I figured one or all of you assholes must have used all the hot water in the morning. It happens."

The band exchanged looks. Auranna didn't quite know if she should share their experience on the bus to the others yet. She decided she'd tell them after the concert, then figure out what to do about the bus's interior, pending their reactions.

They finished up the rest of their coffee and headed back to the venue. The first act was playing as they arrived. The women went into a tent with their trunks and sat down at the makeup mirrors, while the men went to their own tent with several groupies in tow.

Carrie shooed out a few groupies from the women's tent, telling some of them to try again after the show, then went about conducting her own sort of experiment, touching Stephanie in places where the coffee had landed. Carrie was awestruck at how cold her skin was, and still hadn't shown a trace of red burn marks. After applying their corpse paint, Auranna tried something new: she grabbed a set of tweezers from one of their bags and laid the metal points against Stephanie's bicep.

"You tell me if this hurts at any point, Steph. I mean it," Auranna told her.

She pushed, scraped, and stabbed across the bicep. The skin didn't turn red.

"Could you feel that?"

"I feel what you're doing, but it doesn't hurt. It just…was."

"Carrie, can you please bring me some water and soda?" Auranna asked.

When Carrie left, Auranna pulled her chair in front of Stephanie's so their knees touched.

"I'm only experimenting, my love."

She pulled Stephanie's neck closer with her right hand and met halfway to kiss her while putting her left hand under Stephanie's skirt and over her underwear, exploring with her fingers. Stephanie quivered and moaned into Auranna's mouth. Auranna tried to pull away, but Stephanie grasped Auranna's hand between her legs and held the back of her head. Auranna pushed back harder, managing to free herself from Stephanie's clutches and put both hands on her shoulder.

"Alright, so I'm guessing by your reaction that you felt *that*?"

"Mmmmm, of course, my Queen."

"Oh. That again. Um…one sec, please."

Auranna stood up and pulled Stephanie along with her.

She hugged and put her hand up the back of Stephanie's skirt, feeling around the coccyx for a tail.

"You better quit fucking teasing me and commit or I'm going to explode," Stephanie said, though Auranna detected a demand more than a light-hearted request.

"I think you've done enough exploding for one day. I'm testing what you can feel, and I thought you might be someone else for a second. It appears you can't feel temperature or pain, but your nerves aren't totally dead."

"No, they are not. Remedy that for me, ya damn cunt-tease."

The blunt profanity sounded strange on Stephanie's lips. Auranna held Stephanie's gaze in all seriousness.

"Hold on, Steph. This is important. We can go crazy after the show tonight. Now, did you taste the coffee in my mouth?"

"No."

"Interesting. And you're still not hungry?"

"Not in the slightest. I haven't felt hungry even for a moment since the bus."

Auranna sat back down in her chair. Carrie came in with the water and soda.

"Thank you, Carrie. I think I got my question answered already. She can't taste anything, either. No pain, no taste, no smell, no hunger. Altogether bizarre."

"Think she's got a virus?"

No, Auranna thought.

"Possibly. Let's see what happens tonight and how she feels tomorrow before we start considering any trips to the hospital. Get your gear on. Sounds like they're wrapping up out there."

Auranna reminded Carrie where they were to look during the show, out where the crone had stood. All they could see was an ocean of random metalheads, no different than any other crowd at one of their concerts. They played for two hours and nothing changed around that spot, other than the usual movement of people meandering in, out, and around the grounds.

During one of their heaviest, more intricate songs, Stephanie motioned to one of the techs to bring her the wireless bass. She continued playing seamlessly and surprised them all—band and crowd alike—by jumping down onto the ground. The security staff didn't know what to do as she slipped over the metal barriers and into the crowd. The fans pushed away just enough to give her room to walk and play.

The song came to the part where they would exhort and whip the crowd into several mosh pits. Stephanie put herself into the swirl and played in the middle while the metalheads pushed, careened, and pounded into each other around her.

Stephanie became an angel of death, strumming discord into the humans surrounding her, but she was merely human herself and succumbed to the need for primal, physical contact. The frenzy lost what measure of control a mosh pit could have and became tighter and more violent.

Stephanie maintained every note despite taking elbows and forearms to the head and torso. Auranna looked in dismay at fresh blood—not only the fake blood they poured on themselves throughout the show—streaming down Stephanie's face. She seemed to enjoy every moment of it, though.

Auranna smiled at the theatricality that the crowd embraced, then looked back at the spot by the mixer tent. There was still nothing out of the ordinary. During one of Alex's thrashing solos, Auranna walked back to Carrie and shrugged her shoulders. Carrie nodded her head and mouthed with exaggeration "after the show." Auranna nodded and continued through the song.

Through the last hour, Stephanie played inside the crowd to the limits of the wireless tech. Auranna wanted to join her, but knew it would be far too dangerous for the band leader to put herself out there. Who knew what they'd do to her? She envied the joy and rush Stephanie must have felt in that moment but didn't care for all the groping and body shots she also received.

During the break before their first encore, Stephanie managed to find her way back to the stage. She stood alone, soaked in blood: hers, theirs, the fake. She received thunderous adulation, through which she played an extended intro to "Sublime Suffocation"—one of their favorite encore songs. Stephanie's momentum carried them through three encores. They could have done more if the organizers and staff weren't so tired and actively signaling them to get the fuck off the stage. The lights switched to blinding, metal-killing white as soon as their last song ended. The speakers were all cut, despite the continued ravenous chanting of the crowd.

Eventually the cacophony dissipated and the band—along with Lisa and Joel—gathered outside the bus. Gerald made a show of pointing at his watch. Auranna let Stephanie on first so she could wash off all the blood she'd caked on during the performance. Auranna gathered the others.

"I know this is going to sound strange, but...do you see any blood, or gore, or anything on these steps? Besides what's dripping off Stephanie?"

They all shook their heads.

"No chance you smell anything...strange coming from the bus?"

They all leaned in closer and inhaled, then shook their heads.

"Damn. Alright, on you go!"

If nobody but her could smell or see anything, she couldn't very well convince them to burn the bus down and get a new one. And it seemed like Stephanie didn't care about any of it. Auranna wondered if she'd need to find a comfortable and inconspicuous way to plug her nose until she could deep-clean it. She conjured the image of old cartoons where they closed their nostrils with gigantic laundry pins and wondered if that really worked. While the others sloshed through and sat in Stephanie's insides, Auranna pulled Joel aside.

"Can you take a couple of seconds of video of the bus, especially around the floor?"

"Sure, Aura."

"Thank you. Okay, can you play it back for me?"

"What are you looking for?"

"I...don't know. I don't see it in the display, anyway. Thanks for humoring me."

Lisa came to them after they'd eaten and asked if she could interview Stephanie following her insane performance. Auranna said it would be okay as long as Stephanie approved. Carrie motioned for Auranna to join her on the couch.

"Alright, I didn't see anything the whole time around that spot. Did you?" Auranna asked.

"I did! During the heaviest, most emotional part of 'Metamorphic Maculation' when Steph was in the middle of the pit, I saw a woman standing where you were in the field. Then she wasn't there! I don't mean she walked away or ducked down or anything. She was there, then she *wasn't*!"

Auranna laid back in the sofa in thought.

"Did you...how did you know that was going to happen?" Carrie asked.

"I didn't. I had a...vision about that place. That spot. I didn't know what I would see, if anything. Hey, Lisa, can you come over here, please? Carrie, pull out that photo, would you? Lisa, take a look at this photo. See where I'm standing? Can you make a note of this spot and get a camera set up on it for our entire concert tomorrow night?"

"Why on Earth would I do that?" Lisa balked.

"Because it's easy to erase useless digital footage if nothing happens, but I have a feeling your tits are going to stiffen if what I think will happen happens. It would only be for the one show. Can you do that, please?"

"Alright. I'll get a camera set up on a tripod. But you better make sure none of you knock into it during one of your more...rambunctious sets. These cameras could feed us all for a month on their resale value."

"Thank you, Lisa. Carrie, same thing tomorrow night, please. I would have been more on top of keeping my eyes on that spot if Stephanie hadn't left the stage like that."

"No doubt, Aura. I warmed up some water for your teas and honey."

"Thanks, sweetheart," Auranna kissed Carrie's cheek and went to the kitchen area to find her mug. She hoped the tea and honey inches from her nose would overpower the stink of festering vomit, excrement, urine, and blood that had been moldering in the sunlight for half the day. Stephanie walked out of the bathroom wrapped in a towel, drying her hair with another.

"Hey, Steph, Lisa wants to interview you tonight."

Stephanie wrapped the second towel over her hair and hugged Auranna from behind. Her hands explored up her stomach and cupped her breasts. Auranna grabbed Stephanie's wrists and pulled them back down to her hips, surveying the bus to see if anyone had been watching.

"Rotting Christ, Stephanie, not now! We're not alone! And... Look, this place reeks. I'm not going to be able to—"

"Fine! I'll figure some way out of your goddamn teasing tonight."

"I didn't mean—!"

Stephanie stormed to the front of the bus to do the interview. Lisa was aghast that Stephanie wanted to do it in a towel, but then shrugged and told her it would appeal to the fanboys and girls buying the documentary, then talked with her at length about the night's performance. Auranna sighed at Stephanie's erratic, unreserved personality shift, then sighed again when the smell of her teas did nothing to mask Stephanie's innards spread throughout the bus.

After drinking, she hummed to herself as she looked through her duffel for a shirt she was going to be okay burning later. She pulled out an old Cradle of Filth T-shirt and put it on, along with her oldest, rattiest pair of sweatpants. She resolved to spend the next day with the cleaning crew helping them out—not that they could see what she'd be cleaning—then set a bonfire outside with all the soiled material. She even considered inviting some of their more devout ritualistic fans to dance around the fire.

It was Stephanie's turn with the big bed, which was for the best until Auranna could clean it up. Auranna laid down on one of the smaller beds and covered her face with the blanket, hoping it would shield her from the stench only a foot below. It didn't do much, but it was a slight improvement. She dozed through the movements of everyone else as they prepared themselves for the night and milled about.

She woke several hours later to something crawling into her bed and restricting her with its coils over the blanket. The fabric tightened around her face and Auranna thought she might suffocate. She wriggled her arms up and out of the blanket and pulled it down from her head to find Stephanie snuggling her. Auranna sighed and hugged her closer. She kissed the top of her head and fell back to sleep while concentrating deeply on the black adder, the snake-man-demon in Hell, and Stephanie's many, many dead babies.

CHAPTER SEVEN
DAEMONIUM

WHO'S THE DEMON HERE?

AURANNA WOKE AGAIN, ONLY WITHOUT the blanket or any of her bandmates in the nearby beds. She moved to roll over and found Stephanie still clung to her side. Auranna composed herself, mentally preparing for the explanations sure to follow. Stephanie startled awake and couldn't understand all the blackness around them so Auranna hummed for her while stroking the back of her hair.

"It's okay, my love. I'm here. Listen close, please, because things are about to go to Hell, and I need to prepare you. Just follow me. I'm not completely well versed on the rules, but I'll share what I can. At some point we won't be able to talk and hear each other, but we can communicate through our minds. You'll understand when that happens. It'll be like we're curled up inside each other's skulls. But there will be other voices as well. I know that sounds insane. Trust me, it's not the most insane thing down here. Stay close to me. I need to talk with someone."

Stephanie huddled against Auranna as close as possible while they disembarked from the bus.

"Holy fucking hell..." Stephanie muttered as the bus disappeared behind them and she took in the full view from the jagged outcrop of rock they stood upon.

"It is."

"'It is,' what?"

"Fucking Hell. I mean, I *think* this is Hell. It's not like there's a big road sign that says 'Welcome to Hell, population everyone, ever, except Jesus' or anything like that. All I can tell you with any certainty is that things will hurt you here. It allows you to feel pleasure and passion, but never without an equal or worse dose of pain afterwards. I can remember a few of the more pleasurable trips, but only after some amount of time has passed. The nightmares are more memorable than the fantasies."

"I don't get why I can feel cold down here, but not back home? And the air is fucking hot? What's going on? Was Dio describing this sensation in 'The Last in Line?'"

"I only have theories. I can't explain the temperatures. Don't worry about it. Things are about to become so painful they'll take your mind off the cold real quick."

"Why did you bring me here?"

"Oh, Steph, I didn't intend to bring you here. I didn't even know it was possible. I wanted to talk to the thing that bit you and see if he could explain your new...form...back on Earth. I didn't expect you'd be able to follow me."

"Are you...a demon? Have I been fucking a demon? Is that what's happening to me?"

"I'm...not sure. I thought that maybe you were the demon earlier when you took on the crowd. It's hard to make sense of this place. Oh, time does weird things, too. We could feel like we've been here for fifteen minutes, a couple hours... I once fell for hours until I woke up in the dressing room the other night and startled you. I'm pretty sure whatever happens here with you and me, we'll wake up in the bus before we've even reached our destination. It's very dreamlike. But I wish I could tell you that you won't feel anything happening to you—like a dream. This place…hurts."

"That's great to hear. Thank you for bringing me here."

"I said I didn't mean to. And I'm just trying to be honest with you—so you're not caught off guard. Expect no mercy. Only one being I've met here has ever not hurt me, and I still paid for it afterwards."

"Your rape demon?"

"I told you; she didn't rape me. I…almost want you to experience what I did with her…but we need answers first. And, I hope, really fast."

"Anything you can handle, I can, too."

"It's not a contest. Here, let's experiment again. I'm not sure if things will be different for you down here than your present state on Earth. Could be you'll have nothing to worry about."

Auranna pulled Stephanie around to face her and kissed her, then continued where she left off between her legs in their dressing room tent. Knowing the "dream" wouldn't progress until they ventured into the forest, Auranna was in no particular hurry, so she brought Stephanie to climax. Stephanie leaned on Auranna after and held their foreheads together.

"Fucking finally," Stephanie sighed. "You're not done experimenting, are you? You can test your theory again if you want. Or I can test it on you. Over and over—"

"I wonder if uninhibited lust is going to be your cross to bear. Now, for the second experiment…"

Auranna lifted the back of Stephanie's hand and bit into it. Hard. Stephanie hissed and pulled it away.

"Okay, so, unfortunately, you can feel pain. I'm sorry. But, if you're able to look on the bright side, we're not actually dead. We are essentially dreaming, so if you need some sort of solace or place for your mind to go when you're getting tortured, try to focus on that."

"Can't I stay behind? Or try to wake myself up?"

"I wish. Don't you think I tried doing that the first dozen times I ended up here?"

"How long have you been coming here?"

"Hard to tell with any certainty. I have very vague memories of coming here when I was growing up in Finland, learning to play my guitars...but a lot of the memories unravel if I focus on them. Now, I've never 'brought' anyone with me before. So please, stay very close to me. And pray we don't run into Him tonight."

"Since when are you the praying type? And where are we supposed to go? This is all cliffs and...oh. Into that forest that's blacker than your guitar. Wonderful."

"You're lucky to be here with me, all things considered. I had to figure so much of this out on my own. And I still don't know what's going on, most of the time. That's another thing—the 'people' we come into contact with in here will be frustrating and vague. They never give you a straight answer."

"So, you brought me to Hell to ask someone a question that you know won't get answered straight?"

"Hey, you crawled into my bed. How many times do I have to say I didn't intend this?"

Stephanie kissed Auranna, then hugged her from the side in preparation for entering the forest.

"Well then, all things considered, I'm glad to be here with you as my tour guide."

Auranna walked them into the forest. She turned to show Stephanie that the forest ate up the path and they couldn't run back outside. Stephanie mouthed something to her, but no sound came out.

– This is the part where you use your mind, my love. –

– Oh my god, that feels so strange! It's like you're hugging my brain! –

– You'll get used to it, and you don't need to shout. I can hear you clearly even if you 'whisper.' Now, you see those orange lights? We need to walk towards them, one at a time, until one appears to get closer. Then if we go towards it, we can talk to the being that dominates that light. –

– Oh fuck! What are all those red eyes? –

– Unfortunately, they're always part of the pain equation. If the demons we talk to don't inflict enough pain, they'll make up for it. They're mostly claws and teeth. –

The Slut Queen brings another slattern.

This one has protection. Something is wrong.

No one escapes His punishment. Protection won't save her. She will come to hate the Slut Queen for allowing the torture.

This one's love is pure. It will not break.

All love breaks. One way or another.

– Ignore them. It's the giant red eyes we want to avoid at all costs. I pray again that He does not show Himself. –

– Stop using that word, Aura. 'Pray.' It's annoying me more than these whispers. Hey, that light moved closer. –

– Alright. Try not to think about what's crawling all over us. I imagine it's going to be snakes again. Brace yourself. I'm so sorry for the pain you're about to endure. –

They walked, then trudged over and through the snakes that piled up around their feet, up to their ankles, calves, knees, and thighs. When they reached the light, the snakes commenced biting them. Auranna gritted her teeth through the pain, while in her mind Stephanie screamed as she had on the stage when the black adder had bitten her. At least the situation played out like Auranna had theorized and she could take pleasure in that. She saw the black figure of the snake-man slither towards them.

My Queen. My heart fills with joy that You sought me out again.

– Mine, too, my friend. Could you kindly call off your nest?

I do apologize, my Queen. I endeavor to keep You from further injury from the imps. They are more savage than our love bites and...

– Nnnngh...fine. I get it. Thank you for your consideration. I need...fuck! I need to ask you what you did to Stephanie. When you bit her on Earth with your black adder? –

I only wished to give You Your desire on Earth that I could not give You here.

– Right...right...motherfuckers...I mean the snakes, my friend, not you. Now, what did your adder...actually do? I thought I sucked out the poison. –

That was not poison, but it did its work regardless of Your efforts.

– What work was that? –

Once You woke her from death, whenever that would be, she would be Yours.

– She was already mine, as it were. I don't own her, but we were already together. –

You wished her to experience this place with You. With Rachel.

– So, you made her a partial zombie? ...Oh, goddamn, that bite really hurt...right through my...Nnn...So I could bring her here without her becoming a part of His army? –

She has my venom running through her, but I did not let her become completely wild. It is regrettable I had to go about it this way. But our powers are limited. Almost all things given must exact a payment.

– Well, you chose the best senses for her to keep. I guess. Are you Alice Cooper, by the way? Ow! –

Thank You, my Queen. I exist to serve until He calls us forth. And I am not Mister Nice Guy, though sometimes I try to be, as You have discovered.

– Sure...sure...oh...god...could you, please...call them off now? Send us home? –

Of course, my Queen. Nothing would bring me more— No!

– Oh please no. –

The snakes stopped biting, retreated back to their lord, and disappeared. The giant red eyes appeared in its place. The wind brushed past Auranna towards Stephanie panting and in pain on the forest floor.

– No, my Lord! No! Take me! Do whatever You wish to me! Don't hurt her! I'm begging You, my Lord! Oh! Please! No! Leave her alone! –

Auranna watched in horror as Stephanie's body stiffened and rose up to the eyes, stories above her head. Stephanie disappeared from view. Auranna flooded with remembrance of all the horrible things He was going to make Stephanie feel. But she knew, too, that her imagination didn't come close to the real thing.

The blur of a fleshy mass smashed to the ground in front of her. Stephanie lay broken in a heap at her feet.

The giant red eyes lowered and regarded Auranna.

What did you do to her?

– I...I blocked Your influence over her. You can't have her as part of Your army... –

Your hesitation betrays you. You did nothing. This is the work of another.

– I don't know anything about that. I shielded her. She will never be Yours. –

That may be, for now. But you... You are most assuredly mine.

Auranna closed her eyes as the wind picked her up and ravaged her. It was almost as bad as the first time He seized her, back when she was twelve. Almost. When He finished with her, He flung her down next to Stephanie, then faded and disappeared.

– Ar— ...Are you there, my love? –

– Yeah. I've never felt so much pain. –

– I know. I'm sorry. I'm so sorry I brought you here. –

– Oh fuck. Look at you, Aura. You look like Cannibal Corpse wrote "Frantic Disembowelment" about you. When do we get to wake up? I can't even move. –

– Those little red eyes getting closer are sure to do the trick. I'll see you on the bus. –

Auranna sang in their minds Stephanie's favorite part of "Jet City Woman" as the imps tore them apart.

CHAPTER EIGHT
FOETIDUS

OH GOD, THE SMELL

STEPHANIE WOKE CLUTCHING AND TEARING at Auranna in a desperate attempt to avoid the claws and fangs of the imps. Auranna put her arms over hers to control her flailing. She cooed and hummed for her, bringing her panic down and her awareness back to reality. Stephanie shook for a few seconds, then stilled as the visceral sensation of pain faded.

"Would you two fuck quieter and stop thrashing around over there?" Alex hissed from his bed.

"We're *not*, Alex," Auranna whispered back. "She's having a nightmare."

"Oh. That's good, then. Make sure she writes it all down when she's finished." His voice trailed off in a yawn and he went back to sleep.

"That's actually a good idea," Auranna whispered to Stephanie. "So many of my lyrics and imagery come from that place. I'll often write it all down in the front of the bus before it disappears from my consciousness."

"I'll do it tomorrow. Let me lie here with you. In peace. Please."

"Of course, my love."

"Is it even safe for me to sleep?"

Auranna paused for a moment, forming her response.

"I wish I could be certain about any of this. I wish I could tell you 'yes.' I'm sorry. Tonight was the first night I sought my own passage to the dreamworld. And it's hard to compare, but it felt like He punished me more than usual for doing so."

Stephanie didn't close her eyes until Auranna hummed for her and put her to rest. Auranna soon followed peacefully into sleep and woke again—unscathed—in the morning.

In the next town, the band sat around another diner table for breakfast. Auranna decided to tell them about her visits to Hell—how she pulled Stephanie along with her, and what had happened with the snake and bus. As expected, they stared at her in utter disbelief. She shook her head.

"I know. I *know*! It's insane! It *really* is! But until Stephanie experienced it independently of my thoughts and dreams, I thought I was always hallucinating. Only really, really vividly."

"If everything's as painful as you say, how are you so blasé about this?" Carrie asked.

"It's hard to explain. The pain is literally indescribable. My lyrics only brush the surface. But it's hard to get emotional over something that I've been forced to numb myself to over eighteen years or be seen as a raving lunatic."

"Well, your lyrics make more sense now; more than you just being a rebellious Scandinavian princess, anyway," Alex said.

"She's a *Queen*," Stephanie piped up from Auranna's side.

"Oh, right. A queen. Of *Hell*. Of course. Pardon me, your *High*-ness."

"Alright, cut it out," Auranna interjected. "I don't know why they call me their queen. That aspect of this still makes no sense to me."

"Hey, you don't think...?" Desmond hesitated mid-question, looking between Carrie and Alex, "...she must have sold her soul to Satan to play guitar? Her world-beating talent would make so much more sense!"

"Uhh, no, Dez. I did not 'sell my soul' to play guitar. I've been playing since I was ten. My grandmother taught me while my mother and I followed her on world tours. You know this."

"Worse players than you have been playing since they were two. You are godlike, Auranna. And not in the way music fans dub their favorite bands as 'godlike' and make it meaningless. Come on, Alex, you know it's true. You're the most trained of any of us in theory and craft. She couldn't be as good as she is with only daily practice and dedication—like she claims."

"What did you think I was doing before you just learned about this?" Auranna asked. "Cheating with recordings? Why can't someone be great without something supernatural going on? Satan and the demons have never brought up anything about my soul or guitar-playing."

"Oh, you're not only a tourist down there? Satan is *talking* to you?" Alex asked.

Auranna wasn't sure if that was incredulity in his voice, or jealousy.

"I guess. For all I know it's only a powerful under-demon or something. They don't wear nametags. I assume it's Him from the amount of pain He puts me through compared to anything else in there. Oh, and He has a real problem with the idea anyone has more authority than He does. So I connected the dots."

"Can...will you take us...or at least *me* with you next time?"

"You don't fucking want that, Alex," Stephanie murmured, "trust me. I can't feel pain here, but I felt every ounce of it down there. The torture itself, it's...unfathomable to what could even be achieved on Earth."

"Oh, yeah, our undead bassist! We're like a black metal wet dream!" Carrie said, throwing her hands up in the air.

"Just need to burn some churches and murder each other, right?" Stephanie said, sitting up to rest her chin on her palm, directing a murderous look toward Desmond.

"What are you looking at me like that for? Why would you kill me?"

"For stealing my cupcake from the fridge last year, motherfucker," she said with an evil smile.

"Oh, speaking of burning," Auranna distracted to avoid bloodshed, "Stephanie and I need to burn some of our clothes, some sheets and blankets, the big mattress, and all the carpet in the bus. It's still covered in Stephanie's insides and the cleaning crew won't be able to see or smell it to be able to clean it up. But *I* sure as hell can."

Alex thought about it for a second, then snapped his fingers.

"I've got it! We set fire to the bus and roll it into a decrepit, abandoned church in a field in the middle of nowhere and use that for our next album cover!"

"Fuckin' poser," Desmond muttered.

"I was kidding about the black metal thing, Alex," Carrie said.

"No, no, it's perfect! I promise not to murder any of you, but I'm loving the burning church idea, Carebear. We pass abandoned churches all the time! I'll verify that Zeal & Ardor didn't use a similar image on any of their EPs. I'll see if I can find any abandoned churches this week. We can get Gerald to order us a new bus. We were going to do that for the next tour, anyway, right? We'll get it ahead of schedule. Carrie, can you talk to the other bands and see if they can make any room for us after we burn it all down?"

"Good idea. Now that the thought of murdering each other and burning churches to increase our metal cred is out there, I want to be as far away from you jerks at night as I can," Carrie said while standing up from the table. "See you all at sound check."

"Well, if you're all done not believing me, I'm going to go help the cleaning crew and talk to Gerald about picking up new carpet and a mattress," Auranna said. "Might be tough to convince him since he can't see or smell anything."

Stephanie trailed behind Auranna but kept her impish smile directed at Desmond until they left the diner.

"Fuck, was that all made up so she could justify killing me?" Desmond asked.

Alex shrugged and fished out his wallet.

"Shouldn't have touched her cupcake, dude."

"Your black glow is mesmeric, my Queen," Stephanie said wistfully as she followed Auranna out of the bus with an armful of soiled sheets and blankets.

"Alright," Auranna said as she dropped her pile of their still-dripping clothes into a makeshift burn pit, "what is that? You called me 'Queen' even before we went to Hell. Where did you get that?"

"It sounds better than calling you Goddess. Or Demon. Or Whatever You Are. It's nice and clean. You're the Queen of Metal, and apparently some of those things in Hell. I've never had something to call you like you call me 'your love.' I like it."

"I would like it if those...things...weren't always calling me that. When you say it, it worries me you might become—or already became—one of them, too."

"Well, can't you just pretend I'm one of your fanatical metalhead geeks? I'll worship you better than all of them combined until the day I die...again."

"But you're not like them. Or weren't, anyway. That's one of the many reasons I love you. I'd rather you kept calling me Aura, please. If anything, I'd like to not be reminded of Hell every time you say 'my Queen.'"

"Fair enough. I can relate to that now, unfortunately."

"Thank you. Now let's get at that carpet."

"Here? It's pretty early, but I'm up for it if...Oh! *That* carpet! Sure."

"Goddamn, Steph! You're pissing me off because you're concupiscent as a teenager since you turned and I've got adulting to do. Quit tempting me!"

"I knew you wouldn't be able to resist using 'concupiscent' after you wrote that song about your lust demoness the other day," Stephanie frowned.

"It's appropriate. And come on. We're covered in 'you.' I smell your insides. I'm surprised you can be so lascivious around this."

"Blame your snake friend, I guess. And hey, lady. You have the love I ne—"

"Hey! Careful with those lyrics, Steph. A lawyer might hear you..." Auranna winked, appreciating Stephanie's sentiment all the same.

"All I know is I can't fucking wait for tonight," Stephanie continued. "No concert to be at tomorrow! We're staying in a real bed in a hotel. A little privacy for once without someone yelling at us to get on the motherfucking bus..."

They wrestled the mattress out, then pulled the carpet up and carried it together to the pit. Auranna's heart pounded from the exertion and watching Stephanie's T-shirt cling to her tight with sweat, and her red hair getting stuck randomly around her beautiful face. It reminded Auranna of seeing Stephanie covered in blood in the audience and wanting to take her right there. The knowledge that the liquid stains all over Stephanie's clothes weren't only sweat and blood stopped her from acting on the rush of lust.

Auranna couldn't wait for the hotel, either, and the high-pressure shower spray to truly wash away the last couple of days.

She did a final check inside the bus before marching out with Alex's lighter. In Auranna's absence Stephanie retrieved two broken fence boards from the parking area's designated bus enclosure. She stabbed one board into the center of the pile, then tied the second board to make an inverted cross using some of the soiled clothes.

"You think Satan would go easier on us if He saw this? Should we dance around it naked like witches? Would it call forth your lust demoness?" Stephanie said with a hint of malice in her arched eyebrow.

"Hell if I know. We're not witches. Next time I'm in Hell I'll look her up on my phone and see how to get her to come to us. You think there'll be reception down there?"

"Maybe Steve Jobs is down there ruining Hell as he ruined Earth. Anyway, light this shit up so we can get to sound check on time."

Auranna lit the pile, then verified to make sure no one would be able to see them. Satisfied, she nodded to Stephanie. They took off their clothes—as covered in filth as everything they'd hauled out of the bus—and threw it all into the fire.

"I really should have chosen a different shirt, knowing I was going to burn it," Stephanie said. "You chose Cradle and I left my fucking Zeppelin shirt on. Why didn't you stop me?"

Auranna shrugged, looked at Stephanie for a moment, then back and forth between their underwear and smiled. They threw their underwear into the fire, danced around it for a few seconds, then ran back into the bus for clean clothes, laughing the whole way.

After putting on fresh T-shirts, Slipknot for Auranna and Danzig for Stephanie, they opened all the windows and walked back outside to their fire. The cleaning crew came running at the sight of black smoke, then looked puzzled at the two of them. Stephanie hooked her thumb over her shoulder and shrugged.

"Fuckin' skunk! Hopped on while we were out to breakfast and we left the door open! Stupid us!"

The crew sniffed at the open bus door before entering, then shrugged back. Stephanie smiled and gave them a thumbs up as if they were so good at cleaning there'd be no trace of odor to worry about ever again. She took Auranna's hand and they walked together to the stage area, leaving the cleaning crew to do their work and the bonfire to burn itself out naturally.

Auranna worked with Lisa and Joel to find an unobtrusive area to place their tripod and keep it recording the spot she showed Lisa the night before near the mixer tent. She grabbed a tech who didn't seem to be doing anything at the moment and asked him to stand on the spot so they could focus the camcorder. Satisfied at the placement, she ventured to Stephanie sitting on the edge of the stage and stood between her dangling legs while the other three worked their instruments. Auranna glided her hands along Stephanie's thighs and around to her butt.

"You walking out again tonight?"

"Why not? I fucking loved it," Stephanie said while squeezing her legs around Auranna's torso as she imagined the pleasure. "All the rush of being out there in that mess, none of the pain from getting beaten up by overzealous metalheads."

"I wish I could be out there," Auranna sighed.

"If you did go out there no one would touch you. They'd fall on their knees and worship the ground you walk on. I'm only the bassist. Most of them can't even hear what I'm doing. I'm nothing to them."

Auranna always found it disheartening to hear her bandmates devalue their role in the art of making their music. Moreso, she hated that it was, in many cases, true to the way fans saw them.

"Not after last night, Steph. You were everything to those people. Anyway, it's been a couple days, and you still haven't eaten anything. You may not be hungry or able to taste anything, but I don't think that means you can ignore sating yourself. You've got unlimited freedom to eat the healthiest foods in the world and not dread their awful tastes. Will you try to eat something before we play? I don't want you passing out in the crowd. Who knows what could happen if you did?"

"Alright. That sounds wise."

"Another thing, when you're out in the crowd, avoid that spot, over there, close to the mixer tent. Carrie and I are...experimenting."

Stephanie looked back at Carrie, her expression stricken with fury.

"Oh, whoa, not that kind of experimenting. Poor word choice on my part, Steph. Wow. Please don't kill our bandmates. I kind of like them."

"Fine. Me, too...I guess."

Auranna regarded her girlfriend for a moment.

"I think our snake friend put a little lust and jealousy demoness in you. I'm growing worried for the safety of anyone that comes between you and me."

"They better fucking *not*."

Stephanie's tone sent shivers up Auranna's spine.

"Damn. This is getting dark. Let's get ready for the show, ok?"

Chapter Nine
Vespertilio

Bat, Head Intact

NEWS OF STEPHANIE'S BEHAVIOR THE night before had carried across their fans' social media feeds and the crowd chanted for her to join them from the beginning of the show. Auranna enjoyed seeing her gain so much attention and popularity. Would that they could all leave the stage at some point.

During their performance of "Bitter Benevolence" a cauldron of bats swirled around Auranna through her blistering solo, electrifying the crowd. Auranna had no idea where they came from but their timing—like they were summoned by the screeching of her black guitar—was too perfect. She played along as if it was all part of the production. The band exchanged quick looks and shrugs at the unexpected stage effect. After the song ended, deafening reverence from their fans ensued.

During a slower part of the next song, one of the bats dropped and landed on Auranna's headstock. Astonished, she backstepped from the mic stand to Carrie.

"Are you seeing this?"

"Seeing what?"
"This bat on my guitar!"
"I don't see it!"
"Really? Did you see the ones from before?"
"Of course! Everyone did!"
"But you can't see *this one*?"
"No! Stop distracting me!"

She went to Alex and asked the same thing, but he couldn't see it either. Despite Auranna's movement the bat remained rested and watching her. During a break in notes, she put her hand out to let it hop on. When it did, she felt the same uncanny sensation as when she'd interacted with the two-headed spider. It was there, but had no weight to it. It crawled up her arm to the shoulder and stopped there. Auranna wondered if she was going to see something and pass out on stage again, but nothing happened.

Stephanie came back to the stage for the first encore and wiped her blood off on each band member. The audience went wild for it. During the final song of their last encore, the bats descended around each of them, grabbing their shoulders with their feet and flapping their wings as the band poured the last of their energy into their instruments. As their final notes reverberated from the sound system, they'd never heard a louder reaction at a show, even at the bigger venues. All the bats disappeared into the night, except for the one no one could see, which made itself a comfortable perch on Auranna's shoulder underneath her hair.

Auranna dropped her guitar onstage without thinking and hopped down. She climbed over the metal barricades and glided through the crowd. Stephanie was right about them not touching her. She held her hands out for their reverent touch only after proffered. She received the most awe-struck reactions from the metalheads in the back. She relished every moment of it as she circled the field and all the way back to the stage for a final bow and exit.

She found the band on the bus waiting on pins and needles to get to the hotel. Stephanie hugged her and followed her to the kitchen for her teas and honey. All but Auranna talked about the great show and asked who arranged the bats. She knew they wouldn't believe her if she said it had some connection to the invisible bat still perched on her shoulder. Stephanie, however, noticed and cooed at it, letting it crawl onto her finger as she and Auranna sat in the living area with the others.

"What are you doing, Steph?" Alex asked.

"Playing with this little bat, genius. I'm surprised Aura didn't bite its head off when she had the chance."

"I would never hurt an animal. I don't care how much metal cred it garnered," Auranna muttered.

"What— ...you mean you see it, Steph? I assumed Auranna was hallucinating onstage," Carrie said.

"I resent that, Carrie. Have you ever—in all our years together—seen me on drugs? But who cares anyway? You all didn't believe us this morning. Pretend we're hallucinating and go about your lives," Auranna said.

"Are you still butthurt we don't believe you both traveled to Hell and that you literally talk to Satan?" Desmond asked.

Auranna sighed, then recoiled a little when she saw the dangerous look Stephanie gave to Desmond. Auranna nudged her to stop. Stephanie broke from her angry trance and smiled at her, then laid her head on Auranna's lap.

"You guys slowly turning on each other is great," Lisa said. "Provides a lot of material we can use in this documentary. People that aren't even your fans will watch if there's drama. What did you say about traveling to Hell and Satan, Dez?"

Desmond shared Auranna's story from the morning, often broken by Lisa's laughter, which she promised she'd edit out later. Lisa then asked Auranna if she could do another one-on-one interview to clarify some of the finer details of such an outrageously clichéd story—a world-famous musician outwardly confessing to convening with Satan Himself. It was too perfect!

"No. Talk to me after you've watched the video from the concert."

"We're here, gang!" Gerald called from the driver's seat. "Don't break any furniture in your rooms, please! The new carpet is going to cost a lot already!"

They ran into more than a few metalheads in the hotel who had traveled from smaller towns to see the show, so they signed autographs and took photos. Not removing their corpse paint and show attire until they arrived in their hotel rooms turned out to be a great idea after all, though it made for an awkward check-in process.

Stephanie offered her room to Joel so he wouldn't have to double up with Lisa. Joel accepted her offer without hesitation, and Stephanie rushed to Auranna's room, buzzing with anticipation. She slid through the door before it fully opened, then pushed Auranna into the door to close it, locking both bolts and the chain lock.

"No more teasing, no more innuendo, no saving it for Hell," Stephanie said breathlessly between quick, wet kisses. "Get on that fucking bed, Auranna."

"Can't we both at least clean off our paint, first?"

"No. I'm done waiting."

"Are you...okay? This is getting a little...rape-y for my tastes."

"Did you resist your demon bitch this much? Do you love her more than me?"

"Of course not. But is it too much to ask that I don't have to look at your blood-soaked corpse paint the whole time? Your true countenance is pulchritudinous."

"Put your fucking lyrical thesaurus away. Get on the bed before I pick you up and throw you on it."

Auranna lost patience with Stephanie's aggressive attitude. She brushed past her to get to the bathroom; she wanted to at least wash her face. Stephanie grabbed at Auranna's Iron Maiden T-shirt from behind and pulled her back. The sickening tear emanating from the neck of one of her all-time favorite T-shirts boiled her blood.

Auranna shot her lithe fingers to Stephanie's throat and pushed her back against the wall. Stephanie licked her lips and smirked, thrilled with the rough play. She put her hand over Auranna's, encouraging her to tighten her grip, while simultaneously stretching to get at Auranna's lips. Auranna teased a little longer, bringing her lips within millimeters before pulling away again.

Stephanie pulled Auranna's torso into hers with no attempt at slow seduction. Auranna surged with unexpected pleasure as their battle ebbed and flowed along different areas of their bodies.

Auranna locked eyes with Stephanie and squeezed her neck harder, brushing past the point of playfulness, while her free hand worked its way underneath Stephanie's shirt and around the back to unsnap her bra. If Auranna was strong enough, she would have loved nothing more than to tear it off with her teeth. Once the bra unsnapped, Auranna tore Stephanie's shirt off and found two points to fulfill the urge to bite.

"Don't you ever...tell your Queen...what to do," Auranna growled, biting Stephanie's shoulder, neck, and finishing at her ears, tugging and licking around the lobe.

Stephanie moaned through it all, urging Auranna to push past the initial hesitancy. Stephanie had always been so bashful that she could never bring up with her lover what she wanted to try. The lack of inhibition made her curse herself in the moment for her painfully shy personality—she was missing out on a world of masochistic wonders most of the world would never have the guts to attempt, let alone bring up with their lovers.

Auranna let go of her neck and thrust her tongue into

Stephanie's mouth while they tore off the rest of their clothes. Stephanie pushed Auranna back onto the bed and straddled her. Auranna's hands, fingers, and tongue delighted in the strange cold of Stephanie's entire body.

Stephanie conjured some of what Auranna had felt with the demoness but was no match overall. Auranna lied to her lover, though, and agreed that she'd beaten the Devil, but, really, Auranna had unlocked something in the way Stephanie took pleasure from every movement. She found herself wanting to please Stephanie more than find pleasure for herself. Auranna still came when Stephanie climaxed with Auranna's hand clasped tightly around her neck and her face glowing a lovely shade of purple.

Was this always inside Stephanie but she could never admit what she wanted? If so, Auranna wanted nothing more than to give it to her. She wished to thank the snake-demon for bringing Stephanie's true desires to the surface.

As they lay sprawled in bed, coming down from the rush, breathing hungrily and working up the stamina to go again, Auranna noticed a slight movement over by the hotel dresser. The little black bat perched on it, watching them. Stephanie noticed Auranna's gaze and followed it.

"Oh, I was wondering where that little guy went," Stephanie said.

"It's watching us."

"So? What's it gonna do, tell its friends?"

"The others couldn't see this one, just you and me. It's likely a demon. I'm worried whatever it is will take us to Hell for another visit. I don't want to go back there again any time soon."

"Maybe I can shoo it away."

Stephanie untangled herself from Auranna's sweaty body and approached the dresser.

"Go on! Get out of here! Stop watching us! You're ruining the mood!"

The bat didn't move. Stephanie picked it up and put it in the bathroom, then shut the door. She turned around to get back into bed for round two, but stopped as something caught her attention from the bathroom.

"What the fuck? Did you hear that, Aura?"

"Hear what?" she replied from the bed.

"Come over here. There's a fucking horse or something inside the bathroom."

Auranna joined Stephanie and they placed their ears against the door.

"I don't hear anything."

"I could have sworn..."

"You are doing a lot of that lately—"

The door flew open, causing both of them to fall onto the bathroom floor tiles. Before them was a pair of goat hooves. They craned their necks up to find a naked woman with curled horns, black eyes, and giant leathery wings. Her tail twitched down between her legs, then lifted Auranna's chin.

"My Queen," Rachel said with an unearthly voice.

CHAPTER TEN
Polypus

Sexy Octopi

WHEN AURANNA AND STEPHANIE GOT up, they stood a foot shorter than the creature. Stephanie adopted an attitude of defiance, staring directly up into the creature's black eyes.

"Are you the fuck-demon Auranna won't shut up about?"

"My love, you bring her up more than I have."

"What do you want, slut? Why are you here?"

The creature had been maintaining eye contact with Auranna, but turned to regard Stephanie.

"Mm. I did not know Your bassist was so noisome. She is always the quietest during all the band interviews. This is the one You wished to join us while we experienced all our bodies' transformative pleasures?"

"Noisome? You bitch, I'll cut your tail off and fuck you with it if you think you're going to do that with her again!"

The creature's long tail whipped around to constrict Stephanie's torso, pinning her arms to her sides, and lifted her up to eye level.

"Yes—noisome. When I hear your voice, my ears are filled

with noise. You have no dominion over me or our Queen. You were made to serve. You will silence yourself or be silenced."

"Don't you fucking threaten me, harpy! Aura, tell her to let me down!"

Before Auranna could say anything, the end of the creature's tail jabbed a pressure point on Stephanie's neck and she went limp like a doll. Rachel carried Stephanie past Auranna and laid her down on the bed. Auranna sat down and put her hand on Stephanie's head, then pulled the blanket over her.

"I know she can't feel temperatures, I just think she looks so cute while she's all snuggly and sleeping. She was so sweet before the bite. It was—"

"I know what it was. The snake endeavored to present You a gift and failed. Too hostile, too independent, too licentious, too defensive. She was meant to serve You with pleasure, without pain, but not change otherwise."

"Do you think I interfered by sucking out the venom? Maybe it was supposed to have more time to change her. Regardless, that demon gravely mistook a wanton thought I had in Hell during our...encounter. He shouldn't have interfered, for his part."

"He only meant to serve his Queen, as do I. I was sent here by the one who cannot speak. I came through the ritual portal You opened by burning and dancing around the inverted cross."

"We were fooling around!" Auranna threw her hands in the air. "We're not witches! We have no idea about rituals and spells and that sort of thing!"

"Regardless. Here I am. Did You enjoy my display during the show? I have been to dozens of Black Aura concerts and always thought they lacked a bit of...flair."

"You've been to— ...what do you mean?"

"I used to be a girl named Rachel, and I was one of Your biggest fans. It was only a few nights ago when I was taken to Hell, but an eternity has passed while I have been down there."

"Taken? Did you happen to be standing sort of close to the mixer tent?"

"I am unsure," Rachel shrugged. "I was not taking note of my positioning when I was taken."

"So, you were sent by one who doesn't speak?" Auranna put her fingers to her mouth to think. "Was it the old woman with the barbed wire through her lips?"

"Yes."

"That's my grandmother. She showed me where the people are disappearing from our concerts. I think. I'll be sure once we review a recording. Why did she send you?"

"She does not speak. I do not know. She pulled me from the forest and pointed at the open portal."

"Dumb question. Sorry. Um, are you here forever?"

"I am unsure. This is the first time I have been back since my transformation."

"How did my grandmother find you? Hell has got to be immense. Right? You happened to be so close to her?"

"Her aura matches Yours. It is like a beacon. It is how we are able to find You when You are brought down. It is also how we find You here."

"So, I'm like a flame to a moth?"

"Yes. To Your army."

"My army? I thought you were all in His army."

"He may command it, but You are who we follow uncompelled. We are bound to You. Your grandmother has entreated the spider and me, but for what, we are unsure. He lets her be as far as we have seen. He may not even be aware of her presence."

"I still don't understand what my grandmother and I have to do with all this. Or why people are disappearing from our concerts."

Auranna ran her hand down Stephanie's back, then stood

and paced the room.

"All I remember before being violated and remade by our Lord was Him saying I was a currency. He did not elaborate."

"Currency? He kind of hinted at something like that before."

"You have played over a thousand shows. You have likely banished over a thousand souls as payment for something."

"Banished? Why would I ever do that? How could I?"

"Perhaps He will elaborate with You someday, my Queen. None of us know the 'why' of any of it and we dare not question Him to find out."

"His abuses are too much to bear. I don't desire to speak with Him."

"I believe, if nothing else, Your grandmother wished You to be aware of Your power. To continue? To desist? We are unsure without her ability to speak."

Auranna stopped pacing and folded her arms, frowning.

"It seems like sending you here has created more questions than answers."

"I apologize, my Queen. Is there anything I may do for You? I do not know when I will be called back. My only wish is to please You."

"Can you change Stephanie back to the way she was before the bite?"

Rachel shook her head.

"Do you think..." Auranna considered, "if it's possible here—and not contingent on being in Hell—you could make Stephanie feel as you made me feel? It might quell her lust, at least."

"Or make it worse."

"We could ask her."

"I am afraid her own desire is not her goal. She is devoted to You and You alone. Anything I could do with her would only complicate such a singular, aggressive disposition. It would likely affect her negatively."

"You're making me feel selfish for what I thought would be a generous thing..." Auranna shook her head and walked towards the bathroom. "I need to shower and get ready for bed. Can you watch her while I'm doing that?"

"She will not wake until the morning. I will accompany You to the shower."

"Uhh...mmm...don't take offense but seeing you here in the real world... It's a little...unpleasant."

Rachel disappeared in a puff of smoke and materialized in front of Auranna. Rachel's tail whipped past her and turned on the shower.

"My Queen," Rachel said, walking towards Auranna as she backed herself towards the shower, "I have dreamed of Your music for an eternity. Please play it for me again."

"It's...your eyes. They're all black. Your hooves might crush my feet. I mean, in Hell, I didn't have much of a choice, and my feet would have healed afterwar—"

"You do not desire me?"

"You don't need to look so offended, Rachel. Can you remember when you were still human? Would you have wanted to have sex with a goat, rat, ram, bat...thing?"

"You wound me, my Queen. I am but what He made me. Because of *You*."

"How many times do I have to say it? I am not *choosing* for any of this to happen!"

"Be that as it may... Do You not remember...this? I do not recall such hesitation before..."

Rachel's tail snaked up Auranna's leg and caressed her. Auranna couldn't help warming to Rachel's new form of persuasion. She remembered how good they made each other feel in Hell. At least on Earth there would be no pain afterwards, Auranna convinced herself...

She stood on the rim of the bathtub and looked into the black abysses that must have been the former home of mesmerizing eyes. She slid her hands over Rachel's ribbed, curled horns, down her pierced face, her neck, cupping her breast. Her fingernails made soft tinging noises against each gigantic piercing, and the sensation reverberated from her fingertips to every other nerve in her body.

The demoness drew her close, closer to the double-forked tongue waiting behind yielding lips. The tongues wrapped perfectly around whatever they touched, as intimately and autonomously as the tentacles of an octopus. Auranna would know, after their tours of Japan. Even so...the sight of the wings, hooves, and horns made the experience...unnerving.

Rachel followed Auranna's eyes and their reaction to each of her extremities. She flapped her wing to turn the light switch off and commenced their music.

More satisfied and warmer than their previous encounter, Auranna watched Rachel morph back into her bat form, then roost over her collarbone after Auranna slipped on her Abigail Williams T-shirt. Forgetting sleep, she remembered they needed to go over the new footage with the documentary crew and knocked on Lisa's hotel door. Joel let her in.

"I thought you had your own roo—"

Auranna trailed off at the sight of Joel and Lisa's pale faces. Lisa was watching the footage from the concert. Auranna sat on the bed next to her.

"How did you know to put the camera on that spot?" Lisa asked.

"If I tell you, you're going to laugh like you did on the bus."

"I...I'm really hoping you put a trap door there and you're all fucking with me."

"I'm not into pranks all that much, Lisa."

"If it's not a prank, I don't know how I can't turn this in to the police."

"Why would you do that? The video could easily be counterfeit. You'd be wasting their time. They wouldn't believe you any more than you believed me."

"Aura... This is—..."

"So, what do we do now?" Joel asked.

"Put it up on YouTube," Auranna suggested. "The video could earn over a million views and get your brand out there before you release your documentary. Make it all cryptic and ethereal."

"I don't feel right exploiting it if I know what's happening," Lisa mused, but brought her finger to her lip and tapped it in thought.

"When it was rumor and innuendo, and you could blame my band, you seemed okay enough to exploit it."

"Yes. But then, I wasn't involved in the conspiracy. I was doing my journalistic duty."

Auranna folded her arms and tilted her head.

"So you're personally involved and you've grown a conscience now?"

"Whatever. You're right about the pre-exposure, though. We'll make up a stage name on social media in case the angry parents want to come after me."

"We are who we are in times of danger," Joel muttered.

"Joel, that's one of my favorite non-metal songs of all time. Did I tell you that at some point?" Auranna asked.

"No. Just thought it was apt. Heard it from *The Devil's Rejects*."

"That's one of my favorite movie soundtracks! We should talk later sometime."

"Joel, quit interacting with the subject. We're going to

need to keep our journalistic distance now that we've seen this. Operate the camera around them and shut up."

"You sure you don't want to show this to the police? Even if they think it's made up, we could convince them to keep an eye on that spot with this footage," Joel said.

"You still want your salary? It's contingent on completion of the documentary. Keep your mouth shut about all of this."

Auranna rolled her eyes, then winked at Joel as she got up to leave.

"I'm playing in the crowd tonight. I'll go out during 'Abhorrent Aberration.' If you want some great crowd footage get Lisa and follow me with the camera," Auranna told Joel over continental breakfast with Stephanie. To avoid more arguing, Auranna asked Rachel to wait near the tour bus in her bat form.

"What, are you directing now?" Stephanie mumbled into a piece of bread with what she derisively called "birdseed" baked into it, enveloping a handful of raw almonds.

"Happy to see you're taking advantage of having no taste," Auranna said. "What's with the bad mood?"

"Get away from us, Joel. The grownups need to talk."

Stephanie's scowl curdled the milk in his coffee and he walked away briskly, then she turned her scorn to Auranna.

"Why didn't you wake me up? Or tell that bitch to undo whatever she did? I can only imagine what you did with her. And right after we…"

Stephanie's eyes became wet and she covered her face

with the bread. Auranna hated nothing more than to see Stephanie sad. She got out of her seat and on her knees to hug Stephanie tight.

"My love, I'm sorry. I didn't ask her to show up or knock you out. Especially knock you out. I did ask her if she would pleasure you as she had me, but she was convinced that won't make you happy."

"She's fuckin' right about that, at least. I don't want anything to do with her, and I don't want her touching you again."

"I'm afraid of what she would do to you if you tried to attack her."

"Then tell her to leave us alone and I won't have to!"

"I've already asked her to remain as a bat while she's on Earth. Anyway, can we forget about her and focus on tonight? I'm wading into the crowd during our last song before any encores. I'm letting you know so you don't bang into me like you have been with, well, everyone else below the stage."

The look Stephanie gave to Auranna in the hotel room the night before crawled back across her face.

"After the show I'm banging you in the dressing room. Make sure Carrie doesn't stay in there too long."

"Admittedly I'd be into that prospect if I wasn't so apprehensive about your aggressive attitude and behavior."

"Be as apprehensive and alliterative as you want, just get yourself into that room after the show. My blood is at its ultimate boiling point after getting jacked around in the crowd. I want to experience you as close to that moment as possible."

Auranna matched Stephanie's scowl.

"What did I say about telling your Queen what to do?"

Stephanie's frown softened and she sniffed away angry tears.

"I thought you didn't want to be called—"

"It's growing on me."

"Probably just trying to impress your batty slut."

Auranna's own blood boiled at Stephanie's new unnatural jealousy. They loved each other but their relationship had never been mutually exclusive. Until now, they'd been open to occasionally enjoying groupies and roadies together. Auranna recalled a time early in the tour when they had a four-way with two of the female riggers; all the awkward, extra limbs and how they must have looked like two octopi copulating.

Auranna shook that memory out of her head and refocused on the problem at hand.

"I'm not doing anything with you tonight. Not until you—"

"Morning, ladies," Alex interrupted, holding a bowl of cereal and the world's driest-looking bagel. "Trouble in Hell?"

They both turned their scowls on him in slow-motion. He stepped back and joined Joel across the room.

They looked back at each other. Their lips quivered almost imperceptibly. Auranna cracked first, then both laughed. Stephanie smiled like her old self.

"Alright," Auranna said, "we have two hours until rehearsal. Your Queen commands that you return to our hotel room for make-up coition, or I'll have you thrown in the dungeons."

CHAPTER ELEVEN
Lepores Pati

Suffer the Bunnies

WHILE STEPHANIE CRASHED HER WAY through the crowd during "Abhorrent Aberration," Auranna moved calmly towards the spot near the mixer tent with Joel and Lisa in tow. No one dared touch her as she played her black guitar and growled into the headset. She wore tattered white rags over a black bra under an excessively torn, bloody skirt with nylons and no footwear. When they briefly crossed paths, Stephanie wiped the blood collected from the crowd and her own veins onto Auranna's face and rags; her red handprints soaked into the white linen.

Many fans gaped in awe, while others bowed to her in reverence. Even the mosh pits on Auranna's side of the crowd calmed themselves as she approached. Their adulation from such close proximity hit different than what she received on the stage. All the words she'd read about herself in magazines, social media, all the fan adoration—it had always been from a distance she couldn't close. She often helped at the merchandise booths but even there the table between the staff and fans forced distance. Seeing the love and devotion in each of their eyes from so close was something else entirely.

A carnal lust built up in her chest the deeper and closer she got to her fans. She understood now—deeply and irrevocably—what Stephanie meant about her blood boiling while playing inside the crowd. The sweaty mass of devotees didn't faze her as she thought it might. After her experience on the bus with Stephanie's insides, she wondered if she'd ever be offended by mere smells again.

Auranna wanted to share her passion with every single person in the crowd with whom she met eyes. Stephanie could only be feeling it stronger as she made physical contact with them, but Auranna feared what she might do if anyone touched her in that state of exhilaration. Would she be able to restrain herself?

Her purpose came back to her, and she resolved to be steadfast in her goal that night. She moved through the parting crowd until she neared the mixer tent. She nodded for Joel to zoom out and launched into her melodic solo. She kept her gaze down on her guitar to avoid making eye contact with the person who'd chosen the wrong spot to enjoy their music.

As the song ended, she looked to Joel, who nodded. Auranna made her way back to the stage from the other side of the mixer tent, determined to absorb the new form of adoration. She never wanted the night to end.

In the middle of their third encore the impatient event organizers put up the blinding white lights and pulled the plug on the equipment. The band tossed out gear from the stage, then Auranna and Stephanie meandered around the crowd and let them touch their hands. She relished their skin on hers as she imagined a small part of their worshipful essence transferring into her. After glad-handing with the VIPs in the back and signing gear for the backstage-pass-holders, Auranna grabbed Stephanie's hand and pulled her toward their dressing room. Desmond, Carrie, and Alex stood in front of the door with frowns and folded arms.

"We need to talk, you two," Carrie said.

"Not now, Carebear," Stephanie replied, already getting fidgety.

Auranna needed Stephanie, though she was better at hiding it from her bandmates. She attempted to shimmy past them to the room. Auranna couldn't wait to hear the lock slide into place, then she'd grab Stephanie by the throat again...

Desmond put his arm across the threshold.

"It's boring when you're in the crowd. Do you two realize that? No one is watching the stage when you're out there."

"Don't be a bitch, Dezzie. You can always start your own band if you need to be the center of attention."

"It's not about that, Stephanie. The band is all of us, not just Aura, and not just your new undead bullshit."

"Bullshit? You still think we're lying?"

"Umm, Dez, we all saw the coffee did nothing to her, and Aura still has a burn on her arm from that same coffee," Alex said.

"Aura brands herself; she could have done it afterwards to sell it. Stephanie could have paid off the waitress to bring cold coffee. Look, that's not the fucking point! It's like when we're in the studio. I come into an empty room early, lay the drum tracks, then check out. I'm a goddamn afterthought, and you're bringing that to the shows now!"

"Maybe you shouldn't have become a drummer, Dez-*zie*," Stephanie said, reaching out and patting his cheek. "Can we get out of this fucking gear, now? Please?"

"It's not only Desmond," Carrie said. "At least he's nearly centered on the stage. The keyboardist is always on the side. A quarter of the audience can't see me, and I'm the last one anyone's looking at during a metal concert. We may as well play recordings while you two are out there having the time of your lives."

"Alright, before this becomes like every band's ego-driven downfall, let's breathe for a moment," Auranna interjected. "We're all paid equally. We've always talked an equal amount of time in the documentary and during full band interviews—let's talk to the roadies tomorrow about some stage work and what we could do to give you all the same experience Stephanie and I are having. I would never dream of keeping that from you.

"Now, your Queen commands you to move aside. We'll see you on the bus."

She brushed past them and locked the door, aware of the looks she earned by referring to herself as their queen right after calling them her equals. She meant every word but the next few minutes would be worth their scorn.

"Was Stephanie choking you, Aura?" Alex asked as the bus door closed and Gerald pulled them onto the road.

"What?" Auranna asked, still dazed and coming down from the dressing room.

"Your neck is red. Are those fingermarks?"

"Oh." Auranna rubbed her neck, reveling in the memory of spurring Stephanie on to squeeze tighter, still marveling that she'd gone so long in life without discovering such a wonderfully dangerous kink. "Yeah. Mind your own business."

"Why? Because 'our queen' commands it? Because you two sometimes act like we're not here?"

"I'm sorry. I wish I could explain what's going on with

us, but that would require you to believe the recent accounts we shared. Thankfully, I don't need you to believe our words anymore. Joel, can you please play what you captured tonight for everyone on the big screen?"

They gathered around the living area TV and witnessed a woman with a Black Aura T-shirt disappear from beside the mixer tent. Everyone around the spot seemed transfixed on Auranna and didn't react to their fellow fan's sudden disappearance, nor her T-shirt faux paus.

"There isn't a screen cut or tear that shows any editing whatsoever. Not even a digital distortion or suspiciously grainy bullshit to ruin it!" Lisa said. She tapped Joel's thigh, and the light on his camcorder came on. "How does that make you all feel?"

Auranna went to the kitchen area for tea and honey while they reacted to it.

"That doesn't prove any of that Hell business," Desmond said. "It has to be something else. Magicians make their living doing shit like this every day. Visual effects artists could do it just as seamlessly."

Stephanie flipped out a blade from her pocket and cut across the back of her forearm. The others recoiled around her.

"What magician is making this not hurt? You can't explain this away."

"Maybe you're both on drugs, despite what Auranna says," Desmond tried to explain it away. "Why the fuck are you carrying a knife around anyway? Maybe that's a movie knife with a little spout for the blood. Maybe you numbed your arm in the dressing room before getting on the bus. Maybe it's some undiscovered long-COVID symptom. It could be a dozen other things. I refuse to believe in this Satanic bullshit."

"Dude, most of our music is—"

"It's the *genre*, Alex! Are you falling for this, too? I know you romanticize the eighties and early-nineties mythology but *come on*! Hell and Satan *are not real*!"

"I oughta cut out your blasphemous tongue, Dezzie. That'd prove this isn't a movie knife," Stephanie said, licking the knife with the same murderous grin she gave him in the diner.

"Stop looking at me like I'm the crazy one!"

"Holy Christ, this is fuckin' *gold*," Lisa whispered a little too loudly to Joel.

"You! Shut up!" Desmond pointed at Lisa. "You're probably behind all this! Trying to put a wedge between us to manufacture drama into your fucking documentary!"

"Dez, calm down, please," Carrie said. "I don't know what's happening here, but you freaking out isn't helping."

Desmond looked at her and the rest of them in utter disbelief. Auranna sat next to him with her mug and tucked her legs underneath her, then put her free hand on his shoulder to reassure him.

"We already discussed how messed up this all is. I wish I could show you with your own eyes what I didn't mean to show Stephanie. But I would never put any of you through the torture of Hell if I can help it. Even if it was the last and only way to prove to you what's going on. I'd rather you persisted to think me and Stephanie non compos mentis than ever subject you to that place.

"And, unfortunately, your belief in us is the lesser of our concerns right now. We have the matter of our disappearing fans to deal with. *That's* real. We know where it's happening. It's in the same spot every show. I don't know the why or how, though. Will you please help me figure this out? For the sake of our fans? They are not...treated well down there."

Rachel's little bat wings fluttered from her perch in a dark corner of the bus. Auranna looked at her sadly.

"You just admitted you know where these missing people are, Aura," Carrie said. "Lisa, can you edit that out?"

"Oh! Why, *sure*! There's nothing interesting about that at all! Onto the cutting room floor it'll go!"

"Forget it, Carebear," Stephanie said. "No one would ever believe the 'where' of it. The fucked-up part is because they're all such pious puritans, the pigs, politicians, and parents actually *do* believe in a real Hell and yet they *still* wouldn't believe us. All of you just watched real video evidence and you continue to think we're crazy."

"No, that's Desmond who's crazy, remember? Try to keep the accusations straight for cohesion," Lisa said.

Auranna patted Desmond's shoulder and gave him a kiss on the cheek, then got ready for bed as the rest of them continued to argue. It was Desmond's night for the big bed. He deserved it after today, she thought, and he'd be the first to break in the new mattress. She actually enjoyed the small beds whenever Stephanie felt like cuddling or hearing Auranna hum. At least *before*, when it was cuddling and nothing more—out of respect for their bandmates. She wondered what was in store for her that night. She put her fingers to her own throat and squeezed a little.

Auranna woke to the sounds of a struggle from the back of the bus in the big bed. She sat up and rubbed the sleep out of her eyes. Alex and Carrie slept soundly. Stephanie wasn't in her bed. In her extra-long black "Heartagram" shirt and nothing else, Auranna crept to the big bed.

There was a two-person-sized mound under the covers. Auranna wondered if Stephanie ever held a flame for

Desmond, or that she was even remotely bi, since she'd never once said or acted affirmatively on either account. A choking sound came from one of them under the covers.

An unexpected flash of jealousy hit her. What kind of sex-crazed, Auranna-obsessed undead girlfriend was Stephanie? And how dare she use their newly-discovered kink on a man? Auranna couldn't help herself. She hoped Desmond would only be boffing a groupie he smuggled on board. It wouldn't be the first time. Auranna lifted the covers to reveal Stephanie, in her bra and pajama bottoms on top of Desmond wearing a Mayhem shirt, choking him with both hands. Rachel was strapped down beneath the back of one of Stephanie's bra straps in her bat form.

Auranna put her hand on Stephanie's shoulder and the bus disappeared. All four of them fell five feet to a black, rocky terrain. Rachel burst into her demonic form, breaking Stephanie's bra strap and landing on top of her. Rachel's wings covered Stephanie and Desmond, who hungrily sucked in air once Stephanie's grip had released from his throat.

"Get off me, slut bat!" Stephanie cried as she rolled over and away from both of them.

Auranna helped them up and looked at Stephanie, bemused. "Steph... Why were you trying to kill our drummer?"

"Yeah! What the fuck is wrong with you?"

"Quiet down, Dezzie. I was doing us all a favor. I didn't feel like spending months trying to convince you. This gets us right to the fucking point."

"What does? Where are we? Oh, what the fuck are *you* supposed to be!"

Desmond hopped back from Rachel as she righted herself, whipping her tail around and flapping her wings to hover a few feet off the ground.

"Settle down. She's with us," Auranna said, calming him with a hand on the shoulder like she had on the bus.

"Um...Jesus. Well, uh, I'm De—"

"I know who you are, Desmond Fuller—legendary drummer for Black Aura. I apologize for playing a part in this noisome creature's ruse, though she did not offer me a choice when she grabbed me and stuffed me into her bra."

"You better stop with that 'noisome' line, you giant-horned...batty... Uh...big-titted... Sexee~ee~ ...Christ, Aura. Down here she's... Unlike on Earth... I mean... I want... Can I...you know, take you behind that little rock outcrop over there, Rachel?"

"My Queen is all I desire."

"You bitch! I just accepted you—called you sexy—and this is how you repay—"

Desmond pulled Auranna aside while Stephanie yelled up at Rachel.

"Aura, what in the actual fuck is going on? Everything's so cold and dark!"

"Are you in denial? Look at the red horizon. The bleak cliffs. That black forest waiting for us to amble inside. The hot air even though your skin is cold. Stephanie has brought you to Hell. I'm sorry she did it without ask—"

Desmond wheeled around, pulled Stephanie away from her shouting bout at Rachel and punched her in the jaw, knocking her down. In response, Stephanie pulled the knife she'd shown them in the bus earlier from her pajama pocket and flung it into Desmond's heart. He screamed and staggered backwards. He ripped the knife out and looked down at the black blood seeping out, hissing as he touched the wound.

"Wha—Why would you do that, you bitch? You've killed me!"

"You seem pretty upright to me, Dezzie. Since you keep doubting your own eyes, maybe your nerves will wake you up. Do you fucking believe us now?"

"Huh—how am I not dead?"

"Alright, Dez," Auranna said. "This is a dream-version of Hell. Here's what I know..."

She explained to him what she'd taught Stephanie a few nights before.

"Rachel is a demon, but she started as one of our biggest fans. She was standing on that spot I showed you but it was several shows ago. They all get pulled down and twisted into these creatures.

"There are a couple new wrinkles I'm learning tonight. Stephanie was able to bring more than her clothes. I didn't know we could bring objects like knives. And you were able to follow us despite not having been tainted by a demon. Stephanie was bitten by a demonic snake. I have no idea if that will make anything different for you.

"Now, before you apologize for disbelieving us, am I forgetting anything? Rachel? Stephanie?"

"Yeah," Stephanie said. "Time has no meaning. And I don't think any of us will be hurt this time," she added confidently. "Last time you thought about snakes, Aura, so of course there were nothing but snakes biting and moving inside and out of our..."

Stephanie threw up at the memory coming back on her.

"Bleh, I don't remember eating that. Anyway. While I was choking Dezzie I was thinking about something that couldn't possibly hurt us."

Auranna shared a look with Rachel.

"I'm afraid to ask..." Auranna said.

"Why? I thought about bunny rabbits! The cutest, most loveable things in the world! What could they even do to us?"

Desmond shook his head and groaned.

"Someone's never watched *Monty Python and the Holy Grail* or *Re:Zero*. You've doomed us all."

"Shut up! What would *you* have thought of?"

"Not something with sharp teeth and strong jaws that do nothing but chew all day. Couldn't you have thought of a sock puppet or a stuffed animal?"

"When you get around to forcing Alex or Carrie down here, you try that. Now, do you believe us, and we can get out of here?"

"I could still be dreaming like a normal person…"

"You're going to wish that's all this was," Auranna said. "Let's get it over with."

As they walked towards the forest, Desmond glanced at Stephanie's broken bra strap and partially open cup.

"Uh, Stephanie, I can almost see your—"

Stephanie pulled the cup fully open.

"There. You've seen my nipple. It's old news now. Concentrate on freeing your mind for when the hurt starts. Or, if it gives you comfort, think of my nipple, I guess."

"You said they won't hurt—"

"The cute little bunny rabbits won't. But the creatures that wake us up will, and He might."

"Who might?"

"He that you can't deny further. Pray we don't run into Him."

"Stop plagiarizing my Hell-tour speech, Steph," Auranna said over her shoulder with a little smile.

She stopped at the edge of the forest and held out her hands for Stephanie and Desmond on each side, while Rachel hovered in front of them. They stepped into the black void.

CHAPTER TWELVE

Delıramentum

Is She For Real?

STEPHANIE EXPLAINED IN MINDSPEAK HOW the dim orange lights in the distance worked for Desmond, who had shrunk in fear once they traversed beneath the oppressive, taciturn canopy, and the imps filled their minds with harsh whispers.

More who will come to hate her. Why does she torture them so?
It is not our Queen's fault. Her slut damns them all.
The false queen allows it. She was broken long ago. She will never act.
Others involved. She must act.
She doesn't care about any of them. She loves only music and sex. She will fail them all with her inaction.

– Aura, does He always wait for us to talk to the demons first? That's what happened last time, anyway. – Stephanie asked, doing an admirable job ignoring the imps.

– If I had to guess based on my previous visits... It's like He doesn't know we're here until we find and talk to one of the demons. Then He punishes us for interrupting whatever He's doing. Again, if I had to guess. I cannot, nor will not, speak for Him. –

– Oh, my head. This is amazing and repulsive. It's like the backs of my eyes are vibrating while I 'listen.' – Desmond thought.

My Queen. A light has moved closer to our direction of travel. I suggest preparing Yourselves.

– Against the onslaught of cute bunny rabbits? What are you all so afraid of— –

Instead of the anticipated cuddly fur balls softly and lovingly rubbing the sides of their feet when they reached the light, squishy, squeezing, slick, sloppy, sucky arms slid around their ankles and pulled them to the forest floor. The tentacles writhed around and through them, constricting and leaving painful hickies over and inside every inch of their bodies.

– You...made a mistake...Steph. These aren't...ugh... – Auranna shivered violently in both extreme pleasure and pain.

A bobbing creature slimed its way towards them. It had eight arms that attached beneath what was once a beautiful woman's head, with the mesmerizing, psychedelic eyes of cuttlefish. Her skin changed various luminescent colors in the blackness. The three bandmates would have been dazzled if the occasional sucker didn't latch onto their eyes and disorient their sight. The tentacles pulled away from Auranna's face but didn't let go anywhere else.

My Queen. I have conversed with others in Your army and many have never met You. I am humbled to be the one You chose this day.

– You were supposed to be rabbits. What happened? –

We would not deign to listen to the noisome thoughts of our Queen's doxy.

Rachel laughed from above them, then vanished.

Oh, poor Rachel. One ought never to laugh down here. He will chastise her before He turns His attention to You.

– Our time grows short. Why are you here? No offense, but

we really were expecting rabbits. –

You thought of an octopus when You touched Your doxy's shoulder, as there were eight limbs in the bed.

– Keep calling me that, you—Ooow! Keep those out of my ears! That doesn't shut off my thoughts, bitch! Aagh! –

– Quiet, Stephanie. Don't invite more harm. Umm, octo-demon? How did you come to your form? –

In conversing with Your army's conscripts, it seems to come down to His whims. We see no pattern in His— No!

Her legs shriveled and she disappeared along with the hundreds of tentacles that had been having their way with the three of them for what had felt like hours.

Desmond cried and curled into a ball after the suckers' retreat.

– Dezzie, I wish that was going to be the worst of it, but—oh shit. – Stephanie thought.

A whoosh of wind lifted Desmond from the forest floor.

– You will live, Desmond! It's only temporary! – Auranna cried.

She watched his body rise into the blackness despite his struggles.

Imps came from everywhere around them on the ground. They tore and cut Stephanie and Auranna to pieces, taking their time while screams flooded their heads, filling them with doubt, distrust, and dread.

After an excruciating, seemingly endless amount of time Auranna's body parts reformed. When the wind forced her pieces back together like an impatient jigsaw puzzler, it was an opposite but equally painful sensation as being torn apart. A leg pushed into and fused with the middle of her spine. An arm jutted from where her left breast should have gone back, and her left breast molded into her calf. Only her head remained correctly intact as the wind pulled her up to His disapproving eyes.

You continue to waste my time. First the half-soul slut, then this puling, mewling soul in a live vessel. You must pay your currencies without deviation. I do not desire half-measures. Bring me my untethered souls. The time I will put your army to use draws nigh. Do not interrupt me again.

– My Lord, I beg You, please don't hurt my friends. Please don't hurt me. If You would but tell me why and how You use me, I could endeavor to fulfill my bargain to You more efficaciously. Whatever that bargain may have been... –

The eyes regarded her with...amusement?

You believe me to be a fool—that I will assist your ultimate goal to free your army. Put those hopeful thoughts out of your mind. You are beyond redemption now. And no one shall catch your fall.

Auranna cried while her mind petulantly forced her to think exactly as He surmised. His eyes smiled as the wind made her long for the tentacles.

Auranna woke convulsing on the bed, trying to put her body in any position that would make the excruciating pain echoing through her even an iota easier to bear. Stephanie frantically felt over her entire body to make sure no part had been left behind for the imps to devour. Desmond laid under her with wide open eyes, streaming tears, while his mouth hung open, soundless. Rachel fell from the air in her full form on top of all three of them. Her wings came to rest over the entire bed, constrained by the narrow space.

"What in the name of Rotting Christ is going on back here?" Alex said as he lifted a wing. "A four-way with a Comic Con tryhard? I didn't know you ladies were bi. Can I get in on this like Desmond?"

Rachel picked herself off the bed and looked down at Alex.

"You will never know our Queen in that way."

"Jesus, Aura. You've got other people calling you a queen now, too?"

"I think she started it," Auranna said as she pulled her long shirt back down to her knees and helped Stephanie off Desmond's body.

"No. Your army has called You Queen from the beginning."

"When was the beginning?" Auranna asked.

"Time has no meaning in Hell. Some spoke within the army of a time before Black Aura."

"I thought we were your first band, Aura..." Stephanie said.

"You are. I don't know what she's talking about."

"Details were not explicated," Rachel said.

"Just like they're not explicating right now," Alex said. "If you weren't all having what looked like an amazing ménage à quatre, what the hell—?"

Carrie turned on the light and gasped. Alex's mouth hung open as he looked at Rachel in more stark contrast than shadows and dim passing street lights. Carrie reached for his sleeve and pulled him back, fearing for their lives. Rachel's black eyes observed them without expression. Alex shrugged off Carrie and approached. He reached out and touched her skin. She grabbed his hand and twisted when he touched the large ring hanging from her nipple.

"Ow! I'm sorry, I just...I thought this was a body suit or something. Your skin...There's no seam anywhere on your body!"

He circled around her and found no zipper. He dropped down on his back and propelled himself between her legs.

"No zipper there!"

Rachel lifted her hoof to stamp down and crush his head, but Auranna grabbed Rachel's calf and caressed it to calm her down.

"Get out of there, you perv!" Carrie said as she pulled him from the stomping area. "Aura, what's going on? Who is this?"

"This is the bat you guys said you couldn't see the other night. I'm unsure why you can see her now."

"*She* was perched on your guitar?"

"Well, not like this, of course. She can metamorphose into a bat. Wouldn't you be more comfortable that way, Rachel?"

"You've *named* her!" Alex said.

"No, she has a name. Had? Anyway, she's one of the missing people from our shows."

"My Queen, I am ashamed to admit our Lord punished my impertinence with both pain and irony. After He had His way with me, He wished me to discover the true meaning of humor by walking the Earth in this form until He calls me back to Hell."

"Goddamn, you even *talk* like Aura!" Alex blurted.

Stephanie leaned over Desmond and shook him. His eyes were still leaking and he hadn't shut his mouth.

"Hey. Hey, buddy? I'm sorry for all that. Can we move past this and help Aura solve our problem?"

Desmond blinked and closed his mouth, then turned to Stephanie with a withering glare. She smiled and gave him a double thumbs up to welcome his forgiveness. He sprang up and pushed her to the floor, straddling her as he choked her. Auranna put her hand on his shoulder but he shook it off.

Stephanie laughed under his hands.

"Sorry, Dezzie, you can't hurt me up here. If we ever go back there together, you can take it out on me. Right now you're just dangerously close to getting me off. If only your fingers were a little...more...feminine...Mmm~mmm~..."

Desmond let go, slapped her, and rolled off to the side. He hugged his knees and stared into nothingness. Alex put his hand on Desmond's shoulder.

"What's going on, Desmond? Couldn't handle two stunning metalheads and whatever Rachel is supposed to be?"

"Shut the fuck up, Alex. Isn't Rachel enough for you? Do you still not get where we were?"

"You were in the big bed. I'm skipping my turn tomorrow, by the way, unless one of you burns the sheets."

"You jackass, it's not a *joke* anymore," Desmond sniffed. "I met...Him... It's all true. Aura and Steph weren't making any of it up. Hell is...it's...it's not a *word* anymore. It's a real *place*."

"Alright, fine," Alex said with a smile. "Then take me there. I want to meet Him."

Desmond's dead stare into Alex's eyes sucked the humor out of his face.

"No, you don't. Even if I hated you to your core and wanted you to die, I would never want you to see those...eyes. Or feel what He made me feel."

"You lived, though. Come on, let's do this! Let me and Carrie see this place."

"Don't speak for me, Alex. *I* don't want to see it," Carrie said.

Desmond got up and put his drummer's iron grip around Alex's skinny guitarist's biceps.

"I wished I had died. Even in the unreal state we were in, I wanted to die more than anything. But if I did, I would be in for an eternity of the same pain. He...promised me that."

"I'm still interested. If Aura is drawing so much of her inspiration from this place, I've got to see it for myself. A lot of what she writes might make a modicum of sense, then."

"Do not insult our Queen," Rachel said.

"Wasn't intended," Alex said, waving her glare off with his fingers. "Come on, we're all family here. If you suffered for our art, Aura, I will gladly suffer for it as well."

"There will be nothing glad about it," Rachel warned.

Desmond gave up on convincing Alex and walked to the living room with a notebook and started writing and drawing.

"Aww, see? I want that! Instant inspiration!"

"Alex, I'm saying this as your best friend and, if you wish, sister," Auranna said, "please calm yourself. I will not take you on a tour of Hell. But we will share with you what we saw and if possible, what we felt. Carrie, you may also ask us anything."

"I…I think I'm going to see about joining a new band. You're all insane. As soon as Gerald stops in the morning I'm packing up and leaving."

"Don't do that, Carebear," Stephanie said. "We need you. Come here! Feel Rachel up a little and you'll understand. We're not all insane."

"Steph, you're turning into the Mad Hatter in front of our eyes. And Rachel… she's probably covered in RealDoll skin or something," Carrie said. "She could still be in a costume."

"I wish it were so," Rachel said forlornly. "I cannot fathom leaving this bus. I am a prisoner here as much as I am a prisoner in Hell, only…"

"Only less of a rape-y Satan, am I right?" Stephanie smiled. "Hey! You can let loose at every show! Everyone will think you're in costume and you won't be out of place at a metal concert! Oh my lord, if you could flutter down from the rafters during 'Hellacious Heresy' you'd set the crowd off into even more of a frenzy! You could walk out among the crowd with us. Our fans will love you!"

"…I…will consider this, noisome doxy."

Stephanie pretended to punch Rachel's stomach, then laughed and held out her hand for a peace shake. Rachel took it reluctantly. Stephanie shook it, then pulled Rachel down to her eye level and whispered.

"Aura is still mine. Remember that, Rachel."

"It looks like none of us will be able to sleep for the rest of the morning," Auranna said. "Let's all sit down in the living area and see if we can compose anything from Desmond's notes. I look forward to hearing what he'll create."

Alex and Carrie sat on the couch while Joel continued sleeping on it. They discovered earlier in the tour that he'd sleep through anything and everything. They could sit on top of him and he'd snore away. When they were all seated in the living area, the bus started swerving and Gerald fought to get it under control. Auranna looked to the front of the bus to see Lisa turned around in the passenger seat. She stared at Rachel with a dropped jaw, along with Gerald and his wide, panicky eyes in the rearview mirror.

"Let's get it a little under control, Gerald! We're trying to compose some fucking art back here!" Stephanie called to the front.

CHAPTER THIRTEEN
MORS VOLUNTARIA

SUICIDAL HOPEFULNESS

GERALD MADE AN ABRUPT STOP and emergency exit off the tour bus after seeing Rachel. Stephanie ran after him along the highway shoulder at three AM in her pajama bottoms and torn bra. Lisa slapped Joel several times, yelling at him to wake up and unlock the case in which he kept the cameras. Alex wouldn't stop staring at Rachel. Carrie punched his arm, then pulled her In This Moment blanket from her bed and draped it in front of Rachel's naked body. Auranna cradled Desmond's head in her arms as the imagery he drew brought the painful memories of Hell flooding back.

"Alex, I see the way you stare at me. You cannot see through this veil," Rachel said. "This is..."

Stephanie pulled Gerald back onto the bus by the arm.

"—'s only a new actor for the tour! We met her at the hotel, and she said she'd act for free if we let her stay on the bus outside of the shows. Jesus, Gerald, I can't believe you thought she was a real demon! Are you sure you weren't smoking something with Lisa before we took off tonight? That's reckless endangerment, you know."

"She...she looks so... That costume is too good...too real..."

"She's a self-employed creature designer. Stan Winston is her hero. We're going to help expose her to the country in hopes she'll get noticed by Hollywood. Um, 'expose' might have been the wrong word."

"Real or not, can one of you help me wake this lazy sack up so I can get some footage of her? This documentary is going to have *everything*!" Lisa clasped her hands in delight.

"Calm down, Lisa," Auranna said. "Rachel will look like this tomorrow and the next day. You'll get your footage. Anyway, don't you have a phone? Gerald, can we get moving again?"

"Uh...sure...sure, kid. Let me catch my breath."

Stephanie brought him a glass of water.

"Thanks, Stephanie. I'm sorry, I'm not trying to look, but you're kind of popping out there," Gerald said as he turned his reddening face away.

Stephanie looked down and chuckled. Out of consideration for their already-distracted driver, she pulled a Warlock T-shirt out of her duffel and covered herself. To solidify the ruse, Stephanie went and hugged Rachel.

"They didn't mean anything by their reactions, Rach. Your design work is otherworldly."

As the riggers and roadies emerged from their buses, Auranna surprised them by standing at the stage site before any of them arrived.

"Morning, everyone. I wish to ask you all a favor before you set up the stage..."

Later that night, Black Aura performed the entire show from within the crowd. Desmond set up on a small, low stage in the center, close enough for fans to touch his sweating, muscular back as he played. Carrie wasn't far from him on her own platform, accompanied by a lone security guard standing at her back to keep the gropers away. Alex moved around the audience as Stephanie and Auranna did, but he earned more of Stephanie's treatment than Auranna's reverent walks. He never complained about the extra female attention, although at times the intensity of it threatened to disturb his rhythm.

Rachel flew in, around, and above the crowd throughout many songs. Auranna had requested not only setting up the extra stages and hiding the cords if they didn't have transmitters, but also a fake set of riggings to make it appear as if Rachel couldn't possibly be flying without their assistance. Rachel called forth her bat cauldrons from different locations during several climactic choruses throughout the night.

Auranna played beside each band member in turn—to give them respite—as no one dared get within a couple of feet of her. It also ensured maximum exposure for both the fans and her bandmates to connect on that deeper level of reverence.

After two and a half encores, the band gathered in the men's dressing room.

"So, was that everything you dreamed it would be?" Auranna asked.

"I felt a little awkward with the security guard there, but it was better than being on the stage, for sure. I wish I could be more mobile," Carrie said.

"Why don't we buy you a keytar, then?" Desmond suggested. "Have you ever played that way?"

"I'm sure I could get used to it..."

"There you go, Carebear. You'll have metalheads smashing

and groping you in no time," Stephanie said as she slipped on her Anthrax T-shirt. "The security guard makes us look soft. I'm sure Aura could arrange for you to not feel the pain..."

"Stop trying to damn our bandmates, Steph," Auranna said. "And since when do you undress around the guys?"

"Once Desmond saw me, it became three of four of you who've seen my tits. Plus Gerald and Rachel have, and I caught Joel and Lisa lingering on me before Gerald mentioned my bra coming apart. Might as well cut to the chase with Alex and get it over with."

"Thanks for keeping me in mind," Alex said. "I still looked away. Nothing seems to faze you now, but it wasn't that long ago you'd turn bright red if anyone mentioned anything remotely sexy. It...feels wrong to me."

His consideration caught Stephanie off guard, and she gave him a hug. Auranna put her hand on Desmond's back.

"How do you feel? You shook off playing your composition at the two-hour mark. Too soon?"

"It lacked something, and it bugged me in the runup to it."

"Take your time. I appreciate your instinct not to put out an unfinished piece."

Stephanie punched Alex's arm.

"How about you, then?"

"I'm bothered by Rachel's presence," Alex said. "No offense, Rachel, you did an amazing job out there. The bats are cool, but it's pushing us into gimmick territory. Roaming and interacting with the crowd is special enough and it enhances our cred, whereas your presence...detracts... I'm sorry to be so blunt about it."

"I care not. I will confine myself to the bus until I am called back Home. Forget that I am here."

Auranna's heart weighed heavy for Rachel's forlorn and downcast expression before she turned away.

"That's not your home," Auranna said, slipping her hand in Rachel's and pulling her back to the group. "My heart wishes Alex was wrong, but my mind knows he's right. However, you can play it more lowkey by walking around the edges, taking pictures with fans. Enjoy the show without being part of the show. Can we try that tomorrow night?"

Rachel nodded.

"Anything else on your mind, Alex?" Auranna asked.

"I want you and Stephanie to take me to Hell. I *must* feel more connected to our music, and I want inspiration for my own."

"If you wanted to discover Hell with me, I would show you what it's all about," Stephanie said, "but Aura is the one that makes it happen. I thought that having Rachel with me, then touching the person and thinking hard about bunny rabbits would do it."

"Bunny rabbits?" Carrie tilted her head.

"It didn't work. Cephalopods attacked us instead, thanks to Aura's thoughts superseding my own. If it happens again, tell Aura what you want before trying to get down there. All that you fear most...you'd best keep it hidden."

"If you thought you only had to touch me," Desmond said, "why were you choking me?"

"The cupcake."

"It's all a moot point, anyway, Alex," Auranna said. "I am not taking you to Hell. Desmond and Stephanie were accidents. If you want it only for inspiration, try reading the bible."

"I'm going to pretend you didn't just suggest that," Alex rolled his eyes and crossed his arms.

Aura fixed Alex's eyes to her own and said with a deep finality: "Tours of Hell will not occur again."

Auranna woke to something poking her ribs. She focused in the dark to find Alex kneeling next to the bed in Stephanie's Danzig shirt.

"I'm ready. Take me there," he whispered.

"I told you 'no,' Alex. Go back to sleep. And you'd better give that shirt back to Steph. I don't think she's going to appreciate you stretching it out."

"Please? How does it work? Do I need to touch you?"

He put his hand on her bare shoulder.

"Here? Do I need to touch somewhere else? Do you have to touch me? How does this work?"

"Get your hand off me and forget it."

"Was sex involved? Do you have to be a virgin to make it work? Are lesbians considered virgins? All four of you were on the bed when it happened, right? Do I get in bed with you? Please tell me you're bi and that's going to be the way to Hell."

"I'm losing patience with you. I feel you've been secretly hoping that last part was the way regardless of whether I take you there or not."

"Come on, stop holding back your gift. I don't care how it's done, just get me there."

"Please stop. I need you to understand I come out of there far worse off than anyone else. He...punishes me for interrupting Him. It's like surgery with no anesthesia. You'll feel knives pierce you deeply, and that will seem pleasant when it really starts."

"I'll protect you."

"You have no idea what you're talking about."

She ripped her shoulder from his eager hands and pulled her Slayer blanket over her head. He lingered next to the bed for a few moments, then slunk away to his bed. She considered granting his wish, if only to shut him up and put the fear of Hell in him. But she hadn't wished that experience for Desmond; she didn't wish it for Alex or Carrie.

She wouldn't take anyone there again, willingly or not; even her enemies; even rival poser bands who fronted their Satanic worship with no heart or soul behind them. Those bands wanted their T-shirts to sell at the same Hot Topics from which they purchased their "metal cred." They grew up in banal suburbia. They weren't actively tortured for eighteen ongoing years by The Being they "worshipped" so vociferously.

Touring with other metal groups over the previous decade exposed them as the imposters they were to Auranna, specifically when they tried to metal-splain Hell to her. She furrowed her brow and nodded at them while the dreamworld haunted her memories. Some of them weren't so obsessed with Him, though. She respected them more for playing with the genre's imagery for no other reason than they felt like it.

She didn't blame Alex for obnoxiously insisting on being sent to Hell. He only just discovered he'd spent his time in the band playing the part and not feeling the pain. Nobody liked being a poser, especially someone as earnest as Alex. He believed himself to be an authority to the lower-tiered or up-and-coming bands with whom they toured the world. What credit did he have now?

It didn't matter. Auranna determined she would never allow him the sights, sounds, and feelings he foolishly thought he desired.

"Oh, *come on!*" Stephanie shouted from the bathroom. "What fresh hell is *this*?"

Carrie rubbed her eyes free from the blissful sleep of someone who'd never felt or seen Hell. She yawned and shuffled towards the commotion, as if someone shouting on a metal band's tour bus was nothing to run towards with alarm. Desmond, however, seemed as if he had either not slept at all, or his sleep troubled him all night.

"What's going on, Steph?" Carrie asked as she entered the doorframe, then ran out of the bathroom and threw up into a trash can.

Lisa snapped her fingers at Joel while they fumbled to get dressed. They were both shirtless except for Lisa's purple bra. Joel pulled out his camera and pushed by Desmond and Stephanie into the small bathroom. Lisa leaned in behind him and gasped after adjusting her glasses.

Auranna pulled Desmond back, then squeezed behind Lisa and Joel. In the shower stall, blood splattered the walls in spurts and sprays. Alex slumped splayed on the stall's floor. The drain drank the blood dripping from his forearms and neck, soaking his illicit Mayhem T-shirt with the album cover for Dawn of the Black Hearts.

"You fuckin' poser," Stephanie muttered, but sniffed as she felt his face. A spurt of blood from his neck wound flecked her Leviathan shirt.

Auranna noticed a folded piece of paper with blood spatters in the sink and picked it up. It was titled: "*A tout les amis.*"

"Little on the nose, Alex," Auranna sighed, then opened the flap. "'Find me,' it says. Motherf—"

"What does that mean?" Lisa asked.

Auranna's shoulders slumped. She crumpled the note and spiked it back into the sink, then went to sit on the couch to hug Carrie as she cried. Joel lowered himself on the couch on the opposite side of the bus and kept them in frame.

"What happened with him? Why would he do that?" Lisa asked.

"He didn't listen to our warnings," Desmond said. "Fuckin' idiot."

"Looks like we'll be taking a trip back after all, Aura," Stephanie said after washing the blood from her hands. "Better get going so we can get him back in time for sound check."

"I don't think it will work that way. He's *actually* dead. I can't fathom how we would even begin trying to get to the real Hell. Let alone finding him. Let alone bringing him back."

Rachel clopped forth from the scene in the bathroom and stood with Carrie's blanket covering her. Auranna regarded her for a moment.

"Rachel, when you came to us, what was that like? You mentioned my grandmother pointing for you to go through a portal. Was it that easy?"

"Yes, my Queen. Moving through the portal was instantaneous."

"Queen? Grandmother? Portal? What are you all talking about?" Lisa asked as she finally pulled on a shirt.

"Why don't you preserve some measure of mystery in the documentary?" Auranna asked. "Stop interrupting us while we contemplate."

"Maybe finding him will be easier than we're making it," Stephanie said. "Let's look up a psychic. See if we can talk to his spirit and discover his location down there…"

"What makes you so sure he's in Hell?" Carrie asked, utterly distraught.

Stephanie, Auranna, and Desmond turned to look at her, their eyelids half-closed in answer to her absurd question. She closed her mouth and wiped back her tears.

"Alright, Desmond and Carrie, delay sound check if you have to while Stephanie and I find a psychic. Maybe it will work, maybe it won't. It's worth a shot, at least."

"We'll follow you and Stephanie," Lisa declared, not to be left out.

"Suit yourself."

"I shall remain here and see if I may fashion more functional attire to fit around this figure," Rachel said.

"Don't cut holes in my clothes, Rachel," Stephanie said. "Though my Dimmu Borgir gear would look good on you..."

"Rachel, I don't suppose you would... Never mind. I'll take care of it when we get back," Auranna said.

In anticipation of the hot weather that would ramp up throughout the day, Auranna wore a white Deafheaven tank top over black, torn jeans. Without the use of their shower for the foreseeable future, she applied extra deodorant and set off with Stephanie towards the closest psychic that popped up on their phone search.

The psychic operated from a rundown trailer on the outskirts of the town. Stephanie knocked but no one answered. She called the number from the website and waited for a few seconds while Lisa and Joel recorded the property.

"Hello, Mrs. Voiannt? We're standing outside your...facility and we're in need of your services. ... I'm sorry we don't really have time to make an appointment. This is an emergency. ... Need you to talk to someone for us ~*from beyond the grave*~, if you will, though he's not buried yet. Not sure if that complicates things for you. ... No, I'm not joking. Don't you hear that sort of thing every day? ... What kind of psychic are you? ... If you call the police I'm going to give you a negative review on your Yelp page. ... That's what I thought."

Stephanie hung up and smiled at Auranna.

"She needs a few minutes to clear the dining table. Probably setting up her clichéd crystal ball and turban; getting that magnet ready under the table to pretend items are moving on their own..."

"Why did you suggest this if you don't believe in it?"

"Just because this psychic doesn't seem legit doesn't mean I don't believe in it. Especially now, right?"

The door opened but no one stood in the frame. They glanced at each other, then walked inside the dark room, followed by Lisa and Joel. Black curtains were drawn, and incense burned from a shrine near the table. Auranna smiled at the opened box next to the burner that read "Psychic Soul Incense." A disheveled woman was absorbed, slipping on rings and bracelets, though she had the good taste not to wear a turban.

"I do apologize. I haven't had a paying customer in two weeks. Now you were saying something about a—"

Mrs. Voiannt saw Auranna and screamed.

CHAPTER FOURTEEN
Nudus

Isn't This What You Came For?

THEY HELPED MRS. VOIANNT UP from the floor and sat her in the table's head chair. Stephanie flicked a bit of water into her face from the trailer's kitchen sink while Auranna sat down across from her. The woman woke and recoiled again, but kept her scream minimized to a gasp.

"What's wrong, Claire? We're not going to hurt you," Stephanie said.

"Huh—how did you know my name? I don't post it on the website."

Stephanie looked at Auranna and rolled her eyes. Auranna smiled and clasped her hands together on the table.

"Why all the screaming and fainting, Mrs. Voiannt?" Auranna asked as Stephanie sat down between them. Lisa and Joel positioned themselves at the back of the trailer's living area to capture the table and everyone seated.

"You—your aura. It's *pitch black*... I've never once in all my years of study come across someone like you."

"It's beautiful, isn't it?" Stephanie said while tracing Auranna's body with her eyes.

"That's not the word I'd use for it. It is a grave meaning—she has no soul. Yet she lives. A living death-aura. It doesn't make any sense."

"On any other day that would interest me to learn more, but we're in a hurry and we must find our friend. He passed away only this morning," Auranna said.

"Does he owe you money and you need the combination to his safe? That's the most common reason people come to me after someone's death."

"Nothing like that," Auranna waved her fingers. "I don't know how much you need to know to commune with our friend. Please tell us what you need from us."

"Do you have anything of his?"

Auranna and Stephanie looked at each other. Stephanie shook her head. Auranna felt around her jeans but found nothing. Then she noticed her hands.

"Oh. I guess in the events of the morning I didn't get around to washing my hands. I still have some of his blood on my fingers from his note."

"Blood?" Claire flinched. "I sort of meant like a watch or maybe his car keys. No one has ever walked in here with fresh blood of the victim on their person."

"I imagine this should make it easier, though, right?" Stephanie shrugged.

"Um. You mentioned a note... Was this a suicide?"

"Mmm, yes and no?" Auranna said.

"It was or it wasn't."

"Well, not really... His intention wasn't death, per se. He thinks he's only a tourist in Hell. He's expecting to come back."

Mrs. Voiannt stared at Auranna, unable to process that information.

"So, can you scrape some of this dried blood on her hands

into a bowl and, I don't know, do some witch-y, pagan-y stuff with it? A spiritual summoning with his liquid remains?" Stephanie offered. "Oh, does the witching hour not draw near? I didn't check. Does the time zone matter with that?"

"I've got to update my website to be more specific about what I can and can't do..."

"Good idea, but right now we need to find out where our friend is in Hell," Stephanie continued, "like, a geographical location or...even a landmark. Or which of Dante's circles he's in? We don't know much about it ourselves. It's so dark down there and you can't get far without something torturing you. We'd like to avoid that part, if at all possible. Oh, and we need to be able to find him without running into Satan. He'll fuck everything up."

Claire's mouth quivered while she listened to Stephanie's nonchalant account of her experience in Hell, but she fanned out her Tarot cards, blew on them, then rang a bell over the deck. Auranna and Stephanie cocked their eyebrows at her but continued their conversation.

"Oh damn. He's going to be in purgatory, isn't he?" Auranna asked. "Is purgatory connected to Hell physically? He might be one of those trees that get stuck there for committing suicide, the more I ponder..."

Claire shuffled the thick cards on their ends.

"I'll see what kind of answers the deck—" she started, but Stephanie ignored her.

"That's all based on books and shit written by men, Aura," Stephanie said. "It's quite possible purgatory and the circles don't actually exist. At least when we were down there all I remember seeing were cliffs, a big flat plain between them, lots of rocks, and the black forest. Maybe that's all Hell is?"

"I disagree. Rachel and the other demons spoke of their communions with the rest of my army. They may occupy a completely different area. When they're banished or disappear from our sight, they must be going somewhere...And what of the red-tinged sky? Where and what are the infernos that illuminate against the inky black void?"

Claire split the cards into three stacks.

"Do you think Hell is as clichéd as fire and brimstone and all that?" Stephanie shrugged. "I mean, I didn't smell sulfur or anything, but that could go along with my loss of taste and smell? Although I was able to feel pain down there that I can't feel up here... Oh, god, I'm remembering the smell of His wet fur. It was like sun-spoiled mayonnaise in rotten egg salad and—"

Stephanie put her hand over her mouth to keep back a heave. Claire overreacted to Stephanie's near-expulsion and swept the cards onto the floor in an effort to protect them.

"Don't think about Him. Let's think about Alex..." Auranna said with a cocked eyebrow at Claire's commotion.

"Those were all dream visits, anyway," Stephanie continued. "What if those were images our brains made for us and Hell is completely different?"

Though the sweep resulted in a violent spread of cards on the floor, every one of them landed face down, except two.

"Hmm...maybe. Who's to say?" Auranna put her fingers to her chin in thought, then snapped them.

"Rachel! The portal! She existed in my dream only as far as I knew but manifested after coming through the portal! A physical being could travel between those two locations like she did! I think I know how we can recreate that portal."

They stood up, put some scattered cash on the table, and turned to leave.

"Wait, don't you want—" Claire sputtered.

"So we go through the portal, find him, and drag him back to Earth? I hope it's that easy, Aura."

"Nothing about this will be easy. I want to discuss some things with Rachel before we make the trip back to Hell, though. Do you think we should bring her with us? After what Satan did to her, He might punish her even worse. He could add an elephant trunk to her face to truly make her miserable. I feel so sorry for her, you know? The poor—"

Lisa and Joel backed out of the front door, capturing the discussion. The two women slammed the door behind them and continued their conversation outside, and Mrs. Voiannt was forgotten. Her hands quaked while she pulled the last cigarette out of a pack and almost burned her nose attempting to light it with a match. Her normally deft fingers dropped the match on the cards. A blue fire spread over the deck. The flame remained contained to the edges of the cards, never touching the floor.

Remarkably, the cards didn't burn at all, save for the two that had landed face up. The upright Tower and reversed Magician disintegrated, then the fire snuffed itself out. Mrs. Voiannt blinked at the unexpected show, looked at the unlit cigarette, then crumpled it and vowed to quit.

Auranna and Rachel sat together in the field hand-in-hand while the roadies built up the mini-stages and larger stage with Desmond, Carrie, and Stephanie helping. Once the opening acts witnessed all of Black Aura in the crowd during the previous show, they begged to take part in the same way for their own shows and joined in the extra construction that the roadies never anticipated when the tour started.

"Rachel, you said it was instantaneous to walk through the portal, but did it hurt? Did it feel like anything? Do you think our corporeal forms will be able to withstand the transition?"

"My Queen, I do not know the how of things. I do not know if I am alive or dead. One could not say I died in the conventional sense. I am unsure of my soul's status. I am unsure what Your new knowledge of being soulless means, or how Your doxy having only half a soul works either."

"Please stop calling her that. I love your outfit, by the way."

Rachel pilfered a white XXL Black Aura T-shirt from the merchandise boxes and tore it into a tube top to cover her breasts and snugly fit underneath her wings. She tore up a black tablecloth from the vending services, made a skirt out of it to cover her hooves, and cut a hole out for her tail.

Though she had many animal protrusions—her wings, horns, tail—the hooves shamed her the most. Everything else could be passed off as realistic costume design, but the hooves could only be believable if she were a full-time ballerina walking on her toes inside the "costume." Not to mention the backwards angle of the knees...

"You look badass, Rachel. Seriously. I can think of many more mortifying ways to be stuck here in a non-human form. That poor octo-demon, for one. Anyway, did Satan warn you against coming back to Hell when He was...admonishing you?"

"He only said He would call me back when Your army was needed."

"Who the hell is He fighting, anyway? Do you think it's as simple as a battle between demons and angels?"

"From my comprehension and communing with others in Your army, a multitude of angels were cast from Heaven. One religious devotee of Your music who had been twisted into a featherless dove-like creature with olive branches for feet quoted that it was a third of all angels, from the book of Revelation. Many felt as Satan did and were punished in equal measure. More still were mindless sycophants of neither God nor Satan, and they were cast out for their lack of obsequiousness all the same. Satan often engages in skirmishes against these other heretics who wish to rule Hell as He does."

"Another book written by men, yet some of the details ring true. I wonder if others have traveled through the dream-version of Hell as I do. Perhaps that's where so much of Hell's culture is gleaned. How many writers and scholars were posers, and how many had a true experience, I wonder?"

"Maybe You could ask them, if You meet them down there."

Auranna texted her bandmates to gather by the tour bus.

"I'm unsure what will happen to us once we walk through this portal, Rachel. I pray we don't become trapped. Oh, by the way—I can't believe you cleaned Alex up and put him neatly in his bed while we were gone! I was going to ask you but that would have been unfair of me. Did you read my mind?"

"No. The smell reminded me of the rotting flesh and wretched afterbirths of death in Hell while I was working on clothes to cover my form, so I took care of it. I am partial to this reprieve of fresh air on Earth and he was soiling it. Beyond that, cleaning up after a corpse is not the work of a queen."

"I wouldn't have minded at all. That was going to be nothing compared to what Stephanie and I cleaned up in the bus before you arrived..."

"Are you sure about this, Aura?" Carrie asked as she helped

pile debris in the makeshift pyre pit.

"I'm curious more than anything. Perhaps we'll find more information that can help us free our fans from Hell? And if we happen upon Alex, we'll bring him back to us."

"I wonder if this idiot will come back to a newly formed body or if he's going to look like a cut-up zombie when his soul returns," Desmond muttered as he pulled Alex's body off the bus. He laid it on Carrie's Nightwish blanket a few feet away from the pit.

"What should we do if you don't return before we're supposed to be on stage?" Carrie asked.

"Get on the bus and leave until the fans' pitchforks are returned to their hooks. Then come back here incognito and wait for our return," Auranna replied.

"How long do you want us to wait?" Desmond asked.

"It's up to you two. Play it up to the press if you have to. We could sell more records if it's found out that we disappeared under mysterious circumstances. Share the profits until we return, and if we don't, then don't worry about us."

Carrie looked perturbed at Auranna's offhand dismissal of her concern.

"Aura, why are you being so callous?"

Stephanie returned with two fence boards and planted them as an inverted cross in the center of the pit, distracting Auranna from answering a question she didn't expect to sting.

"Are we forgetting anything before we start the fire?" Stephanie asked.

"Um. Well, we did that little dance, didn't we? But we were...naked..."

"Oh God, yes! This gets better every single second," Lisa grinned from Joel's side, adjusting her glasses to make sure her view was clear and focused.

"You better blur us out, Lisa. I don't care that you've all seen me, but I don't want the rest of the world ogling my tits," Stephanie said.

"Sure, sure. It's not like a documentary with full nudity of internationally renowned, hot musicians would sell any better," Lisa waved her hand dismissively.

"Goddamn it. I don't like how she's changed once things took a turn," Stephanie muttered to Auranna.

"I know, Steph," Auranna whispered, "but the better her documentary does, the more our legend grows. Imagine the adulation... The passion... The dressing rooms during a full arena tour... The chokers I'm going to buy for us..."

"Alright, you've sold me."

Stephanie and Auranna pulled off their clothes and lit the fire. Auranna looked at Stephanie and nodded, then they danced around the flaming pit. Nothing seemed to happen. They all looked at one another.

"If You are expecting a cartoon portal to appear in the natural world, You will be disappointed," Rachel said. "You need to walk into the fire through the cross. That is where I came out, anyway, and saw You running towards the bus."

"Lovely," Auranna sighed. "We'll either walk into the burning pits of Hell or I'll burn to death attempting to walk through two flaming fence boards."

"That's the spirit, Aura," Stephanie said as she pulled her clothes back on. "Who has Alex's guitar? Thank you, Carebear."

Stephanie slung her bass and Alex's guitar over her shoulders. Auranna did the same with her black guitar after getting back into her white tank top and jeans.

"I hope he's drawn to these, and we can get the hell out of Hell," Stephanie chuckled.

Auranna grabbed Stephanie and Rachel's hands and pulled them towards the pyre. She looked over her shoulder at Carrie and Desmond.

"Did you remember our dance? Keep the fire going and dance around it every few minutes to keep the portal open.

Time is different in Hell—we might only be gone a minute."

Carrie's sad eyes nearly caused Auranna to stop but her companions pulled her into the fire.

Auranna writhed and rolled to put out the fire on her skin. Rachel wrapped her in her tail and set her upright. Auranna hadn't caught fire—it was so hot that her mind reacted to the catastrophic change in temperature. She expected to feel cold, like in the "dream" version of Hell, but the true heat of the underworld smothered her. It was all the more uncomfortable that it had no actual effect on her skin, but felt like it should; an inescapable, invisible sensation of burning alive. Their clothes caught fire and the flaming linen fell from their bodies. Their guitars clattered to the ground when their leather straps burned up.

"No! My Satyricon shirt!" Stephanie cried as her fingers futilely closed around the floating, ashen remains.

Her cries mixed with billions of wailing souls both distant and ever-present, despite no crowds to be seen. Auranna grew self-conscious, like the souls were begging her for help. The feeling overwhelmed her, like the first bursts of applause after their initial song in a sold-out stadium. All she could do to center herself was hold up the devil's horns, lower her head, and close her eyes. It didn't have the same calming effect in Hell.

"This place sounds like the living embodiment of the *Obscuritatem Advoco Amplectère Me* album by Abruptum," Stephanie said as she picked up her bass and Alex's guitar.

"Only this is slightly less unhinged."

"That's a hell of a reference, Steph. How long have you been committing that title to memory to work it into conversation?"

"Have you never talked to any of our metalhead fans for more than a couple minutes? It's an unending trivia contest with them you didn't even know you were playing. They've always got to know more than the next metalhead, and they explode in their studded leather if they can stump an actual metal musician. I have to keep myself primed for these guys. I imagine it's what bible-thumpers have to prepare for whenever they start throwing verses at each other to win arguments."

"I usually let Alex go head-to-head with those types of fans," Auranna said as she stooped for her own guitar. "I prefer the fans who are so awed into silence that they can barely lift their pens to ask for an autograph. They're so cute."

Auranna took in the real Hell as she laid the lower part of her guitar's neck over her shoulder. The ember sky was brighter, and defined the landscape better; still the same jagged cliffs and open plains, but there was no forest to become lost and tortured in. Twenty yards up a slope a hooded figure leaned on a staff. Auranna recognized the tatters immediately.

"*Mummo? Oletko se sinä?*"

"What are you saying, Aura?" Stephanie asked while she positioned the guitars on each of her shoulders and adjusted for comfortable balance.

"I believe that's my grandmother. I asked if it's really her in Finnish. She can't answer but I was hoping at least for a nod."

The figure disappeared in a puff of smoke and reappeared inches from Auranna's face. Her long, cold fingers grasped Auranna's chin and examined her closely from under her black hood.

"I guess Rachel's not the only one with that Nightcrawler ability," Stephanie said. "Can she bamf us to Alex?"

"What are you talking about?"

"Nightcrawler. From the X-Men? A lot of metalheads try to throw in... Never mind. Um, ask her if she can find Alex and bring him to us or us to him."

"*Mummo, tiedätkö, missä ystävämme Alex?*"

Auranna's grandmother didn't nod or shake her head.

"Ask her if there's a purgatory?"

"*Onko täällä kiirastuli? Helvetissä?*"

She shook her head once.

"Okay. Is there a waiting room here? Like in Heaven? Maybe he hasn't been processed yet and we can find him there?"

"*Onko täällä odotushuonetta?*"

She nodded.

"Wonderful! Where can we find this place?" Stephanie asked.

The crone pointed in a direction.

"You could have asked me. I have seen this place you speak of—a 'waiting room.'" Rachel said.

"Okay, well, pipe up when you have useful information next time," Stephanie said as they began marching.

"I am afraid it will not seem so useful when we get there," Rachel confessed, but no one was listening.

"*Mummo? Mistä löydämme vaatteita?*"

"What are you asking her?" Stephanie asked.

"I asked her if she knows where we may find clothes or rags to cover ourselves."

"What do you care? Rachel and I have seen and had every inch of you. Are you afraid someone will take a photo of you down here and send it to Earth? Let your body breathe, you know?"

"I perceive millions of eyes on me, leering, imagining those inches, coveting them..."

"How is it any different than when you wear lingerie outfits in front of all our fans?"

"I'm trying not to overheat. Singing and playing lead guitar is incredibly—"

"—Incredibly taxing on you. Yes, we heard your interview answers with Lisa. That lame excuse accidentally validates what I'm saying. It's fucking hot! Why do you want to add clothing on top of that?"

"I would…I'd feel more comfortable in front of my grandmother, okay? Did you walk around naked in front of yours?"

Stephanie rolled her eyes and tore strips of rags off of the crone's robes, who didn't seem to notice. She fashioned the strips around her and Auranna's chest and created makeshift loin cloths.

"You want me to make a set for you, Rachel?"

"I care not down here."

"Suit yourself. Can I at least ask you to carry Alex's guitar?"

They marched onward, ignoring the wails of all the lost, twisted, and moaning creatures along the path.

"I can't wait to draw and write this all down," Auranna murmured.

"I wonder if we should have brought food and water?" Stephanie mused.

CHAPTER FIFTEEN
AESTUS

HELL IS HOT... AND CROWDED

AURANNA LET GO OF HER grandmother's hand and waved before her ragged figure disappeared in a puff of smoke to return to the open portal. It wouldn't do for the unguarded gate between Hell and Earth to allow any of the underworld's monstrosities through.

At first indescribable, Stephanie reminded Auranna of the most apt description of their situation as from Carcass' "Cadaveric Incubator of Endoparasites," like the band had been to Hell and seen the creatures with their own eyes. Maybe they had.

"Getting any closer?" Stephanie called up to Rachel, who circled above them.

"If you ask that again I will cast you down this cliff."

"Do you think we'll be able to find any water down here, Aura?"

"You must stop asking me all these questions, Steph. This isn't like the dreamworld. I'm just as lost as you."

Stephanie massaged her own breasts, then squeezed around the areolas.

"Think we could get either one of us to lactate? I'm not getting anything here, though..."

"That would be a waste of time to attempt without medical guidance or drugs. If we focus on getting to Alex as quickly as possible, we can stop worrying about thirst."

"A crying baby can coax lactation," Rachel said from a few feet above them. "Your doxy whines so much it may be the answer to Your thirst problems."

Auranna frowned at Rachel's poking at Stephanie. Stephanie took a swing at Rachel, but she lifted out of range of Stephanie's bass and hovered a few paces ahead of them.

"If it comes to it, you can drink my blood first, my Queen," Stephanie offered while staring daggers at Rachel.

Auranna stroked the back of Stephanie's sweat-soaked hair and smiled. That would be as effective as drinking salt water, but Auranna appreciated the thought.

No day & night cycle or dimming of the fiery light marked the passage of time for them. It seemed like they walked for hours. They pushed off monstrosities that made for their legs and blocked their path, using the guitars to keep the slimy appendages at bay.

When the attacks ceased for a brief reprieve, Auranna plucked a few strings.

"Tuning's all gone to Hell," Auranna quipped, trying to keep their spirits up.

"You're thinking if we play, Alex will be drawn to us? Good idea," Stephanie said as she stopped to work the headstock of her bass. "I hope this heat doesn't damage the wood too much."

"Damaged or not," Auranna said, "playing guitars that have literally been through Hell should propel us up there with the true legends. Maiden, Metallica, Sabbath, Slayer, Pantera, Priest, Zeppelin. Imagine being the second-most-legendary band starting with the word 'Black.'"

"You don't need to list the legends to someone in a metal band. And Zakk Wylde would have something to say about the 'Black' thing."

"I know. I'm only talking to keep myself moving and pass the time. And don't set your sights any lower than Sabbath, Steph. We'll get there."

"I'm dying of thirst and talking makes my mouth drier. I don't know how you stand it, Aura."

"We're dying of everything. I'm beginning to almost miss the dreamworld, so I don't have to feel this horrid heat anymore. I feel all this fire around us, all the time, but I can't see any actual fires."

They dragged on for several more hours, playing snippets of their music in hopes Alex might hear. Before long Auranna and Stephanie could hardly move or play. Their knees scraped the ground as they lowered into a crawl. They were so thirsty...

The familiar sound of a guitar reached them from up the path and grew closer. A group of four men and a woman approached them, naked but for their instruments.

Auranna recognized them.

"Anders! Devil's Sorrow! What on Earth—I mean, what in Hell are you guys doing down here?"

"Auranna Korpela and Stephanie Creighton of Black Aura! What a small underworld this is!" Anders responded in a thick Swedish accent and a friendly smile.

"Hey guys! You're a sight for dry eyes! I still remember our tour together a couple years ago with fondness," Auranna said to the rest of the band. "We should do it again next year. If you're free, of course."

"It would be our pleasure!" Anders said. "But perhaps we shall save deciding who will be headlining until we plumb these depths for all they are worth. What are you two doing down here alone? Where are your bandmates?"

"I would say it's a long story and you wouldn't believe us, but obviously since you're down here, too, I'm sure you would," Auranna said, then pointed down at their nude, glistening bodies. "Did you all dance naked around an inverted cross back in Sweden to get here, too?"

Devil's Sorrow exchanged glances, then laughed heartily into the void.

"What's so funny?"

"We are naked because Hell burns our clothes off. Did you two dance naked on Earth? That is a classic beginner's mistake!"

"Ha ha ha, yes, we're such fools," Stephanie said, too exhausted to be good humored amongst their mirth. "Where did you get the manual that told you how to get here?"

"We received guidance from Bathory. They taught us everything—including the importance of bringing water, silly girls."

Anders motioned for their drummer to come forward. He pulled the chain from across his back around to his chest and revealed five canteens. He gave one to Auranna.

"Drink quickly when you open the cap. The temperature will evaporate it if you dally," Anders warned.

Auranna offered Stephanie the first pull, then followed suit. She extended the canteen back to Anders.

"No no, you keep that. Consider it a professional courtesy; homage to two Queens of Metal. Do not expect such kindness going forward, however—we are coming for your sales records. Now if you will excuse us, we have inspiration to mine further. Good luck, girls!"

Auranna matched Anders' smile and they embraced. She and Stephanie bumped fists with the rest of the band as they continued down the path in the opposite direction. Their music faded into the distance as Auranna and Stephanie trudged onward.

After several more hours passed, Rachel dropped down and told them the waiting room was ahead. When they arrived, their mouths gaped at the long line snaking hundreds of times, like how a small child would see a three-hour line at Disneyland. The souls crushed into each other front to back for several miles by several miles. There had to be dozens of millions of souls.

Imps kept order at the edges of the macabre procession, pushing and punishing souls that fell out of line. Auranna, Stephanie, and Rachel continued walking until they came to the "processing" area where imps sat behind thousands of pedestals. It reminded Auranna of airport security. Several empty door frames with no walls were lined up behind the imps. Souls were herded and forced into specific doors through which they disappeared.

"Looks like queueing for weeks is the first form of torture," Stephanie said.

"We can't wait this long for him. He should be towards the back of the line."

"Over one-hundred-fifty-thousand people die per day, my Queen. He may be in the back, but he will still be buried," Rachel said.

"Curse God. Too many people die...All these fools dying for a lie," Stephanie said.

"Destruction of these souls has already begun, Steph. No need to rub salt in their wounds. Rachel, can you lift me while I carry Alex's guitar?"

Auranna took Alex's guitar from Rachel and handed her own to Stephanie. Rachel picked Auranna up and flew over the vast miles of souls while she played Alex's sections of their music. While she glided above them, the wailing and confusion on the faces of the people in line amused her. So many of them thought they'd been pious enough in their lives, or their deathbed recantations and last-minute panicked prayers would have been enough to get them into the other place.

Politicians, heads-of-state, judges, lawyers, priests, reverends, nuns, celebrities, pundits, CEOs, wage slaves, infants, children, bible-thumpers, atheists, suicide-bombers, every religion with a hat, every religion without a hat, Christian rock musicians, metalheads, punks, furries, gays, straights, drug-users, sobers, writers—it seemed no one was "safe."

After an hour of strafing the line near the back, an arm popped up from the sea of bodies and its owner jumped up and down. Rachel lowered them to hover above Alex's head.

"I knew you'd find me, Aura!"

Auranna dropped Alex's guitar onto his head on purpose.

"What was that for?"

"Shut the hell up, Alex! It should be obvious! Hold your guitar in the air and play it so Rachel can come back for you! We'll see you in a hot minute!"

Rachel dropped Auranna off with Stephanie and went back over the crowd.

"Time for the trek back, my love. Here, have some more water."

"Think it's odd these imps are ignoring us?"

"They look pretty busy."

"You'd think Jesus dying for all these peoples' sins would have saved them, right?"

"Let's not keep kicking them while they're down. They have an eternity to ponder all the things they did to land them here. Except for the clueless children."

"Yeah. They didn't stand a chance because of a snake in a tree and a fucking apple, and their parents didn't make the binding choice on their behalf to baptize them."

Stephanie ranted against the evils of religion, even mentioning a Pat Benatar song that Auranna had forgotten, until they met with Rachel and Alex at the end of the line, then they walked back to the path that led to their portal. Stephanie pushed Alex roughly from behind.

"The hell did you think you were doing? Asshole!"

"You wouldn't bring me here, so I did it myself. I didn't think I'd be in a line the whole time. Now that I'm out of that marching band, I can study this place. Thank you so much, ladies."

"Do you realize it's not even guaranteed that you'll get to come back? I did this more for information-gathering than rescuing your selfish ass," Auranna said.

"Next time take me to Hell your way, when I ask."

"I might now, so you can feel His wrath. You'll wish you were back in that line just to be out of His sight."

"You seem fine after so many supposed years of interacting with Him."

"I would not be so fine without our music as an outlet. Without Stephanie. Without Carrie, Desmond, you—even though I want to let these monstrosities have their way with you right now."

Alex ignored her pointed statements.

"Goddamn, this place is amazing. It...doesn't quite match your lyrics though..."

"God certainly did damn this place. As far as my lyrics, I've only been in the dreamworld. This is my first time in Hell as a living soul. Oh wait, that psychic said I don't have one of those. What in Hell am I? What in Hell are you for that matter? I mean, you're not translucent but can you feel anything without your corporeal body?"

"Nope. I can't even feel my feet touching the ground. Oh. Can I borrow some of your rags? I'm the only one with my junk hanging out."

"Fuck you, Alex," Stephanie snapped. "I danced naked—unnecessarily I might add—in front of Joel's stupid camera to help save you. The whole world is going to see me; you can stay naked for a few hours."

"We only get a few hours here? Damn."

"Shut up. What do you think this is? You're dead, we're alive, we'll just stay happily in Hell?"

"Mary's Blood. No way you're catching me off guard with Japanese metal trivia, Steph, but I welcome you to keep trying," Alex said. "Is it too much to ask that I can stay a few days to soak all this in?"

"Keep it up and we won't even attempt to bring you back," Auranna said.

"You sure are butthurt about it. You don't have any wounds or anything. I thought you'd have been torn to shreds like how you described it at the diner."

Stephanie swung her bass around and smashed Alex's face. It pushed him back but didn't have an effect on him beyond that.

"You ungrateful shit! We risked our lives to get you out of here. We almost died of thirst! Be thankful for the short time you're down here, at *our* discretion!"

Auranna might have admonished Stephanie for also not appreciating Alex's sacrifice for inspiration that would only improve their musical endeavors, but Stephanie had a point and Alex's whining was pissing her off as well. She changed the subject before developing the inkling to join in on bashing Alex's smug face.

"I admit I expected Him to notice us by now. I don't know what He's waiting for. Stephanie even laughed and nothing happened, unlike what happened to poor Rachel."

"I wish you'd have brought a notebook. Damn," Alex

shook his head.

Auranna snapped her fingers, disregarding Alex's petulance for the sake of opportunity.

"Another experiment!"

"Here, Aura? I don't want to have sex in front of Alex, he's going to try to join in," Stephanie grimaced.

Auranna backhanded Stephanie's arm.

"Whenever we return from the dreamworld, we bear none of the inflicted wounds. We bring with us only what we remember feeling. I want to see what happens when we leave Hell."

She stopped Alex, grabbed the neck of his guitar, and cranked the tuning peg of the low E string until it snapped. She unwound it from the peg and handed the string to Alex.

"Find an empty space on my back and take your visual notes on my skin."

"Are you sure? If you take this with you..."

"Well, make it pretty, at least," Auranna smiled and sat down on the edge of the cliff their path followed. With a view of the plains below, Auranna removed the rags Stephanie had fashioned into a top and used it to tie up her hair.

Alex knelt down and cut into her skin words and imagery of the true Hell. Stephanie and Rachel bent over his shoulders to watch.

"If only we had a camera, Aura," Stephanie said. "With the blood dripping down your back around your tattoos and what Alex is drawing this would make one of the greatest album covers in metal history. The end of your ponytail soaking up your blood is particularly exquisite, like crimson red tips. Hell of a job, Alex."

"I shall not pine for the puns in this place," Rachel said and flew ahead of them while Alex finished up.

"Um, Aura, I don't know if you want to tie that top back on and smudge the markings up," Stephanie said.

"Then I'll leave it off. Alex is going to see us when he

watches the documentary anyway."

"You both can stop making me out to be a pervert. You ladies take me too seriously sometimes. I'll walk behind you."

"Thank you, Alex. Perhaps I'll let you through the portal after all."

Auranna smiled over her shoulder, took a pull from the canteen, then offered it to Stephanie before they made to catch up with Rachel.

"That was strange, writing without being able to feel the string or your back."

"What does it feel like to play?" Stephanie asked.

"Let's find out."

Alex played part of his extended solo from "Torturous Tenderness" since it didn't require the low E string.

"Hmm. Lacks emotion," Alex said. "Like my fingers knew the notes but not what to do with the space in between."

"I was going to say... It did lack something," Auranna said. "I can't wait to hear what you come up with when we return, though. You, Stephanie, and Desmond could do a little more of the heavy lifting with concepts and composition in the studio now that we've a shared experience for inspiration."

"How long do you think Carrie will be able to go before she's begging for her own tour?" Stephanie asked.

"I bet you your Xasthur T-shirt it's before the end of the tour," Alex said.

"Ok. If it's after, I want the Pick of Destiny you have locked in your little safe."

"That's only a movie prop."

"Signed by Jack Black and Kyle Gass. I want it!"

"You're not even a guitarist!"

Stephanie stopped and stared fire into Alex's eyes, causing him to throw his hands in the air.

"Um...you're a *bass* guitarist, is all I meant. I thought you'd be more interested in the little bit of Lemmy's mustache I have in that Ziploc bag."

"I steal sniffs of that bag sometimes. I might as well own it already."

"How long have you known the code to my safe?"

Stephanie shrugged and pushed a monstrosity away from her legs with her bass.

"These demons lack the energy of the ones in your dreamworld, Aura."

"Don't jinx us, Steph. I didn't say as much myself, in case it brought us more pain down the line."

"You guys are overselling the pain. Desmond is a baby."

Auranna turned around and stopped in Alex's path, not caring about exposing herself. She met his gaze with such intensity he didn't get the chance to see her body.

"Alex, no words in your or my language can describe the pain adequately. Not even the goregrind bands accurately portray the horror…but I guess that's as close as I could describe it. And you'd still need to crank it to eleven to get to what He can do to you."

Stephanie nodded.

"There's no such thing as 'overselling' the pains of Hell…when they notice you," Auranna said and turned back around.

Alex kept his mouth shut for once, likely sensing how upset he'd made Auranna, who rarely snapped at any of them, but she was certain he still didn't believe her. How could he until he'd suffered the same?

They continued for another few hours until they reached Rachel and the crone.

"Quickly," Rachel said. "Let us not press our luck that He will continue ignoring us."

Stephanie put her hand on Alex's shoulder and kissed his cheek.

"I hope to see you on the other side, ya fuckin' jerk."

She went through the portal, followed by Rachel. Auranna

hugged Alex then pushed him through before he could say anything. She turned to her grandmother and peered into the black void beneath her hood, hoping to catch a glimpse of her once-familiar face.

"*Mummo*. Something doesn't feel right. This has been too easy... Is there anything you aren't telling me?"

The void stared back at her.

"*Valehteletko minulle*? Are you lying to me? Do you know why I have no soul? Do you know anything about my army and being a queen? Is there any way you can answer me here, on Earth, or in the dreamworld?"

The crone shook its head once.

"To which question was that an answer?"

The crone put her staff into Auranna's chest and pushed her back through the portal.

CHAPTER SIXTEEN

ORANDI

DELIVER ME, O METAL GODS

STEPHANIE CAUGHT AURANNA AND DRAGGED her out of the pyre. Rachel pulled the Nightwish blanket out from beneath Alex's body, rolling him onto the grass, ignoring his grunt of surprise, and put it around Auranna. Lisa brought water bottles to them while Carrie and Desmond put their clothes back on.

Auranna stifled her giggles and Stephanie cackled at the two of them.

"I adore that you both put aside your dignity to keep our portal open," Auranna said. "I feel bad now telling you that nudity was unnecessary. Probably the dancing, as well."

"I adored it, too," Lisa said, staring too long at Desmond.

"What the—then why—?" Carrie blushed bright red and looked fearfully at Joel's camera.

"We didn't know at the time, either. We met Devil's Sorrow while we were down there and they laughed at us, too," Stephanie said. "They gave us this nice canteen, though."

"Where did you get those rags?" Joel asked.

"From Aura's grandmother. I'm surprised they came through—Hey!"

The rags turned to ash and scattered into the breeze.

"Where's *my* blanket, Rachel?" Stephanie whined as she shielded herself from Joel's camera with her upside-down guitar.

"Get one yourself, doxy. The bus is right there."

"Joel! Turn that fucking camera off!"

"Okay, Joel, I think we have enough," Lisa said, twirling her finger around her hair.

"I know that signal by now, Lisa!" Stephanie yelled and ran towards Joel. "Turn it off! I'll roast you both in Hell!"

Joel ran backwards but kept the camera on her. Before reaching him, he turned and ran to the bus, then stopped before the door and started laughing like he couldn't keep the joke to himself anymore.

"Okay, okay, I was kidding, Steph. I stopped recording when you asked me to. See?"

She punched his shoulder and stormed onto the bus.

"How long were we gone, Carrie?" Auranna asked.

"About five minutes."

"Five min—! It's not like we had our phones down there to check, but it felt like at least twelve hours. I'm so relieved, though. There's still plenty of time to prepare for the show toni—"

Carrie cut Auranna off by giving her an unexpected, tight hug.

"Careb—"

"Shut up," Carrie sniffed, then looked at a nearby rustling.

"So, is anyone interested in what happened to me?" Alex piped up from the grass.

Joel and Lisa ran over with the camera as he picked himself up. Carrie pushed between them and embraced him, then punched him. She stamped onto the bus without a word, shaking her hand.

"How do you feel? What did you see down there? What was it like to die?" Lisa asked.

"First, I floated up to a sea of clouds. There was a giant golden gate and a little podium in front of it, overseen by a white-bearded white guy with large white wings. He looked at me for a millisecond and said: 'Metal musician. Nope.' Then he pushed a button and a trapdoor opened under my feet! I fell through a hole with fire growing ever closer, until I came face-to-face with... Him..."

"What did He look like?" Lisa asked, unable to hide her eagerness.

"I'm kidding. You remember that movie *Ghost*? Of course you do. Well, those black, moaning shadows came up from the shower drain and pulled my soul straight down and I found myself in a long line for processing. You should have heard the wailing and cursing from all the people that somehow thought they shouldn't have been down there.

"Get this—remember that politician who died last week? He was in the line passing next to my position and—I shit you not—he thought he'd put enough money into that little begging bowl they pass around at churches to cover up all his sins. It was hilarious!"

Lisa continued asking him questions as the three of them made their way onto the bus.

Carrie returned from the bus and handed Rachel's clothes to her, and Desmond gave Auranna a new white tank top and jeans.

"My Queen, Your back is no longer bleeding," Rachel said. "In fact, the blood is desiccated."

Carrie and Desmond examined Auranna's exposed skin.

"That's amazing, Aura," Carrie said. "Who did that?"

"Alex. We should have brought a notebook along with our guitars, apparently."

Desmond picked up Auranna's guitar and inspected it.

"It's...warm. Even in this breeze."

"I can't wait to play it tonight."

Auranna boarded the bus and found Alex.

"You still have that string?"

"No. I threw it off the cliff when I finished."

"Pull the other end of the string out of the bridge and touch up your work, please. I want a picture of your music dripping down my back for our next album cover, like Stephanie said."

At Auranna's request, a roadie put a barrier around "the spot" before the show. She hoped this would break the curse and a fan wouldn't be taken that night.

Alex didn't need corpse paint for the performance, as his skin hadn't regained its color. He had Rachel stitch up his forearm and neck after Carrie refused to help. During the show his forearm stitches kept popping and black blood would run down his arms, hands, and fingers, all over his guitar, which increased his ease of play, as if the Hell-christened guitar thanked him for his blood sacrifice.

Auranna and Stephanie noticed a change in their instruments as well. Stephanie's bass drank the blood of the fans as she bashed gleefully through the mosh pit, while Auranna's guitar remained pristinely blacker-than-black and bent with her movements to allow for easier shredding. All three of them played with otherworldly fury and speed.

Carrie and Desmond struggled to keep up but performed admirably. However, in the middle of the second encore,

Carrie's keyboard malfunctioned from the strain and sweat she coated the keys in. Auranna praised her afterwards for not panicking, while also playing into the moment by destroying it in front of the aggressive crowd. The keytar was available for pickup at their next tour stop, anyway.

Carrie responded that she never felt as close to the fans as when she destroyed her instrument.

Back on the road after the amazing show, Auranna lay awake in her small bed. It was Stephanie's turn in the big bed since Alex lost his privileges for killing himself. Auranna dreaded falling asleep. Satan had to have known what they did, and even if He didn't, she would surely call Him in her sleep inadvertently, plagued with so much worry.

Carrie exited the bathroom after her shower and smiled "goodnight" at Auranna before climbing into her own bunk across the aisle and quickly falling asleep. Utter exhaustion claimed her and Desmond. The other three Hell-troopers promised to slow the tempo back to normal to avoid burning them out—except for their solos.

Desmond slipped into the bathroom and turned on the shower. After a short pause, Lisa crept towards the door and looked around, then unbuttoned her blouse, laid her glasses on a nearby shelf, and slunk into the steaming bathroom.

Auranna was happy for them and fell asleep with a smile, forgetting for a moment the nightmares that awaited her.

The black forest loomed, menacing overhead when she opened her eyes. There was no pretense this time. No walking off the bus. No chance to wander anywhere but forward. She faintly remembered the first time she'd ever entered the dreamworld starting out this way, only at that time she hadn't known what awaited inside the tree line yet. Her preteen curiosity pulled her in, then. Now, the only thing putting one foot in front of the other was the desire to get things over with as soon as possible.

Among the groaning trunks, the cold intensified. It was only uncomfortable before. This time it stung. In moments, frostbite seeped into her. Even her life in Finland couldn't have prepared her for the cold, like the vast expanse of outer space. Was this happening because of her Celtic Frost T-shirt? She wondered...

The lights were nowhere to be seen. Even the imps weren't there to taunt her with their contradictory debates. She looked behind, and miles walked were little more than feet gained. The only thing keeping her oriented was the forest floor that sent pins, needles, knives, and swords through her frostbitten feet.

– Is it You, my Lord? Did I anger You? –

Something without form hit her in the front like a giant fist, then knocked her around on the ground for what felt like an hour. A day? She lost track of time as the wind buffeted her. When it stopped, her fingers, toes, ears, nose, and nipples were long torn off. The frostbite didn't numb the areas of loss—she experienced every ounce of pain.

– Are You done? May I return home, my Lord? What have I done to anger You so? –

The giant red eyes appeared in front of her. The wind came back for its customary abuse, only it had new holes to violate. It constricted her everywhere, twisting her skin and breaking her bones.

You did not pay the currency tonight.

– You will get no more souls from me. –

She thought the wind couldn't get any worse until it grew

thorns. She despaired without a place to deposit her mind during the torture. The agony was too much. Nowhere to escape, her screams caught in her lungs and suffocated her.

You endeavor to restrict my army's growth. Do you intend to renounce your image? Change your lyrics? Will you reform as a Christian Rock band?

Mirth projected through the red eyes. Auranna struggled to mindspeak through the pain.

– Do You ever intend to tell me why I am building this army? Why do You need me when the Gates of Hell feed You one-hundred-fifty-thousand souls a day? –

The mirth disappeared and anger returned.

Enough questions.

– Where is my soul, my Lord? –

It will be returned to you when my army is complete. You will not ask another question.

– I never offered my soul to You, my Lord. I do not understand... –

Bring me my souls! You do not need to understand! You will not dare conduct another performance without paying or this will have felt like a baby's soft hand grabbing your finger!

Hands she had never seen before caught her and the wind left her body. His long claws pierced her while He squeezed, thoroughly breaking the rest of her bones, and He threw her to the forest floor like a discarded candy wrapper.

She lay in the blackness, consumed with suffering for minutes. Hours? Days? An eternity?

The air warmed after a time. One eye had been pierced and exploded by one of His claws. The other witnessed the orange lights return, but movement was impossible.

Where were the imps to finish the job? She hadn't seen their little red eyes all night. Why hadn't she woken up yet?

– Rachel? Stephanie? Desmond? Can anyone hear me? Please save me... I die in this human shell... –

The silence almost hurt as much as His wrath. She greatly feared dying alone. Dying amongst her friends, in front of an ocean of fans, with her instrument in hand, playing her most personal music for the world to hear—that was the only way to die.

What had she done to deserve this? Did she foolishly sell her soul as a child? She couldn't believe that she wouldn't remember such a thing. She still had childhood memories of *äiti* in Finland and following *mummo's* tour across Europe. She remembered her mother explaining how her grandmother practiced guitar every day since she was ten years old and became one of the world's foremost female guitarists. Auranna told herself she'd become one of the world's foremost guitarists, period. Fuck the condescending gender tag, she'd thought when she plucked her first string.

She'd write. She'd draw. She'd compose. She'd lead. She'd design the band's attire including their corpse paint in order to look unique from every other black metal band's designs. She'd forgo drugs and alcohol. She'd take care of her body. She'd take special care of her instruments. She'd help the roadies. She'd work the merchandise stands before she became so famous she distracted from the opening acts and they begged her to stop. She wanted to be the hardest-working musician in the industry.

It was a matter of personal pride that she'd never asked for help. Why on Earth would she ever sell her soul to Hell? To Him? How and why would that shortcut ever occur to her? Why had He brought her down to the dreamworld after her mother vanished?

She recalled her *äiti* and *mummo* arguing backstage at a tour stop in Norway before *mummo's* band played. It was the first night Auranna watched a show alone. Without her mother to keep her backstage, Auranna ventured out into the crowd. It was also the first time she saw *mummo* play from the audience's perspective. She and her mother had been adamant that Auranna was in danger if she ever disappeared into those aggressive masses of hot fury.

Mummo had screamed at her for an hour once Auranna was found. She didn't say so, but Auranna always sensed her grandmother blamed her for her mother's disappearance, since it happened that night.

Crying was beyond her, lying broken upon the dreamworld's ground. Wherever her heart had been squished and moved to after all the compression damage, it grew heavy remembering her mother. She hoped her *äiti* never came to know Hell; not like Auranna and her grandmother.

Did Auranna invite Satan into her heart by writing Him and Hell into her lyrics? She didn't worship Him. She was only fascinated by the mythology and imagery, and that only came about because of her repeated and unwanted trips to the dreamworld throughout her teen years. The Satanism seeped into her conscious. She never sought it out until so much had permeated her mind that she thought she might as well make lemonade with the lemons she'd been given and write the best damned Satanic songs on Earth.

Perhaps she'd have put equal energy into God if the imagery was more than clouds and boring angels. "Go to Heaven for the climate, Hell for the company," Mark Twain had said. When Auranna read that line, she'd added the limitless goldmine of lyrics to the short list of benefits to the otherwise torturous vacation destination that is Hell.

– ...God? Are you...Oh god, how cliché is that? I'm sorry, God. It's rude of me to ask for your help now when I never once prayed to you in my life. I apologize for bothering you. Forget I said anything. –

She lay and thought more, quickly putting out of her mind that she had just been crazy enough to attempt a real prayer. Perhaps new lyrics would come from the pain. At least she'd get something out of it all besides the realization that Satan became defensive easily. What did a supreme being such as He have to be so defensive about, anyway?

Her mind drifted to the spider, the snake, and the octopus. She concentrated on them. They could keep her company. But she couldn't reach their lights...

Three of the orange lights moved closer to her. She thought extra hard about them, and the lights drew in faster until the scattered pieces of her body were engulfed by tarantulas, snakes, and tentacles. Their caretakers appeared above her as the bites and sucker hickies commenced. All of it tickled in comparison to His wrath.

Almost.

– My friends, only for tonight, might I entreat you to call off your brethren? I am...*shattered*. –

Our Queen, we would love nothing more than to ease Your suffering. However, we cannot break His rules. He decrees we must punish You to speak with You, or He will make our own suffering magnitudes greater.

– I sympathize, my friends. I truly do after tonight. Is there any chance you could wake me? How does that work? I haven't seen the imps anywhere... –

We are unaware of their location presently. We apologize, our Queen.

– I understand. While I would love nothing more than to speak with you three—oh, sorry, four. I would love to speak with you all, but I cannot bear this pain any longer. Please...leave me. –

Yes, our Queen. We desire to see You in Your full glory when You lead Your army.

– Lead it? –

The three creatures disappeared with their minions into the void. The orange lights retreated to their starting positions, far, far away from her.

Auranna's mind neared its breaking point—she wanted to pray again. Only she didn't know any true prayers, or how to make it sound less like desperate begging. The bible bored her and had not provided her with ironic inspiration as she'd hoped after she'd stolen one from a hotel when she was sixteen. Hymn books, on the other hand...

She couldn't remember a single one other than Black Aura's two covers, but their versions wouldn't help her. She plumbed her mind for the next best thing—metal lyrics.

She recited "Call From the Grave" and put extra emphasis on the prayer to the God of Heaven.

Nothing. So much for Bathory saving her life again.

She sang "Hallowed Be Thy Name" in its entirety, first as close to Bruce Dickinson's voice as possible, then with Dani Filth's shrieks that she could mimic far easier. Neither version worked.

She sang every song she could think of that mentioned God or Heaven, even tangentially; even the songs in Finnish and her broken Swedish and Norwegian. Nothing worked.

Perhaps Metallica would get her out of this impossible Hell. She sang "One," praying for death that never came.

Losing hope, she sang "Fade to Black." It became clear music wouldn't save her, but it was also the only comfort she had left.

How could she be so stupid? There was one person left in Hell that could help her, and Auranna had forsaken her.

– *Mummo. Mummo*, I beg you. Please find me. Please free me. –

To Auranna's surprise, the orange lights spun, rose into the black canopy of the forest, and disappeared. She perceived the rustling of detritus that decorated the forest floor from far off. The movement picked up speed and volume the closer it got to where she lay. She didn't want to imagine what horrors could possibly be in store for her next.

A white-blue light grew as it approached, displacing the decay around it. It outlined a human shape. Ten feet from Auranna's body, in the sight of her one good eye, the light dropped to the ground and shone up at the shape.

It was Auranna.

CHAPTER SEVENTEEN
Ecclesia

The Metalhead's Hell

AURANNA STARED UP AT HERSELF looking down at herself. Only...the Auranna standing over her wasn't...quite... She was a little off. Her eyebrows didn't match. Her chin wasn't the same. Many features matched but some were broader, older—

There was a familiarity Auranna couldn't deny was her own blood, but through a distorted mirror: her grandmother, before whatever turned her into a shambling, silent husk.

Tyttärentytär.

– *Mummo?* What happened to you? Where are your robes? Where is the barbed wire sewing your mouth? Where are your desiccated wrinkles? –

Olen pettynyt sinuun.

– Disappointed? What did I do? I've only ever tried to make you and *äiti* proud of me. –

Älä puhu hänestä.

– What do you mean? I miss her so much sometimes. Don't you ever—? –

Sanoin, että älä mainitse häntä.

– Okay! I won't mention her. *Mummo*, I beg you to wake me up. I'm so... –

Olet niin heikko.

– You find me weak? That's not fair. I've endured so much... –

Jatkaa maksamista. Äläkä unohda enää.

– I do not wish to keep paying the currency. I already told Him... –

Her grandmother bent down and grabbed her by what was left of her shirt. The uncanny specter tightened her fist in the fabric, bringing Auranna's broken face within inches of hers.

Vastarintasi on turhaa.

– I recognize it's futile. He's made that clear enough. I shall endeavor to stop...disappointing you so. Please. Please, *mummo*. Is there anything you might do to wake me up? –

Auranna's grandmother dropped her to the ground, then walked away. The light that had descended with her arrival and illuminated her from the forest floor rose and followed her. Fingers snapped and all light went out.

Auranna bolted upright, bullets of sweat flying over the bed and spattering the wall at her feet. Her body had been in so much pain for so long, it made her nauseous to be cut off from the sensation so abruptly. She rushed to get out of her tiny, drenched bed and burst into the steaming bathroom, diving for the toilet which greedily devoured the contents of her stomach. The strength went out of her and she fell on her butt, leaning her back into the wall. Her head lolled to the side to find Desmond and Lisa in the shower staring down at her in shock, confusion, and embarrassment.

"Cute tat, Lisa," Auranna said as she pulled herself up. "Sorry to interrupt."

She closed the door behind her and took some deep, steadying breaths, thankful to be out of the dreamworld at last. She wrestled off her soaked, stuck Celtic Frost shirt and Megadeth underwear, then rifled through her duffel for a notebook and new clothes. When she stood up with all three items acquired, a cold hand touched her shoulder.

"Aura, come to bed with me. I've been waiting for you," Stephanie said.

"Would that I could, my love. I am...unable to sleep right now."

"I didn't have sleep in mind. You won't need those clothes..."

"I know. I meant it both ways. I just threw up and my head hurts. I promise we can spend extra time in the dressing room after the next show."

"Your skin is all wet... Oh, you're so pale! Let's get you to bed for real."

"No!" Auranna hissed. "Let me be!"

Stephanie backed away, hurt as if Auranna had slapped her. Auranna had only seen Stephanie upset a few times since she'd known her, and it crushed her to have been the cause. She reached out to grab her fingers and seek forgiveness, but Stephanie had already turned and disappeared into the back of the bus. Auranna pulled on the fresh underwear and an extra-long Overkill T-shirt.

She passed Rachel, who stared into the passing black landscape from the living area, and sat down in the passenger seat in the front. She opened a fresh page of the notebook and put pen to paper but couldn't move it. Anger bubbled up the longer she stared at the mocking, empty lines.

"Hey, kid, can't slee—?"

"Quiet, Gerald."

Sweat soaked her new clothes. Her body fought her mind to not give life to what she'd endured—to not remind it of all the pain. She was equally compelled to release her pain—but to manifest what happened into words was to endure it all over again. If she couldn't get it out, though, it was all for nothing. Auranna wondered if using her treatment in the dreamworld as inspiration justified it. She pressed harder and harder into the page on the ball of the pen until it snapped. Ink splattered all over her face and arms, white shirt, and the dashboard.

None of the ink touched the paper.

She lifted the notebook and smashed it onto the dashboard as hard as she could, making Gerald jump in his seat. She brought it down again. And again. She needed to scream at the top of her metal-goddess lungs but feared waking most of the bus's occupants. She stared at the smeared splotches on the dashboard. It almost looked...beautiful. An ink-stained mess.

Auranna rolled the window down and frisbeed the notebook into the night along the empty highway. She closed the window and shakily ran her fingers through her hair. The horrified tears she couldn't shed in the dreamworld spilled out in great, quaking sobs. She grasped her hair and squeezed to the roots, seeking to cause tears of a different kind; to get her mind out of Hell. Gerald reached across and put his hand on her shoulder.

His warm, calm touch was the life preserver she'd been missing. Her tears intensified but they were more in relief than despair. She stood up to hug him, causing him to swerve a little before getting back in line. Auranna giggled into his shoulder at the sound of Joel rolling off the couch during the abrupt swerve. Gerald laughed with her, then harder still when they realized it still hadn't woken him up.

"Jesus, kid, you're burning up," he said after she let go of him. "Let's get you to a hospital."

"For a fever? We can have the medic look at me at the next stop."

"You're not impressing anyone, Aura. If you're sick, this whole operation comes to a screeching halt. We all depend on you. Not to mention your thousands of fans that are coming to see your band. I'll get us to the next closest hospital. Now go lay down until then."

"I can't. I can't sleep," she nearly wept again as the memories pushed back into her consciousness.

"Then at least grab a couple of blankets and plant yourself here in the passenger seat."

The doctor and nurses admonished Auranna while administering a cocktail of antibiotics and helped to wipe the ink off her face and arms. They scoffed at her tattoos and brands, and the stupidity of etching lyrics into her flesh with a guitar string and bringing on an infection. They advised her to take a short break from touring until the fever went away. She nodded and smiled, but she was really only thinking ironically of the lyrics from "Clean My Wounds" by Corrosion of Conformity. As she left the hospital she shook her head at Gerald's concerned expression.

"Want me to have Alex start making calls to cancel the show tonight?" he asked.

"No. We're not canceling anything. The show is still on."

"Are you cert—?"

"No cancellations."

She resolved to try and sleep. Gerald was right. There was no stand-in for her if she pushed herself too hard. However, what drove her more than losing peoples' jobs and disappointing her fans was the threat of what would happen to her if the payment wasn't made at the show. She sort of understood His tantrum—to be denied anything from anyone—but why would her grandmother have brought up the payment? Didn't she want Auranna to put an end to their subservience? Wasn't that why she showed Auranna where the disappearances were happening? Why did she send Rachel to Earth or help guard the portal so they could return from Hell? What she'd finally spoken in the dreamworld indicated no desire to help whatsoever...

Auranna went to the back of the bus while Gerald got them onto the road again. Everyone had gone to sleep, including Desmond and Lisa. She crawled into the big bed with Stephanie. Most nights that they slept together Stephanie would roll her head into Auranna's chest to hear and feel her humming, but Stephanie faced away and shrugged Auranna's hand off her shoulder.

Auranna whispered into Stephanie's ear.

"I'm so sorry. The infection and fever were speaking, not me. I'd love nothing more than to sleep next to you."

Stephanie still didn't turn.

"You are my air," Auranna choked as her heart spoke. "I can't breathe without you."

"...that's not fair...my Queen."

Stephanie rolled over and laid her head in her customary place while Auranna hummed them both to sleep.

The band gave Auranna a sick-pass for the day in hopes she'd feel better with some rest before the actual show. Despite the well-meaning intentions, prepping for a metal show was loud work, and Auranna couldn't sleep easily through it. She stepped off the bus in her Oranssi Pazuzu T-shirt and sweatpants and looked towards the town. She thought about talking to another psychic. One who might be a little more helpful, and perhaps get through a card reading without spilling them all over the floor...

She checked her phone and found a psychic advertising services on the far edge of town, which was enough of a distance there and back to fill the rest of the day until the opening act, a perfect distraction. While she walked, people in passing cars stared at the tattoos and brands on her arms. For the first time in her life, she was self-conscious about them. She folded her arms and kept her eyes on the buildings and sidewalk instead of the streets or fellow pedestrians.

Halfway to the psychic's location, she passed a church with the front door propped open. Her pace slowed until she stopped a block past. She looked down at her shirt. '*Taivaan portti avautuu*' played in her mind. She stood there for a moment, then turned back.

Out of place and even more self-conscious the moment she stepped inside the church, God judged Auranna quickly and harshly. As she looked around, she had to squint; the off-putting white room amplified the sunlight that came through its ample windows. She hugged her arms tighter to cover as much of them as possible, then turned to leave.

"Hello, miss! Welcome! Please, come in," a man called to

her from the front.

She spun around to find where the friendly voice had come from. He was roughly fifteen years her senior in a white button-up shirt and open collar, standing behind one of the front pews.

"Just straightening out these pews before our special session this evening."

"I'm sorry to intrude, father. I was—"

"This isn't a Catholic church, miss. You can call me Pastor Levi."

Jesus and the other statuary in the front of the church and the figures in artwork along the side walls stared, their eyes following her movements. Auranna detected harsh scowls behind their placid, white faces.

"Um. I'm so sorry. I don't know why I walked in here. I was on my way to—"

"Psychic Spira Chulis?"

"How did you know?"

"Based on your arms I'd guess she's more up your alley than I would be. But please, come sit! Perhaps you walked in here for a reason."

Auranna took one more look over her shoulder, silently praying for Stephanie, Carrie, or even Lisa to rescue her at the last moment. She took it as a sign when they didn't and shuffled her way up to the front pew. She didn't know what to do with her hands when she sat down, so she grasped the bench on both sides of her knees.

"What were you going to ask Ms. Chulis, if you don't mind my asking?"

"Um. Well. Sir. I don't suppose you can see auras?"

He smiled and shook his head.

"You see, I... Well, mine is black."

"Ah. You feel you have no soul? You're aimless and lost?"

"All of the above, I guess. I don't feel like I don't have a soul, if that makes any sense. I'm afraid I sold it but I really don't remember doing so...or what I'd have even asked for if I had."

"I see. A psychic told you this? About your 'aura?'"

"Yes, sir. And my girlfriend sees it as well."

Auranna expected a punitive frown from him at that, but he acted like it was nothing. The statuary frowned at her orientation, though. She was sure of it.

"Is she psychic, too?" Levi asked.

"She's undead or partially-dead or something like that. We're not sure. We weren't at the psychic to talk about my aura, though. After my friend committed suicide..."

Auranna scratched at the branded inverted cross on her forearm as the pastor gave her an unearned look of sympathy.

"Well, he wasn't dead long. We went in after him and pulled him back out. Thankfully there's no purgatory or we'd have gone to Hell for nothing. He's paying for it now, though. He looks dead. He's not healing at all."

Levi shook his head loose after a moment.

"I'm sorry, I must have misheard you. Your undead girlfriend sees your black aura, and you just pulled your friend out of Hell—personally—after his suicide?"

"You heard me fine," Auranna confirmed before she tumbled into explaining in detail what had happened in the dreamworld the night before that led to her current despair. "...that's when I started to pray to God, but I cut myself off for being selfish and rude. Do you think he would have answered my prayer if I'd completed it? Is there a prayer I could learn that would protect me from Satan punishing me ever again?"

Levi regarded her with a fearful amusement, maintaining his composure as only a professional man of faith could.

"I... Well, there certainly are prayers that would protect you from Satan, but they're more for pushing him out of your mind and resisting his temptations. You said he *physically* attacked you?"

"Yes. Though I'm always technically asleep when He does,

so I'm not sure how you'd define it then. To clarify, consent would not have been proffered if I'd been awake, either. The concept of consent doesn't apply to Him, or stop Him, rather. It's not a temptation or a choice on my part, as you imply."

Auranna hugged her arms and pulled her posture inward. Levi wasn't staring at her chest, or her flesh riddled with blasphemous iconography. In fact, he never broke eye contact with her whenever she summoned the courage to meet his. But admitting what Satan had done to her made her feel guilty in the place of holy worship, as if she invited the torture and indignity on herself with her appearance and profession.

"Consent? Oh oh oh! Now I think I'm getting it. Someone raped you and you feel aimless and lost as if he took your soul from you and you don't know how to get it back, and you want to know if God would have answered your prayer to make the man stop if you'd completed it," Levi sighed in satisfaction and sat back more casually into the pew as if he'd solved a hard riddle. "You don't need to speak to me in metaphors, miss, though I'm still puzzled over what you meant by pulling your suicidal friend out of Hell. Oh, unless you mean...you talked him out of it. Of course! That must be it."

The statuary knew she didn't speak in metaphors. Auranna could almost hear them, shouting for her to leave the sacred place.

"I'm trying not to embellish my story, so you won't decide not to help me. If you can. I'm not sure. That's not fair of me. You don't know me, why should I expect you'd help me? I knew this was a mistake. I'm sorry for wasting your time. I've got to get back to the venue and—"

"Venue? Ah, you're a fan of that satanic Black Aura band playing tonight? I should have guessed with your arms. You look exactly like my daughter wants to. She's yearned to see that band for years. I grounded her and tore up her posters and the tickets. She says she won't forgive me now, but I know she'll thank me someday. I hope to open her eyes during the special session tonight for the concerned citizens of this town about allowing that band and others to play here. You should come to the service, too, and forgo that corrupting influence. It's clearly had a negative impact on you already."

"How...cliché. Did you watch *Black Roses* recently?"

"Excuse me?"

"Never mind. Again, I'm sorry for wasting your time. Thank you for humoring me and listening to my story. Good luck with your daughter. You'll have your work cut out for you earning her forgiveness."

The judgments from God, artwork, and statuary lifted their oppressive weights from her chest the moment she crossed the threshold to the outside, allowing her to breathe normally again. She didn't feel like repeating herself to the psychic and walked back to the venue instead, back to the one place she belonged.

CHAPTER EIGHTEEN

POENA

PUNISHMENT RENDERED

ABIGAIL PEEKED DOWN AT HER phone. Only a few hours before the venue opened, another couple before Black Aura stepped onto the stage. Or in the crowd, if the rumors and social media postings were true and not doctored for publicity.

Her son-of-a-bitch father blathered on about the evils of metal music and the dangers of letting it in their town, and how the mayor should be ashamed of granting the permits to hold the concert. Every one of the adults murmured their agreement throughout his speech. It was like he watched *Footloose* but turned the movie off before the pastor's change of heart; all he'd gotten from it was a splash of inspiration to tear up her room and tickets. She regretted recommending he see it to open his worldview and soften the landing when she planned to ask for permission to go to the concert with a "pretty please with extra chores on top." Clearly, he'd missed the message.

Rebecca had to buy a new pair of tickets quietly to avoid suspicion from her own parents. Abigail's best friend had been much smarter than her, faking her sickness to avoid coming to the lame, puritanical browbeating and fire-and-brimstone nonsense. Abigail needed to make her own escape.

She moaned and held her stomach. Her mother glared at her sideways without taking attention away from the speech.

"Are you okay, Abigail?"

"Daddy's sermons from the Book of Revelation make me sick. It's too gruesome," she whispered and moaned again. "Can I walk home and lay down?"

"I guess your father can continue at home for you, later. You'd better be there when we get back or I'm adding two weeks to your grounding, and your father will be free to add whatever he wishes on top of that."

"I'm just going to lay down, Mom."

"Alright. Take some of the pink stuff when you get home."

"Calamine lotion? How would that—" Abigail faked a heave as if she really thought about drinking that.

"Pepto, Abigail! Now get out of here before you throw up in the House of the Lord."

Abigail held her stomach while she passed through the door and down the street, then walked normally out of sight of the church.

Pssh. Revelation. *Yeah right*.

Rebecca's house looked like all the other houses in their town. Homogenous and safe. A good Christian house. It made her sicker than if she really had drunk Calamine lotion, or listened to her father's overbearing rants from Revelation.

"Abby, get your ass in here!" Rebecca said after opening the door. "We need to get our corpse paint on and arrive early. Maybe the band will greet people during the opening acts. I read that Auranna likes to work the merchandise booth sometimes."

"I wish we could buy more posters, but that asshole would

rip them all up again. What are you planning to wear?"

"Normal clothes."

"At a metal concert? What the hell, Becky?"

"Think about it, dummy. We come home late at night with our normal clothes and corpse paint washed off, we can tell our parents we heard something 'scary' outside, so we stayed at each other's houses until we knew our parents would come back from that meeting. Come home in the metal gear and we're fucked."

"What would I do without such a smart best friend?"

"You wouldn't be going to this concert tonight. I ordered a whole bunch of black and white makeup—it's up in the bathroom. Get going!"

With most of the adults who'd be offended by their makeup in the church, they walked easily and openly to the venue. Every block they closed, more young adults and teenagers in makeup and metal gear—as well as normal clothes like them—joined the procession. Abigail followed the general congregation towards the front entrance, but Rebecca tugged at her sleeve and pulled her towards a different line.

"Becky, that's the backstage pass line! We can't get in there with normal tickets! Don't make me stand there while you try to 'convince' the guard to let you in."

"The only things I'll need to convince him are *these*," Rebecca said while pulling open her denim jacket.

Abigail gasped, blushed, and looked away.

"What? The tickets are in here," Rebecca winked and pulled two tickets from the inside pocket.

"Backstage passes! How? When? How could you afford—? What?"

"Early birthday and Christmas present. I used the money I was saving for a car."

Abigail hugged her wonderful friend tight.

"Kiss her!" a random metalhead in the line said to the laughter and approval of others.

Abigail scowled at him, but Rebecca locked eyes when she turned back and shrugged, then gave her a quick kiss on the lips, earning a cheer from the line. Abigail's eyes widened and she froze in place. She hadn't expected to have her mind blown before Black Aura even started playing.

Rebecca chuckled and pulled Abigail's arm to the line, handing her one of the passes.

"Um. Really, Becky. This is... I can't—"

"Don't overthink it, Abby. Have fun! It'll be like your last night on Earth before you're grounded for life!"

"You're right. They're going to kill me if they find out. Might as well earn it."

Even with the backstage passes, it was like they were getting away with something forbidden. They walked around the venue and saw some of the opening bands spread out, relaxing while the roadies moved with purpose and sometimes anger when a visitor got in their way. They explored everywhere, expecting to be told at any time to stop and leave the area—but no one did.

From one of the buses in the back a man with a camera walked backwards while a procession of six people and a winged demon filed out towards the venue. Unable to keep her eyes off the demon in the torn clothing, she was oblivious to the fact Black Aura was passing her within arm's length until Rebecca shook her out of her trance.

"That was them! The whole band! Come on, we have to follow them!"

Other pass holders mobbed the band. Most had their shirts and passes autographed while a few bolder visitors offered body parts to be signed. Abigail and Rebecca pushed their way through the crowd in a bid to see the band from closer up.

After Auranna signed a metalhead's butt cheek, she looked up and around for the next person. She made eye contact with Abigail for a brief moment and smiled, then turned to sign another fan's shoulder blade. Abigail froze in place for the second time that night.

The band expertly signed while moving bit by bit, so they never actually stopped. Eventually they split up into dressing rooms. A few female fans huddled behind Alex and Desmond as they went into the men's dressing room and were allowed in. The males had no such luck trying to get into the women's dressing room. Rebecca pulled Abigail by the arm towards that very room, holding up her pass to whoever wanted to see it.

In a state of elation and disbelief that no one tackled them from behind, they opened the door and slid inside. No one grabbed them by the shoulders and tossed them out on their butts like Abigail expected.

Three Queens of Metal sat in front of mirrors, applying their corpse paint after tying their hair.

"I have no idea why those groupies are still flocking to Alex. He looks like a damn zombie. Does his dick even work?" Carrie said.

"You can thank Alice Cooper for that," Stephanie said.

"Oh hi!" Carrie looked up through the mirror. "Never mind that necrophilia talk. I love the dea— Dammit, Steph! I meant, I love your paint, girls."

"Thu—thank you," Rebecca said, likely blushing as much as Abigail beneath the black and white makeup.

"Do you want to put mine on?" Stephanie said and laid back in the chair.

They exchanged shocked expressions, asking with their eyes: which one of them should be the one to do it?

"I'll make the decision easier for you. One of you can do mine, one of you can do Carrie's."

They awkwardly split up. Auranna stood between Carrie and Stephanie in the mirror, intensely inspecting the girls' faces as they worked. Abigail occasionally returned her gaze, awestruck.

"I agree with Carrie. Great job. Why don't you copy what you did onto theirs?"

Auranna went back to applying her own.

"So, are you girls from around here or did you drive in from another town?" Stephanie asked.

"We're from here, ma'am," Abigail said.

"Please with that 'ma'am' shit," Stephanie said. "Makes me feel old."

"I'm sorry, ma'— I mean, miss."

"Jesus, 'Steph' is fine. Are you the pastor's daughter or something? Who talks all respectful at a metal concert?"

Abigail's face burned at the thought that she had given herself away. The paint had done nothing to mask her like she'd hoped; being a pastor's daughter was more than skin deep.

"Just giving you a hard time, hun. We tour all over the country. These smaller towns have all kinds of people like you. It's nothing to be ashamed of."

Auranna leaned back from the mirror with half of her paint on and stared a little harder than before at Abigail. Abigail's face was on fire, and she feared her paint melting off. She grew ever more breathless from the incomprehensible and wonderful turn the evening had taken, but her embarrassment kept trying to ruin it for her.

"You have his eyes," Auranna said and went back to her painting.

"Whose eyes?" Stephanie asked. "Are you going to tell us she's your daughter and you remember the dad's eyes?"

Abigail detected a note of jealousy in Stephanie's voice that revealed her joke would also be a devastating possibility.

Auranna slumped her shoulders and stared sideways at Stephanie, then backhanded her thigh.

"No, she's the pastor's daughter, like you said. I met him today."

"Yuh—you met my...dad?"

Rebecca looked at Abigail and mouthed 'wow!'

"What did...I mean...how did you—?"

"Oh, I wandered into his church. I told him about some things going on in my life and he listened. He kept thinking I was speaking in metaphors, though, so he didn't *listen* listen, you know?"

"Yes. Yes, I do know."

"He said he tore up your posters and tickets. How did you get in here?"

"Um...my best friend."

Rebecca smiled while she continued with Carrie's paint, pretending to be too absorbed.

Auranna sat back in her chair to finish the other half of her paint. Abigail tried to keep her mind on the task at hand. *Be cool*, she told herself.

"*My* dad was like that," Carrie said. "It was Otep stuff in my room. He said I would burn in Hell. Messed my room up. He wasn't a pastor or anything, but just as pious and God-fearing. I ran away from home and became a roadie until some union snob caught me and kicked me out. I stole a keyboard from this jerk player in some shitty band who spit on me for tripping over his cords."

Stephanie cackled and smeared the paint. Abigail started to apologize but Stephanie waved her off.

"Looks cool, hun. Now no one will mistake us for twins. Not that my red hair wasn't already a dead giveaway. I was remembering when we got revenge on that asshole who spit on Carrie. When we were opening early in our career their band was between us and the headliners on the bill. All five of us put together a little money and paid a roadie to program the guys' keyboard to only play fart sounds."

Carrie laughed and Auranna smiled. Stephanie stood up after Abigail's finishing touches on her paint.

"Speaking of bands below the headliners, you girls want

to meet the band that plays right before us? Coolest fuckin' dudes in the world. Come on, I'll introduce you."

Auranna grabbed Abigail's hand.

"We'll be right behind you, Steph," Auranna said, then pulled Abigail closer. Abigail's heart nearly smashed through her ribs. "Your father is a nice man. I hope you know he loves you and he honestly feels like he's protecting you. You look like a nice girl in corpse paint. Maybe you can tell him how normal we are, especially after you meet the other bands and fans, too. We're not literally worshiping Satan. It's a genre we love. Does a murder mystery writer murder people?

"Whether you tell him or not, and whether he grows to accept us in our entirety, always remember where his heart is. Plus, if you act extra sweet while you're grounded, he might shorten the sentence."

Auranna smiled. Abigail didn't know what to say.

"Strange words from the Queen of Metal, right? Well, take it for what it's worth to you. Tell your dad I said: 'Next time I'm going to Miss Chulis.' He'll know what it means."

Auranna led Abigail by the hand to another room where Rebecca was busy getting her shirt signed by the band Stephanie wanted them to meet. So much for minimizing the evidence...

Abigail couldn't believe the one-eighty switch in Auranna's personality once her pick swept across the strings of her blacker-than-black guitar. How on Earth could her voice *do that*? She seemed so normal—soft-spoken even—backstage.

Recordings did her voice no justice. Live...it was *alive*. The raw emotion and powerful, vivid lyrics projected the images right in front of Abigail's eyes and put her in touch with feelings she didn't think possible.

After the first song onstage, the band left to roam the crowd, as the rumors had said. Stephanie was a wrecking ball with all the large metalheads in the pits, dishing out as much as she took. Fans didn't know if Alex's stitched wounds were fake and whether the seeping blood was a prop, but they were swooning to catch a drop of it. It delighted and disgusted them. Carrie was less sure of herself with a keytar and remained close enough to Auranna to take advantage of the crowd's reverence and less-aggressive behavior when she passed by. Desmond played with fury, but his face was blank most of the time, as if haunted by the music itself.

Abigail and Rebecca pushed through the crowd to get a glimpse of each of them in their element. The jostling and pushing took some getting used to. She felt better about it when she started pushing back. Several times Rebecca's body pressed into her own. Rebecca had taken on a strange glow since their quick kiss. They'd been friends since the second grade and turned into best friends shortly after. Abigail never thought anything about their relationship beyond that. Whenever the pit moved close to them, Rebecca moved away from Abigail less each time. Then she could tell Rebecca actively sought contact. Rebecca played it off by looking away, but during one of the melodic breaks in "Insightful Incision," their eyes locked and they couldn't look away. Auranna's shriek brought them out of it and they continued their quest to reach her. Abigail was shaken and tingling from the shared moment. *What does it mean that I want to touch Becky again*, she asked herself.

Away from the swirling movement of the pits, the crowd hardened into a brick wall when Auranna passed through a section. No one could move or keep their eyes off her, as if she were Medusa turning them all into stone. Rebecca pulled Abigail's arm in a strategic attempt to get ahead of Auranna's movement. They stopped at a spot close to the mixer tent as that seemed to be Auranna's current path.

The crowd parted as Auranna came closer and closer. Another couple of steps and she'd be close enough to touch. With a mind of its own, Abigail's hand sought Rebecca's. She relished Rebecca's soft and sweaty skin touching hers.

Auranna's solo invaded Abigail's mind and the music drove her thoughts, directing her: *turn to Rebecca and return her kiss from earlier*. She fought through that temptation, at first. Then she wondered if it really was a temptation or if it simply felt…right.

She turned away from Auranna's captivating presence with effort and found Rebecca looking at her with a shyness she had never showed in all the years they'd known each other. Abigail smiled and squeezed her hand, which Rebecca returned.

In the middle of her solo, Auranna looked up from her guitar at them. Her eyes flew open, and a whisper of pain hit her note. It was the last thing Abigail experienced before the world turned black, red, and hot.

CHAPTER NINETEEN

OCULOS

EYES OF ANGELS

ABIGAIL AND REBECCA HELD HANDS near the mixer tent, then in a blink they stood on the stage looking out over a mass of black shades, punctuated by five glowing, pulsating silhouettes moving between the shades. The speakers behind them weren't playing the music they were listening to only a moment before; their heartbeats matched the aggressive but dull rhythm that echoed through the crowd.

Abigail ripped her hand from Rebecca's. Rebecca didn't seem to notice as she took in their new black surroundings.

"Abby? What's going on?"

"I don't know. I'm sorry I thought about you that way."

"What way? What are you talking about?"

"Out there, I wanted to... I mean...I felt compelled, as if Satan himself were guiding my thoughts, to, um, kiss you, and...maybe more. I never imagined that we'd be punished so immediately. My dad doesn't preach hate for that sort of thing, but maybe he's wrong."

"Umm, I don't think that's what's happened. I was already thinking that way earlier and we were fine."

"You were?"

"Yes, Abby. Can we focus on what's happening right now? This is... I don't know what this is."

Abigail bit her lip and looked around. Small red eyes stared at them from the backstage area. The black sky disoriented with its lack of stars and moonlight. A red-tinged glow burned around the edges of the visible sky, over the edges of some distant cliffs and what looked like the black outline of trees.

"Do you think someone slipped something in our drinks before the concert started?" Abigail asked.

"I don't think there are any drugs that would cause us to have the exact same hallucination."

Abigail gasped when she noticed the five glowing silhouettes staring at them up on the stage, seamlessly playing as they moved and glowered. She huddled into Rebecca and they held each other in dread. Abigail started reciting every prayer she could remember. She blathered until the words stopped coming out of her mouth.

– Prayers aren't going to help us. Shut up, Abby. –

Aghast at Rebecca, Abigail mouthed more empty words. She pulled back from her embrace and tugged at Rebecca to face her. Rebecca mouthed "what?" but her voice didn't follow either.

– What? –

Abigail shook her head. Rebecca's voice didn't enter her ears. It came from the center of her mind.

– Can you hear me, Becky? –

Rebecca's eyes grew wide.

– Yes. How did that happen? –

– I don't know. Are we in... Are we being punished in Hell? None of this is how Dad describes things in the Bible, though. –

The bible will not help you here, Abigail.

Giant red eyes appeared above the black shades in front of

the stage and squinted at them with malice.

Rebecca is correct. Your prayers will not, either.

The voice wasn't pleasantly in the center of their minds as when they thought to each other. It snaked in and around the brain, slipping through the folds, pulsing and squeezing to the dull thrum of the music.

– Who are you? Why are we here? – Rebecca thought.

Your queen settled her debt to me with you two. I am pleased.

– Our queen? – Abigail asked.

The air around them compressed and lifted them off the stage, then carried them out into the shades to where they'd been before—where they'd endeavored to meet Auranna. He thrust them within inches of the silhouette, but it continued playing aggressively, observing them with indifference.

The wind threw them back towards the stage. Abigail's back cracked against the edge of it. Rebecca's leg snapped gruesomely against a large speaker. Their screams drowned each other out in their minds.

– I don't understand! She sacrificed us? She seemed so friendly! –Abigail cried through the pain.

You are nothing but a currency to her. You will meet the others she has paid with soon enough.

Abigail prayed furiously once she found the inner strength to stop howling in pain. In her own desperation, Rebecca joined her. The eyes laughed and the sound tore through their minds like nails on a chalkboard. They persisted in finishing the recitations. Abigail searched her mind for every tangential protective prayer that she could muster. One of them had to work.

– 'See, I am sending an angel ahead of you to guard you along the way and to bring you to the place I have prepared.' –

An angel! I could not have thought of a better choice, I must confess. Changing you into angels would give me some small memory of Home every time I look at you. Which type shall it be, though?

You frantically imagine yourself as an armed archangel, so you may strike me down. I admire the thought. I do miss some of them. Archangel Jophiel was my personal favorite. What she could do with that flaming sword...

That, however, is not the angel you shall become. Nor shall you be cherubic babes, nor even humanoid. Shall it be the many-winged monstrosity? Or...the eyes?

Abigail wasn't sure what he was referring to, or where they were described in the Bible. Pain exploded from every part of her body as she was stretched. And stretched. And stretched. Their screams filled each other's minds while the red eyes laughed with all the pleasure of a child playing with goo.

They were pulled and pulled like putty into long strips of flesh, then wrapped around each other in dozens of layers to form a sphere. Eyes manifested from every inch of their skin. They blinked and their vision multiplied to see in all directions. The eyes pressed into the ground painfully as they poked and rubbed the grimy stage surface. Abigail shifted to lessen the discomfort, but that only irritated new eyes as the sphere rolled.

Their minds snapped and they wailed to no avail. The wind punted their sphere up the cliffs, and they landed in the black void of the forest's canopy.

The girls disappeared, then flashed before Auranna's eyes, their faces distorted with terror. Her guitar sprouted dozens of eyes which stared at her accusingly as she wrapped up the song through muscle memory. Her legs wobbled like jelly, and she feared passing out like the concert when the spider was made.

She slumped down to her knees and fell backwards, looking up into the night sky. Of all the places the girls could have been standing, why did they have to choose *that spot*? She couldn't imagine the horrors Satan would inflict on the daughter of a pastor. Would that she could take their place. Auranna's grief was instant, her regret debilitating. Why was she left to feel the guilt of all these tortured souls? Why couldn't Satan take only her?

The night sky grew closer and moved as if she were lying on a conveyor belt. A dozen hands lifted and guided her towards the stage, her first experience of crowd-surfing. Most of them touched her reverently, but for one who couldn't resist touching her butt. Why couldn't that one have been standing in the spot instead of the girls?

Her body met the hard floor of the stage. For the first time in her professional life she didn't feel like playing. The torture of the night before; the horrors she imagined would befall those poor girls; the confusion over her grandmother's contradictory involvement; Stephanie's transformation; Alex's body not healing after regaining its soul; Desmond's dead-eyed stare after suffering His wrath; the thousand souls she'd condemned to an eternity of pain and torment for she knew not what—it all weighed on her.

It was all her fault somehow. The ultimate frustration lay in knowing that, but not how or why it was so.

She'd had enough. It was time to find out.

But first, the crowd chanting her name brought her to her feet. While her bandmates attempted to make their way through the crowd, Auranna began a solo instrumental she'd never shared with anyone. She channeled her rage and frustration into symphonic fury. Her bandmates stopped trying to reach the stage and simply became part of the crowd. She blessed them all with a performance that would overwhelm any demands for an encore.

A strong urge to smash her most prized possession on the stage nearly overtook her before sense brought her back from the brink. She needed her guitar for what was to come. She didn't know exactly why, but the feeling was overwhelming in its certainty. She handed her axe to the master tech, grabbed an innocuous emergency guitar, finished the solo, then dashed it to bits on the stage. Her fans erupted at seeing a side of her no one in the world had ever seen. Auranna had never felt so much anger. Musicians were absolute morons to her for smashing their instruments regularly. At least Carrie's was already broken when she'd shattered hers. Were those moronic musicians right all along? It was so cathartic—as if months' worth of expensive therapy unloaded inside of thirty seconds.

After saluting the jubilant crowd with only the headstock of the poor guitar, she took the feeling of fervent desperation to the dressing room. She tempered the thoughts of the pain that was sure to come with pleasure, ravaging Stephanie—to Stephanie's utter delight—for an extra hour past road call, ignoring the pounding on the door. The bus wouldn't leave without them, no matter how much they yelled and threatened. Auranna deserved to be selfish once in her forsaken life.

Stephanie clung to Auranna's arm affectionately as they got on the bus. Auranna ignored the annoyance from her bandmates and Gerald at their dallying after the show. *Let them be mad*, she thought. She needed to build up her armor; coat herself with positive thoughts and feelings to protect her from the coming pain.

She sat on the couch next to Rachel. Stephanie held tighter as her jealousy reared its ugly green head. Auranna chose to ignore that as well and allowed her to continue. Stephanie's love, regardless of how it could be interpreted after her transformation, soothed Auranna's rage.

"Rachel, I'm going to Hell tomorrow morning. I need answers. I want to free my army. I want to free you. I want to cure Stephanie. Will you journey with me?"

"Yes, my Queen. I would be honored to aid You in any way possible."

"You're not going anywhere without *me*, my Queen," Stephanie chimed in as if Auranna was choosing between the two of them.

Auranna realized Joel had been recording them the whole time with Lisa sitting close by, ready for an interview.

"Joel, I don't suppose you have an extra camera we could take with us down there? Something you wouldn't miss if it melted or became irretrievable?"

"Yes he does and that is an *amazing* idea. Why didn't we think of that the last time you went to Hell?" Lisa said. "Joel, get one of the backup cameras charged and put in an empty memory card. Which one of you will be recording? Stephanie? Go with Joel so he can show you all you need to know about the best footage. Focusing, DPI, that sort of stuff. If you don't adjust the exposure down there, you probably won't capture anything."

Stephanie grumbled and followed Joel. Auranna squeezed Rachel's hand in thanks, then went to sit in the passenger seat in the front.

"Sure is taking a long time to get out of here, Gerald."

"Don't give me that, kid. If you and Stephanie had come to the bus earlier, we could have been at the front of the line rather than the back. We're still technically on time, but barely. I'm getting messages from the front bus drivers that there's a barricade on the road out of town and they're only letting cars through one at a time. Likely a DUI trap after the concert."

"Think we can get to the next stop by early tomorrow?"

"What's your hurry? It's a rest day."

"I want to hurry up and rest."

Gerald chuckled and shook his head.

"I'll never get you kids no matter how many years I drive you around this country."

A couple hours passed and the DUI checkpoint only had a few more buses to go. Cars were cleared quicker. Each bus parked longer as the police searched every part of them.

A police officer stood off to the side while his colleagues worked, talking to a familiar man. Auranna touched Gerald's shoulder to ask him to let her off the bus, and approached the man. The officer stood at attention to block her, but the man came around the side and nodded.

"Pastor Levi, good evening," Auranna said.

"I wish I could say it's good, miss."

"What's going on?" she asked, guilt piling up. She wanted to cut out the veiled conversation and get to the point, but she also didn't know if she could handle hearing him say it out loud.

"My daughter and her friend didn't come home tonight. We're seeing if anyone has any information. Unlikely though it is, she might have gone against our orders after all. We're hoping someone saw them at the concert."

"Pastor, can I speak with you on my bus? In private? The line isn't moving very fast."

"Your own bus? Oh. You know, for all the riddling you were doing in the church, I never put two and two together when you talked about having a black aura."

"I apologize if I deceived you with who I was."

"No, no. I don't believe you were trying to. I wasn't thinking about it that hard," he said distractedly as he scanned the vehicles, searching for any sign of his daughter.

"I'm not trying to deceive you tonight. Please join me on my bus, away from the honking horns and cool night air."

Levi snapped to attention when he realized Auranna was alluding to knowing more. He asked the officer to come get him if they found any useful information while he was gone and followed Auranna onto the bus. He made to leave when he glimpsed Rachel but Auranna put her hand on his shoulder.

"It's okay, Pastor. She's a part of all this. I need you to sit down with me. I have information about Abby and Becky."

"How do you know their names?"

"Please, sit next to my friend Rachel. I will go over everything with you."

She guided him to the couch and turned to Lisa.

"Lisa, please keep your cameras off for this. This is a private matter. Don't let Alex come up here, either. Rachel is enough of a shock to deal with."

Lisa grumbled and pulled Joel away with her while twirling her hair. Auranna rolled her eyes at the implication Joel would keep recording even from the kitchen, then knelt down before the pastor and told him everything.

After he'd called his wife to tell her that he was following a lead on their daughter, Levi sat back, patience running out on his face. They were well past the checkpoint. He'd chosen to stay and listen to Auranna's story to its completion.

"None of this makes any sense. I'm having a hard time believing a single part of it."

"I understand, Pastor. None of it makes sense to me, either. But I'm going to find answers as soon as we're far enough away from town. If I can find the girls and bring them back, I want you here for it. I'm...uncertain what their condition may be once I find them."

"You propose to literally travel to Hell, find them, and bring them back? The blasphemy and heresy I've heard today is staggering. I'm disappointed at the number of drugs you all must have taken to get to such a state of psychosis."

"We're a clean band. We sometimes have a little alcohol, but I need to protect my voice, and we're all professionals. This is our job and we take it seriously."

"Too seriously. The things I read about in your music's lyrics and imagery while I prepared my sermons have haunted me for the last four weeks. But then, I knew in the back of my mind that you were simply confused young people rebelling against religion and authority. Now I'm not so sure."

"We're not confused. Well, *they're* all not confused. I definitely am the more I journey to the dreamworld. I come away with more questions than answers. I hoped that by writing everything out when I returned things would come together someday. But I grow impatient now, and I want to put a stop to what took Abby and Becky. All you'll have to do is stand outside the portal. I plan to return with them within minutes, if it's anything like last time."

Levi sat in silence while Auranna brought him bottled water. He regarded Rachel with skepticism.

"I'm not saying I believe any of this, but—"

"Hell is real in the bible, is it not?" Auranna asked with an edge she hadn't meant to let escape. "Why are you having such a difficult time believing this?"

"It's more of an idea, though that's not entirely accurate to say, either. I don't believe it's literally beneath the Earth's crust any more than I believe Heaven is in the atmosphere above the clouds. They're real, but not in the physical sense like one could decide to go there anytime they wanted to. But then there's her..."

He looked at Rachel again.

"When you were taken, did you feel...pain?"

"No. It was instantaneous. The pain only started when He

turned His gaze to me."

"You mean Satan."

"Yes."

"Was it—?"

"You desire some comfort in your daughter's anguish. I can offer none. The pain is indescribable. She will wish she were dead, and you would wish the same if it meant ending the suffering she endures."

"I would trade places with her if—"

"No, you would not. The pain breaks you immediately, completely. No human could have the will to choose it, if they knew how it felt. I believe the only reason our Queen has not crumpled after eighteen years of it is Her lack of a soul, but that does not mean She cannot feel the pain inflicted from Him and Her army."

"Your queen and her army?"

"Oh right," Auranna said, "I left out that little detail, didn't I? I can't say I understand it either, so I didn't want to get stuck in the weeds discussing it. Don't look at me that way, Pastor. I'm no queen, no matter how much the demons keep saying it or how much I play along with Rachel and Stephanie. I hope you didn't get out of this whole thing that I have some delusions of grandeur about my place down there."

"I only met you today. I don't know what you hope to get out of all this."

"Let's start with your daughter and her friend."

CHAPTER TWENTY
HYMNUS

A HEAVENLY VOICE

EVERYONE ON THE BUS, EXCEPT Gerald, who'd departed for breakfast, gathered in an empty field near the next town. Pastor Levi fumed in the cold morning as Stephanie tied the shorter of two planks pilfered from a nearby fence to the bottom fourth of the longer upright board. Auranna assured him it was necessary and to stop letting his 'Bible-brain' interfere with what was happening. That only made him clutch his pocket Bible tighter.

As fire engulfed the blasphemous inverted cross, Stephanie removed her clothing. Though surprise should have been beyond him at that point, Levi gasped and shielded his eyes.

"Steph, you don't need to strip down, remember?" Auranna said. "And you're embarrassing the good pastor."

"Fuck that. I'm not letting my clothes get burned up again. I can't find that Satyricon shirt in print anymore. Hell can't have my Metallica shirt, too. Carrie, do you have our canteens ready?" Stephanie asked once her clothes were safely removed and in a pile away from the pyre.

The only one of them that seemed like a normal human being brought four canteens on a chain, one each for Stephanie and Auranna, and for Abigail and Rebecca if they could be found.

"Why do you need those?" Levi asked Auranna.

"There's no water in Hell, as far as we know. We almost died of dehydration in a matter of hours."

"I meant the guitars."

"Oh. Hell is a vast place. It would still take luck, but if your daughter hears our music it may draw her to us. Don't get your hopes up—it's only a theory. It did come in handy when we brought Alex back from Hell's waiting room."

Levi regarded Alex's neck and arm wounds again, yet another thing he had a hard time getting his head around. The young man should be dead... He *looked* dead.

Rachel removed her clothes, revealing even more painful-looking piercings than what was visible on her face. How could someone do that to themselves? Why? It sickened him. A hundred sermons came to him over the course of Auranna's blasphemy. He couldn't wait for them to stumble into their perverse fire, and he could call bull-spit on the whole thing. Then he'd return to searching for Abigail and Rebecca in earnest. These people had wasted enough of his ti—

Rachel and Stephanie disappeared through the fire, followed shortly by Auranna. He looked at Desmond, Carrie, Alex, Lisa, and Joel in turn, all standing there as if it was like any other day in their lives.

His Bible-brain shut off and he ran through the fire after them.

Levi hadn't planned his landing when he'd run through the portal and ended up stumbling into Auranna. Both their clothes burned up and their naked bodies collided and crashed to the ground. She gave him a pained smile as he lay on top of her.

"If I'd known you endeavored to join us, Pastor, I would have stepped out of your way. ...I really hope that's my whammy bar poking through my thighs."

Levi blushed and scrambled away from her. He turned from the three women so they couldn't see his unwanted protrusion. He cursed his body for its inappropriate reaction.

"It's alright, Pastor," Auranna said. "You may block yourself with one of these canteens until we find some rags. I'm sorry we didn't plan for your intrusion."

Eager to cover and forget, he looked around. All his years of study proved him right. Hell was dull, desolate, and devoid of God's blessings. He found no humor in the idea of Hell and was under no delusion there would have been little devils with pitchforks dancing and poking people, surrounded by literal fire in a cave-like atmosphere, or a large satyr commanding all of it. Satan would look like any other angel, he believed.

Part of him was relieved that he hadn't been mis-imagining Hell or portraying it falsely to his congregation. The other part despaired that it was a real, physical place he could feel and see with his mortal body. Were Abigail and Rebecca really being tortured here? It dawned horribly upon him that Auranna hadn't been lying now that he'd seen it for himself, and the weight of that realization came crashing down on his chest.

"Here, Pastor," Stephanie said as she offered him a long rag. "Do you know how to fashion a loin cloth? I can do it for you, but your blushing might catch these rags on fire."

Levi looked back to find Stephanie and Auranna in crude tops and loincloths. Rachel remained nude. A fourth figure joined them. Rags covered it completely, its face hidden beneath its hood.

"We'll look away while you figure that out," Stephanie said as she walked back to their little group and gazed out over the black plains below.

Levi tied the cloth around his hips to cover his shame.

"Thank you, um, sir? Ma'am? ...Are you Death? Thanatos isn't depicted like you, but you do resemble many interpretations of Death's robed form."

"She's not Death, Pastor. She's my grandmother...I think... She's unable to speak so I can't ask her for sure. But her face looks very much like her, so I don't believe it to be coincidental.

"*Mummo*, we come for a different purpose than last time. Do you remember the forest that you found Rachel in before you sent her through this portal? Can we travel there? Is it far from here?"

The hooded figure nodded once.

"I need to learn to stop asking you multiple questions at once. Will you guide us there?"

She shook her head once.

"Why not? Is it too painful? I know you've been there. You visited me last night in your younger form, remember? You said some very unkind things to me in my agony."

She shook her head once.

"'No,' you don't remember?"

She remained still. The performance from the night before crept up on Auranna, channeling unnatural anger. Getting answers from her grandmother was tedious as it was unhelpful.

"If you won't help us get to the forest, can you point us in the right direction? Is there anyone who can help us?"

The hooded figure grasped Rachel's wing and pulled it open. She touched several points on it, then traced a path between them.

"What does that—?" Stephanie started.

"Silence, doxy. She is drawing a map."

"You fucking call me that one more time..." Stephanie muttered and walked off, plucking her bass strings.

She brushed past Levi as he watched the old woman draw on the demon's wings. Once she finished, Rachel flew up into the air. She whistled at Stephanie to move in a different direction. Auranna said something in an unfamiliar foreign language to her grandmother, then went to stand at the edge of the cliff. She looked out across the black plains for a moment, then held up her pinky and index finger and bowed her head. A solemn, blasphemous prayer from the world's most famous Satanist struck Levi as poignant and unholy.

"Follow us or go back through the portal, Pastor," Auranna said as she turned down the path.

The fleeting image of being back in his comfortable home with his wife nearly pulled him towards the portal, but then he conjured Abigail's face. He wasn't blind to her distancing herself from the family, from the Lord. She spent as much time as possible with her friend Rebecca. Maybe they were done looking up to him and Him, but that was no reason to waver at the edge of safety and suffering. Levi would save them, or die trying, with or without the Lord's help.

He picked up the pocket Bible that remained after his clothes burned and followed Auranna and her strange friends.

For hours they walked, pushing off molasses-slow, moaning monstrosities that reached out for them as they passed. Levi couldn't tell if they were damned souls or demons. He said small prayers for each of them. The prayers kept his mind sharp and distracted from the nightmarish sights, sounds, and smells of Hell.

Auranna and Stephanie absentmindedly played their instruments, which lacked any of the fury or heresy they had when they were plugged in. It almost sounded...

"Beautiful."

"Hmm? What's that, Pastor?" Auranna asked over her shoulder.

"Your music. It's beautiful. I listened for a very short time to a Black Aura song after Abigail started putting up posters of your band. I thought it was horrible, horrid screeching and screaming without purpose. But stripped down to this...without lyrics, especially, I like it."

"Thank you for your compliment. That's all we wish, like any other musicians. Here, does this sound familiar?"

She played the most gorgeous version of one of his favorite hymns growing up. Stephanie joined her. It almost brought him to tears.

"A cover song we did early in our careers. A lot of bands cover well-known properties to cash in on someone else's success. We decided if we were to cover anything, it would be lesser-known work, anonymous and uncredited. I stole a hymn book from a church in Tennessee during our first tour and we covered two songs on later albums. I imagine you'd find it delicious to see metalheads thrashing in jubilation to hymns, if you could get past that look of disapproval as soon as I said 'stole.'"

"I don't imagine you or they absorbed their messages, though."

"Probably not. Nine out of ten people can't comprehend the lyrics of a metal song without them being written down. Most people are responding to the music and my voice, regardless of what comes out of it."

"What's your favorite non-hymn, Pastor?" Stephanie asked.

He thought about it for a moment. The only time he chose to listen to mainstream music was during their once-a-year vacation road-trips. He needed something to keep him awake during the longer legs once conversation had exhausted itself. He refused Abigail's choices of rock and metal, but they always agreed on one song. He loved the lyrics; she loved the music.

"'Spirit in the Sky.'"

"Probably should have been able to guess that," Auranna said with a wry smile.

They played it to perfection. Tears evaporated off his cheeks as he remembered singing it together with Abigail in the car.

Auranna and Stephanie looked at him while repeating a few bars, inviting him to join in. He blushed and shook his head. They continued walking and playing the same bars over and over until it started annoying him, then he realized they weren't going to stop until he did it.

He conceded, took the cue, and started singing. The women harmonized with him through the choruses as they marched on.

As enjoyable as it had been, Levi lost hope that his singing or their playing would draw Abigail to them. They didn't tire through several hymns he asked them to play with his direction, but he was tired of singing himself. The hot, dry air made his voice hoarse, decreasing his morale.

Auranna picked up the vocals for him and sang like an angel, better than anyone in his choir. She put more feeling and emotion behind each word than any in his congregation ever mustered. The more she sang the more he rethought the harsher sermons that had been running in the back of his mind since he'd seen her enter his church with her unholy tattoos, brands, inappropriately tight devilish T-shirt, and lazy, baggy sweatpants.

And now she was in this horrible place, willingly helping him find Abigail and Rebecca. Was she actually an ang—?

No, he thought. *She caused this. She can't be an angel.*

Rachel dropped down and put a stop to their play.

"Down this cliff, there is a place Your grandmother pointed to. The only cliffs I've known are the ones at the edge of the forest. To descend, I do not know what awaits us."

"Don't you remember when she brought you to the portal?" Stephanie asked.

"That was like a puff of smoke from one place to another."

"Why couldn't she do that for us instead of all this walking?" Stephanie whined.

"I am of this place, you three are not."

"Can you bring us down there, Rachel?" Auranna asked. "If it tires you, we can attempt to traverse it ourselves."

"I will do it. I do not desire to see my Queen injure Herself.

I fear the mortal consequences upon our return. It is not like Your dreamworld, as Alex's art carved into Your back proves."

"Fair enough. I'll go first. You go last, Steph. I don't want the good pastor to be left alone."

Stephanie nodded as Rachel lifted Auranna and flew out of sight down the cliff.

"Goddamn bitch is too eager to hold my Queen..."

Levi cleared his throat, avoiding getting entangled in the bizarre idea that Stephanie was jealous of a demon.

"How long has Auranna been coming to Hell?" Levi asked.

"This is only the second time," Stephanie said. "I'm unsure if her dreamworld is Hell or not, but she's been going there since she was twelve. She told me she was studying 'The Number of the Beast' by Iron Maiden shortly after her mother's disappearance and she was taken to the dreamworld for the first time."

"When did you stop believing she was crazy?"

"I never believed she was crazy. I believed she had a perfect imagination for our type of music and never thought any of it was literal until I was bitten by a ghost adder, blew out my insides and hundreds of baby snakes, and died in our tour bus."

He cocked his eyebrow. "Auranna never mentioned that part. Only that you were undead or half-dead."

"We don't know what I am. I don't really care, as long as that slutty bat bitch doesn't come between us. Anyway, do you have any idea why that song would cause Auranna to be taken?"

"I'm sure you can guess I don't know the lyrics or have ever heard it. But the number you're referring to... I'd rather not discuss it."

"Have a little hexakosioihexekontahexaphobia, Pastor? I guess that's only natural."

Before he could respond to Stephanie's absurdity, Rachel

appeared and picked him up from behind, wrapping her arms beneath his armpits and around his chest. On the flight down he tried to put her breasts pressing into his bare back out of his mind. He thought about some of his older congregants out of their Sunday dresses. It helped immediately.

Rachel placed him down next to Auranna, then took off one more time. Was that exhaustion he noticed in her breathing? Or anger at having to carry Stephanie?

It must have been the latter, because Stephanie swung her bass guitar to strike at Rachel's head mid-flight. Rachel's wings lost control and they tumbled into the side of the cliff, rolling the last few dozen feet to the bottom.

CHAPTER TWENTY-ONE
ADVOCATUS

LAWYERS IN HELL. PUNCHLINE COMPLETE

MERCIFULLY, THE CANTEENS SURVIVED THE fall. The bass guitar, Rachel's wings, and Stephanie's leg did not. Stephanie crawled towards Rachel with rage in her eyes. Even an exposed femur wasn't enough to halt her fury.

"I told you to stop calling me that, you goat bitch! Piss me off again and I'll cut out your tongues!"

Auranna got between them, putting her hands on Stephanie's shoulders to stop her from any further assault, then looked at her leg.

"I can see your bone, my love. Please stop struggling."

Levi knelt down beside her.

"Put something between her teeth."

Auranna looked around but couldn't see anything both soft and strong enough—nothing that could do the job like a leather belt or wooden spoon. She snapped her fingers, pulled the pocket Bible from Levi's hand, and put its spine between Stephanie's teeth.

"Pray, Stephanie. This is going to hurt," Levi said.

Levi snapped the bone back in place. He expected Stephanie to cry out but instead she whimpered quietly. She tossed the Bible away in disgust and leaned up in a sitting position.

"We've been through much worse, Pastor," Auranna said, noting his confused expression. "Are you also a doctor?"

"I used to be an EMT to help pay for rent during college. I'm surprised I remembered how to do that after so long."

He got up to retrieve the Bible. Auranna caressed Stephanie's forehead and kissed her, then slapped her, much to Levi and Stephanie's surprise.

"You deserved that," Auranna said, then made the rounds to Rachel and her broken wings.

She didn't look to be in any pain outwardly, but her face conveyed a tremendous amount of sadness. One of her horns had broken off, in addition to her mangled wings.

"I don't suppose you can fix her poor wings?" Auranna asked Levi.

"I'm sorry. I mean, I could probably set the bones, but they won't be useable."

"Do not pretend to care for me further. I deserved this," Rachel said.

Auranna slapped her across the face, too.

"No, but you deserved at least *that*. Steph asked you to stop demeaning her. I also asked you to knock it off. Now, is this out of your systems, ladies?" Auranna raised her voice to address both of them. "Have you screwed us all over enough? Can we finally move past this insane jealousy and figure out how to proceed?"

Stephanie folded her arms and frowned at the black sky. Rachel stood up and Levi involuntarily cringed as she reached behind her back, grasped one of her broken wings, and, together with her prehensile tail, snapped the wing off. The pain no longer hid behind her face. The demon winced and wisps of tears evaporated from the voids of her eyes.

She handed the wing to Levi.

"You may fashion a brace and cast with the bones and flesh."

Rachel approached, then loomed over Stephanie, staring into her eyes. Levi was unsure if there would be violence or not. Stephanie recoiled as if she expected the same.

"Stephanie," Rachel said earnestly, then turned to leave. "I shall scout ahead. Follow my hoof prints in the dust."

Auranna shook her head and helped Levi secure Stephanie's leg.

"Just another day nursing the easily bruised egos of like-minded friends and colleagues," Auranna muttered.

Auranna and Levi took turns carrying Stephanie on their backs as they followed the hard-to-see hoof prints. Whichever one wasn't holding Stephanie had to stoop down to perceive anything with only the dull red glow of the horizon to light the way.

"I'm imagining the sour look on Lisa's face when she realizes we forgot to bring that camera," Stephanie said from Auranna's back. "The flash may have come in handy, at least."

Stephanie abandoned her broken guitar. The one not carrying her lugged the canteens and Auranna's guitar. They traded off every mile—or what felt like every mile.

One transfer—before Stephanie climbed on Levi's

back—she and Auranna embraced and kissed. When Auranna took the lead to track, Stephanie spoke to Levi from his back.

"Do we make you uncomfortable, Pastor? I mean, amongst the millions of things that crawl down here that could make you uncomfortable?"

"Not at all, Stephanie. My church is inclusive."

"Just pretend that part of the bible doesn't exist, eh?"

"I tend to stick to the New Testament of the Bible. The lessons in the Old are often archaic and don't have much bearing on our modern lives. You and I might laugh ourselves silly over the rules and laws in the Old Testament, including those in Leviticus—beyond the passage you reference. It saddens me that so many believers will scoff at almost every other rule in the Old Testament yet cling desperately and blindly to that one single passage as if Jesus Himself spoke it."

"You're a pretty cool guy, Pastor. I'm sorry we met under these circumstances. I took exception to your ripping up our band's posters in your daughter's room, though. You know what that did to most of us back home? It made us join metal bands."

Levi chuckled at the thought of Abigail rocking in front of thousands of fans.

"She's a good makeup artist. She might have a job waiting for her in Hollywood when we get her out of here," Stephanie mused.

"If."

"When, Levi. *When*! Have a little *faith*!"

They caught up to Rachel several miles after their groundbreaking tumble. She stood in front of a black building that stretched on for many miles more. Auranna caressed Rachel's shoulder in thanks, just above her missing wing's stump. Stephanie asked Levi to stop in front of Rachel and held out her hand. Rachel regarded it, then took it.

"We already shook once, Rachel. Don't let there be an incident that requires a third."

Rachel nodded, then offered for Stephanie to lean against her as they continued, taking her turn shouldering the group's burden. Levi couldn't lie to himself that he hadn't enjoyed carrying Stephanie mostly naked through the horrifying plains of Hell, but a hundred-twenty-five pounds was still a lot of weight to carry that far regardless of how often he and Auranna swapped, especially because Auranna's thin frame didn't seem to handle the weight that well. He admired that she never complained, though. Their deep love carried them far.

Levi was irrationally disappointed there was no air conditioning inside the building—it was as hot inside as it was outside. An endless set of rows were occupied by an endless payroll of lawyers, all hunched over their work, carving words into the backs of humans shackled to the floor. The humans' wails filled the walls.

The group walked to the large desk near the front door where a man with a Shakespearean mustache and a powdered wig furiously wrote on what could only be stacks of human skin. Each time he finished writing, the skin-parchment disappeared, then he wrote on the next one underneath.

He stopped for a moment to regard the company before him, then looked back down and continued writing.

"The soulless one, the half-soul, the soul belonging to a bastard, and a pious, pure soul. What are you doing here? How did you get through customs?" the man asked, never pausing his writing.

"Um. We haven't died, um, sir. We're...visitors," Auranna said.

"One of those idiotic metal bands, no doubt. I've shooed out so many musicians over the centuries, I should set up a sign. Maybe I'll nail it to Paganini's forehead right outside that door. Now if you please, we are very busy here."

"Who...are you?" Stephanie asked.

He sighed but kept writing.

"I am Marlowe Goethe. I keep track of the souls sold to our Lord, and the lawyers behind me codify the contracts before they are sent to Him for a final signature. Now, if you please."

Levi couldn't believe his ears. He wondered how he'd incorporate all of this into a sermon. Of course, the reality of it was horrifying, a perfect metaphor in front of his very eyes, but he'd have to find a way to convey it so that he wasn't dismissed as exaggerating by his congregation.

"Souls sold? Do you remember all of them, or is there a file system or something?" Auranna asked.

Marlow Goethe sighed and yelled for one of the lawyers to come to his desk.

"Marshawn, will you please answer these bothersome visitors' questions so I may get back to work? Thank you!"

The young lawyer smiled and gestured for them to follow him away from Goethe's desk.

"Another metal band come to sell their souls for greater guitar skills and worldwide fame? I love it! Your ilk makes up about nine percent of the souls we deal in. So much raw passion. Such inconsequential power to grant for an eternity of our Lord's possession, to do with as He pleases."

"Um, Marshawn, we're not here to sell our souls. I don't even have one," Auranna said. "We were guided here by my grandmother. Perhaps you can find my soul here, though? Or my contract? Auranna Korpela?"

"Sure thing! Let's have a look, shall we?"

Marshawn led them through the aisles of wailing souls struggling against their restraints.

"Um, is this going to take much longer?" Stephanie asked.

"Are you in a hurry? Time has no meaning, and we don't have computers down here. If Hell were on Earth, so much of this would be unnecessary! But then I'd be out of a job..."

"You...get paid?" Levi asked.

"Lawyers get paid in...less pain...than the others, as long as we work for it. Don't laugh too quickly. It's not that much less pain. And we're still in Hell, so... Sort of takes the punchline out of the joke, right?"

"Not really. People like you screwed us over our first record deal," Stephanie said. "Desmond told that fucker to 'go to Hell.'"

"S'all part of the job, miss. Too bad you didn't have a better one on your side. I'd have got you—"

"Okay, Fletcher Reede. Just help us find my soul," Auranna said.

"What do you suppose Goethe meant when he said 'the soul belonging to a bastard?'" Rachel asked Marshawn.

"You're one of the souls that slipped through by the machinations of those below Satan—the ones cast out when God purged Heaven of the non-lickspittles."

"What does that mean?" Rachel asked.

"What are you hung up on?"

"You're saying Satan doesn't own my soul?"

"Not at all, ma'am. You aren't a true demon."

"There are *others* who buy souls?" Levi pushed to keep the conversation going.

"Oh yes. They are often the quite-desperate type, as well. They'll buy weak souls who sell for ridiculous reasons, such as another bite of delicious cheesecake, or one single night with a beautiful person—which often lasts all of twenty seconds for the males, and not even a hint of an orgasm for the females. Tickets to a single regular season sporting event. An extra snow day to delay a homework assignment. Imagine anything someone might pray to God for, however trivial, and an equal, if not higher, number of people will sell their soul for it."

"People's prayers are not trivial," Levi admonished. "There is often more behind them than the words convey."

Marshawn put his hands up and smiled.

"S'all the same to us down here, my friend. And there's a third of all the angels who once resided in Heaven who were cast out and will buy these 'trivial' souls to build armies to fight Satan for supremacy.

"See, early on Satan knew He would be overwhelmed by these bargains, so He outsourced the 'lesser ones' to some of His friends, and the other cast-out angels took much of it up on their own. The problem with God is that he doesn't ever outsource prayers. So many go unanswered not from 'lack of caring' as it's often said by disgruntled mortals, but because most people are dead before his attention ever turns to them."

Auranna stopped and sat down, holding her hands to her forehead.

"We still looking for your soul, ma'am?" Marshawn paused in his walk and came back to them.

"Whose souls are in this warehouse? I mean, who do they 'belong' to?"

"Why, our Lord Satan, ma'am."

"If the one who took Rachel's soul is not Satan, then we're wasting time. My soul resides with the same bastard. You don't keep records of the fallen angels' souls other than Satan's, correct?"

"That's correct, ma'am."

"Fuck!" Auranna hit her head with her fists. Levi grabbed her hands and helped her to her feet.

"Auranna, I'm sure this is all very meaningful to you, but you told me we were here to find my daughter. Is this helping us right now?"

Auranna let the frustration over their wasted efforts go as she met Levi's eyes.

"I'm sorry, Pastor. You're right. Rachel and I are being selfish. We should have turned back hours ago. This knowledge doesn't help us free those souls whether they're owned by Satan or not. But at least we know we're wasting our time here. Satan must not have dominion over Abigail and Rebecca. But we still need to find the forest."

Marshawn guided them back towards the exit, then stopped six mutilated mortals short of the end of the aisle. He looked down at the back of the soul in front of him and traced the contract carved into its flesh.

"Ah! Korpela! How fortuitous! Oh, but alas, it is not Auranna. I apologize, ma'am."

"Is it Fiia? That's my grandmother's name!"

"No, it's not Fiia, either. It's Pihla."

Auranna covered her mouth with her hand and tears evaporated off of her cheeks as quickly as they streamed out.

"*Äiti!*"

Auranna knelt to look the hunched soul in her eyes, but it was clear that she was nothing more than a mindless husk.

"Who is eye-tee?" Levi asked.

Auranna sniffed and put her head against the hollow woman's head.

"My mother."

Stephanie lowered herself next to Auranna and hugged her tight. Rachel put her hand on Auranna's shoulder.

"What does her contract say, Marshawn? Why did she sell her soul to Him?" Auranna asked, consumed by long-repressed bereavement over her mother's disappearance.

"'I, Pihla Korpela, sell my soul to His Lord Satan Helel Baphomet Diabolos, in exchange for the protection of my daughter Auranna Korpela's soul from all corruption from Him and His fallen brethren on Earth and in Hell. May her grandmother Fiia Korpela's authorized deal with any others of the fallen ones not overrule the protection codified in this contract, signed before our Lord.' Then there's her signature, Marlowe Goethe's, and Satan's, neat as a bow."

Auranna shook with dry sobs. Levi put his hand on her head and said a small, silent prayer for her mother.

"I'm sorry our time together has come to an end," Marshawn said. "If there are no other questions, I'll bid you a good eternity."

"The forest," Levi said. "There is a forest we're trying to get to. Is there a faster way we could get there besides walking?"

"I suppose that could be arranged. Which forest are you hoping to enter?"

Levi and Marshawn looked at Auranna in question. She shook her head.

"I don't know what any other forest would be like... Mine makes you cold but the air is hot. It swallows you whole with no exit. You're surrounded by orange lights that lead you to whichever is the most relevant or talkative demon of their army at the time. It must be ruled over by one of the fallen angels."

"I'm sorry, ma'am, none of that is enough for me to help you."

They walked to the exit door, frustrated and drained. Auranna snapped her fingers.

"Marshawn! Wait, come back!"

He returned in good cheer, happy for more distractions from his eternal boredom and pain.

"Our name, Korpela—it means 'dark forest' in Finnish. Are these forests tagged somehow?"

Marshawn gave them a sympathetic look, like a doctor giving unwelcome news to a waiting room filled with a patient's family.

"I'm afraid—the scene inside here notwithstanding—Hell is not as organized as all that. There are no maps, there are no road signs, there are no posts in front of forests with names on them. I am eternally sorry I couldn't be of more help to you."

"One last thing, Marshawn," Stephanie said. "Is there at least a way back up to the top of the cliff?"

"Oh, well certainly! Come outside with me. I'm overjoyed to provide some measure of help today after so much disappointment."

Marshawn cupped his hands and called to the top of the building: "Abaddon! Devland! Helmer! Runihura!"

Four terrible winged figures that resembled gargoyles descended from the top of the warehouse.

"Was that some sort of Satanic Santa Claus call for his 'reindeer?'" Stephanie asked.

"They will take you to the top of the cliffs. Safe passage, friends!"

Marshawn waved as the gargoyles picked them up in their claws and made for the cliff that Rachel and Stephanie had fallen down without grace. The beasts dropped them at the cliff's edge, then flew off and out of sight over the black plains.

CHAPTER TWENTY-TWO

ROTA

WHEEL OF TORMENT

AURANNA GREW IMPATIENT AT LEVI'S protestations on the way back to their portal. He finally complied with their empty-handed return when she showed him three of the empty canteens, and the half-full fourth.

"I promise you I'm not done, Pastor. I plan to take this straight to the source, now that I know we're not dealing with Satan Himself anymore. I will try to find a landmark within the dreamworld that can guide us. Perhaps I can prompt the fallen angel to say something relevant or the souls inside will help us."

"I thought you would never return there after last time," Stephanie said from her back.

"Things are different now, Steph. I will endure anything that fake-Satan throws at me."

"I'll be there with you, my Queen," Stephanie said as she kissed Auranna's ear.

"Not this time. I'll take the good pastor with me. We need

complete concentration, and your leg is a hindrance, to put it bluntly."

Up the path along the ridge, her grandmother stood vigil in front of the portal. Auranna's blood boiled at the sight of her. She offered the last two drinks of water to Stephanie and Levi and let her rage carry her the rest of the way.

At the portal, Stephanie climbed on Rachel's back and they passed through together. Levi looked at Auranna with a sympathetic, pleading quality that she couldn't deal with in the moment. She shoved him through before he said another word, then turned to her *mummo*.

"*Akka*! What did you do to my *äiti*? To your own *tytär*?"

Her grandmother didn't move. Auranna knocked away her gnarled staff, then grabbed her robes and twisted them. The crone put up no resistance. Auranna pushed her towards the edge of the cliff.

"What was she protecting me from? Why did she name you in the contract? What deal did you make with the fallen angel?"

Her grandmother's head lowered.

"Was that sadness, *mummo*? Regret? What did you do to her?" Auranna screamed into the void under the hood.

Auranna knew she wouldn't ever hear a word in return, which angered her even more. She wanted to shove her fingers through the barbs in her lips, rip her jaw open, and force the answers out of her. Murderous intent crossed her mind; to throw her grandmother's body over the cliff. But then, she wasn't just her grandmother anymore and she'd likely escape the fall in a puff of smoke. Auranna backed up, then cast the crone to the ground in a heap.

"*Rakastin häntä niin paljon*! I loved her so much! How could you take her away from me?"

Auranna raised her guitar—blacker than the black sky she held it up against—and brought it down repeatedly on the mound of rags and bones that was once her *mummo*. There were no muffled sounds of pain nor protest. A soft, cold hand brushed across the top of her foot just as Auranna turned to leave her grandmother behind for good. She looked down at the skeletal fingers of the monster that had taught her everything she knew on the guitar.

The touch was almost…affectionate.

"It's too late for that, *mummo*. Continue to burn."

Auranna kicked the hand away and went through the portal.

Auranna brushed off Rachel and Stephanie as they attempted to catch and pull her from the fire. Carrie rushed over with a fresh change of clothes as their Hell-fashioned garb turned to ashes, but Auranna held up her hand. She stormed onto the bus and got into the shower, not bothering to wait for it to warm up, and cried beneath the water until she pruned up and dried out like the husk of her mother.

In a fresh In This Moment T-shirt, jeans, and a straight, high ponytail, she approached Levi as he recounted their experience to Lisa in the living area of the bus. Lisa asked questions breathlessly, eagerly gathering a fresh perspective from someone she hadn't interviewed hundreds of times that year and didn't give her sarcastic answers as Alex had.

"Are you prepared to die for Abigail, Pastor?" Auranna interrupted, annoying Lisa.

"Of course. Would I have followed you to Hell if I wasn't?"

"That was a walk in the park, Levi. And you didn't believe us even as you approached the flames of the inverted cross.

Knowing you can trust me now and I have no reason to exaggerate, you must know where your daughter is right now will hurt. It will hurt so much you'll wish you were dead, and you may wish for others to die in your stead. You may beg for it, because it will feel like an eternity. I am a queen down there but that offers me no exceptions. If anything, I've only been tortured more uniquely. Physically. Verbally. Sexually. Psychologically. And yet there is no imagination on Earth that can conjure that suffering accurately. They will delight in your pain more; I am sure of it—a man of the cloth. Their enemy.

"I don't wish to see you broken. I don't wish to watch what they will do to you—what they'll force me to see them do to you. They'll do it all in front of Abigail, and even with all this I tell you, that isn't the worst of it. The worst is the knowledge that Abigail has already gone through everything I told you, and you will see her in a broken state that will never not know such pain. She will be changed. Maybe not right away, but for the rest of her life she will remember it, and so will you.

"You may find solace in the understanding that you will not actually die when I take you to the dreamworld. You will wake as if from a nightmare, but you will remember every pain inflicted, of every kind, for quite some time. I am 'used' to all this and yet almost every part of me wants to stop helping you, to stop looking for a way to help my fans, Rachel, Stephanie, to stop all this bullshit, if it meant I would never have to go back there again.

"But I am prepared to die for my band, my friends, and my fans. For the short time I met her, I considered Abby a friend and we both know she's a fan. I consider you a friend. I will do this for you and her. But none of that is as important as understanding what it means when I ask you: Are you prepared to die for Abigail?"

Stephanie buried her head in Rachel's single broken wing

and sniffed. Rachel humored her for a moment before pulling her out and kept her at arm's length. Carrie and Desmond wiped away a couple of tears. Even Lisa sniffled while twirling a finger in her hair. Alex put his cold hand on Levi's shoulder.

"I am prepared to die, Auranna Korpela, for my daughter and her friend."

Auranna nodded and called Gerald on her phone.

"Hi, Gerry. Are you in town picking up supplies? I'd like you to pick up a lemon, an apple, and pineapple from the store. Thank you."

Auranna ignored the perplexed looks on everyone's faces and texted a message to him to clarify: *Ask for those things at an army surplus store. Pick up one of each. I will pay you back if you have to 'convince' the clerk to give you the real ones. They CANNOT be inert. Expect a much larger bonus at the end of the tour for this favor, my friend.*

"Pastor, if you want to bring anything with you, it will travel with us. I'm bringing one of the spare guitars and the fruit. Carrie, take Stephanie into town to get her leg fixed up. Rachel, figure a way to get Alex to stop bleeding all over the place. Desmond, see if the techs can work these dents out of my guitar. I want it ready to go for the show tomorrow night. Lisa and Joel, can either of you tell me where my antibiotics are? I seem to have misplaced them. Maybe the camera footage will help."

"How can you think of a show during all this?" Levi asked.

"The fans are my 'flock.' I won't fail them here on Earth any more than the ones trapped in Hell. I'm sure I don't need to explain myself further to you."

Auranna sensed Levi tense up as he lowered himself to lay at her side on the big bed. A satchel with the fruit and one of the throw-away emergency guitars were strapped across her Ghost T-shirt. The pastor clutched a large bible he brought from town to replace the little pocket one he'd dropped inside Hell.

"Relax, Pastor. Imagining and bracing for the pain is futile. I need you to concentrate on Abigail and Rebecca. I will do the same. We must be in contact when we fall asleep. Here."

She reached for his hand and laced their fingers together.

"How am I going to fall asleep?"

"Before we try sleeping pills, I want you to keep concentrating on the girls. They need you now."

"Is sleep really part of the…ritual?"

"I don't know. That's the only way I've gotten there, except when I took Stephanie and Desmond. That might have had more to do with Rachel's presence. I wish I didn't sound like I was making this all up as we go along…"

She began to hum as she would for Stephanie. Levi turned to look at her.

"It's in the background, Levi. Focus on the girls. Not on me."

She hummed "Spirit in the Sky" for a while until she drifted off to an undesired sleep.

Auranna grabbed Levi's shirt and pulled him back to her.

"Do not be so eager to enter that forest, Pastor. Time has no meaning here, much like the other place. Do you remember everything I told you in the bus?"

"I believe so. I'm thankful our clothes didn't burn off this time."

"They may not be on you long. The imps' claws make short work of fabric. As we get closer to that forest, I fret I haven't prepared you well enough for—"

"Your eyes communicated everything while you were warning me this morning. I am prepared."

"No, you're not, but I admire your courage. Anyway, things may happen to you, to me, to us, to Abby and Becky...I want you to know I will not feel less about you if you do or say anything that you think might save you."

"What will you do with the guitar?"

"I don't know. It soothes me to feel the strings under my fingers, as much as your bible soothes you. Having an anchor to something you love helps in the worst of times, wouldn't you agree, Pastor?"

Levi looked around again, then turned towards the forest and clutched his bible to his chest. Auranna put her hand on his shoulder, and they ventured into the enveloping black trunks.

– Pastor, think about Abigail and Rebecca as much as possible. Walk towards one of the lights until one approaches. –

He took several steps and despaired when the lights wouldn't respond.

– Do not give up. I have banished over a thousand souls

that make up these lights. Do not think about the things crawling over your skin. Ignore the red eyes in the canopy. Think only of your daughter. –

The Queen brings more fools to torture.

She bears worse torture than all.

She deserves it. Anger consumes her now. She will blunder and fail them all.

Her resolve strengthens. She will understand why she must take up her crown.

Deluded. Foolish. Vain. Selfish.

After what could have been minutes or hours of overlapping debates by the piercing whispers of the imps, a light finally moved closer. Levi ran for it, breaking free of Auranna's grip on his shoulder. She nearly crashed into him when he stopped short of the glowing orange sphere.

The sphere grew larger. It resembled a rubber band ball, in both color and the texture of hundreds of elastics overlapping each other. A smaller orange sphere birthed from the bottom of the larger, expanding sphere and acted as a spotlight for Auranna and Levi to see the being before them. Thousands of eyes lined each band.

Our Queen, we are overjoyed to see You! Father, we lament your presence.

– Abigail! Rebecca! I hear you! Are you inside the sphere? Why do you lament me? –

We are the sphere. And we are compelled to inflict pain by Him.

– Abby, Becky, you don't have to! Please fight against the urge to harm your father. Pastor, whatever you need to say, say it before he takes them away! –

– Abigail. Rebecca. You have been made an Ophanim! A Throne! A Wheel! You are an angel second only to God Himself! Pray to Him! Speak with Him! –

Our Lord will punish us for praying to your lord. He has done so for an eternity.

– God hears you! He feels your pain! I feel the pain behind

your voices! –

You do not, father. And god does not. But you will.

– You are a protector! You are strong! The fallen angel you think you serve was a fool to turn you into an angel of God! You can break free! –

We are not literal angels. You are a fool for coming here.

The sphere shrank to the size of Auranna and Levi, then hovered above them as if held by...

The wind violently plucked Levi from the ground. Auranna wasn't fast enough to grab his flailing hands, but even if she had, it wouldn't have saved him. Father and daughter disappeared through the canopy.

Alone, the imps spared Auranna no torture. Panting and pained from thousands of cuts and tears, she lay on her back, waiting for Levi to be thrown back down to the forest floor and join her.

She pulled the guitar neck out of her abdomen with difficulty, yanking a portion of intestine with it, and laid it across her torso. Catguts ran through her mind, then she remembered it had been only sheep and cow intestines that were used as early instrument strings. She plucked her intestine but there was only a sickening squelch where she morbidly expected a musical note.

Auranna grimaced as she moved aside her intestine to grasp the neck of her guitar. She plucked several songs with her fingernails, annoyed that she didn't affix a pick through the strings over the headstock. Not that she couldn't play without a pick; it simply hurt more when she had hundreds of cuts and the music vibrated through every incision; through her hands, up her arm, into her heart.

Auranna played every song of Black Aura's debut album in order. Each time she finished a song, it saddened her to imagine what the fallen angel was doing to the girls and Levi, and that she had no way of knowing how long it would last, or what was in store for her turn. She played the same album in double time, then quadruple time. Amused through the pain and the flesh of her fingers sloughing off, she played the songs in reverse order, and her finger bones became more effective picks. On the third playthrough, boredom took over and she played the next song backwards. It filled her with sorrow, reversing the song from when Abigail and Rebecca were taken right before her eyes.

Somehow the song sounded more beautiful to her that way. She hummed with the notes backwards. It was like a whole new language. She had to bring the new playstyle to the band, to see if they'd join her in making an experimental album.

Something unlocked in her thoughts while reverse-playing. All of the people she banished were brought to Hell by *her music*. It wasn't a matter of standing in that spot. The music had to cause that spot to activate.

For ten years, the music carried the band forward, always letting the news of their fans' disappearances pass through them as an inevitability, just as she'd come to think of all the times she'd been pulled into the dreamworld against her will. It all seemed inevitable, and she had no control over any of it, so why act worried?

Playing the same songs, over and over, throughout ten years with the band—it was all they bothered with. Fans grew restless if they tried something new, so they always stuck to what was on the released albums. No experimentation. No live jamming.

Except the last concert when she broke the mold, played her new solo instrumental, and smashed a guitar to bits, eliciting a response unlike anything she'd ever experienced. Now, playing her music in reverse... It was fresh. Exotic. They were all the same notes being used, and yet...

What are you doing? How is this happening?

The fallen angel's voice smashed into her head, interrupting her.

What did you do? How did you break my control? Where are the girls and pastor? Answer me!

The red eyes descended and loomed over Auranna's body.

What did you do?

What had she done? He lost them?

– You can't find them? –

Do not play coy with me. Tell me what you did with them.

Auranna could only guess in the moment, but it clicked in place what she had been doing when he interrupted her.

– I've learned to transport people throughout Hell. I can now effectively lead our army, dropping soldiers into places our enemy won't see coming. I'm so close to perfecting it. I wanted to test it tonight. Once it's ready, I'll be back to lead. –

The angry air squeezed around her. She played another song backwards and the air's force disappeared. Taking advantage of the unexpected swap in power dynamics, Auranna reached into her satchel.

– My Lord, do You know about the fruit in my satchel? It may be the knowledge You are seeking. –

His eyes flared with rage and squinted at her.

Why would I ever fear fruit? You are deceiving me. Your punishment will be like nothing you have ever known.

– I do not doubt that, my Lord. –

She pulled out the apple-shaped grenade, holding it upwards between the eyes after pulling its pin.

– If you were truly Satan, you would know how much knowledge comes with fruit. –

The grenade exploded in the palm of her hand, bursting shrapnel and flames into the red eyes and tearing through her arm, body, and mind.

CHAPTER TWENTY-THREE

RETROSUS

BACKWARD LOGIC

AURANNA WOKE WITH A VIOLENT start much like those she'd get on a normal night, before deep sleep had set in and something in a dream triggered her reflexes; a ball thrown at her head or trying to catch herself from falling. She bucked off the two bodies tangled and stretched across her and Levi on the bed.

"Ow! What was that?" one of the bodies whined.

Levi felt all over his body, flexing what were broken bones only a moment before. Auranna peered down between her feet to see two naked young ladies helping each other off the floor and Carrie bringing blankets to them. Auranna rolled on top of Levi and smiled down at him, her long ash blond hair providing a veil of privacy for those behind her. When he tried to get up, she pressed him back down, keeping him from seeing too much too soon.

"Patience is a virtue, isn't it, Pastor?"

"They're decent now, Aura," Carrie said.

Auranna kissed Levi's cheek and rolled off of him. She sprawled out on the bed, staring at the ceiling and basking in the joyful noise of their reunion.

Auranna had never been hugged so many times in a day as by Levi, Abigail, and Rebecca before Abigail's mother arrived. After the girls were nearly hugged to death themselves, Levi pulled Auranna aside.

"No more hugs, Pastor. You're all squeezing the metal right out of me."

"Auranna, if you need my help to rescue the others, please call me. I can't repay you in any other way. The power of prayer was with us. You'll need my help, and I don't think you'll want to find another person of faith to try to convince, if you should find yourself in a desperate hour. You'll never walk alone. You can always get a hold of me."

Auranna cocked her eyebrow and glanced down at her Ghost T-shirt. *There's no way he could have known those lyrics... Of course not.* She shook her head at the thought, then shook Levi's hand.

"Thank you, Levi. I've got your number and will call if needed. If you ever want to talk to someone about what you saw or what you felt, or anything else that bastard did or said, you know I won't laugh or disbelieve you. The only way I've remained sane so long through all this is by utilizing my music and band as an outlet."

The girls interrupted one last time to hug them both, then piled into the family car. Abigail's mother was more than eager to get the girls home, forget the nightmare, and leave the tour bus behind.

Stephanie hobbled over in a walking boot supporting a proper cast. Auranna put her arm around Stephanie's shoulders as the car disappeared from sight.

"I heard a little of that. Was that all you needed? Prayer?" Stephanie scoffed.

"Hell no! But I didn't want to spoil their moment."

"Oh good. You know, even the way you talk has changed so much lately, just like those demons and Rachel. I wasn't sure if you were going to tell us you're preparing to convert us to a Christian rock band or request we all become actual demons… Anyway, are you going to brief us on how you did it, then?"

"Yes. I'll give you all my instructions soon. Meanwhile, we need to figure out how to get to that God-damned forest, wherever it is in the real Hell."

For the following show Auranna directed the roadies to put up another heavy obstacle on "the spot." Enough bolstering her army. She knew what would be in store for her when she went to sleep, but resolved to put up with it for the endgame she had in sight.

Stephanie's walking boot allowed her some freedom of movement, but she kept to only one mosh pit for the duration of the show. Fans fought to get rowdy with her, and she obliged as best she could. Rachel gave up on trying to hide Alex's unhealing wounds and applied tourniquets to his arms and neck. He hadn't died of blood loss yet, so he shrugged when she made a joke, in her way, about cutting off the flow altogether. Throughout the day he didn't feel anything differently, so they left the scarves tied on while he played, too. Alex's change from living, to dead, to living in a dead body confused them all, but Auranna was thankful they could at least converse as usual and he still hit all his notes.

Desmond became more himself the further his mind got from the memory of his journey in the dreamworld. He and Lisa hid themselves less once Auranna knew, and they endured excessive ribbing from Stephanie and Alex.

After the show, Stephanie said she didn't feel like fooling around with the awkwardness of the giant walking boot and went straight to the bus in hopes of helping it heal faster. She didn't register the pain, but she didn't like the loss of mobility during the show. As much as she couldn't feel it, pushing things farther than she already did was liable to make the bone set poorly.

Auranna and Carrie removed their corpse paint and attire in the dressing room together.

"Carrie... I've been trying to think of the best way to ask you this, but I haven't come up with anything, so here it goes: Will you go to Hell with me?"

"I'd love to, but I was asked by a senior and he rented the limo already."

Auranna backhanded Carrie's arm and laughed, then leaned against the table, crossing her arms.

"I honestly didn't want to involve you in any of this. I didn't want to involve any of you but look at where we are. And now I believe I've found the key to bringing our fans back from Hell, and I need you. *They* need you."

"I know I'm in your metal band, Aura, and all that entails, but I'm a scaredy-cat. The way you and Stephanie described the pain... I couldn't survive any of that."

"We're still alive. And it's not *my* metal band. It's *our* metal band. They're our fans. They're your fans. I'm not saying that to guilt you into helping. I'm saying that because you are as much a part of the band as I am, as the others are. If I felt I could do this alone and take all the pain on myself, I would, willingly, to protect everyone I care about. But I believe we'll be more effective together than I would be solo—just how we are as a band."

"That's touching. Doesn't make me want to go to Hell, though. Especially after your speech to the pastor."

"Okay, Carrie. I do understand. I've said I would never force anyone to go there, not even my worst enemies. Well, I'll see you on the bus."

Auranna crouched next to Carrie's bed as the bus drove to the next town. She thought of her grandmother while touching Carrie's shoulder. The drowsiness from her after-show teas and the weight of the guitar on her back helped push her to sleep. Gerald swerved to miss something on the road, causing Auranna's hand to slip over Carrie's breast.

Carrie's eyes flew open and she shot up, clutching her chest with both hands.

"What the hell are you doing, Aura? Over ten years I never thought you'd try something like that! Stephanie since she's changed, I would have believed, but I thought you respected me more than to touch me in my fucking sleep."

"That was an accident, Carrie. I merely meant to touch your shoulder. I beseech your mercy and ask that you accept my contrition."

"Why are you talking like that? Why are my boobs so cold? I don't see my breath in the air. Why is it so dark outside...?"

Auranna lowered her head in shame.

"You didn't..."

"Carebear—"

"Don't you fucking 'Carebear' me! You said you'd never force your worst enemies to come here! What the fuck am I, then?"

"You're one of my best friends. And what I actually said was I'd never put any of you through the torture of this place if I could help it, and I intend to keep my promise. I meant every word I said about needing your help to free our fans. I was afraid that if you weren't going to help us my plan would never work..."

"None of this had anything to do with me! It's *your* situation! *You* sold your stupid soul to become a Metal God! Not me!"

"I did not sell my soul. My soul was taken from me for someone else's stupid deal. I'm dealing with the consequences and trying to keep others from paying for them on my behalf."

"Again, what does that make me then?" Carrie stormed around the bus, looking for anyone else to talk to, or shout at. She threw objects around when it fully sunk in that they were alone in some kind of Hell and there was no good way of waking up from the situation.

"Carrie, I want you to do something. Grab a knife from the kitchenette, please. I want you to stab me. I will show you that ultimately you have nothing to fear here."

Carrie pulled out a long chef's blade and looked at it, then Auranna. Auranna stretched the V-neck of her Blasphemy T-shirt to expose the upper half of her chest. Carrie rushed forward and stabbed her. It was quick but it certainly wasn't once. The coroners would have called it a crime of passion, the wounds feverish and sporadically scattered across the torso. Carrie dropped the knife after a dozen or so stabbings and held her blood-covered hands to her mouth as she took in what she'd done. Auranna coughed up black ooze.

"I meant, like, once, Carebear."

Auranna smiled through the black liquid pushing between her gritted teeth.

"It doesn't hurt?"

"It hurts terribly. But I won't die, and when we wake up, the wounds will be gone. The memory of them—and that look in your eyes—won't disappear so miraculously, but I'll live, and you'll realize you haven't actually stabbed me."

Carrie picked up the knife again and pressed it into her arm. She dropped it before it broke the skin.

"I'm so sorry, Aura, I didn't realize how much—"

"I asked you to do it, sweetheart. Now let's move on. I need you to do me a big favor and listen to the rules of this place—not that you aren't already doing me a big favor by being here. Always, always keep in the back of your mind that this is not the end, or eternal for that matter, because it feels that way sometimes. We will be back on the bus at some point as if time hasn't even moved. That said, here's how things work as far as I can tell..."

After Carrie's orientation, Auranna approached the opening of the forest with more confidence now that she had a pick with her. She positioned the guitar in front of her and held out her elbow for Carrie to grab, then walked inside.

Carrie recoiled at the red eyes peeking out among the black branches.

She brings another slave. Another she doesn't care about.
She loves them all. She will save them all.
Delusional—

Auranna played a random song from their catalog backwards and watched the imps skitter off. The familiar sensation of insects and other creepy crawlies over her lower extremities were gone as well.

– You're getting off pretty easy, Carebear. No snake bites or octopus hickies. –

– Oh my God! That feels so strange! –

– You don't need to shout. I can hear you at any volume. –

– Sorry. So, when does an orange light approach us? –

– They're not marked. I just have to... Wait. Do you see that one that's slightly whiter than the others? I'll wager that's the one we seek. –

The light reacted to them differently than the others ever had. Instead of waiting for them to slog through whatever horrors it kept in company, it approached them. Auranna's eyes grew wide at this unexpected circumstance and readied the guitar in case of a sudden onslaught.

The light fell to the ground in front of them and illuminated her *mummo*. Carrie held Auranna's arm tighter.

Tyhmä lapsi.

– *Mummo*, I grow tired, please use English. –

Foolish child. You withheld another payment. He will punish you for many eternities.

– No, he won't. It's time for us to march against his enemy. I'll lead them. But we must prepare. I wish to speak with him. –

– What are you talking about, Aura? – Carrie asked.

It pained Auranna to deceive Carrie, but she needed her genuine reaction to seal the illusion Auranna was trying to sell. If Carrie knew what she had planned, she might give it away by thinking it in front of them. Carrie was also the only one passive enough not to foil Auranna's plan by fighting back.

– Quiet, slave. Speak when spoken to in the presence of my grandmother and our lord. –

Carrie's grip loosened on Auranna's elbow, but Auranna squeezed her muscles and pulled Carrie closer to her side.

– Call him forth, Fiia. The time grows near. –

Her grandmother disappeared into the blackness, taking

the light with her. Carrie yelped as the wind pulled her away from Auranna. Before getting dragged into the air more than a few feet, Auranna played another of their songs backwards. The wind dropped Carrie and she crawled back to Auranna and hugged her leg. Auranna put the quick thrill of Carrie's hand wrapped around her inner thigh out of her mind and stared defiantly at the angry red eyes manifested before them.

– No more, my lord. You will not abuse me or my slaves again. I call upon you to prepare my army. Gather them in the forest. –

The wind probed around her, searching for an opening to grab and punish her. She concentrated on not flubbing the backwards notes.

Amusing. You wish to lead the charge against my enemy? You have embraced your purpose and endeavor to earn back your soul? Defeat my enemies and it will be within your grasp.

– Wonderful. Now I need three things from you before I can hope to begin our conquest. First, I must know the location of this forest in Hell. How may I lead if I don't know how to get here? –

I shall station some of your conscripts at the entrance.

– That's not enough, my lord. I require a beacon against the black sky to guide me. Do you wish me to get lost in Hell and die from dehydration before I ever reach you? –

It shall be done.

– Thank you. Second, my band of slaves will join me. I will use them to strengthen my army and move soldiers about the battlefield in less than the blink of an eye. You will give them the same protection you will give me so I can lead most effectively and efficiently. They can't be worried you will harm them when they arrive, or their performance will suffer. –

You are trying my patience, but I will acquiesce to speed my victory.

– Finally, I request that you tell me why you own my grandmother's soul. What did she buy from you? –

What all talentless musicians are willing to sell their souls for.

– I may have guessed as much, but how do you come to possess *my* soul, then? –

You do not require this knowledge to lead.

– Knowledge wins wars, oversights cause downfalls. I know my soul is protected, but I don't understand how it came into your possess— –

Enough. Seek the forest and prepare to lead.

– Let me speak with my grandmother one more time, my lord. –

Enough! You may avoid your punishment now, but when I find the way through your protection you will pay for every single impertinency! Begone!

Auranna woke with her hand still lingering over Carrie's breast. Carrie gasped and rolled out of the bed. Auranna held her hand out for assistance, kneeling awkwardly on the floor, but Carrie pushed her down instead. Carrie ran back to the other beds, waking their bandmates up.

"Guys! Guys! Wake up! Auranna has damned us all! We're her slaves! She's sold her soul to lead an army in Hell! We're all fucked!"

Rachel clip-clopped over from the living area and grabbed both of Carrie's arms.

"Do not blaspheme our Queen."

"It's alright, Rachel," Auranna said as she picked herself

up off the floor. "Carrie, I'm so sorry. I needed your genuine reaction to sell the plan. You were perfect. As for what the plan is, all of you gather around. Our ritual will involve blasphemous prayers..."

CHAPTER TWENTY-FOUR
Negotium

Soulful Negotiations

THE BASTARD FALLEN ANGEL—WHOSE pronouns Auranna no longer capitalized in earnest—had been too cagey when she brought up her soul in the dreamworld for her to glean any useful information. It bugged her the more she thought about it. She decided she'd talk to Marlowe Goethe or Marshawn before bringing the whole band down with her to Hell—maybe they could shed some light on her soul's situation.

At the next tour site, before anyone woke up and once Gerald went to sleep, Auranna slipped off the bus. Under the cover of pre-dawn she sneaked to an unoccupied area of the field and set up an inverted cross. She lit it and began to remove her clothes when a voice from behind startled her.

"Heading off to Hell alone?" Lisa asked. Joel stood behind her while recording, her ever-present shadow.

Auranna lowered her shirt and sighed.

"What do you want, Lisa? I'm in a hurry."

"Stephanie forgot to take this camera with her last time. Can you please take it with you and record what you see?"

"Why don't you send Joel in with me?"

"He's a wuss. Doesn't want to get flayed or impaled or whatever the hell else goes on in Hell."

"And you?"

"I'm the director. That's not my job."

Auranna smiled at Joel's eye-roll.

"Give it to me, then. I'll put one of these canteens beneath my armpit."

"That's the spirit! Give it to her, Joel."

"One condition, you two. Stop recording me when I undress. You got enough of the nudity already."

"Sure thing. Turn it off, Joel," Lisa said, twirling her hair with a finger like no one knew what that meant by then.

Auranna removed her clothes, picked up two canteens and the camera, and walked into the fire.

She didn't disappear and reappear in Hell so much as walk straight into the burning pile of wood and fall backwards, out of the pit and into the dew-covered grass. The cross only went up to her chest but she smelled burning hair. She felt her eyebrows and ponytail then slapped between her legs when she realized where the odor actually came from.

"Are you alright? That looked and smells like it hurt," Lisa said as she picked Auranna up by the armpits.

"I'm okay. I wonder if I didn't make the cross tall enough? I don't believe Stephanie bothered measuring before..."

Rachel approached from the bus while Auranna pulled her clothes back on.

"Did I miss something, Rachel? The portal didn't appear."

"When I went through the first time, Your grandmother brought me and guided me through. Each time we went afterwards, she was there. Perhaps it is anchored to her. I do not know why it would not work now."

"Oh. This is my fault, then. I may have shut the way for

good after coming back the last time."

"Why do You seek passage back to Hell alone? Shall I accompany You, my Queen?"

"I would be glad for your company, Rachel, but for your broken wings. I would have preferred to get in and out quickly. But now..."

Auranna ate breakfast at a diner alone in an Agalloch T-shirt. It was easy to dismiss Lisa and Joel from following her by saying she was only getting breakfast and a bikini wax to fix what the pyre had done. Rachel had been harder to dissuade, but she reluctantly obeyed her queen in the end. After she'd filled her stomach, Auranna needed answers. She searched her phone for a local psychic and found one. She walked for a mile before finding an unlit open sign and a note on the door that said the psychic was on vacation.

Dejected and frustrated, she walked to the outskirts of town, then into a wooded area, hoping nature would offer some hint of a clue. It occurred to her she could pull up dozens of "paths to Hell" on her phone, but she didn't have time to go down rabbit holes that would more likely than not lead to nothing. She could call Pastor Levi for guidance, but he knew as much as she did at that point about how to get to Hell.

Suicide crossed her mind, but she dashed that thought quickly. Alex was a lucky bastard. And she didn't want to come out of it in the sort of living Hell he came out of it in, though he seemed to have kept his good humor. Auranna also crossed the dreamworld off the list. She needed to get to Hell without the fallen angel or her grandmother's knowledge.

A fallen log in the forest provided a brief respite. She lay back on it and stared into the canopy, wracking her brain. It was like being back in the dreamworld, desperately conjuring lyrical prayers that did absolutely nothing to help other than to pass painful eternity.

She wondered how Robert Johnson knew which Crossroads to go to in order to make his deal with the devil. Or was it Tommy Johnson? Maybe there was a portal there she could use. Would the devil they'd talked to come to her? Or another demon? Would it care she didn't have a soul to barter? She stopped thinking too much about it after a moment of clarity. All the Crossroads gave the Johnsons was the blues.

As it always did if her mind wasn't focused on a specific task, music crowded out all other thoughts. Her lips moved with lyrics, but only a whisper escaped. She sang Black Aura, other bands' music, and new music she would have furiously jotted down in her notebook if she hadn't chucked it out of the bus on that midnight highway.

A fallen tree branch cracked a few dozen feet away. Auranna lolled her head to the side to see a magnificent black stag at full alert from stepping on the branch. His deep black eyes met hers for a breathless minute. She would have given up a lot to scratch his muzzle. As much as she adored animals of all types, they gave her a wide berth. Before, she passed it off as having strange pheromones, if only to make herself feel better for scaring so many of them off. When that black adder passed through her arm, it stung worse than if it'd bitten her.

In a perverse way, she welcomed the animal attacks in the dreamworld. They hurt unbearably, but it was the closest animals ever got to her. When Stephanie had been going on about bunny rabbits, Auranna cursed herself for not thinking of that sooner.

Now, she realized as she shared the moment with the majestic stag, it sensed her aura, and that was what frightened animals away. It made perfect sense. Animals could intuit and sense things humans couldn't. They knew she was trouble.

A semi-truck back along the main road downshifted as it eased into town, causing the stag to bound deeper into the forest and disappear. Auranna sat up and thought more about its blackness and eyes. It reminded her of the goat imagery from Bathory merchandise. She laughed at the ludicrous thought that if she were a cartoon, a light bulb would have popped into existence above her head.

She pulled out her cell phone and sighed in relief at the two out of four bars for service, then dialed an old friend.

"Anders! How the hell are you? ... I apologize for calling you so early in the morning in Sweden. Thank you for taking it, though. I need your help. Well, I need Bathory's help, if you catch my drift. ... The way we used before is closed to me now. I fucked up. What can you tell me about the way Devil's Sorrow travels to Hell?"

After a stop to pick up some supplies, Auranna checked into a roadside motel. It smelled funny and seemed like the cleaning staff only came through once a week, if that. She made a mental note to give a nicer bonus than the previous year to the bus cleaning crew once the tour ended.

She moved some furniture to the side of the room and took

a painting down from the wall. Her phone chimed and Anders' email came through with scanned photos of the Latin passages and symbols to use to draw a portal to and from Hell. The portal would stay open both ways as long as the symbols drawn on the surface were left undisturbed.

Anders recommended chalk; easier to clean up afterwards, he'd said. Then he recommended permanent marker to draw coordinates, symbols, and the phrases required on her skin since she could lose the cell phone in Hell, and paper might burn up as easy as clothing. She remembered that pocket bible surviving with Pastor Levi, but what if that was protected by Heaven? She didn't muddy the waters bringing it up to Anders, and decided it was better to not chance unholy paper going up in flames. Besides, the motel room's bible that she could have experimented with appeared to be stolen, perhaps by a young teenager dreaming of metal godhood...

The more information Anders gave her, the more Auranna believed she and Stephanie had done absolutely no witchcraft of their own to get to Hell before; it had all been her grandmother.

Getting coordinates close to the Soul Warehouse would be relatively easy—Anders had already travelled there with his band, and she didn't need to spend valuable time explaining the location to him. The damned lawyer, Marshawn, had said they weren't the only ones to find that warehouse, after all. She needed to recite a long, specific phrase while imagining the place she wanted to go. It worked like how she gained an audience with certain beings in the dreamworld.

After drawing the symbols in a circle on the wall, she called Anders to go over a final check to make sure she didn't miss anything. She didn't plan to be gone long, so didn't prepare any water.

Auranna took a few deep breaths and stepped through the wall.

The warehouse stood only a half mile away. Close enough, Auranna thought, then dropped her arms in annoyance at her clothes burning off again. Why didn't she take advantage of the hotel room and take them off before walking into the portal? If she didn't have a dozen other things on her mind at the time…

She sighed and took note of the portal's location. On the walk to the warehouse, Auranna looked for anything to cover up; she didn't want to have a conversation naked. The hairband holding her ponytail had burned off, so she positioned her long, wavy hair over her chest. Among the myriad of horrors that reached for her as she journeyed through Hell, a particularly aggressive monstrosity managed to grab her upper leg. She kicked it away, then tore its meager, tattered rags away from its skin. The fabric was only long enough to tie a weak knot around her waist. Close enough, she thought again, and continued on her way.

After several more skirmishes with horrid, forlorn demons, she made it to the warehouse. When she entered, Marlowe Goethe worked as diligently as before and didn't bother looking up as she approached his desk.

"Mr. Goethe, I request to speak with His Infernal Majesty, if you please."

"That 'love metal' band from your homeland that perverted the pentagram? They don't live far from you. Why come all the way here to—"

"Please, sir. I'd love to see them again, but I didn't mean

H.I.M. I meant *Him*. Your boss. Your Lord. *Our* Lord. Beezle-fucking-bub. How do I obtain an audience with Him?"

"You have no soul to barter, Miss Korpela. He will be uninterested in speaking with you."

"I believe He will, soul or not."

"One of His intermediaries will be the judge of that. You are not an exception simply because you've misplaced the essence of your humanity."

"Please, no intermediaries. Will it hurt you to grant this request?"

"It certainly will if He believes I've wasted His time."

"It will not be a waste of our Lord's time, I promise."

"You have nothing to back your promise, as I said. Now leave me to my work. The lottery in one of the Earth countries has crossed an historic threshold and millions of fools are practically throwing their souls at us. Most of them have already sold their souls for other nonsense, so it takes a little time to sort through them all for that lucky winner."

Auranna pushed off of the desk and looked around. She didn't think it would help, but she walked to her mother's husk. It was still bent naked over a sawhorse-like structure with her hands and feet shackled by chains to the floor, providing no slack.

When Auranna knelt down to look at her face to face, the eyes had more life in them than they did last time, though not by much. Auranna looked over her body; the contract etched into the flesh of her back, the gruesome signatures slashed at the bottom, and many more bruises and wounds than she'd seen before. Was she simply inattentive last time or were the signs of a beating new?

Pihla's expression changed, like she recognized Auranna, but then she turned her head away from her daughter's hopeful gaze. Auranna put her hand on her mother's shoulder.

"*Äiti*, please don't turn away. I haven't seen your face in so long. I'm so sorry for whatever *mummo* did to put you here. I... Why couldn't you have told me what you were planning? I would never have let you throw your soul away for me. At the very least we could have found another way. I know I was only twelve, but... Oh, if only I knew why you did what you did!"

Pihla didn't look at her, but her skin shuddered beneath Auranna's touch. A few tears dropped to the floor and sizzled away. Auranna laid down and positioned herself underneath her mother's face. Pihla had been more beautiful than Auranna or her grandmother. She could see it even in the dark, reddish glow of the warehouse and the advanced aging done to her skin by Hell's atmosphere and the gravity of such an abominable, torturous position.

"*Äiti*, can't you look at me? I haven't seen you in eighteen years, yet I've seen *mummo* several times since her death. I might have killed her for good, by the way. I learned about your deal with Satan to protect me from her. When she didn't deny it, and after the harsh words she had for you and me, I snapped... I beat her with my guitar. I think she's dead because the portal to get here was gone when I tried it this morning."

Pihla's tears fell onto Auranna's cheeks and sizzled.

"I'm sorry if my beating *mummo* to a second death saddens you. You would never be here if it was not for her, though. Granted, I never would have found out about my role in damning so many souls to Hell without her guidance. But at least I can still see her in the dreamworld, if I need to again. And I've finally found out how to avoid that fallen bastard's abuse. He can't hurt me anymore.

"I desire to save you, though I don't know how, yet. I promise on my soul—wherever it is—I will save you."

Auranna lifted herself up to Pihla's face and kissed her forehead. Auranna's own tears disappeared in little puffs from her temples. She sniffed and rolled over to look at the chains a little closer. She gave up on the idea that she could help pull her mother's wrists between the shackles; they were clamped tight enough to cut into the flesh.

Someone kicked into her side and fell, landing partially on her and partially on the hard warehouse floor—Marshawn sprawled in the pathway.

"Oh, the soulless one! Welcome back! Sorry to trip over you. I took for granted an eternity of walking up and down these aisles with no obstructions, and I apologize. Entirely my fault. Here, let me help you up!"

Auranna caressed her mother's back once she returned to her feet, hoping her touch provided some small token of solace through such torture.

"What brings you down here, Ms. Korpela? Just visiting your mom?"

"I wish to speak with our Lord. Goethe turned me away."

Her mother stirred under Auranna's fingertips. Auranna thought she must like the contact and continued caressing her back.

"Meeting with the Boss, eh? Can't say it'll be easy. Didn't Goethe mention intermediaries? He's got a lot of them, I'm sure one is around here somewhere..."

"I don't want to speak to intermediaries. I want to speak to Him directly. I need a favor from Him."

Marshawn's eyes grew wide and he laughed a big, hearty laugh, as if he hadn't heard a joke that good in a century.

"A favor? He doesn't do favors. He bargains. He buys. He doesn't entertain anything outside of that. I'm afraid that without your—"

"—without my soul. I get it already. Isn't there anything I can do? The matter I wish to discuss is of great importance to Him, really."

"You could walk to Him, but that could take years. He's deep down there, across the Plains, across the Desert, across the Frozen Tundra. I don't know why He likes it so cold, to be honest."

"Is there a spell I could cast or a chant that would put me in front of Him?"

"Even if there were, you'd freeze on the spot. You think this heat is unbearable? At least we can function here. Paying a visit to the Prince in person is perilous and pointless."

Auranna sighed in defeat.

"Alright, I give up, can you arrange for this intermediary, then?"

"No, but Goethe can. I'll let him know!"

Marshawn left the aisle and walked with purpose towards Goethe's desk. Auranna was about to follow when fingers caress the top of her foot. She looked down to see her mother's hand, reaching for her with all the length she could muster against the taut shackles.

"I will see you again, *Äiti*. I love you."

Auranna bent and kissed her mother's shoulder, then followed Marshawn to Goethe's desk.

"Your intermediary will meet you outside. I certainly hope you do not plan to waste His time, as He will punish all three of us if you displease Him," Goethe loathed to inform her.

"Understood, sir. Thank you. Thank you, Marshawn."

Auranna leaned against the outside of the building for the intermediary. The monstrosities that populated the grounds of Hell oozed closer to her as she waited. Every couple of minutes she moved a little further down the wall to evade them. After what must have been an hour, she had the thought that they might be herding her somewhere. She walked along the side of the building for a quarter of a mile before thirst crept up on her. Not knowing how much further she had to travel, she looked back to the approximate location of the portal.

Her audience would have to wait. How arrogant was it to not bring a canteen? To assume her sojourn to Hell would be as quick as an errand to pick up an energy drink from the convenience store? She turned back, stepping over, around, and on the slow denizens of Hell. One managed to tangle itself around both of her legs and drop her to the ground. Others were surprisingly quick to clamber over her before she had the chance to get up. Their bodily fluids covered and slowed her. She gagged at the pungent smell and unpleasant feel of their disgusting, slimy bodies.

They were too heavy to push off and she couldn't crawl out from under them; the worsening dehydration had zapped her arm and leg strength. Struggling and continuous gagging intensified the thirst. Her breakfast left her body in a goop she hardly noticed expelling and couldn't discern among the rest of the ooze covering her.

Grappling with suffocation and dehydration, Auranna gave up. She despaired at failing her mother. Her fans. Rachel. Stephanie. The band. All she put herself through to figure most of it out, only to have it all end beneath the slowest, ugliest, most revolting creatures imaginable.

An undignified death for the undisputed Queen of Metal.
What the hell did I lead us to?
She hummed to herself the whole Alice in Chains song that her last thought triggered while she waited for death. What would happen to her if she died in Hell? Would she still end up in the waiting room or was she being punished enough already? She had no soul to transfer from the corporeal world even if she had died on Earth. Would anything happen at all? *This*, for eternity?

Even if that was to be her fate in the afterlife, it was not acceptable to her that it started there. Auranna remonstrated herself that she had given up so easily. If she was going to die, it would be with a guitar over her shoulder in glorious harmony with her bandmates. Any fans not attending the final performance would lament missing her die for her art. Her death would mean something. Not this...lonely and disgusting forfeiture.

With fury she only conjured on stage, she pushed the monstrosities off. Her death growl powered her movements as a martial artist's controlled expulsions of air help them to breathe during combat. The rag tied to her waist got caught and she left it behind, sprinting along the wall back to the entrance with all the energy she'd found in her emergency reserve.

The monstrosities stopped following her once she reached the corner. She collapsed to the fetid earth that clung to the slime of bodily fluids covering her. Her face landed close to something furry and cloven. She craned her head up to see a large demon, similar to Rachel, but without the piercings and wings. Though its body was no less attractive than Rachel's, it was covered in a patchwork of scars, tears, and cuts, all oozing black blood. Its horns curled out of its forehead at different angles, but didn't seem like they grew that way naturally, as if centuries of abuse had positioned them in their current state. Auranna couldn't help but wonder if this one would make her feel as Rachel had, although pleasure was the furthest thing from her body's capacity at the time.

The demon reached down to help Auranna to her feet and assisted further with its long, prehensile tail when she struggled to remain upright.

I am impressed, Auranna Korpela. Lesser beings would have given up.

"Are you...Him? Am I speaking to Him or are you simply a conduit?"

She is named Molly, but you speak to your Lord. Make your plea. I machinate against my brothers and sisters, and I will not allow you to distract my attention long.

"My Lord, if one were to grant You the unsolicited favor of weakening one of Your brothers, would it earn that devoted servant a reward?"

I am not in the reward business, and you have no soul to proffer. I have no need for your service.

"Your Majesty, my soul lies with one of Your brothers. I mean to earn it back."

Your soul once procured—what is it worth to you?

When Auranna entered the portal, she believed the return of her soul was the only thing she would ask for. After being inside the warehouse again...

"Redeem my mother's soul and send her to Heaven, that I will take her place upon my natural death."

Your soul would be more valuable to me than Pihla Korpela's, but it is not corruptible by me and my kin under the terms of the contract. Your mother envisioned this very circumstance and protected you against throwing your soul away for any reason, even to save hers. Regardless, I cannot deliver her to Heaven. That must ever be earned, not granted.

"There must be something I can offer You to grant my wish."

I care only for souls. You cannot offer yours. Find me another.

Before Auranna could answer, the beautiful, mutilated demon disappeared in a puff of smoke. The air of protection Auranna felt in the demon's radius vanished along with them, and the monstrosities surrounding her moved in for another attack.

She ran towards the portal.

Auranna fell through the portal onto the floor, face-first. Dust kicked up from the ancient motel carpet and caused her to sneeze repeatedly. She pushed herself up off the floor and saw all the dust had caked with Hell's dirt onto the slime left all over her body by the monstrosities. Woodstock '94 had cleaner audience members.

She took a long time in the shower. The slime sloughed off easily enough, but covered the tub in colors that reminded her of Stephanie's expulsions on the tour bus. As much as she figured the hotel cleaning staff wouldn't care due to their level of pride in their work already, she felt bad leaving behind such a mess and got down to scrub the muck off the sidewalls, pushing it all down the drain if it didn't want to get there on its own.

Now she needed to solve the naked problem. The single towel she used to dry off wasn't big enough to let her comfortably walk the rest of the way across town back to the tour bus. There were no fancy bathrobes to steal. The shower curtain was translucent. She rolled her eyes at overthinking everything when she noticed the top blanket on the bed. She wrapped it as a makeshift dress beneath her armpits, then lamented becoming the saddest, most pathetic version of Cinderella in history.

Auranna put her wallet and phone in the bag of supplies and left after clearing off the chalk outline of the portal to Hell. On the way back to the tour bus she called the hotel's front desk and settled up over the phone. She admitted to taking the blanket and allowed them to charge the ridiculous fee they attached to the gross, scratchy, ugly dress whose dusty train she dragged behind her.

Auranna boarded the bus to find her bandmates sitting in the living area. They didn't look twice at her strange attire, or the dust and mud that caked her legs, arm, and chest from the walk. It was certainly low on the shock meter for them over the last few weeks—no blood, no viscera, no horror. Even Lisa and Joel didn't keep the camera on her for more than a few seconds, and Auranna thought it was the most "interesting" she'd looked on camera since the tour started.

"Any issues practicing the music like I asked? My army is counting on us," she asked the band.

"A lot of angry looks from the mixers and techs, but we'll be fine. I could play that way in my sleep," Alex said.

"I've got a plan to get us there without all the walking and dehydration. I'll need to make one last trip solo, to smooth out the path. I'll go after the show tonight. Dez and Alex, I'll need your help. Just to get there! Please don't give me those distrustful looks. I'm not going to trick any of you. Carrie, I know I broke your trust, but it—"

"—it was necessary. Like Alex's suicide was necessary. Or you changing Stephanie's personality. Or whatever the hell you did to Rachel," Carrie said with folded arms and hunched shoulders.

"I get it. I do. But let me please insert that you have not suffered even remotely as much as any of them have, Carrie. I protected you. I will protect all of you, now that I know how. I lo—"

"Spare me, Auranna. After this is over, I'm done," Carrie said. "I've already applied to another band on the other side of the world so I can be as far away from you as possible."

"That hurts me more than you stabbing me did, Carrie. We've been together for over ten years. I need all of you. Please don't make tomorrow night our last show together! We have so much more we can do."

"I'm with Carrie, Auranna," Desmond said. "I've seen too much. Felt...too much..."

Tears glistened at the corners of Auranna's eyes, her

pleading lips starting to quiver. Rachel stood up to console her Queen but Auranna waved her off.

"You think I haven't? Everything that's happened to you all has happened thousands of times to me, magnitudes more painful than anything you went through—since I was twelve! We have a chance to end it all tomorrow night. But I can't do it alone…"

"We know you can't," Carrie said. "We're still going to undo what you did to our fans. Once it's done, though…"

"You selfish little twats," Stephanie growled. "She's poured her heart and…whatever is keeping her alive without a soul into this band. Has she ever cheated you out of money? Stopped you from contributing creatively? The big bed rotation was her idea. She cleans the goddamn bathroom like everyone else. She talked some very angry roadies into setting up the show so you could be in the fucking muck with us. She—"

"We get it, Stephanie," Desmond said. "She's a great band leader. Auranna's only half of the problem. Your change has been…jarring, to say the least. Before the change I would have pegged you as the last person in the band to become such a violent, vindictive bitch, even below Carrie. Your face used to turn red as your hair when you said anything worse than the word 'hell.' You were adorable. I don't like you anymore. I don't like Alex anymore. I don't like this band anymore."

A pulsing headache ripped through Auranna's skull. She sat down on the floor and massaged her temples while Stephanie and Alex yelled at Carrie and Desmond. Stephanie slapped Lisa when she wouldn't wipe the smile off her face. The slap succeeded in knocking Lisa's glasses off and cracking them on the floor. Desmond punched Stephanie, knocking her down in front of Joel. Lisa punched Joel for not protecting his boss. Alex had to be restrained by Carrie from going after Desmond, but she looked like she wanted to let him go so he'd get leveled by Desmond, too.

Rachel picked Auranna up from the floor amidst the chaos and led her to the back, hiding Auranna's tears from the rest of the band with her broken wing.

CHAPTER TWENTY-FIVE

ANGELUS

ANGELS AND THEIR CHARIOTS

STEPHANIE LIMPED BACKSTAGE AND TOSSED her replacement bass at the tech's feet rather than handing it over. She pushed roadies and groupies out of the way and slammed the door to the dressing room behind her. The other four already sat on the couch, dejected and miserable.

"That was the worst fucking show I've ever seen," Stephanie said. Her face matched her red hair as she seethed. "*Seen*! Let alone *played*! Is this how you assholes are going to tear this band apart? With the worst performances of your lives? You unprofessional jackasses!"

She limped to the makeup table and flipped it over.

"Half a soul and a broken fucking leg and I had more energy than any of you. You make me sick!"

Stephanie spit on the overturned table and hobbled back out the door. Auranna continued staring at her feet; her eyes unfocused, observing nothing. She'd tapped out of her emotions while she cried in Rachel's arms on the bus before the show and couldn't find the will to care about how awful it had gone. In her moment of weakness, Auranna loved Rachel more than anyone else, but that was a fleeting feeling. Once she returned Stephanie to her old self, her real love for her would return. At least that's what she told herself. Rachel would go back to her life in America, and Auranna would bring Stephanie to Finland and get her reacclimated to the cold and darkness of home.

Only...she wanted to bring all of them with her a few weeks before. Stephanie. Alex. Desmond. Carrie. Her anger at her grandmother boiled over again for getting her tangled up in such a mess. Couldn't she have found some other time and place to put her on the path of saving the fans? *Akka*.

Her soon-to-be-former bandmates got up and wordlessly left the dressing room without undressing or removing their corpse paint. Only Alex remained. He sighed and scooted next to Auranna.

"You saved me from Hell, Aura. I'll never leave you."

It surprised her that she didn't care. Hours before it might have meant something more. She put her wrist over her spiked bracelets and punished herself for not caring. What kind of shit band leader had she become? She'd failed them all. Half of the imps in the dreamworld were right about her. The despair from beneath the obscene monstrosities that'd piled on top of her in Hell returned.

"You're bleeding."

Auranna pressed harder, hoping the bright red would turn darker soon. Alex grabbed her wrist and pulled it away from the crimson-christened spikes, bringing it to his face and smearing her blood over the white of his corpse paint.

"Tell me what you need, my Queen. I hope Desmond was optional for what you had planned."

The sight of Alex—the earnest, educated music

nerd—covered in her blood and calling her his queen brought a twitch to the corner of her mouth. It grew until a smile cracked out from her pursed lips. She leaned over and kissed his cheek.

"You goofy poser."

Auranna and Alex didn't bother undressing from their show attire or washing off their smeared corpse paint and blood. Auranna took the lead as they approached the circle of angels and their chariots. The angels paused from their boozing and idle chatter to regard Auranna in wide-eyed surprise.

"My favorite kind of angels. I wanted to apologize to you all for the poor quality of our show tonight," Auranna said. "I know you traveled a long way to see us."

Alex used their attention on Auranna to sneak around the back of their ring. He crouched down to draw on the ground around one of the Harleys, parked slightly out of the group.

"You know, there are seven charters in Finland. One of them isn't far from my hometown. Let me make our bad performance up to you with tickets to fly to one of their national events next summer. I can get you in contact with some of the members over there."

The angels exchanged skeptical looks. She wasn't sure they were buying it, but they didn't have to for long.

"So, which of you has actually been to Hell?"

"What?" one of the bigger, more dangerous-looking ones said.

"You know. Hell! Isn't that part of your initiation or something? Rotting Christ, it should be! Wouldn't that give you all a leg up at your meetings? You'd shoot right to the top!"

Alex nodded at her and mumbled off the lines from the email Auranna had forwarded to him from Anders.

"Are you threatening us?"

"Of course not! Don't you trust your queen?"

Alex nodded again and hid behind the other bikes as the Harley he encircled with chalk markings disappeared into the ground.

"Hey! What happened to your bike there?" Auranna pointed at the spot.

One of the members pushed through the group and put his hands on his head.

"What the fuck? Where's my fucking bike?"

Auranna squeezed through the onlookers and put her hands on the dismayed biker's back.

"I'll help you find it, friend."

She pushed him into the circle. Next to the circle was the canteen Alex had left for her. She swiped it and stepped down through the portal before anyone else had a chance to stop her.

The biker stood next to his Harley, gaping at the hellscape around him. He held his hands to his ears to block the screams of billions of tormented souls. Auranna arranged her hair over her chest and held the canteen in front of her crotch, then tapped on the man's shoulder. He wheeled around and almost fell backwards off the cliffside. She expected him to be on edge, although not quite so literally. Then she remembered she still had her corpse paint on.

"Whoa whoa, calm down, buddy! I'm not going to harm you. I only need to borrow your ride for a little while."

"Nobody touches my bike."

"I know. That's why I brought you with me. Now take a look around you. Try to keep these landmarks stamped in your mind. I don't have a beacon or anything to bring us back here. Oh, do you carry road flares?"

"The fuck are you talking about, bitch? Where are we? What the hell is going on?"

"Hell is exactly what's going on, sir. You sure whine a lot for a Hell's Angel. Doesn't this excite you? Think of everything you can tell your club when you get back."

He fumbled for something in a compartment of the bike, then pulled a handgun on her.

"Kill me and you won't be able to escape. You'll die of dehydration if those approaching monstrosities don't kill you first. Look at them. That's a horrible way to die. I would know."

"Get me out of here. Now!"

"I will. I need you to give me a ride to that beacon off in the distance. The sooner we get there the sooner we can return to Earth. Get your bike started, please. Time is a factor. I mean, it's not, but your body doesn't know that. It still needs water."

"How long will that canteen last us?"

"Oh, there's no water in it. So, let's get going already."

Likely to his disappointment, Auranna jammed the canteen between his body and hers, leaning back with her hands on the rear fender as they drove. He rumbled through and over many indiscernible beings on the way to the beacon. The creatures' fluids exploded and covered both of them. She didn't mind it so much when she wasn't underneath them, but she couldn't speak for her chauffeur.

"What's your name?" she shouted over the engine's roar.

"Dennis."

"How long have you been an Angel?"

"I'm a Prospect. Not fully patched yet."

"You think this experience will get you your patches?"

"I don't know. A few minutes ago, Hell hadn't crossed my mind. How do you know so much about the Finland groups?"

"I don't know anything about your culture other than you're mostly cool to hang out with backstage and whatever I looked up on my phone before approaching you guys."

"Very manipulative. Guess it worked."

"Guess so."

Auranna cut back on the questions lest she learn something about the man's past or his group's initiation process that would make it easier for her to abandon him. With her band breaking apart at the seams, her capacity for sympathy was at its lowest level. She briefly imagined what it would be like to be St. Peter, deciding who went to Heaven or not. What if he was having a bad day?

"What was wrong with you guys tonight? We've seen a couple of your shows earlier in the tour and the energy was night and day," Dennis asked.

"Band drama. Vacations to Hell. Dead girlfriend and a best friend's suicide. A side demon I may be in love with. Deals with Satan and fallen angels. I killed my grandmother with my guitar. Stuff metal bands have to deal with from time to time, you know?"

"I think I'm going to take us the rest of the way in silence, if you don't mind."

"Silence is a little hard to come by on this thing but suit yourself."

Riding through Hell on a Harley with the hot air blowing through her flowing hair and over her sweaty body gave her a sense of pleasure she hadn't felt in real-Hell yet. The dreamworld occasionally let her have that, especially when she met Rachel. She never thought anything in the real place would be capable of exhilarating her.

If only it was Rachel or Stephanie driving the bike, she'd have something more fun to hang onto than the rear fender, and she wouldn't have to hold back how the vibration against her naked body made her feel. She contemplated buying a Harley once she returned to Finland.

The bike came to a stop in front of the forest that was the source of the beacon. Under Hell's light, the trees were more terrifying than in the dreamworld, like each one possessed the spirit of a different mass murderer. Auranna envisioned darker lyrics for the band's next chapter.

If it survived.

As she got down from the bike, she wiped back a tear reflexively, but it had dried up on her skin and left behind a salty residue. She twisted off the canteen top and a hunk of chalk clattered out. She looked up at the sound of the bike roaring to life again. Dennis smirked over his shoulder.

"That'll teach you to fuck with the Angels!"

He drove back in the direction they'd come from. He'd have an easy enough time following the mangled bodies and tire tracks back to the spot they entered. The portal wasn't on the ground, though. He'd have a hell of a time lifting his bike through it, if he could find it. The markings only showed on the side they were drawn on.

"Impatient idiot," Auranna murmured as she paced out approximately fifteen yards, then a couple extra yards added. She drew a circle and made markings based on the notes Alex wrote on her legs with a waterproof and, thankfully, sweatproof permanent marker. Her legs were the only part of her that weren't either covered in tattoos and brands, or a place she would allow Alex to touch while he drew the markings on her.

Once completed, she moved well away from the large circle and drew a smaller one around herself. She chanted the words Alex wrote on her lower thigh and dropped through.

Rachel waited with Alex near the portal in the parking lot where the Harleys had been. Rachel brought a nicer blanket than the hotel one and wrapped her in it. Auranna reached up and pulled Rachel down by the horn to kiss her on the lips.

"Thank you for following us. You're so thoughtful."

"I live to serve, my Queen."

"Not much longer, I hope. Don't take that the wrong way."

She hugged Alex, thankful his understanding of Anders' notes didn't strand her in Hell like that poor bastard, Dennis.

"I'm glad your notes on my legs were more legible than your carvings on my back. Where'd all the other Hell's Angels go?"

"Ha! They saw that little magic trick and roared off into the night, tails between their legs!"

Alex went to clear the markings on the ground when Auranna caught his sleeve.

"Hold on. I don't know why I'm bothering, though..."

She got down on her stomach next to the portal and poked her head through. There was Dennis, despondent and huddled against his bike near the cliffside.

"Hey, jerk. Would you like a hand back to Earth?"

He jumped out of his skin at her floating corpse-painted head smiling at him. She reached out her hand.

"What about my bike?"

"You lost the opportunity to return with it when you left me behind. Consider it the price for your unnecessary treachery and be thankful I decided to bring you back at all."

She actually believed for a moment he would stay behind with the way he kept looking back and forth between the bike and her outstretched hand.

In the end he chose to grab her hand. With help from Rachel and Alex, they pulled him out, then Alex used his shoe to destroy the circle markings. The three of them turned to go back to the tour bus.

"Hey! What about me?"

"You've got thumbs, Dennis! I suggest you find some branches in the forest over there to cover yourself first!" Auranna called over her shoulder.

Gerald urgently waved for them to hurry and get on once they were within sight of the bus.

"We're on time every night of this tour and you three nearly break the streak with the finish line in sight. Get your asses on here!"

Gerald regarded Auranna as Rachel and Alex climbed aboard.

"What keeps happening to your clothes, kid?"

CHAPTER TWENTY-SIX

CAELUM

SEX AND METAL IN HEAVEN

AURANNA MADE MENTAL NOTES ON where the roadies loaded the battery-powered speakers and amplifiers, freshly charged, as well as the generators, freshly fueled, in case the batteries ran out before their performance ended. The bus was going to be cramped, but soon it would all be over. Lastly, Auranna promised to pay the techs in overtime to re-tune their instruments directly after their last show and put them on the bus.

Stephanie sat on the couch with her arms crossed and her leg petulantly stuck out in the way. Her expression was hostile enough that every roadie remained extra careful not to bump into her cast and none had the guts to complain. Carrie dozed up front in the passenger seat. Desmond sat between Lisa and Joel, talking about their plans after the tour ended later that night. Alex wore headphones and continued to make symphonic sense of what he experienced in Hell.

Rachel stood ever watchful over Auranna since the band's

little brawl the day before. Auranna asked her not to loom over her as if she needed protection from them, but Rachel protested that Desmond had become dangerous. He didn't just hit Stephanie—he slugged her. Auranna reminded Rachel that Stephanie couldn't feel pain and Desmond knew that. Rachel didn't seem to buy it but at least refrained from putting her wing around Auranna whenever Desmond got close.

Auranna may have been fooling herself. She had no way of knowing whether Desmond remembered Stephanie wouldn't feel that hit. He hadn't held back. He also stopped talking to anyone but Carrie and Lisa, which hurt Auranna more than if he'd decked her, too. He and Carrie didn't say one word during sound check, but at least they ran through a few of the songs Auranna requested, much to the confusion of the techs.

Stephanie kept taking her rage out on roadies, techs, and equipment. Auranna spent most of the day apologizing for her and letting them all know that Stephanie only acted out because the tour coming to an end deeply saddened her. No one outside the bus knew that it might also be the end of Black Aura. Would it be at the end of three encores? One? Would Carrie and Desmond even come out at all?

Would they earn the privilege to do so in the first place? If it went anything like their most recent show, Auranna knew there would be no encores, no accolades, no pride to propel them back onto the stage.

When the last roadie left the bus, Auranna stood in the center of the living area and shrieked at her highest octave. Joel dropped his camera on the ground in surprise, earning a punch in the arm from Lisa. Alex ripped his headphones off and stood at attention. Carrie hit her shins against the dashboard and cursed, then sulked to join the gathering. Stephanie unfolded her arms and sat up straight. Desmond continued scowling.

Auranna pushed the loose strands of hair that fell in front of her eye away and stared at each of her bandmates.

"If you're expecting a rousing speech from your band leader after that debacle of a performance last night—to snap you out of your malaise—you're about to be disappointed. I need you to keep your minds on something, though. Our fans... *Your* fans are counting on you. Not only in Hell, but on Earth. You disgrace yourself when you don't give your all for them. I don't know about the rest of you, but I'll damn myself to Hell for eternity before I go out and put on a show like that one ever again."

Before any of them added their two cents, Auranna left the bus and joined the staff selling merchandise as the gates opened.

During every melodic break in all the thrashing, screeching, and snarling, Auranna let her tears flow freely. Black Aura and their fans were everything to her. The looks on each face at the merchandise stand reminded her of that, over and over. It was a lovely bonus that her tears made the corpse paint run, further animating her appearance throughout the performance.

When her voice cracked, she leaned into the rawness and used it to artistic effect, weaving in and out of sadness and anger, infusing the lyrics with profundity. Her black guitar from Hell took in all her emotions, allowing her to play as if possessed. She brought many fans to tears when her sensational solos appeared to torture her, as if her despair were a demon fighting to escape her body.

More than once after their most experimentally fast tempos she collapsed in exhaustion. More than once her fans brought her back to her feet. Each time she rose felt more leaden than the last, until she lost all strength to go on.

The fans were so unsure if Auranna had died that they only looked down at her crumpled form, afraid she might be broken, and touching would only break her further. Alex and Stephanie pressed towards their Queen as soon as it was clear she wasn't getting back up, and they were eventually joined by Carrie and Desmond.

Rachel pushed through the crowd, not caring that her top snagged on a metalhead's spiked leather jacket and ripped it off. She picked Auranna up in her arms and carried her limp body towards the stage, guitar hanging from her shoulder high enough to clear the ground. The sudden, somber silence rang through every ear louder than the cranked-up speakers had over the previous two hours.

Rachel laid Auranna down at center stage and backed away. Two medics burst from backstage, but Stephanie waved them off. Stephanie was more worried than the rest of them, but Auranna had told them to keep the music as top priority the last time she collapsed. Carrie made to stoop down and check Auranna's pulse but Stephanie got between them.

"Get to your instruments. She needs you," Stephanie whispered to her bandmates.

Carrie and Desmond left the stage. Stephanie and Alex stood in their old spots onstage to the right and left of Auranna. Stephanie palm-muted a heartbeat. Alex followed. Desmond and Carrie returned from backstage followed by techs wheeling out the backup drum kit and keyboard, then added to the band's growing heartbeat.

The crowd took up chanting "Aura" to the rhythm.

"Au-ra. Au-ra. Au-ra."

The roadies and techs joined in. Lisa backhanded Joel's arm when he took up the call, but even she got caught up in it.

"Au-ra. Au-ra. Au-ra."

Auranna's eyes opened to painful, blinding sunlight. White clouds surrounded her legs, greatly disorienting her as she got used to the sensation of nothing beneath her feet. Her black show attire stood out starkly against the white of it all. A line hundreds of thousands of people long filed past her towards a gate guarded by two beings that consisted of a dozen white wings each, then a white man in a white robe with a white beard at a drab pedestal blocking the gate.

The line moved forward quickly. For every one person who earned a second glance from the white man, one thousand people fell through a trap door in front of the pedestal. For every five people the white man looked at twice, four of them were pushed back into the trap door by the winged monstrosities. The one in five-thousand-and-five entered the gate jubilantly, never giving a millisecond of thought to the people behind.

Most in the line knew where they were going well before the trap door pitilessly swallowed them. Some were sweating bullets, preparing little speeches and recantations to earn forgiveness. The white man listened to none of them.

"They know what they did," Auranna murmured.

Why was she outside of the line? Shouldn't she have appeared at the end of it like the rest of the new arrivals?

You are not dead, Auranna Korpela.

Auranna spun around but there was no one near her.

"Who was that? Where are you?"

You have work to do. And even had you died, you have no soul. This is all in your head.

"Wait, just this heavenly cliché? Or 'all' as in all the Hell stuff, too? Are you telling me I'm going to disappoint my fans and wake up from an extended dream sequence back at the beginning of the band's existence and all of this was for nothing?"

Yes.

"'Yes,' what? To the first question? Jesus Christ, you're as vague and confusing as the demons through that trap door!"

I am not He. And you really ought to learn to ask one question at a time. The nearer you get to meaning, the sooner you will discover that you are dreaming.

"Who are you?"

I am Archangel Jerahmeel—I have been an interested follower of your life since you were twelve. And recently a pastor has prayed persistently for your lost soul and that you may complete your mission with Godspeed.

"So, you're a fan and you're answering his prayers?"

Not at all. You require no guidance from us. I only surmised you would like to know before you wake up. And...your music is not so...encouraged here.

"That's right. Metal... It's from Hell, after all. I guess you have to follow the rules pretty tenaciously up here. Did you mean to bring up Black Sabbath a minute ago, though? Or were you trying to confuse me with the whole 'dream' aspect?

"No answer, huh? Have it your way. Hey, are people allowed to have sex on the other side of those gates? Asking for a friend..."

Auranna thought she heard a small, satisfied chuckle tucked in the silent answer. The people in the line stopped shuffling forward, turned their heads to her in unison, then chanted her name. Auranna took a few steps backward in surprise, and the last step sent her over the edge of the cloud, plummeting through the sky.

Her eyes throbbed to the pulsing stage. Fuzzy forms of fluorescent white moved in and out of her vision, disappearing and reappearing wherever her eyes moved. The chant of her name continued unabated from where it began in the clouds. After a few moments of paralysis, her fingers curled one by one around the neck of her guitar. In her periphery Stephanie and Alex plucked in sync with her heartbeat. Desmond's kick drum and Carrie's keyboard were discernible in the background.

The chant morphed into cheers as her arms regained feeling and positioned her guitar across her torso. While her legs took a little bit longer to wake up, she wove a new melodic intro from the heartbeat to their favorite encore-closing song, skipping the planned final song on the playlist.

The crowd swelled with each of her movements. She

pushed herself up so her legs splayed in a "W" shape. Her hair hung over her face as she launched from the unplanned intro to the real song. Her other senses took in the fans' electricity and her bandmates' efforts while her hair blocked her vision. It was perfect harmony: singing and chanting from the crowd; her guitar responding beneath her fingers preternaturally and the strands of her hair sticking in her smeared corpse paint; her body regaining strength so she could stand; the smell of a thousand colognes, perfumes, deodorants, and armpits in the sweaty mass in front of her; the wooden stage vibrating its dust beneath the onslaught of the speaker system; and the taste of the dried salt of her tears crusting over her cheeks and lips.

Thunderous, raucous exuberance deafened the venue after the speakers ceased their ferocious euphonious amplification. Auranna was eager to conclude their business in Hell, but she knew if the band didn't satisfy the crowd's lust for more, there was potential for a riot.

While her bandmates played off the fake goodbyes and thank yous requisite of every band that knows full well they're coming back out, Auranna swung her guitar around to rest upside down across her back. She grabbed a water bottle backstage and poured it over her face and hair. A roadie offered her a towel and she wiped off all the corpse paint, then tied her wet hair up in a high ponytail.

Auranna had never performed as a member of Black Aura without corpse paint. She'd been seen in public by random fans at signing or interview events, but the number of fans that had ever seen her real face was miniscule compared to the vast amount of them. Her bandmates noticed as soon as they joined her backstage and did the same, sensing the finality of the gesture.

When they returned to the stage, Auranna tried her best to fight through the dizziness and exhaustion that hadn't magically disappeared when she woke from her...fainting?

Death? Three songs into the second encore, she looked for Rachel. She hadn't moved from the backstage area since Auranna's resurrection, ready to catch her again should she fall. Rachel met Auranna's eyes and knew it was time for the final flourish.

The end of the song required one of Auranna's most technical solos in their catalog, one for which she'd earned a speed title. Her vision blackened halfway through; her legs turned to rubber after three quarters. As she approached the finish, Rachel's bats swarmed around her. So dense no one could see through, Rachel used their cover to enter the cauldron around Auranna's teetering body. Rachel caught Auranna limp in her arms as the final note sounded. The bats disappeared into the night.

Through the final cheers and applause, Stephanie limped to Auranna's utterly spent form in Rachel's arms, kissed her, then left the stage. Alex put Auranna's hand in his for a moment, squeezed, and followed Stephanie. Carrie caressed Auranna's cheek and left with tears in the corners of her eyes. Desmond knelt in front of Auranna's upside down head, put his forehead to hers, then exited.

With help from her tail, Rachel held Auranna's lifeless body into the air, center stage, a sacrifice to Black Aura's fans and the Gods of Metal. Every metalhead in the crowd saluted in their own myriad of ways. Rachel called the bats to cover their withdrawal backstage.

By the time Rachel brought Auranna to the tour bus, the

techs had the band's main instruments re-tuned and placed with the battery-powered equipment. The master tech carefully removed Auranna's guitar from around her torso, did his tuning magic, then placed it with care amongst the other instruments.

In spite of her cast, Stephanie rushed to Auranna's side once Rachel laid her down on the big bed. She put her ear to Auranna's chest, but she heard and felt nothing.

"We must get our Queen to Hell before Her brain dies," Rachel said. "Did you bribe Gerald to stay in town for a few hours?"

"Yes," Stephanie whispered.

"Did Alex finish with the markings around the bus?"

"I did," Alex answered from over Rachel's shoulder. Carrie and Desmond filled out the circle in the cramped space, all of them looking down upon Auranna's deathbed.

"Start reciting. Quickly!" Rachel hissed.

Alex pulled out his phone and chanted the words that would open their passage to Hell. As he finished the last words, everyone but Rachel startled at the sound of a small, forgotten voice from behind them.

"What was all that chanting?"

They turned to find Lisa and Joel still onboard as the light outside changed from starlight black to the dull, reddish glow of Hell.

CHAPTER TWENTY-SEVEN
Salvatio

Imperfect Crescendo

AURANNA WOKE TO THE SOUNDS of Stephanie sniffling, and Lisa and Joel screaming. Desmond attempted to calm them down while Auranna weakly cupped Stephanie's cheek.

"Why so sad, my love?"

Stephanie collapsed across Auranna in an embrace and sobbed heavier. Auranna reached out for Rachel and grasped her clawed hand.

"Looks like I forgot to tell everyone what happens to clothes down here," Auranna said. "Sorry for taking that for granted, guys. Your instruments will work fine for cover if you're feeling like Adam and Eve when they discovered sin."

"Are you okay, Aura?" Carrie asked once she returned with her keytar covering her torso. "Do you think you died?"

"I might have the first time. I'm pretty sure I only fainted the second time."

"Stephanie thought you died," Alex said, covering nothing.

"Is Stephanie a doctor, now?" Auranna asked while rubbing Stephanie's back. "Get up, please, Steph. Let's prepare."

They realized then Stephanie's cast had burned up, and the straps holding the boot together had as well. She grabbed one of the two crutches so she'd have one arm free to carry her bass.

"We're not screwing around here, Aura," Carrie insisted. "Tell me that was planned."

Auranna looked into her eyes once she got up from the bed.

"Did that sort of drama seem like me, Carebear?"

"...I guess not. But I'm worried about what will happen to us here if something were to happen to you. What if we can't get back to the real world?"

"You don't need me to return home, should it come to that. Alex has the chants and markings drawn on his legs as well as mine."

Auranna grabbed her guitar and rested it over her shoulder. Everyone in the bus had already seen her naked at some point or another and she no longer cared about the prying gaze of the billions of souls soughing around Hell. The mission was too important to let prudish thoughts interfere.

Lisa and Joel evidently didn't feel the same as they searched frantically for anything to cover themselves.

"Lisa, Joel, you finally have the opportunity of a lifetime to capture something never before seen on film and you don't even have a camera rolling."

Lisa brushed past Desmond into the bathroom and slammed the door. Her hyperventilating came through loud and clear. Joel regained some of his composure when he realized Alex and Desmond didn't seem to mind losing their clothes, and the majority of the women present weren't interested in what he had dangling between his legs.

"Oh shit. I just thought of something," Stephanie said.

"When we return with the bus our clothes won't reappear."

"I have a roadie guarding a chest with a change of clothes for all of us when we return," Auranna said. "I wasn't counting on two stowaways, but we'll cross that bridge when we come to it."

Lisa came out and stood next to Joel. He gave her a reassuring side-hug around the shoulder.

"Hard to be embarrassed when everyone else is bare-assed, isn't it? Nice tat, by the way."

Lisa glared with an expression only one degree below murderous intent. Rachel put her hand on Auranna's shoulder.

"My Queen, I will go ahead to spread awareness among Your army that You have arrived to lead them to battle. We look forward to vanquishing Your enemy."

Lisa narrowed her eyes at Auranna after Rachel left.

"What did she mean by 'lead them to battle?'"

"Lisa, I'm giving you two choices. You can stay on the bus and return to Earth, or you can follow us and see what Rachel meant. Do what you want, but do not interfere."

"I vote we go back," Joel said.

Lisa looked at each member of the band in turn.

"Joel, you better have a few backup batteries packed on this bus."

Joel sighed. "I want a cut of the documentary."

"You signed an agreement for your salary before we started. Forget it."

"That was before the prospect of filming in Hell. I want twenty-five percent."

"Twenty-five! That's outrageous! Fifteen."

"Twenty-five, or I start smashing the camera."

"Okay, okay! Twenty-fucking-five."

"You all heard that, right?" Joel asked the band.

They nodded while gathering the rest of their instruments. They picked up speakers, amps, and a canteen each.

Desmond enlisted Lisa to help carry his drums. Joel agreed to pull the wheeled generator and whatever could be stacked on it behind him while filming.

Once they cleared the bus and stepped over the markings that Auranna had pre-drawn where the Hell's Angel abandoned her, Alex chanted and sent the bus back to Earth. Auranna led them to the edge of the forest and stopped. She tilted her head to her bandmates.

"Whatever you decide to do after this...I love you all."

Before any of them could reply, Auranna stepped into the black forest.

A small group of animalistic demons gathered inside the entrance. Auranna recognized them from the dreamworld—she'd met each of them at various points since she first involuntarily travelled to the forest. Their forms weren't as scary as they had been in her dreams. She could see them fully thanks to the red glow coming through the canopy, whereas her previous visits had been in near-pitch darkness but for those single orange lights.

The demons approached and grabbed her before she had time to react. She didn't know what good struggling would do—it'd never benefited her much before—so she allowed them to do whatever they were going to do. She feared the violence she had so often experienced at their hands before, but as she braced for the worst, they set her back on her feet.

They had wrapped her in various parts of their bodies: goat fur loin cloth, snake anklets and bracelets, a centipede hairband, and a pair of giant emperor scorpions comfortably sitting over her breasts.

More demons came forward and "clothed" the rest of the band as they too entered the forest. The two-bodied spider approached Auranna and bowed awkwardly.

"Our Queen! We have waited for this day for an eternity. Our Lord has been so overjoyed since You proclaimed Your intention to fight that He has lessened our torture a bit. We are to escort You to Him."

"Thank you. My slaves and I shall follow."

"Your slaves?" Lisa asked.

Stephanie elbowed her in the side and shook her head.

"Don't feel bad, it's all part of the plan."

Lisa scowled, but stopped talking. They passed a thousand demons going deeper into the forest until they came to a clearing encircled by trunks of the ominous trees. In the center, a gorgeous, angelic man sat in a large throne. To his right a smaller throne stood in which an older version of Auranna sat.

The band rubbed their eyes and did double-takes.

"Oh yeah, chin's a little different. Eyebrows, too," Stephanie said after a moment. "Your grandmother before whatever put her in those robes?"

"Yes, my lo—I mean, yes, my slave."

Auranna motioned for the band to stand back while she approached the thrones. A strange sensation crept up her chest the closer she got to the angel—something she had never experienced in her life: attraction to the male form. He overwhelmed her with his beauty, and she began to indulge in her mind giving him everything he wanted.

Her eyes flitted to her grandmother, who was taken from Earth at a relatively young age and seemed to be fully preserved. Stronger than the draw to the gloriously chiseled being to her grandmother's left, Auranna stared at "herself" and came back to who she was, and all the people she was fighting for. She determined to look only at the ground when speaking to the angel.

She knelt before them.

"My lord, I have prepared my slaves to help strike fear and death into the hearts of our enemies. I beg your indulgence as we prepare our ritual."

"What does this ritual do?" the fallen angel asked.

"They'll dance as marionettes to our sound. Command me where you want your army to attack, and I will send them to however many hundreds of locations they're needed. In stealth, they could kill the enemy before they have a chance to react, no matter how many of them there are. I know it will look and sound strange, but I promise you immediate results. When our ritual is finished, my enemy shall know complete and utter defeat."

"Fail me, Auranna Korpela, and your soul will be mine forever. I may not be able to corrupt it, but that will not stop me from devastating your physical body and keeping your soul locked away. You will know torment like no other in Hell has ever known. Your grandmother will join you at my feet as every pain known to man and demon will be inflicted upon you both over ceaseless eternities."

Auranna lowered her head from her kneeling position, hiding her hatred from his enchanting, haunting eyes. She gritted her teeth.

"Then I beseech you, my lord, to shut up so we may begin the fucking ritual."

Her grandmother put her hand on his forearm when he made to stand and smite Auranna for her insolence. Auranna rose and turned to her bandmates, sweat evaporating from her outburst. She hadn't planned to sign her death warrant so soon, but she couldn't hold her tongue at that moment.

An imp approached her from behind the throne with some strange parchments made of human skin. The dried flesh had markings all over it, presumably the locations of "the enemy." She pretended to read it seriously and nodded until the imp scuttled away.

They set up their equipment at the edge of the clearing, facing the center of it. Alex drew with chalk around the band for their planned getaway. The demon army gathered in front of the "stage," coming into the clearing from the forest. They carried various weapons in whatever their misshapen and malformed limbs could hold. Most were terrified, but some were as stoic as Rachel.

When they had all gathered, they bowed before the fallen angel, then turned to face their Queen. Auranna looked at each member of the band and smiled. She raised her pick to Hell's sky.

"Black Aura, take it from the bottom!"

The band blitzed backwards the last song in their catalog. Auranna's heart leapt as dozens of their demonic fandom disappeared from the clearing. With each subsequent song they played, dozens more vanished.

When they came to "Selfish Sacrifice," the first song that Auranna had become aware of the fans being taken, she sighed in relief when the two-headed spider disappeared.

As they continued, an imp approached the throne and said something to the fallen angel that made his face contort with fury. He surely would have put a stop to Auranna's jailbreak if he wasn't rendered powerless by their music. Like any other spectator, he'd have to wait until the end of the show.

A tear evaporated off Auranna's cheek as Rachel disappeared alongside all the other demons condemned by "Obsequious Obeisance."

Between songs Auranna maintained at least one melody backwards while her bandmates drank from their canteens, and they did the same for her. The field and their canteens neared emptiness around the same time. At the conclusion of the last song, all that stood in the clearing were the thrones, the band, and Lisa and Joel huddled behind the speakers. The "clothing" provided by the army had all disappeared along with their respective demons.

Only one of the thrones was still occupied. Where had her grandmother gone?

In answer, one of the speakers exploded, knocking the band to the ground and interrupting their meandering after-performance play. Her grandmother marched toward Auranna from the fiery equipment.

"Alex, the chant!" Auranna cried.

He got one word in before the fallen angel bridged the gap between the throne and band. In a blink he had Alex's throat in his hand. Auranna looked frantically for the correct words on her legs, but the fallen angel gazed at her and the ink burned off her and Alex's flesh, leaving behind second-degree burns.

Stephanie's bass bent and curved around her arms and legs, restraining her and hurting her broken leg. The strings snapped and lashed across her body, bringing her to the ground. Cords from the equipment snaked around Carrie, Desmond, Lisa, and Joel. Through the pain and thrashing, Joel kept the camera in a death grip angled towards Auranna.

The fallen angel dropped Alex on the ground to be assaulted by his own guitar, the same as Stephanie. Auranna's grandmother ran at Auranna with murder in her eyes but the fallen angel used Hell's air to lift her from her path of revenge.

"I told you you would suffer as your bitch granddaughter for failing me."

He broke Fiia's legs and arms and tossed her at Auranna's feet. All the seductive energy that had encircled the angel was gone.

"Saving me for last, bastard?" Auranna spit.

"I'm savoring the hate that half of your band harbors for you for getting them into this. Enough pain for them all and you will see the other two's love for you evaporate alongside their tears.

"Now, you will tell me what you did with my army."

"Imposter, I know you. I told you my enemy would know utter defeat after the ritual."

"I see you have picked up on the vagueness around here. You will answer straight or your torture will start immediately."

"Everything I've learned was from Fiia. She guided me to your scheme and opened portals to and from Hell."

"The hell I did!" Fiia cried.

The fallen angel loomed over her.

"Is this true, Fiia?"

"No! I've never interacted with her except when You were nearby! I tried to get her to lead Your army without telling her why You couldn't do it Yourself. The army's attachment to her music as part of the ritual meant only she could lead them. If she knew all that, she would have simply refused to help at all! All Your years of torture didn't move her to act until it started affecting people in her inner circle."

"*Akka*! Lying bitch!" Auranna yelled. "You've been traveling around Hell in robes and opening and guarding portals! You showed me where the warehouse of souls was! This is all because of you! You must have wanted to escape, but you betrayed your own daughter to do it! You damned her soul and now I've damned you!"

"She's lying, my Lord! I've never wanted to escape! You know why I sold my soul to You! I gave it to You willingly! This little bitch screwed it all up at the first concert I was to send You souls by standing in the spot You designated! I had no idea my daughter had already protected Auranna's soul, and everything would get so royally fucked up!"

"Who else would know about that spot and show it to me?" Auranna asked. "Who would send Rachel to help me? Who would help us in and out of Hell? The old woman was all wrinkled up but looked just...like...*us*..."

Auranna's hand covered her mouth as understanding and regret settled upon her. The fallen angel smirked. Fiia stared up at Auranna with all the hate in Hell.

"None of this would be happening if you hadn't interfered at that first concert after my deal! I always told you to stay backstage during my performances. You couldn't wait to run around in the crowd the first time your mother wasn't there to keep you back! I was punished when our Lord brought me to Hell and transformed my gift into your curse!"

The fallen angel picked Fiia up with his control of the air and threw her into the broken equipment, all the while keeping his grotesque, glorious gaze on Auranna.

"Where's my soul?" she asked.

"It does not matter, child."

Auranna dove for her guitar but it levitated into the air, just out of her grasp. The guitar swung into her face, knocking her to the ground. It rained blows over her body, as she had done to her own mother; her mother who had only meant to protect and guide her. And this same beating was how Auranna had repaid her? Auranna deserved the pain, but the irony hurt as much as the broken bones.

Stephanie struggled to get up, but each movement caused her nothing but more pain and whimpering. Auranna's guitar broke on the last blow. She looked at her suffering friends, then the angel.

"Please, don't take your anger out on them. Let them go. Do what you want with me instead."

"That was already the plan, Auranna Korpela. Making them watch will torture them as much as you."

Auranna screamed as her first eternity of pain commenced in earnest.

CHAPTER TWENTY-EIGHT
SOLUTIO

FIGURE IT OUT FOR YOURSELF

THE FALLEN ANGEL HELD BACK some. Not a whole lot; only enough that Auranna wouldn't be broken to a point of unconsciousness or death. Compared to the dreamworld, which had no such preoccupation with her corporeal health, the real torture wasn't as bad. But it didn't tickle. All her past experiences and Auranna had only ever grown numb to the debasement, not the pain.

Her screams hurt Stephanie and the others deeper than the cuts passing imps left on their flesh; she could see it in their eyes. The fallen angel had been right about that.

Auranna didn't know how long the first bout of torture lasted. Time had no meaning. It was one of the few things she could count on being consistent regardless of the context of her visits. Time incorporeal notwithstanding, she only reasoned it couldn't have been an actual eternity because all but

Alex would have died of thirst.

At that thought the fallen angel unscrewed all the canteens and gave everyone their last sips of remaining water.

"You will not die of dehydration, though you will all certainly beg for death in any form. I will have minions bring forth Hell's water to keep you from dying once this is gone. I promise you will not like the taste or the way it makes your insides feel, but you will not die. What about food, you all cry with apprehension? Done sparingly, I will feed each of you to each other in small enough parts to sustain this merry band over decades."

He flung Auranna's broken mess of a body into the smaller throne and went to work on Fiia. An imp that had been hiding behind the big throne approached her. In her desperation she tried pleading with it.

"Please go to the warehouse of souls and get me Marlowe Goethe or Marshawn. I must speak with our Lord. Our *real* Lord, not this false one."

The imp stared at her with a malicious grin, its teeth dripping, but it didn't advance on her.

"Wouldn't you rather be working for someone more important? Help me destroy this bastard and you can move on to better masters."

The imp hesitated for another moment, then raked its claws along her arms, desecrating her tattoos. As it reached for her face it exploded, spattering her with black, thick blood and innards. The air pulled her back over to the group.

"Nice try, Auranna Korpela. The imps are mindless. They are what became of those who have been tortured for eternity and becoming one is their only way out. The question is how long you can endure the tortures of the underworld before you start begging to become mindless nothings, too."

If he hadn't primed her for an eternity of suffering through a dreamscape of Hell, he may have been right. She never truly got used to any of the pain, but at least during her previous tortures, she always kept the hope that she'd wake up eventually. Perhaps whoever she talked to on those fluffy, boring white clouds in all their vagueness had agreed she was dreaming everything. Who cared if it was like none of these events had ever happened to her fans, and her band's meteoric rise was all an illusion?

It was all she had left—praying she might wake up to an inconsequential life.

***

Black Aura witnessed their leader endure the worst atrocities they could imagine, and countless more that couldn't be scraped from the bottom of anyone's deepest unconscious. There wasn't even the cold comfort of an end in sight, or the thought she would die, sparing her from further suffering.

Stephanie would blame herself for her own eternity for not thinking of prayer sooner. Praying for anything outside of Hell was a hopeless endeavor, but perhaps praying from inside could work? The longer it took for her prayer to go unanswered, though, the more she cried about its overall uselessness.

Movement emerged from the forest. Stephanie hoped for Auranna's salvation, but it was only the imps hauling buckets.

"Say goodbye to your beautiful bodies, Black Aura," the fallen angel remarked, taking a moment from destroying Auranna and Fiia to survey their expressions. "This liquid will slake your thirst but change you from the inside out."

An imp brought a ladle to each of their faces. The fetid

smell gagged them. Just as the ladles touched the band's trembling lips, the imps were all cast back from the clearing and their buckets of water exploded. Stephanie and the fallen angel scanned around in equal confusion.

Two men in tattered suits emerged from the dark forest and approached the menagerie of suffering. Stephanie rejoiced aloud once she discerned their faces.

"Marlowe! Marshawn! You heard me!" she cried before a wallop of air broke her eye socket. Blood ran into her eye, and she couldn't rub it.

"Enough, Xastraneth!" Goethe chastised the beautiful being. "Still lashing out because Archangel Jerahmeel banished you from his dream apprenticeship?"

Xastraneth puffed up his chest, ready to unleash more of Hell's wind like a petulant child, when a hundred pikes manifested, shooting from the ground and air to skewer him.

"Why don't you wait a moment so we may conduct our business? We'll let you get back to it when we're done," Goethe said, then turned his attention to Stephanie.

"Thank you, Marlowe! I pledge to Satan the other half of my soul to stop the torment of Auranna Korpela!"

Goethe chuckled and looked at Auranna's broken form, then back at Stephanie.

"You might be happy to know your soul is whole again. It was refunded to you when that snake fellow returned to Earth. Which would interest us if—"

"I don't care! Take it all! Break me more! Fucking kill me! Please, save Auranna!"

"I hate to burst your noble bubble, Miss Creighton, but our Lord is not interested in your soul. We are quite full, and He will only listen to the most compelling of requests, especially after Auranna wasted His time during their last meeting. You humans can't be trusted to know your worth. He sent us not because of your prayer alone—but because of its connection to her."

Auranna would have smiled if her face didn't feel like a two-hundred-pound weight rested on it. Talking was going to be painful, but this was her only chance for salvation, even if her fate ultimately lay with lawyers.

"I may have wasted His time, Goethe, but He did not waste mine. He asked me to find Him a soul, then He'd grant me a favor for weakening this…Xastraneth. I have held up my end of the bargain, and I have a soul to give Him."

"We're all ears, Miss Korpela."

"Take my grandmother Fiia's soul."

Fiia screamed in protest.

"She already pledged it to Xastraneth," Goethe said while holding his chin.

"Surely our Lord can overrule that?"

"Our Lord doesn't care for the deals between His lesser brethren and desperate soul-sellers."

Do not speak for me.

The terrible voice filled the mortals' minds. They writhed in agony since none of them could reach up to hold their heads.

Auranna Korpela has weakened my enemy, as she promised. I will listen to her request.

"Thank you, my Lord," Auranna said through raspy, broken breaths. "I ask that You take my grandmother, Fiia Korpela's soul, in exchange for safe passage back to Earth for Stephanie, Alex, Carrie, Desmond, Lisa, and Joel."

Goethe procured a still-dripping parchment and pen, then used Marshawn's back to write on.

"If you can conjure parchment and pen, why didn't you summon a desk?" Marshawn folded his arms and shook his head, leaning dutifully forward regardless.

"Quiet. I'm working out the details with our Lord. Have to get the last names right, you know."

Stephanie couldn't believe Auranna's request. She could have saved herself. She could have included herself in the offer! What in Satan's name was she doing?

"Wait! Why not yourself, Aura? Satan! Include Auranna's release in the contract!"

"It's too late, Miss Creighton. The contract is done. I only need her signature," Goethe said.

"Then take my soul like I asked you to so you can save her!"

"Stephanie, my love," Auranna said through more difficulty. "The injuries we suffer here carry over. It's not like the dreamworld. I don't believe I would survive long, and...I can't live like this."

Goethe and Marshawn nodded solemnly. Goethe approached her and knelt down next to Auranna's body.

"If you'll just sign beneath my name..."

Auranna sighed in pain as Goethe jammed the pen into her broken hand and affixed her mangled fingers around the stem.

"Don't make me lean over to the parchment, Marlowe. Bring it to the pen," she moaned.

"No! Don't sign that!" Stephanie and Fiia cried in unison.

"My friends," Auranna said with the last of her strength, "you were my haven in life. You are my haven in death."

Her final words on the matter were pulled from the very song Stephanie and Auranna intended to play at their wedding, something they joked about many times over the last few years. Stephanie wanted to give her lover the ultimate gift by having Ville preside over the ceremony. Why had it always seemed like the timing was too hard to line up; their friends from other bands too hard to book; why had they waited?

Stephanie cried out in despair as their dream was signed away. Her outcry morphed into a guttural scream when Auranna dropped the pen after it slipped off the end of the contract. Fiia disappeared, and Stephanie only caught a glimpse of her Queen for a split second more before she and the others were back on the bus on Earth.

Auranna's broken form lay next to the hundred-pike statue that was Xastraneth. She tried not to think about what would happen to her upon his release.

You need not concern yourself with him any longer, Auranna Korpela.

"What do You mean?" Auranna said through no less pain. Separate from the dreamworld, the trips to the real Hell proved she and her friends were unable to speak through their minds. Satan, however, had no such handicap, and his words were like a vice squeezing her head tighter and tighter, even when it was good news.

I have trapped his essence in the frozen wastelands, deep beneath the ice. He cannot escape.

"Well, thank You, I guess. So...do I just...lay here for eternity?"

I care not what you do with your time here.

"Lovely."

"Umm, my Lord, I'm sorry to interrupt," Goethe said. "I've received word that we don't have a spot in the warehouse for Fiia's soul without expansion. It's been some time since You've taken a deal directly. Souls have lost their quality these last decades. We thought we'd have more time to plan the renovation. I'm afraid we have to invalidate the contract."

"Wait!" Auranna cried. "Trade my mother's spot! Free her from her contract and return her to Earth! Her contract doesn't apply anymore, now that Fiia and Xastraneth's corruption is off the table."

"I don't like the idea of freeing a soul once sold," Goethe said. "What would all the other souls think?"

Auranna's proposition is satisfactory. Free Pihla and chain Fiia to her spot. We will discuss warehouse expansion later. I may wish to conduct a purge in the meantime. There is a certain grade of soul I would like to maintain in the warehouse going forward. Those sinners that blasphemed the Ten Commandments seemed worthy at the time, but humanity has proved it has far worse to offer.

Auranna felt something shift through the perpetual pain she endured. Her insides stopped pulsing with internal bleeding, organs throbbing, broken bones grinding together every time she moved and torn muscles snapping further with every breath. Her skin's tightness loosened, the heaviness of her limbs lifted, and normality returned for the first time in painful ages. She stood up and flexed everything. Waking up and stretching after sleeping in the same position for an entire night was never so exquisite.

"What happened? How is this possible?"

The terrible presence in her mind disappeared. Satan was apparently done with her.

Goethe and Marshawn turned to leave.

"Wait! What just happened?"

"We're very busy. We must start planning for the expansion. Walk with us if you wish," Goethe said.

She fell in beside them.

"Are you going to answer my question?"

"Let me see if I can figure it out, boss," Marshawn intercepted for Goethe, then turned to Auranna with a pensive expression. "While Fiia and Xastraneth were unable to corrupt your soul, they held it from you. The contract said nothing about protecting your body or mind, and they used that against you. Pihla will wish she had been more thorough in her request. Anyway, without their hold over it and Pihla's release, your soul must have returned to you."

"Why am I all healed up? Stephanie wasn't when she got her soul back."

"It's certainly unexpected," Goethe said. "Perhaps a parting gift from our Lord? I can only imagine very few people in His life have ever offered Him a favor and actually followed through on it."

"So, how did Xastraneth or Fiia take hold of my soul to begin with?"

"It had to have been an accident," Marshawn pondered aloud. "Some sort of loophole once your soul was protected from their corruption?"

"Ah. Fiia spoke of me interfering at her first concert. After pledging her soul to Xastraneth, my involvement foiled her deal somehow. Do you think my soul was sent to him, but my mother's protection kept me from being sent to Hell with it, causing the transaction to backfire? Then it was modified to take both body and soul of my fans when Xastraneth transferred the curse to me?"

"Maybe? We weren't there and we don't have the time to monitor every single soul's interaction in the whole world. We're not 'Santa Clause and Partners.' Anyway, what does that matter anymore? You've got it back and you're whole again."

"Except now I'm stuck here. The notes that burned off my legs didn't come back. And without my mother helping to open the portals, I can't get out that way, either."

They cleared the forest at last. A rush of hot air blew past them and scorched the trees, burning the treasonous forest away in an instant.

"Our Lord appreciates you snuffing out resistance to His rule," Goethe announced officiously. "It's not often He can clear the blight of rebellion without significant use and destruction of His own army. That said, we're lawyers, not chauffeurs."

Marshawn snapped his fingers. Two gargoyles flew up from somewhere below the cliffside to pick him and Goethe up.

"Wait! Where am I supposed to go?"

"You aren't shackled," Marshawn said. "Our Lord said He doesn't care what you do here."

"How else can I get out of here?" Auranna yelled through cupped hands as they flew out of her voice's range. She only made out the silhouette of Marshawn shrugging against Hell's red sky before the gargoyles swept down over the cliff and back to their damned warehouse.

The Satanás-ex-machina was complete as far as Hell was concerned. Auranna stared into nothingness for a time, her mind racing for a solution that didn't exist.

She walked in the general direction of Hell's waiting room, as she was unfamiliar with any other places in Hell except the warehouse and the destroyed forest behind her. She wondered if she'd die from thirst or inattention to the monstrosities along the way. Which would be preferable?

The forest!

She ran back to the edge of its charred remains and searched for the markings she'd drawn to transport the bus when that wannabe Hell's Angel abandoned her. She despaired over the large chalk circle, blown away by the air that destroyed the forest.

She drew in the dirt with her finger, hoping her muscle memory would conjure the correct markings. While it worked for the first couple of lines, causing her heart to race in hope, the rest of the design tumbled out of her head like a dream unraveling the more she concentrated on it.

"No, no, no! Come back!" she cried.

She slumped down to the ground and dropped her hands between her knees, then laid back in the dirt. It occurred to her that she still had one more out—her newly-returned soul. But why would she bargain with it, knowing what waited for her in the end? Even when she ended up in Hell after natural death, she didn't want to be chained inside that warehouse for literal eternity. It was out of the question. Not knowing what was behind the door at the end of Hell's processing line was at least preferable to knowing exactly what it was like to be stored away in Satan's stockroom. Would anyone ever visit her?

Slow, squishy movement pulled Auranna away from her overwhelming hopelessness. She turned her head, Hell's dirt and burned twigs tangling in her hair, to see several monstrosities oozing towards her from angles meant to strategically corner her. She preferred dying on her feet to dying beneath those things, she decided.

Auranna salvaged the will to get up and headed in the direction she remembered the Harley bringing her. She found its tracks just beyond the scope of where the wind scorched the forest. She determined to go back to Hell's waiting room. Maybe she could find more information there? Though if it was anything like her first trip to Hell with Stephanie, she'd be dead from thirst well before halfway. Still, it was something, like the hope she always clung to in order to survive the worst of the dreamworld.

What if it was like the gates of Heaven that Alex had joked about and Auranna had dreamed when she fainted at the concert? Perhaps she'd win the afterlife lottery and somehow earn eternity in "the other place."

Thoughts in that vein strengthened her resolve, and she added new motivations to her will to fight on. What if being a living, soulful person again would cause Hell to reject her and send her back to Earth? Then she could mend the broken bonds of her band. She could reconcile with Desmond and Carrie.

She could reunite with Stephanie.

CHAPTER TWENTY-NINE

LIBERANDUM

FINAL DESPERATION

STEPHANIE'S SCREAM CARRIED OVER FROM Hell's void into the bus, deafening her bandmates. With no concern for her broken eye socket, the lashes from her bass's strings, the imps' claw marks, or her broken leg, she grabbed her remaining crutch, pushed past Lisa and Joel, and half-limped, half-slipped out of the bus's front door into the darkness and cool air.

"Your clothes!" Carrie called after her. "Where's the roadie with that chest Aura mentioned?"

Unfazed by the buses of opening bands and roadies that were only beginning to move after their final show, she trekked on. One bus had to screech to a halt as she crossed too close in front. The buses were making their way to the exit of the fenced yard; the fenced yard with no broken or loose boards, it looked like.

Undeterred, Stephanie put her weight into an awkward run with the crutch, crouching down at the last second and throwing her body into what seemed like the loosest board in the row. All she accomplished was nearly dislocating her shoulder and scraping it up badly. Blood dripped down her arm from new wounds and re-opened old ones.

"Steph, what are you doing?" Alex cried as he ran up behind her and grabbed her arms. He had time to clothe himself before he ran after her, but they were already streaked with his undead, black blood from where the imps had slashed at his flesh, as well as the lash-marks from his possessed guitar strings.

Stephanie shrugged out of his grip and kicked at the boards with her good foot while leaning against the crutch. Her futility and lack of strength didn't stop her. After a blitz of useless kicks, the soles of her foot was as bloody as her shoulder.

She stopped for a moment to regain her breath and what little strength she had. Murmurs flanked her as spectators gathered.

"Is she on drugs?"

"She's bleeding..."

"She's fucking feral..."

"Maybe this is her version of trashing a hotel room..."

Carrie arrived at her side and put a hand on Stephanie's bare back. Her clothes bore the same bloody streaks as Alex and Desmond. She held out a fresh stack of clothing. Stephanie swatted them to the grass and shrugged Carrie's hand away, the bones in her shoulder grinding uncomfortably.

"If you want to help, get me a lighter and gasoline."

Carrie reached out again, in hopes of calming her friend, but there was something in Stephanie's voice and eyes. After watching what Auranna had endured for them and that Stephanie was willing to risk her own soul and death to save Auranna, Carrie's heart broke all over again. She pulled her hand back and ran to the roadies to get what Stephanie asked for.

Stephanie threw her other shoulder into the boards, earning a collection of winces and groans from the people behind her when she bounced off the fence and fell to the grass in a heap. Desmond helped her up, looked into her eyes, then nodded. He turned his back to her and unleashed a kick hard enough to dislodge one of the boards. A second kick did the same to a second board.

Alex grabbed one of the boards and swung it like a bat into the gap of the fence, snapping it into two-thirds of its length. Stephanie took the longer board into both hands and lifted it above her head, then stabbed it downwards. She cried out as splinters drove deep into her palms, and the board didn't break the hard ground. Pushing the pain out of her mind, she got down on her knees and dug in the dirt, ignoring the increasingly muddy blood caking her wounds.

"I see what you're doing, Steph," Alex said as he bent down to dig with her. "Hurting yourself isn't helping, though."

"I'd die to save her, Alex. And if I'm gonna die, I'll die with my boots on."

"That's cute. You're not wearing any. Put your clothes on; Joel is filming you."

"I don't have time! Hours are passing in Hell the longer I take to get back there!"

Strong hands grabbed her under her arms and pulled her away from digging, despite her flailing. Desmond put her in an embrace from behind, strong enough to hold her back as a couple of roadies pierced the ground with shovels.

"I understand, Steph," Desmond said hardly above a whisper. "But you saw her after she signed the contract. She was nearly dead. Even if she's still alive…"

"That's all I need, Dezzie. 'If.'"

Alex plunged the fence board into the new hole, then held the smaller board against the lower portion of the taller one. He nodded at Desmond to let Stephanie go, and she fell onto her clothes that Carrie had brought earlier.

Using her bra and an Iron Maiden T-shirt, she tied the boards in an inverted cross.

Lisa put her hand on Stephanie's shoulder as she stood up. Somehow, Lisa still managed to be all-business with her cracked glasses and bloody clothes.

"I'm not supposed to be interacting with you guys in front of the camera, or I would have said something earlier, but I can't let this continue. Auranna tried this alone, and it didn't work."

"She must have done it wrong. Did she do the dance?"

"I thought you said that wasn't—"

"Fuck what I said. It has to work. It has to," Stephanie cried, desperate tears forming at the news of Auranna's failure. But maybe Auranna really did do it wrong? It was still a sliver of hope.

As Carrie lit the fire, Stephanie tried to remember the exact movements she'd shared with her lover. Now that her soul was whole again, she wasn't able to push out the debasing thoughts of people watching her act like a naked fool. Her skin was no less bright red than her hair, as residual embarrassment of so many eyes on her sunk in.

Satisfied that she'd remembered the dance, though awkward and painful, she performed it alone with her broken leg and crutch. Stephanie didn't wait to acknowledge her bandmates—or for them to join—and hobbled as quickly as she could into the burning inverted cross.

Her vision went black. The board hit back as hard as she crashed into it. She smelled burning hair immediately after falling back on her butt.

Undaunted, she turned to Alex, Desmond, and Carrie.

"Guys, I did this with Auranna and it worked. I need a partner. Or at least two of you need to do it. It will work. I promise."

Stephanie didn't appreciate their hesitation, looking

around at the assholes taking in the show with amusement and mortification, but Carrie surprised her by peeling off her clothes first. While she unsnapped her jeans, Alex and Desmond followed suit.

"What the fuck is happening?" and every other iteration of that statement could be heard murmuring through the crowd.

Though she was no Auranna in terms of vocal range, she still quieted the rising rabble by screaming for them all to shut the fuck up.

Black Aura danced around the cross, which began to fall apart as Stephanie's bra and T-shirt did all they could to hold it together.

After completing the dance as best as she could manage, every wound weighing heavier on her by the minute, Stephanie made for the portal again. She nearly concussed herself when the cross didn't budge, and she was thrown on her butt in the grass again.

Her bandmates sighed and put their clothes back on. Stephanie stared into the cross as it fell apart burning and hugged her good knee while the other leg lay out uselessly. Tears began free flowing. Someone laid a blanket around her shoulders, but she didn't care to look around to see who was trying to comfort her. There would be no comfort in her life unless she saw Auranna again. Even if what Desmond said was true... Auranna needed to know her love wasn't one-sided before the end.

Being the last night of the tour, there wasn't a particular hurry to leave, and the buses remained parked while their occupants talked among themselves about Black Aura's bizarre behavior and imminent downfall.

Stephanie didn't care; let them gossip. If only they knew what had happened to their Queen of Metal, they'd be savage, too. She wracked her brain trying to think of a solution. The harder she thought, the more blanks it drew and despair weighed down on her chest.

This was it. It was all she had.

Except...

Shrugging off the blanket, she hobbled back to the bus, ignoring the onlookers who no longer seemed to be fazed by her erratic behavior but for their amused gazes. Inside the bus, she pulled open the cutlery drawer in the kitchenette and grabbed the biggest knife inside.

Holding the knife out, she pushed the painful thought of accidentally missing her heart out of her head and touched the point over it, feeling its rapid beating through the blade and handle.

Missing... There was no life to miss, without Auranna to share it with...

Measure twice, stab once...

She held her arms out straight, clutching the knife handle with both hands, and closed her eyes.

Alex crashed into her side just as her muscles tensed to thrust inwards. She only succeeded in stabbing her shoulder before they fell to the ground.

"Goddamn it," Lisa said at the front of the bus, standing next to Joel and his camera. "That would have been *so good*..."

Alex pushed himself up, looking down over Stephanie.

"You don't want that. Trust me."

"I know. But without her..."

"Yeah."

Alex helped her to her feet and seemed indecisive about what to do with the knife sticking out of her shoulder. She was covered in blood from her ragged shoulders, shredded foot, splintered palms, and the lash marks still oozing from Xastraneth's preshow. Her cheeks were the bed to rivers of salt. Her eyebrows, eyelashes, and the front of her hairline were singed off. Her broken eye socket swelled her eye shut. She more than likely re-damaged her leg but among the plethora of other injuries it was hard to tell. A headache throbbed throughout her skull, more penetrating than Satan's voice.

Stephanie sat down hard at the little dining table bench, rested her forehead against her bleeding palms, and sobbed.

A commotion came from outside the front door. Carrie and Desmond pushed past Lisa and Joel, filming Stephanie's despair. Carrie held hands with someone Stephanie didn't immediately recognize, her vision blurry and distorted. When he came closer, her despair did a one-eighty so quickly that she thought she might have a heart attack.

Anders looked down at her.

"You and Aura are such silly girls," he smiled.

As Alex drew markings on the bus next to Black Aura's logo, Anders explained to the band how concerned he was about Auranna's request for instructions to get to Hell. He detected desperation in her voice even though she tried to play it down. Once she confirmed she was seeing the trip through, Anders boarded the next flight to the US from Sweden and rushed to get to the venue in case he needed to help get her back. She could have flubbed the markings; lost the location of the portal; or any number of outcomes could have befallen her. And once she was in the portal, she couldn't ask for help.

His worry increased as he raced towards the venue, realizing it was their final show of the tour. He arrived at the bus parking lot to find the buses at a standstill and a gaggle of people talking about Stephanie's self-destructive behavior. Carrie and Desmond spotted him looking over the remains of the burnt cross and brought him to the bus after he asked them who had tried the foolhardy, disproven technique to go to Hell.

Alex nodded that the markings on the bus were done. A roadie brought forth all the canteens that could be scrounged from the remaining agreeable tour buses, linked on a chain, and handed it to Anders. Stephanie snatched one in her free hand and hobbled at the fastest speed she could to the center of the markings.

"Thanks for the highway, Anders!" Stephanie yelled as she stepped through the portal into Hell. She took one look back before disappearing and was disappointed to see her bandmates shoe-gazing instead of following her immediately.

Stephanie picked herself up from the dust that settled over her wounds. She pushed the monstrosities away with the crutch as she got her bearings. It was far more difficult than last time as she dealt with the cut in her shoulder. The forest was gone, but there was evidence of an inferno and the remnants of burned stumps. She checked the ground for tracks, but it was hard to pick up any signs with the monstrosities slugging over everything.

Stephanie heartened to the jingle of Anders' chain of canteens as he entered the portal behind her, but she didn't have time to acknowledge the new arrival; was he alone? Did the others follow? It didn't matter. It didn't change what Stephanie had to do.

She investigated closely the debris-ridden ground, channeling her inner bloodhound. A strange track caught her eye—a small tire. Bare feet followed the track. Stephanie's heart leapt. She knew those feet anywhere—the way each toe curled as well as their individual lengths; the feel of every inch of them through the massages they shared in the dressing rooms after countless shows. During some of the wilder nights of her demonic, hyper-sexualized recent existence, her mouth had come to know them intimately. Those were Auranna's feet, without a doubt.

Stephanie didn't waste time trying to reason how Auranna could be on her feet after what they witnessed her experience in the forest clearing. She "ran" up the path, not waiting for any straggling companions that may have followed her. The longer she used the crutch, the closer it came to feeling like a second leg, and her speed eventually picked up.

The tracks were easy enough to follow in the dull red lighting of Hell's sky because of how unusual they were, but she had no way of knowing how long Auranna would have been able to follow the tire tracks without water. How long had it been for Auranna since the band had returned to the bus?

Though hope increased at each step Auranna kept leaving before Stephanie, she tried her best to temper expectations. What if the monstrosities got to Auranna ahead? What if Xastraneth found her, or another fallen angel or demon? What if she lost the path? What if she mis-stepped and tumbled down one of the cliffs?

Stephanie whapped herself across the face with the canteen, trying to jog loose the stupid questions. There was no reason to doubt anything until the tracks stopped.

Stephanie moved for hours, keeping her head down on those beautiful tracks. As long as they continued, she would. If Auranna could get so far without a canteen, Stephanie would suffer through the same thirst and exhaustion. If Auranna could survive, so would she.

As the miles dragged on, though, the thirst became unbearable. Her vision blurred again. Stephanie didn't understand how Auranna could have possibly survived the distance—on top of everything else she'd suffered—yet the tracks continued ever onward. Stephanie took a swig from the canteen and looked behind her. Anders' silhouette was barely discernible, about a quarter of a mile away. Was there more than one figure? Was that even Anders? Could it be a demon tailing her?

Waiting to find out who the figure belonged to wasn't an option. There was a point between dehydration and death that would no longer be gradual. Auranna could die at any moment. If Stephanie waited—even if it only cost her ten minutes—it could mean all the difference in Auranna's survival, when the canteen finally reached her lips.

Reinvigorated, though hungry, Stephanie went on. She remembered Xastraneth's threat to feed themselves to each other. Would that even work? If she reached starvation, could she simply bite into a chunk of her own flesh to sustain herself for a stretch longer of searching? It sounded so stupid in her mind, but the more she thought about it, the more it made sense.

As she hobbled, she nibbled at her cuticles, tearing away the dead flesh around her fingernails. The callouses at the ends of her left fingers provided spiritual nourishment. She imagined strength returning to her with each morsel she swallowed, and her pace quickened.

Another stretch of painful hours, another swig of the canteen. Stephanie winced at several hang nails peeling back to the first knuckle of several of her fingers as she sustained her hunger further.

As she carried on, an idea formed. She worked the splinters out of her palms with her teeth and spat them out, then tore at the loose flesh around the holes. The skin wasn't dead yet, so it stung mercilessly. But she'd seen what Xastraneth had done to Auranna. Recalling Black Aura's lyrics the last ten years, it was clear Auranna had truly suffered far worse in the dreamworld, where death wasn't possible. The discomfort of eating such tiny bits of flesh was nothing in comparison.

Even though Stephanie's soul was whole again, she remembered everything she said and did when it was cut in half: Foul, lewd, lascivious language. Overdriven libido. Heartless jealousy. Attempted murder of Desmond. Her mistreatment of Rachel, who only ever wanted to protect Auranna, and was willing to go back to Hell multiple times to do it. Everything else Stephanie did that was like her deepest, unchecked subconscious being controlled by a petulant, whiny eleven-year-old.

She wished she could apologize to her best friend Desmond. She wished she could call Carrie her "Carebear" again without earning a disapproving look of contempt. She wished she could help Alex solve his undead problem. She wished she could meet Rachel in real life, thank her, and share their love for Auranna instead of hoping to kill each other.

All of this pain was nothing. It was deserved.

If her Queen could survive eighteen years of every imaginable bodily horror, Stephanie would do the same. Even if it took eighteen years to find her—even if she was dead at the end of the trail—at least she could see her one last time.

The canteen had only about a fifth of the water left. She didn't worry about anyone following her anymore. Anders

had more canteens on that chain but she wondered if eating himself had ever occurred to him on any of his extended trips to Hell before. She wondered if she was simply going crazy and the hunger was only in her head. She looked at the small hole in the fleshiest part of her right hand that she'd torn a hunk from with great effort and pain, and imagined it fueled her, even as the few remaining rational thoughts in her head said she was overdoing it. *It's unnecessary. It's futile. It's stupid.*
Fuck you.
She needs you.
You need her.
She would do this for you.
She had done this for you.
She would die for you.
She died for you.
Don't fail her.
Stephanie flew over Auranna's footprints.

Something white in the blackness ahead. Not moving. Splayed on the ground.

Stephanie's hand was a ragged mess that if it grew infected, she may never play bass again—may never still with the strips of tendon she'd pulled away with her teeth. She had stopped drinking in hope of saving the last drops for Auranna.

Her throat was dry as bone; she couldn't call Auranna's name, if that really was her up ahead. The blurry vision returned. Both her legs were in agony. She had stopped sweating long ago. Despite the boost of hope that she'd reached the end of her chase, her good leg gave way and the crutch clattered over the edge of the cliff. She ate a mouthful of Hell's dust on impact.

She crawled forward. Her arms had a little strength left. More than her legs, anyway. All they'd had to do until then was sway back and forth. Now, they put in the effort to match what her legs had given.

Stephanie thought about the canteen. The tiny amount of water left in there...it wasn't enough for both of them. What if something had befallen Anders behind her and there was no water on a chain coming? If he was on the way, would he know to prioritize Auranna?

Closer.

Closer.

Was this the end of Black Aura? If she reached Auranna, would they die alone in Hell? Where were her bandmates? They should have overtaken her long ago. But...they had broken up. They wanted out. Not that Stephanie could blame them after all she did... But...

If only their band was there...

As all extraneous thoughts other than reaching Auranna pushed out of her mind, she was left with one more.

Why did she think she could do any of it without her bandmates?

Auranna startled awake, puzzled that she wasn't dead. She'd given herself over to it. She'd closed her eyes. She'd waited for the monstrosities to finish the job.

She looked down across the pale, dehydrated expanse of her body to see an unmoving crop of bright, red-dyed hair, and a hand with the most beautiful, lithe, bloody, raggedly-torn fingers she'd ever seen resting around her foot. A canteen was on the ground not far from that hand. The cap was off.

Her lips tore and her throat cracked as she tried saying her name. Nothing came out. Her heart broke that her gifted voice failed her when she needed it the most.

She attempted to lift herself up but her arms and legs had no more strength.

Even though that hand only touched her foot and she would have given anything—even another eighteen years of torture—to see her face once again…that hand was all she needed. She concentrated on her foot, so she could feel the love radiating from that hand.

She remembered…

She remembered my greatest fear…

Dying alone…

Her head fell back and rested in Hell's dirt. She thought about the canteen. Maybe it hadn't evaporated yet. Even the tiniest little drink to get the taste out of two different bodily fluids she'd drunk to sustain herself would have been a second treasure at the end of her life.

Her life…

The endless torture…

Over endless years…

The tribulations…

The despair…

Stephanie's last effort and final touch had been worth it all.

Epicinium

Epic Finnish

Digital Album Review by Stanley Crawford

Upon meeting Auranna Korpela towards the end of Black Aura's most recent and widely acclaimed US tour, I believed the end of her band was coming fast. The constant disappearances of her fans seemed to not weigh heavily on her. She acted aloof and at times I believed she was seeing things. By the end of our interview, she indicated she would die before breaking up her band.

Then she did die on the final night of the concert, at least according to many audience members and witnesses backstage. Roadies reported significant strife amongst the famously close-knit band in the leadup to that night. She collapsed several times between and even during songs, and every witness attested that she couldn't possibly have been acting. The documentary crew had clear footage that backed up these claims. Furthermore, truly bizarre accounts of a mental breakdown of the band, presumably after learning of Auranna's death, dominated music headlines for days.

Miraculously, she and her partner were seen in public a week later coming out of a hospital, but she and the band refused to comment on how she survived, or whether it was all a hoax to help sell the documentary. Weeks after her "resurrection," the band flew to Korpela's home in Finland and began working on their newest album—*Vanquished Fallen*. They completed production in only two months. One might imagine the short turnaround and the events that damaged the band's bonds at the end of the tour would have resulted in a rushed, subpar final product, but the album is anything but!

Filled with the most visceral and imaginative lyrics in not only their own history, but perhaps in *all of metal*, the album evokes fear, terror, pain, suffering, and, somehow, hope and triumph. You might think such a feat impossible with each of the five members penning personal songs outside of their collaborative efforts, but every song builds on each one before it effortlessly.

Korpela's haunting, and, I must say, haunted vocals and masterful solos are the foundation on which the album stands tall, but career-best work from Stephanie Creighton, Desmond Fuller, Alex Kerrington, and Carrie Stafford provide unbreakable pillars.

To read more about our impressions of each individual song and a more in-depth review, as well as my original interview with Korpela, please subscribe to unlock the full articles.

Box Office Wrap-up

...while Marvel's newest offering continues the studio's downward spiral with an opening only worth ten million dollars in the US, mass layoffs are expected to follow the disappointing results, but Disney is steadfast that they will never stop making the same superhero movies despite what an entire nation of fans is signaling to them.

Finally, the little music documentary-that-could, *The Dirge of Black Aura,* continues to earn millions off its miniscule budget despite playing in a limited number of theaters. Strong word of mouth of its racy, violent, and occult material has lovers of the macabre and metal alike scrambling for a ticket at mostly sold-out cinemas. The exclusive, intimate look at one of the world's most famous metal bands as it nearly fell apart is fueling a seemingly endless argument among its fans, old and new: Documentary? Or hoax?

Personal Email
To: auraskorps@jigokurecords.com
From: pastorlevi@hymnalministries.org
Subject: Re: Re: The power of prayer
Dear Auranna,

Though I can tell you are being diplomatic, I can hear you scoffing at my last email from across the Atlantic. I'm not trying to convert you. After what you supposedly went through in that documentary (I've heard...things, but cannot bring myself to watch it. I still blush when I remember our *trip.*), I would imagine I shouldn't have to try to convince you to convert.

I wish you'd open yourself up, at least, to the *possibility* God heard my prayers and took pity on your suffering, and helped you in your later trials, much as He helped return Abigail and Rebecca to us (they both say Hi, btw. Abigail even told me to write btw instead of "by the way." Said I'd be cooler and easier to listen to if I learned to talk and type like all you young people. You will never hear me rapping from the pulpit, tho).

Have you considered my invitation to speak at our church? You didn't answer either way. Some in my congregation thought I made up the whole 'soul warehouse' thing. I've tried to dress it in metaphors, but you have a knack for those hellish ones that I don't. Go toe-to-toe with me on the Bible, though, and I'm afraid you'll lose ;^)

Abigail says she wants backstage passes to your next concert in our town so she can pay back Rebecca. Those two have become more chummy since the incident. She refuses to tell me what changed in their relationship, tho. Maybe u could talk 2 her when u visit?

Think about it, won't u?
Sincerely b4 God,
Pastor Levi

Handwritten Letter Left on a Pillow

Auranna

Meet me tonight at the ice pond that reflects the aurora.

We need to discuss the last thing you said before you signed that contract.

S

Midwest US Television News Broadcast

"Before we send you to a wrap-up of the NFL final scores with Eric Hookenladder, a bizarre story we reported on months ago has gotten even *more* bizarre. From the same site where a man visiting from Arizona claimed witches stole his Harley Davidson motorcycle after slipping him hallucinatory drugs, it's been reported that disgusting blobs of flesh and bones continue to pour out of thin air—according to local police.

"Scientists are unable to explain their appearance. Despite their protestations in the name of science, though, local police have been incinerating the massive blobs after one attempted to engulf an investigating deputy and ate part of his hand.

"Conspiracy theorists and paranormal tourists have flocked to the site despite strong warnings from law enforcement to stay away. We caught up with one tourist dressed head to toe in black gothic attire and they had this to say:"

"Me and my friends thought this had to be the work of something supernatural. It could be the opening through which our Lord Cthulhu emerges and drives the world insane, and we just wanted to be here when that happens, because it would be so cool, you know?"

"Isn't Cthulhu a fictional creation by one H.P. Lovecraft, Eric?"

"Well, Julie, one could say the same thing about the Bible, no?"

"Eric, you can't say that on TV!"

"Oh. Uh...Tonight the Bengals *smote* the Cardinals with a

score of 35-13 and the..."

"Eric, I'm going to have to cut you off while we go to break."

Personal Email
To: auraskorps@jigokurecords.com
From: piercingmetal@hellmail.com
Subject: Your friend

I hope this is your real email address. I couldn't believe the number of gatekeepers I had to go through at Jigoku Records just to get this.

It's been three months since I returned to my real body. I fell over a lot, getting used to walking with my knees facing forward again lol. Tomorrow I'm getting re-pierced now that I'm all healed up from the original ones being torn out. Thank Satan those ones I got in Hell disappeared like everything else.

Is it weird that I kind of miss my tail, though?

Do you remember Elijah and Tristan? The spider boys? They formed a club, if you will, for the survivors. They reached out to me about a month ago. They said it's been hard finding people but the membership is slowly growing. I found I really needed their friendship after what happened, especially after Justin (my boyfriend before I was taken) stopped helping my parents search for me after only a week and ran off with one of my "friends." Made me feel great about myself, that I'm so forgettable... But I'm not the only one who came back. Some people had been missing for years, a decade, even. Some of those stories are worse than mine.

I'm sorry to bother you, I just wanted to reach out to tell you about the club. There's talk of a big event the next time you guys tour the US. Please reach out to Elijah and Tristan before you plan accommodations.

I think about you every day.

I'm sorry. That came out of nowhere. (Why can't I bring myself to erase it lol) You're busy planning your next tour (I adore the new album, by the way). You probably want to shut off that part of your past and my emailing you isn't helping.

I do wish you didn't live half a world away, though. This seems so impersonal. I don't know if you can properly understand how much I appreciate everything you did to save me.

I'm so thankful I met you, my Queen, even though I had to go through Hell to do it.

—Rachel Kimura

Digital Movie Critic's Blog

The continued financial success of the music documentary *The Dirge of Black Aura* had not changed my mind about reviewing this exploitative single-cam garbage from first-time director Lisa Nocnitsa, but so many of the commentariat demanded it that I decided to give you my uncensored thoughts on it here—in an unofficial review.

I firmly fall into the hoax camp of the audience that does not for one second believe the band played and was tortured in Hell. The production design definitely *looks* expensive and realistic enough, which further fuels the theory that Ms. Nocnitsa procured secret donors to pull it off, then played up the "shoestring" budget to increase the documentary's profile and sucker so many of the movie-going public into proving her value to producers as a new director. Personally I can't wait until her next picture with one thousand times the budget crashes and burns and we can be rid of this lying witch's influence.

Though I found the band itself charming at first, their slow unraveling made no sense to me. They seemed far too nonchalant about what they claimed to be seeing and experiencing, even with their lifetime of living and breathing the "metal lifestyle," as I'm often accused of downplaying whenever I bring this up. They are no more different than you and me, and I promise you every "metalhead" who claims to be some devil-worshiping tough guy who would "welcome" the presence of a real Hell and all its denizens is really a mewling baby inside overcompensating for their crippling inner-fears. You will not move me from this stance, no matter how much you all complain to the contrary in the comment section.

Don't get me started on all the nudity and the snuff-film quality of the final "torture-scene." Cheap and tawdry smut. Ms. Nocnitsa somehow convinced those band members and that weird, batty, goat thing in a costume to remove their clothes multiple times to sell more tickets and downloads. No, I do not care that men were equally fully nude. In fact, I'm sure that contributed heavily to the surprising number of female viewers. I'm not saying it wasn't an effective ploy, but that makes it no less contemptuous and soulless exploitation in the name of "art."

As portrayed, Auranna Korpela's sacrifice and the image of the rest of the band walking through that "portal" on the side of their bus would have played better if this was a real movie and not a "documentary" as Ms. Nocnitsa continues to insist, because it all falls flat when they all "reappear" just in time to create a new album and plan another world tour in four months. I don't know which of these two women is more deceiving and cynical. I will never pay money to watch their movies or listen to their albums.

For all the metalheads out there vociferously defending Black Aura and Ms. Nocnitsa's lies, go back to your basements and expend your mental energies on writing a novel if you're so invested in fantasy.

Next week I'll review the new *Star Wars* movie made by the woke executive determined to destroy the childhoods of millions of people by adding a gay main character just to score points with the LGBTQ+whatever-the-hell-other-letters-they-add crowd. I'll "add" a link to the official boycott website below.

Personal Email
To: piercingmetal@hellmail.com
From: auraskorps@jigokurecords.com
Subject: Re: Your friend

I apologize for the rigmarole the record company put you through to get my email. Naturally after the documentary debuted they've been inundated with requests for comments, interviews, threats, boycotts, etc. It's so lovely they finally gave it to you.

I hope you realize it was a good thing that your boyfriend showed his true colors. You could have been trapped in a different kind of Hell; shackled to someone who doesn't deserve to be with you. You deserve so much better. Someone who would go through...lol, I remember you would not pine for the puns in Hell. I'll knock it off now ;^)

If a club for the victims helps you all heal faster, I'm all for it! I will email Elijah and Tristan. Do you have their contact information?

I know you two didn't always get along, but Stephanie wasn't herself when you knew her. Now that her soul has returned, her violent behavior and aggressive personality have disappeared. She's back to the sweet, adorable girl we all remembered.

When I learned what she went through to find me... Well, I hope someday she can tell you the story. She's mentioned a desire to meet you since we returned. You'd like her very much, I think, now that the unnatural jealousy no longer interferes with her personality...

What am I saying? You're talking about a boyfriend and I'm fantasizing about the three of us, like that could work. As if the demon form was really you. I don't even know the real you. After what you said about thinking about me every day, though...

I must confess, I think of you every day as well. Even...towards the end...I felt I might love you. But that's crazy. I only know what you look like in your demonic form. I only know how your demon body feels. Would I even recognize you without those empty black eye sockets, horns, and giant piercings?

Rotting Christ, I can't let it go. I'm sorry. For all I know you might have been forced. You might have been in constant pain. All I was thinking about was the unimaginable pleasure you gave me while you were shackled to that bastard. It may have only been "your duty." If I'm hurting you in any way by bringing it up again, it is completely unintentional. I try to stay away from writing except for our songs for this very reason—I tend to ramble when I'm not focused on music.

Look, I hope this doesn't confuse you, and if I misunderstood your last email, again, I apologize, but...have you ever been to Finland?

Kunnioittavasti

—AK

Hollywood News Report

After the surprise financial windfall of Lisa Nocnitsa's smash-hit *The Dirge of Black Aura*, it came as no surprise when her cameraman argued that he was owed twenty-five percent of the profits. Nocnitsa claims he had already signed a contractual agreement for a lump-sum salary paid at the end of the film for a standard fifty-thousand dollars.

The cameraman, Joel Prescott, claims Nocnitsa made an oral promise to twenty-five percent in front of Black Aura during production, but unfortunately was not rolling film at that moment. Some of the individual members of Black Aura affirmed Mr. Prescott's account, but Ms. Nocnitsa claims that she was both coerced and not on Earth at the time, and therefore is not beholden to any law or agreement on Earth, oral or otherwise.

Mr. Prescott has indicated he plans to sue.

Winter in Finland

Auranna emerged from the studio satisfied. Carrie's new lyrics were immaculate. The song played beautifully. All through the recording of their latest album they were more in tune with each other, preternaturally intuiting each other's thoughts. It cut down on meetings and trying to explain everything to each other, which used to plague their previous studio time. With all the extra studio slots they'd purchased, they started working on the follow-up album, too, which they planned to debut halfway through the upcoming world tour.

During a quiet moment alone in the brisk, invigorating Finland air, Auranna breathed contentedly as she fingered the ring Stephanie had offered to her at the pond. The ring was a black snake with diamonds for eyes, and it coiled perfectly along the length of Auranna's right ring finger. Her white breath roiled over her hand as she recalled the words Stephanie asked that night.

The rest of Black Aura followed her out of the studio shortly after, all bundled up and carrying flashlights. They overdid it a little on the coats, but Auranna knew they weren't used to the winters yet—but probably never would be.

"The more you guys use flashlights, the longer it takes for your eyes to get used to the darkness. The streetlamps reflecting off the snow should be enough. And even then, you've got the aurora borealis to guide you."

"P-p-p-please stop t-t-t-talking and let's get b-b-b-back to your house, Aura," Carrie chattered.

Auranna took Stephanie's hand and led Carrie, Desmond,

and Alex through the snow-covered sidewalks. Stephanie's limp was improving slowly, but two doctors they talked to, one in America and one in Finland, believed she may never walk the way she did before the break. Auranna delighted in offering her shoulder for support whenever Stephanie wasn't too proud to lean on her.

"You think Devil's Sorrow's new album will surpass ours?" Desmond asked.

"No way," Alex said. "Maybe if they'd released it a year or two later, they'd sniff our sales. That documentary ignited everything."

"Guys," Auranna interjected, "were it not for Anders leading you to Steph and me, we wouldn't be here, and our fans would still be in Hell. I don't care about the rivalry. Let's see if we can work out co-headlining."

"I don't think you'll have to twist our arms to agree to that," Stephanie said.

Auranna kissed Stephanie's ear lightly and whispered, "Don't think I would ever discount your role in saving me, my love."

She thought that would bring out another cute, shy smile, but Stephanie only looked haunted as she stared at her deformed hand. Her speed in the studio had been dampened while she got used to strumming differently, but the speed wasn't what defined her skills. When Stephanie played now, Black Aura felt her pain and devotion to Auranna, the band, their fans, and music. Auranna pulled the hand to her lips and kissed the scar tissue.

Stephanie changed the subject.

"Joel is asking if we'll come to court to help him sue Lisa. Maybe without Desmond present, though."

"She's not my girlfriend anymore. The long distance thing wasn't working," Desmond said. "Plus, she's kind of a bitch. It's too bad, too. She did this one thing where she…"

"Okay, okay, we get it," Alex said. "I don't want to imagine that witch and you together."

"Yeah, Joel was a pretty cool guy. I'll go," Auranna said. "If he loses his case...I kind of want to help him out. Honestly, at the core of it all, without him, the documentary wouldn't have happened and our album sales would be maybe a fifth of what they were. Lisa is definitely doing wrong by him."

"I'm in favor of that, even if he wouldn't stop filming us without our clothes," Stephanie said.

"Meh, he wasn't doing it on purpose. Like he could plan for all that, you know?" Alex offered.

"Easy for you to say!" Stephanie said as she backhanded his arm. "He got me most—out of any of you!"

"Come on, S-s-s-s-steph," Carrie said. "If you d-d-d-didn't like all the attention, you w-w-w-wouldn't have done all those risqué photoshoots with so many m-m-m-magazines and websites after your body healed, and the a-a-a-a-album released."

"Hey, I was approached by those people! They promised it would increase interest in the upcoming tour. You don't think that had some small part to play in selling out eighty percent of the venues before we've even started? Honestly I didn't think it would go well with my messed-up eye and all the scar tissue, but the editors forwarded a lot of fan mail that said they dug my scars."

"I-i-i-if you whip your tits out d-d-d-during a show, I'm leaving the b-b-b-band for real this time."

"Knock it off, Carebear," Stephanie smiled as her face turned bright red from more than the cold. "You love us and you're terrible at hiding it."

They stomped their feet before entering Auranna's home. It was still jarring to see a woman already in the kitchen who returned to Earth at the same age she was taken to Hell and was only slightly older than Auranna. They looked almost identical.

"*Hei, Äiti*. How is the *Karjalanpiirakka* coming along?"

"*Näyttää herkulliselta, tytär*. Please remove your jackets and set the table."

"What's that? Is it like that salmon stew she made the other night? That was my favorite thing since I've been here," Carrie said.

"I'll be happy if it's not that cheese that squeaks between your teeth. I can't taste anything, obviously, but I can't get over the texture...and the sound," Alex shivered from the memory.

"I've liked everything so far," Desmond said, "except that salt licorice. Rotting Christ..."

"Hey! She made that from scratch! And it's amazing—you're just a typical American with poor taste," Auranna laughed.

After dinner Auranna and Stephanie excused themselves to take their nightly walk through the snow. Auranna was overjoyed that Stephanie loved the snow as much as she did, even though Stephanie grew up in the American Southwest.

Stephanie wiggled in closer to Auranna's embrace, arm wrapped around her hip, and laid her head on Auranna's shoulder. Whenever she looked at her fiancé's body, her slightly sunken eyebrow, and all the other evidence of what she put herself through to reach Auranna at Death's door, it was all a permanent reminder of what they meant to each other. The scars meant more to her than the ring.

She was happy to hear about the fan support, because she would have some things to say if anyone were to ever comment on the "ugliness" of Stephanie's scars. To Auranna, they were beautiful.

She hummed a few bars of Stephanie's favorite Aerosmith song. Stephanie kissed Auranna's cheek.

"You're my angel, too, baby."

They walked a few hundred yards before a dark figure appeared ahead of them on the sidewalk. The figure's hood obstructed the view of its face. Auranna tightened up her arm a little to bring Stephanie to attention. Their pace slowed.

The figure kept looking down at a piece of paper, then their hood would turn to the side before passing each house's number box. Auranna had a growing dislike for voids under hoods, so she took a few extra steps to the side, making space between the figure and themselves as they pass—

Was that an oversized Black Aura hoodie? It was unlike any she'd seen at the merchandise booths and on their official website's store. Someone who was adept at creating their own clothing made that hoodie.

Auranna turned around, guiding Stephanie to about-face in unison.

"*Hei, oletko eksynyt*? Are you lost, friend?"

An attractive metalhead revealed herself beneath the hood, standing among the soft illumination of streetlamps reflecting off the snow. She had piercings in all the places Rachel wore them, though much less painful looking. Auranna couldn't believe it was the first time seeing Rachel's smile.

There was nothing forgettable about it.

THE END

AUDITE PERICULO TUO SOUNDTRACK {LISTEN AT YOUR OWN RISK}

Unofficial soundtrack to the novel Black Aura

-

Auranna's Theme Song:
"Nutshell" by Alice in Chains

-

The song I listened to the most while writing Black Aura:
"Ascension Sickness" by Abigail Williams

-

Indirect or paraphrased lyrical, titular, and sonic references:

-

Chapter 1:
"Black Sabbath" by Black Sabbath
"*De Mysteriis Dom Sathanas*" by Mayhem
"Black Label" by Lamb of God
"Rose of Pain" by X Japan
References: Black Sabbath, Mayhem, Katatonia, Lamb of God, Immortal, Venom, X Japan, Metallica, Rotting Christ

-

Chapter 2:
"Night's Blood" by Dissection
"*I Troldskog Faren Vild*" by Ulver
"Raped by a Demon" by Obsidian Shrine
References: Dissection, Ulver, Obsidian Shrine

-

Chapter 3:
"Into the Void" by Black Sabbath
"Bleed for the Devil" by Morbid Angel
"Hell Bent for Leather" by Judas Priest
"Somebody Put Something in My Drink" by The Ramones
References: Black Sabbath, Morbid Angel, Judas Priest, The Ramones

-

Chapter 4:
"Runnin' with the Devil" by Van Halen
"Cowboys from Hell" by Pantera
References: X Japan, Van Halen, Black Sabbath, Pantera

-

Chapter 5:
"Genocidal Humanoidz" by System of a Down
"Snakebite" by Alice Cooper
References: System of a Down, Alice Cooper, Death, Exhumed, Rotting Christ

-

Chapter 6:
"Attached at the Hip" by CKY
"Duncan Hills Coffee Jingle" by Dethklok
References: CKY, Dethklok, Rotting Christ, Cradle of Filth

-

Chapter 7:
"Welcome to Hell" by Venom
"The Last in Line" by Dio
"No More Mr. Nice Guy" by Alice Cooper
"Frantic Disembowelment" by Cannibal Corpse
"Jet City Woman" by Queensrÿche
References: Venom, Dio, Alice Cooper, Cannibal Corpse, Queensrÿche

-

Chapter 8:
"Church Burns" by Zeal & Ardor

"Iowa" by Slipknot
"Over the Hills and Far Away" by Led Zeppelin
"Naked Witch" by Danzig
References: Mayhem, Zeal & Ardor, Slipknot, Led Zeppelin, Danzig, Cradle of Filth

-

Chapter 9:
"Boiling Blood" by God Dethroned
References: Meatloaf, Ozzy Osbourne, Iron Maiden, God Dethroned

-

Chapter 10:
"Angry Again" by Megadeth
"To Be Treated" by Terry Reid
References: Megadeth, Abigail Williams, Terry Reid, God Dethroned

-

Chapter 11:
"Freezing Moon" by Mayhem
References: God Dethroned, His Infernal Majesty (H.I.M.), Mayhem

-

Chapter 12:
"Beyond Redemption" by His Infernal Majesty (H.I.M.)
References: His Infernal Majesty (H.I.M.), Rotting Christ

-

Chapter 13:
"Witching Hour" by In This Moment
"Mother" by Danzig
"Poison My Eyes" by Anthrax
"Angel of Death" by Slayer
"What Fresh Hell" by Leviathan
"*A Toute Le Monde*" by Megadeth
References: In This Moment, Warlock, Anthrax, Danzig, Slayer, Leviathan, Mayhem, Megadeth, Dimmu Borgir,

Deafheaven

Chapter 14:
"Warranty" by Slipknot
"Witching Hour" by Venom
"*Obscuritatem Advoco Amplectère Me*" by Abruptum
References: Slipknot, Venom, Nightwish, Satyricon, Abruptum

Chapter 15:
"Cadaveric Incubator of Endoparasites" by Carcass
"What the Hell Have I" by Alice In Chains
"Curse the Gods" by Destruction
"Salt in Our Wounds" by His Infernal Majesty (H.I.M.)
"Hell Is for Children" by Pat Benatar
"I'm Dead" by Mary's Blood
References: Carcass, Iron Maiden, Metallica, Black Sabbath, Slayer, Pantera, Judas Priest, Led Zeppelin, Black Label Society, Obituary, Alice in Chains, Bathory, Destruction, His Infernal Majesty (H.I.M.), Pat Benatar, Mary's Blood, Xasthur, Tenacious D, Motörhead, Spinal Tap

Chapter 16:
"A Dying God Coming into Human Flesh" by Celtic Frost
"Call From the Grave" by Bathory
"Hallowed Be Thy Name" by Iron Maiden
"Hallowed Be Thy Name" by Cradle of Filth
'One' by Metallica
"Fade to Black" by Metallica
References: Nightwish, Celtic Frost, Bathory, Iron Maiden, Cradle of Filth, Metallica

Chapter 17:
"Sweating Bullets" by Megadeth
"Fever" by Overkill

"Clean My Wounds" by Corrosion of Conformity
"On the Road Again" by Willie Nelson
"*Taivaan Portti*" by Oranssi Pazuzu
References: Megadeth, Celtic Frost, Overkill, Corrosion of Conformity, Willie Nelson, Queensrÿche, Oranssi Pazuzu

-

Chapter 18:
"I Love the Dead" by Alice Cooper
References: Alice Cooper, Otep

-

Chapter 20:
"Spirit in the Sky" by Norman Greenbaum
"The Number of the Beast" by Iron Maiden
References: Satyricon, Metallica, Norman Greenbaum, Iron Maiden

-

Chapter 21:
"Angry Again" by Megadeth
References: Megadeth, Niccolò Paganini

-

Chapter 22:
"Spirit in the Sky" by Norman Greenbaum
References: Darkthrone, Ghost, Norman Greenbaum

-

Chapter 23:
"Call Me Little Sunshine" by Ghost
"Ritual" by Blasphemy
References: Ghost, Blasphemy

-

Chapter 24:
"Cross Road Blues" by Robert Johnson
"What the Hell Have I" by Alice in Chains
References: Agalloch, Robert Johnson, Tommy Johnson, Bathory, His Infernal Majesty (H.I.M.), Alice in Chains

-

Chapter 25:
References: Rotting Christ

-

Chapter 26:
"Sweating Bullets" by Megadeth
"Heaven and Hell" by Black Sabbath
"The Metal" by Tenacious D
References: Megadeth, Black Sabbath, Tenacious D

-

Chapter 27:
"Real World" by Queensrÿche
"Opening Night" by Scowl
"Symphony of Destruction" by Megadeth
"Deceiver, Deceiver" by Arch-Enemy
References: Queensrÿche, Scowl, Megadeth, Arch-Enemy

-

Chapter 28:
"Heaven Tonight" by His Infernal Majesty (H.I.M.)
References: His Infernal Majesty (H.I.M.)

-

Chapter 29:
"Die With Your Boots On" by Iron Maiden
"Downfall" by Trust Company
"Highway to Hell" by AC/DC
"Epilogue" by Eluveitie
References: Iron Maiden, Trust Company, AC/DC, Eluveitie

-

Epilogue:
"Angel" by Aerosmith
References: Rotting Christ, Aerosmith

-

Please support the above artists by discovering their music through reputable sources only! Please buy their licensed merchandise!

-

Movie and TV references:
We Are X, Metalocalypse, The Devil's Rejects, Monty Python and the Holy Grail, Re:Zero, Tenacious D in the Pick of Destiny, This is Spinal Tap, Ghost, Black Roses, Footloose, Wayne's World, Liar Liar, The Simpsons, The Santa Clause

-

Please enjoy the above media through reputable sources only!

-

Biblical Reference:
Exodus 23:20
"See, I am sending an angel ahead of you to guard you along the way and to bring you to the place I have prepared."

-

<u>Black Aura's featured songs</u>
"Obsequious Obeisance"
"Forsaken Fury"
"Selfish Sacrifice"
"Sublime Suffocation"
"Metamorphic Maculation"
"Bitter Benevolence"
"Abhorrent Aberration"
"Hellacious Heresy"
"Torturous Tenderness"
"Insightful Incision"

Special Thanks

I want to thank a certain Lounatic, a great critique partner and friend. He introduced me to my editor, Ollie Ander, who keeps me excited through the long, lonely process of writing, even when I feel like giving up. I appreciate her tough editing that doesn't seek to discourage or insult, but to educate and improve the work. I'm not sure if I could have completed this without Lou and Ollie's encouragement.

Ollie is also my marketing material and paperback cover designer and I appreciate everything she does to bring my books to life.

I also want to thank Richelle Manteufel for her support and friendship, and for helping with the back cover material.

Thanks to my alpha- and beta-readers for their patience reading early drafts and providing valuable feedback.

If this was like CD liner notes with the *Inspired by* section listing every band influencing the artists, mine would be pages long of the musicians that have inspired me to hit the Infinite Repeat button on all my devices.

Sneak Peek
Devil's Sorrow

The second track in the Devil's Playlist series

Anders' heart rate strode from *allegretto* to *allegro* as he closed hotel door number 150 behind him. No woman had made him react with such awkwardness since early pubescence. He tried recalling any sort of comparable beauty, but all the faces in dark rooms backstage blurred together over a decade and a half of endless touring. It was like he'd never seen a woman before.

Molly took in the hotel room's surroundings with mild disdain, running her fingers over surfaces, studying the wallpaper, feeling the fabric of the blankets between her sharpened fingernails. She peered through the curtains overlooking part of Helsinki and sighed.

Then she plopped onto the king-size bed and hiked up her gown.

"Let us begin, Hellwalker."

Anders shook his head out of the trance her svelte legs had put him under.

"Uh, wait. I would like to know why you keep calling me Hellwalker? You could have me confused with someone else? A lot of guests at that wedding wander the Plains."

"I do not wish to talk during the act. Come over here and get on with it."

Anders ground his teeth as his chest twisted up. Molly acted like half the groupies he'd ever met who treated him like an unchecked box on a long list of musician body counts. However, Molly's otherworldly beauty demanded something else from him, even if he didn't quite know what it was yet.

"Please cover yourself," Anders said while he approached the bed, turning his head fully away from her exposed legs so his eyes couldn't betray him.

"Take off your clothes."

Anders ignored the directive and sat on the corner of the bed with his back to her. He hoped she couldn't hear his heartbeat or see the sweat across his brow.

"Your heart races. I can feel it through the bed," Molly whispered. Her words inched over his back, up into his ears, turning his brain into mush.

She ran a fingernail down his spine, causing a thunderous shiver that deafened him. He nearly came to orgasm just sitting there. It wasn't unlike the last two seconds of a wet dream, right before one's mind understands what's happening, but it's too late to stop.

"I can make that sensation last all night, Hellwalker. Turn around and I will begin."

Anders stood and went to the window instead, opening the curtains so the cold radiating off the glass would cool him down. It didn't help that Molly's legs were still visible in the reflection.

"I do not understand what you are doing here," Anders spoke to the reflection. She rolled her eyes and sat up but kept her legs open.

"You are boring the hell out of me, Anders Helvete. I only get the chance to visit Earth once a century. All the other men I take need no words."

"Do they survive?"

Molly hadn't expected the question. She frowned at his reflection, then covered her legs in a huff. She got up and took a step towards the door. Anders spun to her.

"Wait! You do not need to leave. I simply have questions. It did not sound like Ferral was in such a hurry..."

She scowled over her shoulder at the mention of Ferral. Even miffed, she was captivating to behold. Anders didn't want to upset her and have her go so soon. Interacting with a non-threatening demon was a gift he would never receive in Hell.

"If that is true," he continued, cautious, "perhaps I could buy you a drink?"

Molly turned on him, withering him with a glare of disappointment.

"You do not have to 'pick me up' to bed me. The bed is right here. I am open to you. I do not understand the hesitation you have, and I do not care to."

Anders furrowed his brow at the rules of consent getting blown up in front of him.

"Perhaps you may find another to...bed tonight. In a bar. Please, let me take you. You can buy if it makes you feel better."

"You have given me no choice, it seems. I will find another who is not such a tease."

"I have not remotely teased you," he showed a bit of exasperation, then reigned it back in. "You have teased yourself with your assumption of me."

Anders didn't want to argue with her and chase her away, no matter how obstinate she was being. He recovered his neutral tone and went by her towards the door. She brushed another fingernail across the back of his hand as he passed. He wobbled slightly and sprang forward to catch the doorknob.

"Please, stop doing that. I know you can be patient, languishing in Hell. Why do you not enjoy your time out of His reach? Make it last for all it is worth?"

Molly only frowned and exited the room without another word as Anders held the door open for her.

About VB Scott

I'm an unassuming metalhead that loves all subgenres and will never pick sides between one band over the other. Good music is good music.

I write in several genres and would love nothing more than for you to follow me as I release more stories that I hope you'll enjoy.

My handle is vb_scottwrites on Threads, Instagram, Facebook. Subscribe to my Substack at vbscott.substack.com

Feel free to contact me through my email address at vbscott.writes@gmail.com

If you enjoyed Black Aura, **please consider leaving a rating and/or review**, as this will go a long way to ensuring more books in the Devil's Playlist series will continue.

Also by VB Scott

Revenge of the Bakeneko
A historical fiction, action-adventure novel set in the early 1700s of Japan's Edo Period

A dice game in the hands of Takana Gozen is anything but a matter of chance. Takana covets golden *ryō* coins almost as much as she hates yakuza, and she is a master at manipulating both as she hosts backroom gambling events to pay off her deadbeat father's debt. She's spent the last eight years wandering the *Nikkō Kaidō* highway, living the life of a homeless vagabond—stealing, cheating, and killing—all in the never-ending pursuit of coin.

Instigated by the lowliest of prostitutes in the brothel Takana's mother runs, a series of brutal, deadly events break Takana out of debt, and she earns the power to oppose the very structures that bound her. The found family she collects along the way looks to her for leadership, and together they form their own *yakuza* clan—the most prosperous and feared in all of Eastern Japan: The Bakeneko Clan.

Takana has trained her whole life to survive deadly encounters, but the risks that come with being a clan head come in more forms than *katana* and *kunai*. Protection, love, compassion, friendship, and sacrifice will all be necessary if she is to survive her new life—a life that proves to be more dangerous and unfulfilling than the old one.

www.ingramcontent.com/pod-product-compliance
Ingram Content Group UK Ltd.
Pitfield, Milton Keynes, MK11 3LW, UK
UKHW030651090325
455944UK00001B/7